W9-CKE-862

Barbara Reber
5 Pine Ave S
Mississauga ON L5H 2P5

"*I'm not forcing you to marry me, Lottie.*"

"That depends on how one wants to define 'force.' Although I'm hardly being carried away in chains, I am not an entirely willing party to this so-called marriage. And if you hadn't found me, I would still be residing happily at Stony Cross Park . . ."

"You weren't happy there. I'll wager you haven't been happy a day in your life since you met Lord Radnor."

Oh, how she longed to contradict him! But it was pointless to lie when the truth was so obvious.

"You'll find life far more enjoyable as my wife," Gentry continued. "You won't be anyone's servant. You can do as you please within reasonable limits. And you won't have to fear Lord Radnor any longer."

"All for the price of sleeping with you," she muttered.

He smiled, all velvety arrogance, as he replied, "You may come to enjoy that part of it most of all."

LISA KLEYPAS

Worth Any Price

AVON BOOKS

An Imprint of HarperCollins*Publishers*

AVON BOOKS
An Imprint of HarperCollins*Publishers*
10 East 53rd Street
New York, New York 10022-5299

Copyright © 2003 by Lisa Kleypas
ISBN: 0-7394-3152-8

To my mother-in-law, Ireta Ellis,
for your love, generosity, and understanding,
and for making me happy whenever I'm with you.

Love from a most appreciative daughter-in-law,

L.K.

Prologue

He was twenty-four, and it was the first time he had ever visited a brothel. Nick Gentry damned himself for the icy sweat that had broken out on his face. He was burning with desire, cold with dread. He had avoided this for years, until he had finally been driven to it out of desperate carnal need. The urge to mate had finally become stronger than fear.

Forcing himself to keep moving, Nick ascended the steps of Mrs. Bradshaw's red brick establishment, the exclusive business that catered to well-heeled clients. It was common knowledge that a night with one of Mrs. Bradshaw's girls would cost a fortune, as they were the best-trained prostitutes in London.

Nick would easily be able to pay any price that was required. He had made a great deal of money as a private thief-taker, and on top of that, he had garnered a fortune from his dealings in the underworld. And he had earned a great deal of notoriety in the process. Although he was popular with most of the public, he was feared by the underworld and detested by the Bow Street runners, who regarded him as an unprincipled rival. On that point the runners were correct—he was indeed unprincipled. Scruples had a way of interfering with business, and therefore Nick had no use for them.

Music drifted from the windows, where Nick could see elegantly dressed men and women mingling as if they were at an upper-crust soiree. In reality, they were prostitutes conducting business transactions with their patrons. This was a world far removed from his flash house near Fleet Ditch, where buttock-and-file whores serviced men in the alleys for shillings.

Squaring his shoulders, Nick used the lion's-head brass knocker to rap sharply on the door. It opened to reveal a stone-faced butler, who asked what business he was about.

Isn't that obvious? Nick wondered irritably. "I want to meet one of the women."

"I am afraid that Mrs. Bradshaw is not accepting new patrons at this time, sir—"

"Tell her that Nick Gentry is here." Nick shoved his hands into his coat pockets and gave the butler a grim stare.

The man's eyes widened, betraying his recognition of the infamous name. He opened the door and inclined his head courteously. "Yes, sir. If you will wait in the entrance hall, I will inform Mrs. Bradshaw of your presence."

The air was lightly scented with perfume and tobacco smoke. Breathing deeply, Nick glanced around the marble-floored hall, which was lined with tall white pilasters. The only adornment was a painting of a naked woman regarding herself in an oval mirror, one delicate hand resting lightly at the top of her own thigh. Fascinated, Nick stared at the gold-framed picture. The female image in the mirror was slightly blurred, the triangle between her legs painted with hazy brush strokes. Nick's stomach felt as if it were filled with cold lead. A servant wearing black breeches crossed through the hall with a tray of glasses, and Nick's gaze dropped swiftly from the painting.

He was intensely aware of the door behind him, of the fact that he could turn and leave right now. But he'd been a coward for too long. Whatever happened this night, he was going to see it through. Clenching his fists in his pockets, he stared at the gleaming floor, the swirls of white and gray marble reflecting the glow of the chandelier overhead.

Suddenly a woman's voice broke lazily through the air. "What an honor it is to receive the celebrated Mr. Gentry. Welcome."

His gaze traveled from the hem of a blue velvet gown to a pair of smiling sherry-colored eyes. Mrs. Bradshaw was a tall, wonderfully proportioned woman. Her pale skin was lightly dotted with amber freckles, and her auburn hair was pinned up in loose curls. She was not beautiful in any conventional sense—her face was too angular, and her nose was large. However, she was stylish and impeccably groomed, and there was something so appealing about her that beauty seemed entirely superfluous.

She smiled in a way that caused Nick to relax in spite of himself. Later he would learn that he was not alone in this reaction. All men relaxed in Gemma Bradshaw's agreeable presence. One could tell just by looking at her that she didn't mind coarse words or booted feet on the table, that she loved a good joke and was never shy or disdainful. Men adored Gemma because she so clearly adored them.

She gave Nick a conspiratorial smile and curtsied low enough to display her magnificent cleavage. "Do say you've come here for pleasure, rather than business." At his brief nod, she smiled once more. "How delightful. Come take a turn through the drawing room with me, and we will discuss how you may best be served." She came forward to slip her arm through his. Nick jerked slightly, checking the instinctive impulse to fling off her hand.

The madam could hardly fail to notice the rigidity of his arm. Her hand fell away, and she continued to chat comfortably, as if nothing untoward had occurred. "This way, if you please. My guests often like to play cards or billiards, or relax in the smoking room. You may chat with as many girls as you wish before deciding on one. Then she will show you to one of the upstairs rooms. You will be charged an hourly rate for her company. I have trained all the girls myself, and you will find that each has her own special talent. Of course, you and I will discuss your preferences, as some of the girls are more willing than others to engage in rough play."

As they entered the drawing room, a few of the women cast Nick flirtatious glances. They all looked healthy and well tended, entirely different from the whores he had seen near Fleet Ditch and Newgate. They flirted, chatted, negotiated, all with the same relaxed manner that Mrs. Bradshaw possessed.

"It would be my pleasure to introduce you to a few of them," came Mrs. Bradshaw's gentle voice in his ear. "Does anyone catch your eye?"

Nick shook his head. He was usually known for his jaunty arrogance, for having the smooth, easy banter of a confidence trickster. However, in this foreign situation, words had deserted him.

"Shall I make a few suggestions? That dark-haired girl in the green gown is exceedingly popular. Her name is Lorraine. She is charming and lively, and possesses a quick wit. The one standing near her, the blond . . . that is Mercia. A more quiet sort, with a gentle manner that appeals to many of our patrons. Now, Nettie—that is the little one by the looking glass—is practiced in the more exotic arts . . ." Mrs. Bradshaw paused as she observed the stiff set of Nick's jaw. "Do you prefer the illusion of innocence?" she suggested softly. "I can provide you with a country lass who makes a most convincing virgin."

Nick was damned if he knew his preferences. He glanced at them all, dark-haired, blond, slim, voluptuous, every shape, size, and hue imaginable, and suddenly the sheer variety overwhelmed him. He tried to imagine going to bed with any of them, and fresh sweat broke out on his forehead.

His gaze returned to Mrs. Bradshaw. Her eyes were a clear, warm brown, surmounted with ruddy brows a few shades darker than her hair. Her tall body was an inviting playground, and her mouth looked plush and soft. But it was the freckles that decided him. The amber flecks decorated her pale skin in a festive spray that made him want to smile.

"You're the only one here worth having," Nick heard himself say.

The madam's fiery lashes swept downward, concealing her thoughts, but he sensed that he had surprised her. A smile curved her lips. "My dear Mr. Gentry, what a delightful compliment. However, I do not sleep with the patrons of my establishment. Those days are long past. You must allow me to introduce you to one of the girls, and—"

"I want *you*," he insisted.

As Mrs. Bradshaw saw the raw honesty in his eyes, a faint wash of pink spread across her cheeks. "Good Lord," she said, and laughed suddenly. "It is quite a trick to make a woman of thirty-eight blush. I thought I had forgotten how."

Nick did not smile back at her. "I will pay any price."

Mrs. Bradshaw shook her head in wonder, still smiling, then stared at his shirtfront with concentration, as if struggling with some weighty matter. "I never do anything on impulse. It's a personal rule of mine."

Slowly Nick reached for her hand, touched it with great care, drew his fingertips across her palm in a cautious, intimate stroke. Although she had long hands befitting a woman of her height, his were much larger, his fingers twice as thick as her slender ones. He caressed the damp little creases on the insides of her fingers. "Every rule should be broken once in a while," he said.

The madam lifted her gaze, seeming fascinated by something she saw in his world-weary face. Abruptly she seemed to make a decision. "Come with me."

Nick followed her from the drawing room, heedless of the gazes that pursued them. She led him through the entrance hall and up a curved staircase that led to a private suite of rooms. Mrs. Bradshaw's apartments were elaborate but comfortable, the furniture deeply cushioned, the walls covered in French paper, the hearth glowing with a generously stocked fire. The sideboard in the receiving room was laden with a collection of glittering crystal decanters and glasses. Mrs. Bradshaw picked up a snifter from a silver tray and glanced at him expectantly. "Brandy?"

Nick nodded immediately.

She poured golden-red liquid into the snifter. Expertly she struck a match and lit a candle on the sideboard. Holding the snifter by its stem, she turned the bowl of the glass over the candle flame. When the brandy was warmed to her satisfaction, she gave it to him. He'd never had a woman do that for him before. The brandy was rich and nut-flavored, its gentle spice drifting to his nostrils as he drank.

Glancing around the receiving room, Nick saw that one wall was lined with bookshelves, every available inch of space occupied with leather-bound volumes and folios. He drew closer to the shelves, investigating. Although he could not read well, he discerned that most of the books were about sex and human anatomy.

"A hobby of mine," Mrs. Bradshaw said, her eyes gleaming with friendly challenge. "I collect books about sexual techniques and customs of different cultures. Some of the books are quite rare. Over the past ten years, I have accumulated a vast wealth of knowledge about my favorite subject."

"I suppose it's more interesting than collecting snuffboxes," he said, and she laughed.

"Stay here. I'll be just a moment. While I am gone, you are welcome to view my library."

She went from the receiving room to the adjoining room, where the end of a poster bed was visible.

The leaden feeling returned to Nick's stomach. Finishing his drink in one gulp of smooth fire, he set the glass aside and went to the bookshelves. A large volume bound in red leather caught his attention. The antique leather creaked slightly as he opened the book, which was filled with hand-painted illustrations. His seething insides tangled in a huge knot as he saw drawings of bodies writhing in sexual positions more peculiar than anything he could have imagined. His heart hammered against his ribs even as his cock surged with aggravated desire. Hastily he closed the book and shoved it back onto the shelf. Going back to the sideboard, he poured another brandy and downed it without tasting it.

As Mrs. Bradshaw had promised, she returned soon, coming to stand in the doorway. She had changed into a thin dressing gown trimmed with lace, the long sleeves draping in medieval points. The white silk garment revealed the pointed crests of her full breasts, and even the shadow of hair between her thighs. The madam had a magnificent body, and she knew it. She stood with one knee eased forward, protruding through the opening of the dressing gown to display the long, sleek line of her leg. Her blazing hair rippled over her shoulders and down her back, making her look younger, softer.

A shiver of longing chased down Nick's spine, and he felt his chest rising and falling in a labored rhythm.

"I'll have you know that I am selective about my lovers." The madam gestured for him to come to her. "A talent such as mine should never be squandered."

"Why me?" Nick asked, his voice turning raspy.

He drew nearer, close enough to realize that she wore no perfume. She smelled like soap and clean skin, a fragrance far more arousing than jasmine or roses.

"It was the way you touched me. You instinctively found the most susceptible places on my hand . . . the center of the palm and the insides of the knuckles. Few men have such sensitivity."

Rather than feeling flattered, Nick experienced a flare of panic. The madam had expectations of him—expectations that he was guaranteed to disappoint. He kept his face expressionless, but his heart dropped in a sickening plunge as she drew him into the warm, firelit bedroom. "Mrs. Bradshaw," he said awkwardly as they approached the bed, "I should tell you—"

"Gemma," she murmured.

"Gemma," he repeated, every coherent thought scattering as she pushed his coat from his shoulders and helped him remove it.

Untying the knot of his sweat-dampened cravat, the madam smiled up at his flushed face. "You are shaking like a boy of thirteen. Is the notorious Mr. Gentry so intimidated by the thought of bedding the famous Mrs. Bradshaw? I wouldn't have expected it of such a worldly man. Certainly you are not a virgin, at your age. A man of . . . twenty-three?"

"Twenty-four." He was dying inside, knowing there was no way he could deceive her into believing that he was a man of experience. Swallowing hard, he said hoarsely, "I've never done this before."

The ruddy arcs of her brows inched upward. "Never visited a brothel?"

Somehow he forced the words up from his aching throat. "Never made love to a woman."

Gemma's expression did not change, but he sensed her astonishment. After a long, diplomatic pause, she asked tactfully, "You have been intimate with other men, then?"

Nick shook his head, staring at the patterned wallpaper. The heavy silence was broken only by the drumming in his ears.

The madam's curiosity was almost palpable. She ascended the moveable wooden step that had been placed beside the tall bed, and climbed onto the mattress. Slowly she reclined on her side, relaxed and catlike. And in her infinite understanding of the male sex, she remained silent and waited patiently.

Nick tried to sound matter-of-fact, but a tremor broke through his voice. "When I was a boy of fourteen, I was sentenced to ten months on a prison hulk."

He saw from Gemma's expression that she understood immediately. The wretched conditions on the hulks, the fact that men were chained together with boys in one large cell, was hardly a secret. "The men on the ship tried to force themselves on you, of course," she said. Her tone was neutral as she asked. "Did any of them succeed?"

"No. But since then . . ." Nick paused for a long moment. He had never told anyone about the past that had haunted him—his fears were not easy to put into words. "I can't bear to be touched," he said slowly. "Not by anyone, in any way. I've wanted . . ." He paused for a moment, floundering. "At times I want a woman so badly I almost go mad with it. But I can't seem to . . ." He fell helplessly silent. It seemed impossible to explain that for him, sex and pain and guilt were plaited together, that the simple act of making love to someone seemed as impossible as making himself jump off a cliff. The touch of another person, no matter how innocuous, triggered a perilous need to defend himself.

Had Gemma displayed a dramatic reaction of horror or sympathy, Nick would have bolted. However, she only regarded him thoughtfully. In a graceful movement, she swung her long legs over the bed and slid to the floor. Standing before him, she began to unbutton his waistcoat. Nick stiffened but did not move away. "You must have fantasies," Gemma said. "Images and thoughts that excite you."

Nick's breath turned shallow and quick as he shrugged off his waistcoat. Remnants of volatile dreams swirled through his head . . . lewd thoughts that had left his body charged and aching in the empty darkness. Yes, he'd had fantasies, visions of women bound and moaning beneath him, their legs spread wide open as he worked himself between them. He could not possibly confess such shameful things. But Gemma Bradshaw's brown eyes contained an invitation that was nearly irresistible. "I'll tell you mine first," she offered. "Would you like that?"

He nodded cautiously, heat spreading through his groin.

"I fantasize about being naked before an audience of men." Gemma's voice was low and molten as she continued. "I choose one that captures my fancy. He joins me on the stage, and performs any sexual act I wish. After that, I select another, and another, until I am completely satisfied."

She tugged the hem of his shirt from his trousers. Nick lifted it over his head and dropped the damp garment to the floor. His cock throbbed painfully as Gemma stared at his bare torso. She touched the heavy pelt of hair on his chest, much darker than the brown hair on his head. An appreciative sound came from Gemma's throat. "You're quite muscular. I like that." Her fingertips ventured through the matted curls and stroked the hot skin beneath, and Nick took an instinctive backward step. Lazily Gemma gestured for him to come back. "If you want to make love, my dear, I'm afraid you can't avoid being touched. Stand still." She reached for the top button of his trousers. "Now tell me *your* fantasy."

Nick stared at the ceiling, the wall, the velvet-draped windows, anything to avoid the sight of her hands at his crotch. "I . . . want to be in control," he said hoarsely. "I imagine tying a woman to a bed. She can't move or touch me . . . she can't stop me from doing anything I want."

"Many men have that fantasy." The backs of Gemma's fingers brushed the stiff underside of his cock as she attended to the last buttons. Suddenly

Nick forgot to breathe. The madam leaned closer, her breath whisking through the curls on his chest. "And what do you do to the woman, after she is tied?" she murmured.

His face darkened with a flush of mingled arousal and embarrassment. "I touch her everywhere. I use my mouth and fingers . . . I make her beg me to take her. I make her scream." He set his jaw and groaned in his throat as her long, cool fingers encircled his shaft and freed it from the trousers. "God—"

"Well," she purred, her clever fingers tracing him down to the hilt and back up to the tightly swollen head. "You are a most generously endowed young man."

Nick closed his eyes, reeling from a powerful onslaught of sensation. "Does that please a woman?" he asked unsteadily.

Gemma continued to stroke him as she replied. "Not all women. Some cannot comfortably accommodate a man your size. But that can be managed." She released him gently and went to a large mahogany box on the bedside table, lifting the lid and searching through its contents. "Remove the rest of your clothes," she said without looking at him.

Fear and lust clashed violently inside him. Eventually the lust won out. He shed his clothes, feeling vulnerable and painfully impassioned. Gemma located what she was looking for, turned, and tossed something lightly to him.

Reflexively Nick caught the object in his fist. It was a rope made of claret-colored velvet.

Perplexed, he watched as Gemma untied her dressing gown and let it fall to her feet. Every inch of her strong, supple body was exposed, including the wealth of vibrant hair at her groin. With a provocative smile, she climbed onto the bed, revealing her generously rounded backside in the process. Leaning back on her elbows, she nodded toward the length of velvet clenched in his fist. "I believe you know what to do next," she said.

Nick was amazed and bewildered that she would make herself so completely defenseless to a stranger. "You trust me enough to let me do that?"

Her voice was very soft. "This will require trust on both our parts, won't it?"

Nick joined her on the bed, his hands trembling as he tied her wrists together and anchored them to the headboard. Her sleek body was completely at his mercy. Climbing over her, he bent his head and kissed her mouth. "How can I please you?" he whispered.

"Please yourself this time." Her tongue touched his lower lip in a light, silken stroke. "You can attend to my needs later."

Nick explored her slowly, his apprehensions dissolving in a flood of heat. Lust roared through him as he found places that made her writhe . . . the hollow of her throat, the insides of her elbows, the tender undersides of her breasts. He stroked, tasted, nibbled at her skin, becoming drunk on her smoothness, her female fragrance. Finally, when his passion built to an unbearable height, he lowered himself between her thighs and pushed into the wet, warm depths he craved so badly. To his eternal humiliation, he climaxed with only one thrust, before he had satisfied her. His body shook with unbearable pleasure, and he buried his face in the mass of her flaming hair as he groaned harshly.

Gasping in the aftermath, he fumbled at Gemma's tethered wrists. When she was freed, he rolled to his side, away from her, and stared blindly at the shadows on the wall. He was dizzy with relief. For some unfathomable reason, the corners of his eyes stung, and he closed his eyes tightly against the hideous threat of tears.

Gemma moved behind him, her hand settling lightly on his naked hip. Nick flinched at her touch but did not move away. Her mouth pressed against the top of his spine, a sensation that shot down to his groin. "You have promise," she murmured. "It would be a shame for your abilities to go undeveloped. I am going to extend a rare invitation to you, Nick. Come visit me from time to time, and I will share my knowledge with you. I have a great deal to teach. No payment will be necessary . . . only bring me a gift now and then." When he did not move, she bit gently at his nape. "After I'm through with you, no woman in the world will be able to resist you. What do you say to that?"

Nick rolled over and pinned her to the mattress, staring down at her smiling face. "I'm ready for the first lesson," he said, and covered her mouth with his own.

Chapter One

THREE YEARS LATER

As was his long-standing habit, Nick entered Gemma's private suite without knocking. It was Sunday afternoon, the time they met almost every week. By now the familiar scent of the place—leather, liquor, the hint of fresh flowers—was all it took to begin the low hum of arousal in his body. His desire was unusually strong today, as his work had kept him away from Gemma for a fortnight.

Since the first night they had met, Nick had followed Gemma's rules without question. There had been no other choice, if he wanted to continue seeing her. They were friends, of a sort, but their interactions were strictly physical. Gemma had evinced no interest in what was in his heart, or even whether he had one. She was a kind woman, and yet on the rare occasions when Nick had tentatively spoken of matters other than the superficial, he'd been gently dismissed. It was just as well, he had realized. He had no wish to expose her to the ugliness of his past or the complex tangle of emotions he kept locked inside.

And so once a week they joined each other in bed with their secrets safely intact . . . the instructor and her ardent student. In the luxurious cocoon of Gemma's gold-papered bedroom Nick had learned more about lovemaking than he had ever thought possible. He'd gained an appreciation of female sexuality that few men acquired . . . the intricacy of a woman's pleasure, the ways to excite her mind as well as her body. He learned to employ his fingers, his tongue, teeth, lips, and cock with both delicacy and strength. Most of all he learned about discipline, and how patience and creativity could make even the experienced Mrs. Bradshaw cry out until she was hoarse. He knew ways to keep a woman balanced on the edge of ecstasy for hours at a time. He also knew how to make a woman climax with nothing more than his mouth on her nipple, or with the lightest brush of his fingertip.

The last time they had met, Gemma had challenged him to bring her to orgasm without touching her at all. He had whispered in her ear for ten minutes, painting sexual images that became ever more exquisitely lurid until she had flushed and shivered beside him.

Thinking of her lush body, Nick turned warm with anticipation, and he strode into her parlor. He stopped short as he saw a young blond man seated on the velvet-upholstered chaise, dressed only in a wine silk robe. It was, Nick noted dazedly, the same robe that he made use of whenever he came to visit Gemma.

She had made no promises of fidelity to him, and he had no illusion that he had been her only lover for the past three years. Still, Nick was startled by the sight of another man in her receiving room and the unmistakable tang of sex in the air.

Seeing him, the stranger flushed and sat up from his relaxed position. He was a stocky, fair-skinned youth, with enough innocence remaining to be embarrassed by the situation.

Gemma walked out of her bedroom, wearing a transparent green negligee that barely covered the crests of her rose-brown nipples. She smiled as she saw Nick, seeming not at all perturbed by his unexpected arrival. "Oh, hello, dear," she murmured, as relaxed and friendly as always. Perhaps she had not planned for him to discover her new *cher ami* in precisely this manner, but neither was she distressed about it.

Turning toward the blond man, she spoke to him softly. "Wait for me in the bedroom."

He threw her a glance of heated adulation as he obeyed.

As Nick watched the man disappear into the next room, he was reminded of himself as he had been three years earlier, callow and burning and dazzled by Gemma's sensual arts.

Gemma lifted a graceful hand to stroke Nick's dark hair. "I didn't expect you to return from your investigation so quickly," she said without a trace of chagrin. "As you can see, I am entertaining my new protégé."

"And my replacement," Nick said rather than asked, while a cold feeling of abandonment crept over him.

"Yes," Gemma said softly. "You have no more need of my instruction. Now that you have learned all I can teach you, it is only a matter of time before our friendship becomes stale. I would prefer to end it while it is still enjoyable."

It was surprisingly difficult for him to speak. "I still want you."

"Only because I am safe, and familiar." Smiling affectionately, Gemma leaned over to kiss his cheek. "Don't be a coward, dear. It is time for you to find someone else."

"No one could follow you," he said gruffly.

That earned a tender laugh and another kiss. "That shows you still have much to learn." A wicked smile gleamed in her clear brown eyes. "Go find a woman who is deserving of your talents. Take her to bed. Make her fall in love with you. A love affair is something everyone should experience at least once."

Nick gave her a sullen glance. "That is the *last* damn thing I need," he informed her, making her laugh.

Drawing back, Gemma casually unfastened her hair and shook it free. "No good-byes," she said, depositing the hairpins onto the table by the chaise. "I much prefer *au revoir*. Now if you'll excuse me, my pupil is waiting. Have a drink before you leave, if you like."

Stunned, Nick stood immobile as she drifted into the bedroom and closed it with a firm click. "Jesus," he muttered. An incredulous laugh escaped him at having been so lightly dispensed with after all they had done together. Yet he couldn't summon any anger. Gemma had been too generous, too kind, for him to feel anything but gratitude.

Go find another woman, he thought numbly. It seemed an impossible task. Oh, there were women everywhere, cultured, common, plump, lean, dark, fair, tall, short, and he found something to appreciate in all of them. But Gemma had been the only one with whom he had ever dared to unleash his sexuality. He could not imagine how it would be with someone else.

Make someone love him? Nick smiled bitterly, thinking for the first time that Gemma didn't know what the hell she was talking about. No woman could love him . . . and if one ever did, she would be the greatest fool alive.

Chapter Two

She was here. He was certain of it.

Nick surveyed the party guests intently as they milled in the gardens behind Stony Cross Park. His hand slid into the pocket of his coat, finding the miniature case that contained Charlotte Howard's portrait. Slowly his thumb caressed the glossy enameled side of the case while he continued to gaze at the crowd.

His two-month search for Charlotte had led him to Hampshire, a place of heather-carpeted hills, ancient hunting forests, and treacherous valley bogs. The western county was prosperous, its twenty market towns abundantly filled with wool, timber, dairy products, honey, and bacon. Among the Hampshire's renowned estates, Stony Cross Park was considered to be the finest. The manor house and private lake were situated in the fertile Itchen River valley. Not a bad place to hide, Nick thought wryly. If his suspicions proved to be correct, Charlotte had found employment in the earl of Westcliff's household, serving as a companion to his mother.

In his pursuit of Charlotte, Nick had learned everything he could about her, trying to understand how she thought and felt, how others perceived her. Interestingly, the accounts of Charlotte had been so contradictory that Nick had wondered if her friends and family were describing the same girl.

To her parents, Charlotte had been an obedient daughter, eager to please, fearful of disapproval. Her disappearance had been a staggering surprise, as they had believed that she was resigned to the fate of becoming Lord Radnor's bride. Charlotte had known since early childhood that the well-being of her family depended on it. The Howards had made a bargain with the devil, trading their daughter's future for the financial benefits Radnor could provide. They had enjoyed his patronage for over a decade. But just as it had come time to give the devil his due, Charlotte had fled. The Howards had made it clear to Nick that they wanted Charlotte found and given to Radnor without delay. They did not understand what had prompted her to run, as they believed she would be well served as Lady Radnor.

Apparently Charlotte had not shared their views. Her friends at Maidstone's, the upper-crust boarding school Charlotte had attended, most of them now married, had reluctantly described a girl who had become increasingly resentful of the way Radnor supervised every aspect of her existence. Apparently the school staff, desirous of the generous financial endowments Radnor provided, had been happy to enforce his wishes. Charlotte's curriculum had differed from everyone else's; Radnor had chosen the subjects for her to study. He had mandated that she was to retire to bed an hour earlier than the other students. He had even determined how much food she should be allotted, after observing during one of her visits home that she had gained weight and needed slimming.

Although Nick understood Charlotte's rebellion, he felt no sympathy. He had no sympathy for anyone. Long ago he had accepted the unfairness of life, the cruel twists of fate that no one could avoid forever. The tribulations of a schoolgirl were nothing compared to the ugliness that he had seen and experienced. He would have no compunction about bringing Charlotte to Radnor, collecting the remainder of his fee, then putting all thought of the luckless bride-to-be completely out of his mind.

His gaze chased restlessly over the scene, but so far there had been no sign of Charlotte. The great house was filled with at least three dozen families, all of whom were attending what amounted to a month-long house party. The annual event was hosted by Lord Westcliff. The daytime hours were devoted to hunting, shooting, and field sports. Each evening had entertainment, such as soirees musicales, and dances.

Although it was nearly impossible to gain one of

the sought-after invitations to Stony Cross Park, Nick had managed to with the help of his brother-in-law, Sir Ross Cannon. Nick had decided to pose as a bored aristocrat who needed to refresh himself with a few weeks in the country. At the request of Sir Ross, the earl of Westcliff had extended an invitation, having no idea that Nick was a Bow Street runner on the hunt for a runaway bride.

The myriad of lights hung from the oak branches caused the women's jewels to glitter madly. A wry smile tugged at one side of Nick's mouth as he reflected how easy it would be to strip these pigeons of their finery. Not long ago he would have done exactly that. He was an even better thief than he was a thief-taker. But now he was a runner, and he was supposed to be honorable.

"Lord Sydney." A man's voice interrupted his thoughts, and Nick turned away from the terrace to face Marcus, Lord Westcliff. The earl possessed a formidable presence. Although he was of only average height, his form was broad and exceedingly muscular, almost bullish in its heavily developed power. His features were bold and decisively formed, his shrewd black eyes set deep in his swarthy face.

Westcliff looked nothing like the slender, fair peers who occupied the first circles of society. Were he not dressed in elegant evening clothes, one would assume he was a dock-worker or journeyman. However, Westcliff's blood was unquestionably blue. He had inherited one of the most ancient earldoms of the peerage, a coronet that had been won by his ancestors in the late 1300s. Ironically, it was rumored that the earl was not an ardent supporter of the Monarchy, nor even of hereditary peerage, as he believed that no man should be insulated from the toils and concerns of ordinary life.

Westcliff continued in his distinctive gravel-scored voice. "Welcome to Stony Cross, Sydney."

Nick executed a shallow bow. "Thank you, my lord."

The earl regarded him with an openly skeptical glance. "Your sponsor, Sir Ross, mentioned in his letter that you suffer from ennui." His tone made it clear that he had little tolerance for a wealthy man's complaint of excessive boredom.

Neither did Nick. He chafed inwardly at the necessity of affecting ennui, but it was part of his ruse. "Yes," he said with a world-weary smile. "A debilitating condition. I have become decidedly melancholy. I was advised that a change of scene might help."

A surly grunt came from the earl's throat. "I can recommend an excellent cure for boredom—simply apply yourself to some useful activity."

"Are you suggesting that I *work*?" Nick summoned an expression of distaste. "Perhaps that would do for someone else. *My* kind of ennui, however, requires a careful balance of rest and entertainment."

Contempt flickered in Westcliff's black eyes. "We

shall endeavor to provide you with satisfactory amounts of both."

"I look forward to it," Nick murmured, taking care to keep his accent clean. Although he had been born a viscount's son, too many years spent in the London underworld had given him a lower-class cadence and woefully soft consonants. "Westcliff, at the moment what would please me most is to have a drink, and to find company with some delightful temptress."

"I have an exceptional Longueville Armagnac," the earl muttered, clearly eager to escape Nick's company.

"That would be most welcome."

"Good. I'll send a servant to fetch you a glass." Westcliff turned and began to stride away.

"And the temptress?" Nick persisted, smothering a laugh at the way the man's back stiffened.

"That, Sydney, is something you will have to obtain for yourself."

As the earl left the terrace, Nick allowed himself a swift grin. So far he was playing the part of spoiled young nobleman with great success. He had managed to annoy the earl beyond bearing. Actually, he rather liked Westcliff, recognizing the same harddriven will and cynicism that he himself possessed.

Thoughtfully Nick left the terrace and wandered down to the gardens, which had been designed with both enclosed and open spaces, providing countless pockets of intimacy. The air was dense with the smells of heather and bog myrtle. Ornamental birds trapped in an aviary chirped wildly at his approach. To most it was doubtless a cheerful clamor, but to Nick the ceaseless trills made a desperate sound. He was tempted to open the door and set the damned things free, but it would have little effect, as their wings had been clipped. Stopping at the riverside terrace, he surveyed the dark sparkling flow of the Itchen River, the moonlight that washed through swaying filaments of willow and clusters of beech and oak.

The hour was late. Perhaps Charlotte was inside the house. Casually exploring his surroundings, Nick wandered to the side of the manor, a residence built of honey-colored stone and cornered with four towers that reached six stories in height. It was fronted with a distinctively large courtyard sided with stabling, a laundry, and low buildings to house the servants. The front of the stables had been designed to mirror the chapel on the other side of the courtyard.

Nick was fascinated by the magnificence of the stables, unlike anything he had seen before. He entered through one of the ground-floor archways and found a covered court hung with gleaming harnesses. A pleasant mixture of smells filled the air; horses, hay, leather, and polish. There was a marble drinking fountain for horses at the back of the court, sided by separate entrances to the horse stalls. Nick walked across the stone-flagged floor with the light, almost soundless step that was habitual for all Bow Street runners. Despite his quietness, horses shuffled and snorted warily at his approach. Glancing through the archway, Nick discovered rows of stalls filled by at least five dozen horses.

It seemed that the stables were empty save for the animals, and Nick left through the west entrance. Immediately he was confronted with an ancient ironstone wall almost six feet high. There was no doubt that it had been built to protect unwary visitors from falling over the steep bluff overlooking the river below. Nick stopped in his tracks at the unexpected sight of a small, slim figure poised atop the wall. It was a woman, standing so still that at first glance he thought she was a statue. But a breeze stirred the hem of her skirts and teased a lock of pale blond hair free of her loose topknot.

Fascinated, he drew closer, his gaze riveted on her.

Only a reckless fool would balance on that uneven wall, with certain death awaiting if she lost her footing. She did not seem to recognize the fatal drop looming before her. The tilt of her head indicated that she was staring straight ahead, at the night-darkened horizon. What in God's name was she doing? Two years earlier, Nick had seen a man standing with that peculiar stillness just before he had jumped to his death from a bridge over the Thames.

As Nick's gaze raked over her, he saw that the hem of her long skirt was caught beneath her heel. The sight spurred him into action. Moving forward in a few stealthy strides, he lifted himself easily, soundlessly, onto the wall.

She did not see him coming until he had almost reached her. She turned, and Nick saw the flash of her dark eyes just as she lost her balance. Seizing her before she could fall, Nick hauled her against his chest. His forearm locked securely just beneath her breasts. The simple action of pulling her body against his was strangely satisfying, like a puzzle piece snapping neatly into place. She gave a low cry, automatically clutching at his arm. The loose lock of fine blond hair blew across Nick's face, and the fresh, faintly salty fragrance of female skin rose to his nostrils. The scent made his mouth water. Nick was startled by his instant reaction to her—he had never experienced such visceral response to a woman. He wanted to leap from the wall and carry her off like one of the wolves that had once roamed the medieval forests, and find some place to devour his prey in private.

She was rigid in his hold, her breath coming in gasps. "Let go of me," she said, prying at his arms. "Why the devil did you do that?"

"You were going to fall."

"I was not! I was perfectly fine until you rushed at me and nearly knocked me over—"

"Your heel is caught in the hem of your skirts."

Moving cautiously, she lifted her foot and perceived that he was correct. "So it is," she said shortly.

Having rescued people from every conceivable

situation, Nick was accustomed to receiving at least a perfunctory show of gratitude. "Aren't you going to thank me for saving you?"

"I have excellent reflexes. I could have saved myself."

Nick let out an incredulous laugh, both annoyed and fascinated by her stubbornness. "If it weren't for me, you would have broken your little neck."

"I assure you, sir, that this so-called rescue was entirely unnecessary. However, since it is obvious that you are going to persist . . . thank you. Now please take your hands from me." Her tone rendered the words devoid of appreciation.

Nick grinned, appreciating the fearlessness of her manner, despite the fact that her heart was pounding wildly against the inside of his wrist. Carefully he loosened his arm and helped her to turn by slow degrees. She wobbled a little and dug her fingers into his coat sleeves in a spasm of anxiety. "I've got you," he said steadily.

She faced him, and they both froze as their gazes locked. Nick forgot the wall beneath his feet. It seemed as if they were poised in midair, in a blue wash of moonlight that made everything look unreal. Recognition shot through him like a bolt of lightning. Incredibly, he found himself staring into the features that had almost become more familiar to him than his own.

Charlotte.

"I've got you," he repeated with a faint smile.

Chapter Three

"Sit," the stranger told Lottie, his huge hands closing around her shoulders and pushing her down. She obeyed carefully, lowering herself to the wall with her legs dangling. The man swung to the ground, landing lightly from the six-foot drop. He held up his arms for her. Lottie hesitated as a cold fist seemed to squeeze around her heart. Every instinct warned her not to jump into his arms. He looked like a predator waiting to snatch her.

"Come," he murmured. The moon struck glints of jolting blue in his eyes.

Reluctantly Lottie leaned forward with her arms outstretched. As she repelled from the stone surface, her hands settled on his shoulders, and he took hold of her waist. He tempered her descent with an ease that betrayed immense physical strength. His hands lingered at her waist, assuring her balance before he released her.

Standing with him on the ground, Lottie was struck by his size. The stranger was unusually tall, with broad shoulders, and big feet and hands. Although he was well dressed, wearing the new cut of coat with long lapels, and loose-tailored trousers, his dark hair had been cut unfashionably short, and his face was clean shaven. That was unusual among the elegant crowd at Stony Cross Park. Stylish gentlemen let their hair grow over their collars, and sported side-whiskers and moustaches. This man didn't even have a wisp of a goatee to soften the obdurate line of his jaw.

He indicated the wall with a jerk of his head. "Why were you standing up there?"

For a moment Lottie couldn't speak as she stared up into his handsome face. Nature had been spendthrift with this man, bestowing him with bold, princely features and eyes as blue and intense as the heart of midnight. The cynicism in those eyes was a fascinating contrast to the touch of humor that lurked at the corners of his wide mouth. He looked to be about thirty—the time in a man's life when he surrendered the last vestiges of callowness and came fully into his maturity. No doubt women of all ages were instantly enthralled by him.

Gathering her wits, she managed to answer him. "I enjoy the view."

"You could obtain the same view from the safety of a window."

A faint smile touched her lips. "The view is far more rewarding when there is some risk involved."

He grinned suddenly, as if he understood exactly what she meant. His roguish smile was dazzling, nearly causing her heart to stop. Lottie couldn't stop staring at him. It seemed that there was something important and unspoken in the air, as if they had once met but she had forgotten the occasion.

"Who are you, sir?" she asked. "I haven't seen you here before."

"Perhaps I'm your guardian angel."

"You don't look very angelic to me," she replied skeptically, making him laugh.

He bowed and introduced himself. "Lord Sydney, at your service."

Lottie responded with a curtsy. "Miss Miller. I am employed as a companion to the dowager countess." She gave him an openly speculative glance. "The guest list for Lord Westcliff's house parties is quite exclusive. How did you manage to get an invitation?"

"The earl was kind enough to offer his hospitality on the recommendation of a mutual friend."

"Have you come to hunt?" she asked. "Is that why you are here?"

"Yes," he said with a puzzling, ironic edge to his tone. "I hunt."

A burst of music came from the direction of the al fresco party, and they both glanced toward the back gardens. "I came to have a look at the horses," Sydney said. "Forgive me for intruding on your privacy."

"Do you intend to return to the party now?"

His dark brows lifted in teasing challenge. "Are you going to climb back onto that wall if I do?"

Good Lord, it was preposterous for one man to possess so much charm! Her lips quirked with an irrepressible smile. "Not tonight, my lord."

"Allow me to accompany you back to the house, then."

Lottie made no protest as he fell into step beside her.

It was hardly unusual to encounter his sort at Stony Cross Park. Most days, one couldn't throw a coin without hitting some brawny male in search of sport. In the past two years Lottie had been approached by many of them. But there was something different about this one. He did not have the sense of ease, the aimlessness of the other aristocrats who frequented this place. She sensed the ruthlessness that lurked just beneath his facade. She did not feel quite safe around him. And yet at the same time, she felt oddly compelled to lure him closer, to make him smile again.

"You seem to have no fear of heights, Miss Miller," he commented.

"I'm not afraid of anything," she said confidently.

"Everyone is afraid of something."

"Oh?" She sent him a provocative glance. "What could a man like you possibly fear?"

To her surprise, he answered seriously. "I'm not fond of enclosed places."

The gravity in his tone made her heart thump heavily. What a voice he had, deep with a tantalizing raspiness, as if he had just awakened from a heavy sleep. The sound seemed to gather at the top of her spine and slide downward like heated honey. "Neither am I," she admitted.

They stopped at the door of the south tower, where many of the upper servants, including herself, were housed. Light streamed from the glittering windows and pooled onto the graveled paths. Now Lottie saw that his hair was not black but brown. A rich, dark shade of brown, the short glossy strands containing every shade between maple and sable. She wanted to touch his hair and feel it slide through her fingers. The immediacy of the urge confounded her.

Stepping backward, she gave him a regretful smile. "Good-bye, my lord. And thank you for being a most agreeable escort."

"Wait," he said, with an urgent note in his voice. "Will I see you again, Miss Miller?"

"No, my lord. I fear my time is fully occupied by the dowager countess."

The words did not dissuade him—she saw it in his eyes. "Miss Miller—"

"Good-bye," she repeated warmly. "I wish you a very pleasant stay, my lord." She left swiftly, conscious of his unnerving regard.

As soon as Lottie reached her room, she locked the door and sighed. Since she had come to Stony Cross Park, she had often been approached by male guests who had made overtures to her. Until tonight she had never been tempted by any of them, no matter how handsome or accomplished. After her experience with Lord Radnor, she wanted nothing to do with men.

Had Radnor been kind instead of calculating, gentle instead of dominating, Lottie would have been able to reconcile herself to the prospect of marrying him. However, Radnor's intentions had been clear from the beginning. He wanted to control every aspect of her existence. He planned to destroy every facet of the person she was and replace her with a being of his own creation. Marriage to him would have literally been worse than death.

Her parents had refused to acknowledge the obvious, as they desperately needed Radnor's financial patronage. And it had grieved Lottie to leave them, as she was well aware of the repercussions they would face. She was often haunted by guilt, knowing that she should have sacrificed herself to Radnor for their benefit. However, the instinct of self-preservation had been too strong. In the end, she couldn't keep from bolting, and somehow providence had led her to Hampshire.

As Lottie had expected, her freedom had come with a price. She often awakened sweat-soaked and cold from nightmares of being dragged back to Radnor. It was impossible to forget—even for a moment—that he had sent people to look for her. Any perception of safety was illusory. Although her life at Stony Cross Park was pleasant, she was trapped here as surely as the birds in the aviary, their wings clipped to make them into animals neither of the ground nor of the air. She could not go anywhere, or do anything, without knowing that she would be found someday. And that had made her doomed and defiant, and unable to trust anyone. Even a handsome young man with haunting blue eyes.

Rather than return to the al fresco party, Nick went to his own room. His trunk and traveling case had already been unpacked by the servants. His clothes were neatly stacked in the mahogany gentleman's chest and hung in the armoire, which was redolent with the scent of cloves.

Impatiently Nick shed his coat, waistcoat, and his gray silk cravat. Stripping off his shirt, he bunched it in one hand and used it to blot the sheen of sweat on his face, neck, and chest. After dropping the wadded-up linen to the floor, he sat on the bed, which had been fitted into an alcove opposite the door. He removed his shoes and stockings, and lay back clad in only his black trousers, his gaze directed at the wood-paneled ceiling of the alcove.

He finally understood Radnor's obsession.

Charlotte Howard was the most bewitching woman he had ever met. She radiated a remarkable force of will that somehow conveyed the impression of movement even when she stood still. Her body, her face, every part of her was a perfect amalgam of delicacy and strength. He wanted to sink inside that vibrant warmth, ride her to peacefulness, and bury his face amid the silky curves of her breasts. He imagined her relaxed and smiling, her skin flushed from his caresses as they lay together in bed.

No wonder Radnor wanted her. And yet in his attempts to possess her, the earl would soon extinguish everything that made her so desirable.

Nick knew it would be relatively easy to whisk Charlotte away to London before the Westcliffs were fully aware of what was happening. He supposed he should do it in the morning, using the element of surprise to his advantage. Deeply troubled, he laced his fingers behind his head. *"I'm not afraid of anything,"* Charlotte had told him. Although he didn't believe that, he admired her for saying it. Of course Charlotte was afraid—she knew what Radnor would do to her when she returned. However, that was not Nick's concern. His only responsibility was to do what he had been paid for.

On the other hand . . .

There was no need for haste. Why not stay at Stony Cross Park for a few days? He would not be required to report at Bow Street for another two weeks, and the woods of Hampshire were far preferable to the soggy, ill-smelling mess of London. If he remained here for an extra day or two, he would be able to learn more about Charlotte. He needed to find out if she was all that she seemed to be.

Rolling to his side, Nick considered the idea. He had never broken his own rules before, one of them being that he never allowed himself to develop personal familiarity with his prey. However, he had never been one to respect rules, even his own.

The thought of Charlotte made him hot and irritable and thoroughly aroused. Gemma had ended their arrangement six months ago, and he had been celibate ever since. It wasn't that he lacked desire . . . in fact, he was burning with unspent passion. And he had met many willing women. But he was not interested in the ordinary or the mundane. He wanted a woman who could provide the sexual intensity he needed. Such a woman would either be inordinately experienced in the bedroom . . . or not experienced at all.

Reaching over the side of the bed, Nick searched in the discarded heap of his clothes and found the miniature. With an expertise born of habit, he pressed the catch of the enameled case and flipped it open. Settling on his back, he stared into Charlotte's exquisite little face.

Is it you? he thought, tracing the line of her cheek with his fingertip. Desire filled his cock and caused it to stiffen unmercifully. His lashes lowered slightly as he continued to watch the tiny painted face, and his hand slid down to the aching jut of his arousal.

As was her daily habit, Lottie took an early-morning walk across the landscape of Stony Cross,

over steep hills covered in heather or forest, past
bogs and ponds and glades that teemed with life.
Most of the guests at the manor, including Lady
Westcliff, slept late and took breakfast at the hour of
ten. However, Lottie had never been able to adapt
to such a schedule. She needed some form of exer-
cise to rid herself of an excess of nervous energy. On
the days when it was too cold or stormy to walk,
she fidgeted inside until Lady Westcliff erupted in
exasperation.

Lottie had devised three or four different walks,
each lasting approximately an hour. This morning
she chose the one that began along Hill Road,
crossed through a medieval oak and hazel forest,
and passed the source of a local spring called the
Wishing Well. It was a cool, damp morning typical
of the beginning of May, and Lottie drew in deep
breaths of the earth-scented air. Dressed in a gown
with loose ankle-length skirts, her feet shod in
sturdy mid-calf boots, Lottie trod energetically away
from Westcliff Manor. She followed a sandy track
that led into the forest, while natterjack toads
hopped out of the path of her oncoming boots. The
trees rustled overhead, the wind carrying the cries of
nuthatches and whitethroats. A huge, ungainly buz-
zard flapped its way toward the nearby bogs in
search of breakfast.

Suddenly Lottie caught sight of a dark shape
ahead. It was a man, roaming through the forest, his
outline partially obscured in the mist. A poacher,
perhaps. Although Lottie stopped at some distance,

he had unusually sharp hearing. His head turned as a twig snapped beneath her boot.

Lottie held her ground as he approached. She recognized him at once, the fluid, almost catlike grace of his movements. He was casually dressed in shirt-sleeves and a black waistcoat, with boots and decidedly ancient breeches. Lord Sydney . . . looking disreputable and indecently handsome. She was surprised to see him there, when all the other guests at Westcliff Manor were still abed. Even more surprising was her own reaction to him, a surge of excitement and gladness.

"Good morning," Lord Sydney said, a faint smile playing on his lips. His dark hair was disheveled, and his cravat had been carelessly tied.

"I wouldn't have expected you to be out at this hour," she said cheerfully.

"I never sleep past sunrise."

Lottie nodded toward the path he had been contemplating. "Were you planning to go that way? I wouldn't advise it."

"Why not?"

"That path leads to marshy ponds and very deep bogs. One unfortunate step, and you could find yourself drowning in mud—that is, if you haven't been done in by raft spiders or snakes." She shook her head in feigned regret. "We've lost some very nice guests that way."

He smiled lazily. "I don't suppose you would care to recommend an alternate route?"

"If you go the other way, you'll come to a bridle

path that leads to a sunken lane. Follow it to the gate-
house garden, go through the opening in the hedge,
and you'll find a path that takes you to the top of a
hill. From there you can see lakes, villages, forests,
all spread before you . . . the view is breathtaking."

"Is that where you're headed?"

She shook her head and replied impudently, "No,
I am going in the opposite direction."

"But who will save me from the bogs?"

She laughed. "You can't accompany me, my lord.
It would neither be seemly nor wise."

If they were seen together, it would cause gossip.
And it would most certainly displease Lady Westcliff, who had warned her never to take a "follower,"
as it was politely called.

"Do you wish to be alone?" Lord Sydney asked. A
new expression crossed his face, so quick and subtle
that hardly anyone would have noticed it. "Forgive
me. Once again I have trespassed on your solitude."

Lottie wondered at what she had seen in his eyes
for that fragment of a second . . . a desolation so vast
and impenetrable that it shocked her. What could
have caused it? He had everything a person required to be content . . . freedom, wealth, looks, social position. There was no reason for him to be
anything other than ecstatic over his lot in life. But
he was unhappy, and everything in her nature compelled her to offer him comfort. "I am rather too accustomed to solitude," she said softly. "Perhaps
some company would be a pleasant change."

"If you're certain—"

"Yes, come along." She gave his athletic form a deliberately challenging glance. "I only hope that you'll be able to keep pace with me."

"I'll try," he assured her wryly, falling into step beside her as she continued her walk.

They approached the trunk of a huge oak that had fallen across the path. Insects buzzed lazily through the rays of strengthening sunlight that streamed in from above. "Look," Lottie said, gesturing to a dragonfly as it flew and dipped before them. "There are more than a dozen varieties of dragonfly in this forest, and at least a hundred different moths. If you come at dusk, you can see purple hairstreak butterflies—they gather right there at the tops of the tr—"

"Miss Miller," he interrupted, "I'm a Londoner. We don't care about insects, except to consider how they may best be exterminated."

Lottie heaved a theatrical sigh, as if vexed by his lack of interest in the subject. "All right, then. I will refrain from describing the many varieties of aquatic beetle we have here."

"Thank you," came his fervent reply. "Here, allow me to help you over that oak—"

"No need."

Lottie hopped onto the fallen trunk and walked along the gnarled surface, showing off her physical coordination with no trace of modesty. When her efforts were greeted with silence, she glanced over her shoulder and discovered Sydney walking right behind her, his footing as sure and easy as a cat's. A startled laugh escaped her as she made her way to the end of the trunk. "You are quite agile for a gentleman of your size."

Lord Sydney let the comment pass, his mouth twisting to indicate that his agility was of no consequence. "Why did you become a lady's companion?" he asked as Lottie jumped to the ground, her feet rustling through the brittle layer of leaves. He followed her, landing in the same spot she had. Curiously, he did not make nearly as much noise as she had, despite the fact that he was easily twice her weight.

Lottie chose her words with great care. She disliked talking about her past—not only was it dangerous but the subject filled her with melancholy. "My family is poor. There was no other choice for me."

"You could have married."

"I've never met anyone that I wanted to marry."

"Not even Lord Westcliff?"

"Lord Westcliff?" she repeated in surprise. "Why would I have designs on him?"

"He's wealthy and titled, and you've resided beneath his roof for two years," came Sydney's sardonic reply. "Why wouldn't you?"

Lottie frowned thoughtfully. It wasn't as if the earl was unappealing—quite the opposite, in fact. Westcliff was an attractive man who shouldered his responsibilities and considered it unmanly to complain about them. In addition to his own strict morality, Lord Westcliff possessed a dry wit and a carefully concealed sense of compassion, and as Lottie had discreetly observed, he employed his courteous manners as skillfully as a weapon. Women were drawn to him, although Lottie was not one of them. She sensed that she did not have the key to unlock his innate reserve . . . nor had she ever been tempted to trust him with the reason for her uncompromising solitude.

"Naturally a man of Westcliff's position would never entertain _that_ kind of interest in a lady's companion," she said in reply to Lord Sydney's question. "But even if we were on the same social footing, I am certain that the earl would never regard me in that way, nor I him. Our relationship—if one could call it that—does not possess that particular . . ." She paused, searching for an appropriate word. "Alchemy."

The word hovered gently in the air, dispelled only by the sound of Sydney's quiet voice.

"Surely alchemy pales in comparison to the safety that he could offer you."

Safety. The thing she wanted most, and could never have. Lottie stopped and stared into his dark face. "What makes you think that I am in need of safety?"

"You're alone. A woman needs someone to protect her."

"Oh, I have no need of protection. I have a very pleasant life at Stony Cross Park. Lady Westcliff is quite kind, and I want for nothing."

"Lady Westcliff won't live forever," Sydney pointed out. Although his words were blunt, his expression was strangely understanding. "What will you do after she is gone?"

The question caught Lottie by surprise. No one ever asked her such things. Perturbed, she took her time about replying. "I don't know," she said honestly. "I suppose I never let myself think about the future."

Sydney's gaze was riveted on her, his eyes an almost unnatural shade of blue. "Neither do I."

Lottie didn't know what to make of her companion. It had been easy at first to think of him as a spoiled young aristocrat, with his beautifully tailored clothes and perfect features. But on closer inspection, there were signs that conveyed the opposite. The deep-cut shadows beneath his eyes betrayed countless sleepless nights. The harsh grooves on either side of his mouth gave him a cynical look that was odd for a man so young. And in unguarded moments such as this, she saw in his eyes that he was no stranger to pain.

His expression changed like quicksilver. Once again he was a lazy rogue with mocking eyes. "The future is too boring to contemplate," he said lightly. "Shall we continue, Miss Miller?"

Disconcerted by his swift change of mood, Lottie led him out of the forest to a sunken road. The morning sun rose higher, chasing the lavender from the sky and warming the meadows. The field they passed was filled with heather and emerald sphagnum moss, and dotted with tiny red sundew rosettes. "They don't have views like this in London, do they?" Lottie remarked.

"No," Lord Sydney agreed, although he seemed distinctly unenchanted by the quiet rural beauty around them.

"I gather you prefer town life," Lottie said with a smile. "Tenements, cobbled streets, factories, coal smoke, and all that noise. How could anyone choose that over *this*?"

The sunlight touched on the mahogany and gold highlights in his brown hair. "You keep your beetles and bogs, Miss Miller. I'll take London any time."

"I'll show you something that London doesn't have." Triumphantly Lottie led him across the sunken road. They came to a deep muddy basin filled with water that spilled from the bank beside it.

"What is that?" Lord Sydney asked, viewing the sloshing hole dubiously.

"A wishing well. Everyone in the village visits it." Busily Lottie searched the pockets of her walking skirts. "Oh, curse it, I haven't got any pins."

"What do you need pins for?"

"To drop in the well." She gave him a chiding smile. "I thought everyone knew that you can't make a wish without a pin."

"What do you want to wish for?" he asked huskily.

"Oh, it isn't for me. I've made dozens of wishes here. I wanted you to have one." Giving up her search for a pin, Lottie glanced up at him.

There was a strange look on Lord Sydney's

face . . . blank, painfully surprised . . . as if he had just been kicked in the stomach. He didn't move or blink, just stared at her as if he couldn't quite comprehend her words. The silence between them became thick, and Lottie waited in helpless fascination for him to break it. Wrenching his gaze away, Lord Sydney gazed at the field of heather with puzzling intensity, as if his mind were striving to wrap itself around something that didn't make sense.

"Do make a wish," Lottie said impulsively. "I'll throw a pin in the well for you the next time I come."

Lord Sydney shook his head. When he spoke, his voice was oddly hoarse. "I wouldn't know what to wish for."

They continued in silence, making their way over a muddy patch and following the sunken road to a footbridge that covered a small stream. On the other side of the stream, a damp meadow beckoned, blazing with waist-high yellow meadowsweet bushes. "This way," Lottie said, lifting her skirts to her knees as they traversed grass and heather and approached a barrier of hedge and fence. "Beyond the hedge, the footpath leads back through the forest to Stony Cross Park." She pointed to the tall arched gate, so narrow that it would allow only one person to pass through at a time. Glancing at Lord Sydney, she was relieved to see that he had recovered his composure. "The only way through is that kissing gate."

"Why is it called that?"

"I don't know." Lottie considered the gate

thoughtfully. "I suppose because a kiss would be the unavoidable consequence of two people trying to pass through it at the same time."

"An interesting theory." Sydney paused inside the narrow gate. Leaning against one side of it, he sent her a challenging smile, knowing full well that she could not go through without brushing against him.

Lottie raised her brows. "By some chance are you expecting me to test it?"

Lord Sydney lifted one shoulder in a relaxed shrug, watching her with a vagabond charm that was nearly irresistible. "I won't stop you, if you feel so inclined."

It was obvious that he did not expect her to take up the challenge. Lottie knew she had only to roll her eyes and reprove him and he would step aside. However, as she considered her response to him she became aware of a painful hollowness inside. She had not been touched by anyone in two years. No impulsive girlish hugs from her friends at Maidstone's . . . no caress of her mother's hand, no sweetly childish kisses from her younger siblings. She wondered what it was about this man that had made her aware of the deprivation. He made her want to tell him her secrets—which was, of course, unthinkable. Impossible. She could never trust anyone, when her very life was at stake.

She realized that Lord Sydney's smile had vanished. Without being aware of it, she had drawn closer to him and now stood within arm's length. Her gaze flickered to his mouth, so wide, masculine,

full. Her pulse escalated to a wild rhythm as temptation exerted a force stronger than anything she had
ever known . . . as strong as fear, as deep as hunger.

"Hold still," she heard herself say. Carefully she
laid a hand on the center of his chest.

The instant that Lottie touched him, Lord Sydney's chest moved beneath her palm in a strong,
quick breath.

The violent thump of his heart against her fingers
filled Lottie with a curious tenderness. He seemed to
be frozen, as if he feared that any movement might
frighten her away. Softly she touched his lower lip
with her fingertips and felt his hot breath fan against
them. A butterfly left its resting place on the gate and
flew away, a trembling stain of color in the air.

"What is your name?" Lottie whispered. "Your
first name."

It took an unaccountably long time for him to reply. The bristly fans of his lashes lowered to conceal
his thoughts. "John."

He was so tall that Lottie had to stand on her toes
to reach his mouth, and even then she couldn't quite
manage it. Catching her waist in his hands, he com-
pacted her gently against his body. Suddenly there
was a strange, lost look in his eyes, as if he were
drowning. Hesitantly Lottie slid her hand around
the back of his neck, where the interlaced muscles
had gone rigid.

He let her tug his head lower, lower, until their
breath mingled and their lips touched in a sweet,
supple kiss. His mouth remained warm and still

against hers, and then his lips began to move in soft brushes. Disoriented, Lottie swayed in his grasp, and his arm slid around her back to hold her securely. Instinctively she nudged upward, straining on her toes as she sought to deepen the tender pressure. But he was careful to keep his passion under tight rein, refusing to take any more.

Gradually she eased away from him, sinking back to her heels. She dared to touch the side of his face, relishing the warmth of his skin against her palm. "I've paid the toll," she whispered. "May I pass through the gate now?"

He nodded gravely and moved away from the threshold.

Lottie crossed through and wandered past the hedge, surprised to discover that her knees were a bit quivery. Her companion followed in silence as she walked along the footpath that led to Stony Cross Park. When they had almost reached the great house, they paused in the shelter of an oak tree.

"I must leave you here," Lottie said, her face dappled by the overhead boughs. "It wouldn't do to be seen together."

"Of course."

A wistful ache gathered inside her chest as she stared at him. "When will you leave Stony Cross Park, my lord?"

"Soon."

"Not until after tomorrow evening, I hope. The

village has a wonderful May Day celebration. Everyone from the manor comes down to watch."

"Will you?"

Lottie shook her head immediately. "No, I have seen it before. I will probably remain in my room with a book. But for a newcomer, the festivities would be entertaining."

"I will consider it," he murmured. "Thank you for the walk, Miss Miller." And with a polite bow, he left her.

After breakfast, Charlotte pushed Lady Westcliff's wheeled chair along the paved walks of the estate gardens. Nick watched from an open first-floor window, able to hear the regal old woman as she lectured Charlotte.

"There is no substitute for daily inspection," Lady Westcliff was saying, gesturing with a bejeweled hand. "Weeds must be pulled as soon as they show. Plants must never be allowed to grow outside their proper places, or they will ruin the proportion of the garden . . ."

Charlotte appeared to be listening respectfully as she guided the chair along the path. The ease with which she maneuvered it belied the vehicle's obvious weight. Her slim arms were surprisingly strong, and she showed no signs of tiring as they proceeded along the hedgerow.

Nick watched her intently as he tried to sort through the anarchy of his thoughts. His usual appetite had vanished after their walk this morning. He had not eaten breakfast . . . had not done anything, really, except to wander around the estate in a sort of daze that appalled him. He knew himself to be a callous man, one with no honor, and no means of quelling his own brutish instincts. So much of his life had been occupied with basic survival that he had never been free to follow higher pursuits. He had little acquaintance with literature or history, and his mathematical abilities were limited to matters of money and betting odds. Philosophy, to him, was a handful of cynical principles learned through experience with the worst of humanity. By now, nothing could surprise or intimidate him. He didn't fear loss, pain, or even death.

But with a few words and one awkward, innocent kiss, Charlotte Howard had devastated him.

It was clear that Charlotte had changed from the girl her parents, friends, and Radnor himself had known. She had become accustomed to living in the moment, with no thought given to the future. The knowledge that she was being hunted, that her days of precious freedom were limited, should have made her bitter and disillusioned. And yet she still threw pins into wishing wells. A wish. The flicker of hope that implied . . . it had struck at his soul, when he had believed he had no soul left.

He could not give her to Radnor.

He had to take her for himself.

His hand closed around the painted wood casement, gripping hard to assure his balance. Otherwise, he would have staggered from the violent surprise of his discovery.

"Sydney."

The sound of Lord Westcliff's voice startled him. Nick was not pleased to realize that he had been so absorbed in watching Charlotte that his customary alertness had vanished. Keeping his face blank, he turned toward the earl.

Westcliff's features seemed even more harshly cut and uncompromising than usual. His dark eyes contained a hard, cold gleam. "I see that you've taken notice of my mother's companion," he remarked softly. "An attractive girl, not to mention vulnerable. In the past, I have sometimes found it necessary to discourage a guest's interest in Miss Miller, as I would never allow any of my servants to be taken advantage of."

Nick returned Westcliff's steady regard, aware that he was being warned away from Charlotte. "Am I poaching on your preserve, my lord?"

The earl's eyes narrowed at the insolent question. "I have advanced my hospitality to you with very few conditions, Sydney. However, one of them is that you leave Miss Miller alone. That is not open for negotiation."

"I see." Suspicion ignited inside him. Had Charlotte confided in her employer? He had not thought that she would trust anyone, even a man as honorable as Westcliff. However, if she had taken that chance, then the earl would undoubtedly offer strong opposition to her being removed from Stony Cross Park. It was also possible that Charlotte had earned his protection by sleeping with him.

The thought of Charlotte naked in another man's arms brought an acid taste to Nick's mouth, and he was suddenly filled with bloodlust. *It must be jealousy*, he thought incredulously. Christ.

"I'll leave the choice to Miss Miller," Nick said flatly. "If she desires my presence—or absence—I will abide by *her* preference. Not yours."

Nick saw from the warning gleam in Westcliff's eyes that the earl did not trust him.

The man had good instincts.

Chapter Four

The English celebration of May Day varied from village to village. It had been derived from an ancient Roman festival honoring the goddess of springtime, and over time each region had added its own customs in addition to the standard Maypole dance and a-maying songs. Nick had vague childhood memories of the May celebrations in Worcestershire, especially the man dressed as "Jack-in-the Green," who cavorted through the village completely covered in fresh greenery. As a small child, Nick had been terrified by the sight of the plant-festooned man and had hidden behind his older sister Sophia's skirts until he had gone away.

It had been a long time since Nick had seen a May Day celebration of any kind. Now, from his adult perspective, the sexual connotations of the holiday were more than obvious . . . villagers dancing with the phallic staffs, the May King and Queen going from door to door and sprinkling "wild water" on the household inhabitants . . . the streets adorned with hoop-shaped garlands featuring pairs of marigold balls hanging in the centers.

Nick stood on a hill near the manor house with a crowd of other guests, watching the riotous dancing in the center of the village. Hundreds of lamps and blazing torches lit the streets with a golden glow. A cacophony of laughter, music, and singing filled the air as women took their turns at the towering May-pole. Blasts from hunting horns frequently punctu-ated the din. Young men danced with ropes woven of tail hair from cattle, which would later be dragged through the night dew to ensure a good milk supply for the next year.

"I expect good hunting tonight," came a mascu-line voice from nearby. The speaker was Viscount Stepney, a brawny young man with a well-known penchant for skirt-chasing. His companions, the lords Woodsome and Kendal, broke into lusty laughter. Seeing Nick's questioning gaze, Stepney explained with a chortle. "The village girls will go a-maying until morning. Catch one of them in the woods, and she'll let you do anything you want. Even the married ones do it—they're allowed to re-move their wedding rings for this one night."

"And their husbands don't object?" Nick asked.

That question made the lords laugh in unison. "Why no," Stepney explained, "they are too busy chasing fresh young tails themselves to give a damn about what their wives are doing. A pleasant holiday, is it not?"

Nick smiled slightly, making no reply. Clearly Stepney and his companions considered it great sport to spend ten minutes coupling with peasant girls in the woods. "A poke and a wiggle," as Gemma Bradshaw had dryly described the lovemaking style of most of the men who frequented her establishment. They had no conception of real sexuality, no requirement of a woman save that she spread her legs. Obviously a quick mating between strangers afforded a certain kind of release. But that was too simple, and too easy, to satisfy Nick. Thanks to Gemma's tutoring, he had developed a complex palate.

The image of Charlotte's face, her dark eyes and pointed chin and sweet mouth, hovered at the back of his mind. Let Stepney and his friends go in search of a quick tail-tickle. Nick had far more interesting prospects.

"Come, Sydney," the viscount urged. "The village girls will become available immediately after the betrothed of May is chosen." Seeing Nick's unfamiliarity with the phrase, he explained, "A lad of marriageable age lies on the green and pretends to sleep. The girls who are willing to marry him race to be the first to awaken him. The first one to kiss him will be able to claim him as her betrothed." He smiled lecherously and rubbed his hands. "And the other girls—all in need of consolation—scatter into the forest, waiting to be caught by enterprising fellows such as myself. You should have seen the one I captured last year—black hair and red lips—ah, what a fine little mount she was. Come, Sydney—if you're fleet-footed, you'll catch one for yourself."

Nick was about to refuse when his gaze was caught by a new cluster of girls grasping the Maypole ribbons. One of them seized his full attention. Like the others, she wore a white peasant dress, her hair covered by a red cloth. At this distance her features were difficult to discern, but Nick recognized her at once. A rueful smile curved his lips as he recalled Charlotte's saying that she intended to stay in her room with a book that night. No doubt the Westcliffs would disapprove of her attending the village festival, and so she had chosen to go in disguise. Fascination and desire swirled inside him as his gaze tracked Charlotte's slim figure. She wound in and out of the Maypole circle, her hands flung exuberantly high over her head.

"I believe I will join you," Nick murmured, accompanying the eager rakes down the hill.

Laughing recklessly, Lottie joined the mass of maidens who waited in tense readiness to race to the village green. From what she had been able to deduce, the betrothed of May was an exceptional catch this year—the butcher's son, a handsome blond lad with blue eyes and a fine physique, and a guarantee of inheriting a profitable family business. Of course

Lottie had no intention of trying to reach him. However, it was fun to join in the game, and she was entertained by the excitement of the girls around her.

The signal was given, and Lottie was carried along with the village girls in a frantic rush. The wildness and noise was such a contrast to her quiet existence at Stony Cross Park that she felt a jolt of exhilaration. She had spent so many years learning proper comportment at Maidstone's, and struggling to remain inconspicuous as a companion to Lady Westcliff, that she couldn't remember the last time she had raised her voice. Caught up in the moment, she howled with laughter and screamed as loudly as the determined brides-to-be around her as the group swarmed over the green. From somewhere ahead, a jubilant cry rang over the crowd. The victor, a robust red-haired girl, clambered onto her new fiancé's broad shoulders, exultantly waving a bouquet of wildflowers. "I did it!" she crowed. "I got 'im, 'e's mine!"

Cheering, the villagers surrounded the newly betrothed couple, while disappointed maidens scattered and ran toward the forest. A host of eager men followed, ready to begin the night's a-maying.

Smiling, Lottie followed at a relaxed pace, having no wish to be the focus of some overexcited lad's amorous attention. In a few minutes, the revelers would pair off, and she would sneak back to Stony Cross Park. Stopping at the edge of the forest, she leaned against a heavy-crowned sycamore and sighed in satisfaction. Her knees were pleasantly weak from dancing and wine. This was the first year she had actually taken part in May Day, rather than simply watched, and it had been even more enjoyable than she had expected. A tune played insistently in her head, and she sang to herself in a whisper, her eyes closed as she rested back against the smooth, mottled bark.

Go no more a-rushing, maids in May,
go no more a-rushing, maids, I pray,
go no more a-rushing, or you'll fall a-blushing . . .

Although all was still and quiet around her, some instinct warned she was no longer alone. Pausing, Lottie lifted her lashes and recoiled as she saw a dark shape right beside her. "Good Lord!" She stumbled backward, and a pair of hands gripped her shoulders, steadying her.

Sputtering in surprise, Lottie flailed at her captor in a bid for freedom.

"Easy," came a masculine voice, rich with laughter. "Easy. It's me."

She gasped and went still, staring up at his dark face. "Lord S-Sydney?"

"Yes."

"You nearly frightened me to death!"

"Sorry." He grinned, his white teeth gleaming in the darkness. "I didn't want to interrupt you."

Lottie laughed and pushed at him, mortified to be caught singing to herself like some half-wit. "How did you find me?"

"It seems to be a talent of mine." Sydney released her and leaned one shoulder against the sycamore, his careless smile at variance with his alert gaze.

Lottie felt for her kerchief, which had been dislodged in the flurry of activity. "I covered my hair—I can't think how you recognized me."

"I know the way you move."

She did not reply, experiencing a mixture of pleasure and uncertainty. There was a compliment implicit in the statement. But he was a stranger . . . he had not known her long enough, nor well enough, to distinguish something so intrinsic and subtle.

"Did you enjoy the May festivities, my lord?" she asked as she tied the kerchief back into place.

"I enjoyed watching you."

Her eyes narrowed in pretend-menace. "Do you intend to tell anyone that you saw me here?"

Lord Sydney leaned closer, as if to impart some highly confidential news. "Not if my life depended on it."

Smiling, Lottie leaned her shoulder against the tree trunk, mirroring his posture. "Are you going a-maying, like the other young men?"

"That depends." A flirtatious gleam entered his eyes. "Are you going to run through the forest in hopes of being captured?"

"Decidedly not."

"Then allow me to escort you back to the house. I shouldn't like for you to be waylaid by some impassioned village youth."

"Oh, I would outrun any of them," Lottie said confidently. "I know these woods quite well, and I am small enough to dart easily among the trees. No one could catch me."

"I could."

"A man as large as you? I think not. In these woods, with all the underbrush, you would be as noisy as a rampaging elephant."

His body tensed subtly, his appreciation of the impudent challenge almost palpable. "You might be surprised—" he began, and paused as he was distracted by a feminine squeal from somewhere to the left of them, as a village girl was "caught" by a randy young man. A moment of silence, and then a loud moan of pleasure filtered through the trees.

When Sydney turned back to Lottie, she was gone.

Laughing inwardly, she slipped through the woods like a wraith, raising her skirts to her knees to keep from being snagged by branches. She maneuvered easily through the maze of trunks and flexible saplings, until finally all was quiet and there was no sign of anyone behind her. Pausing for breath, Lottie glanced over her shoulder. No movement, nothing except for the distant sounds of May Day carousing.

Either Lord Sydney had decided not to give chase, or he had lost her in mid-pursuit. A triumphant smile curved her lips—she had proved her point. Turning, she continued toward Stony Cross Park—and shrieked in alarm as she walked right into a hard male body.

She was caught against a deep chest, a pair of powerful arms subduing her easily. It was Lord Sydney, his low laugh tickling her ear. Stunned, she leaned against him, requiring temporary support as she strove to recover her equilibrium.

"How did you get in front of me?" she asked breathlessly.

"Flank speed." His gentle fingers sought to restore her kerchief, but it slid from her fine, slippery hair, revealing the neat braided coil at her nape. He let the cloth drop to the ground. A smile wove through his voice. "You can't escape me, you know."

The teasing words seemed to contain a hint of warning.

Lottie stood in the shelter of his body, absorbing his warmth, his spicy masculine scent. How had she come to be alone in the darkness with him? She did not believe in happenstance. This could only be a result of her own relentless attraction to him . . . an attraction that seemed to be returned in full measure. As they both fell silent, Lottie became aware of a nearby couple, their entwined figures barely visible through the trees. The muffled sounds of sexual revelry brought a rush of heat to Lottie's face.

"Take me back to the house, please," she said.

Lord Sydney released her. Lottie stepped away, almost bumping against the large tree behind her. Following, he pressed her against the wide trunk, using his arms to protect her from the rough bark. Her breath caught sharply. Her hands slid to his upper arms, where the brutal swell of muscle was manifest through his coat. She knew that he was going to kiss her, that he wanted her. And heaven help her, she wanted him too.

He stroked the curve of her cheek with a single fingertip, so carefully, as if she were a wild creature that would bolt at the slightest sign of haste. Her breath quickened as he touched her chin and tilted her head back in an angle of surrender.

His gentle mouth descended to hers, molding, coaxing, until she parted her lips with a gasp of pleasure. The tip of his tongue stroked the edge of her teeth, ventured farther, brushed the inside of her cheek in a burning, delicate exploration. The kiss made her light-headed, and she wrapped her arms around his neck in a desperate bid for balance. He let her have more of his weight, pinning her securely between his body and the unyielding oak at her back. She twisted and pulled at him, until he made a soothing noise and ran his hands down her back. The slow caress only sharpened her need, making her arch against him in a blind, instinctive search. She felt something against the fabric of her rough-woven skirt . . . the intimate bulge of his sex.

The rigid length of him matched perfectly in the notch between her thighs. His hardness pressed into her softness, his mouth possessed hers with wicked skill, while his arms surrounded her. Sliding her hands into his hair, she curved her fingers around his scalp, beneath the thick locks that gleamed like silk in the fragmented moonlight. A harsh breath escaped him, and his lips slid along her throat. Even in her innocence, she sensed the wealth of experience in his careful touch, the hunger he kept so tightly shackled.

Her peasant blouse had slipped over one shoulder, revealing the white gleam of her skin. His fingers stole to the ribbon of her gathered neckline and tugged deftly, causing the crumpled linen to slide downward. Gradually his hand eased beneath her chemise. Her cool, soft nipple tightened against the calloused pads of his fingers, the peak turning harder and warmer with each circling stroke.

Lottie pressed her face into the crook of his neck and shoulder. She had to stop him now, before her will was completely demolished. "No. Please stop. I'm sorry."

His hand slid from her blouse, and he touched her damp lips with his fingers. "Have I frightened you?" he whispered.

Lottie shook her head, somehow resisting the urge to curl into his embrace like a sun-warmed cat. "No . . . I've frightened myself."

For some reason her admission made him smile. His fingers moved to her throat, tracing the fragile line with a sensitivity that made her breath catch. Tugging the peasant blouse back up to her shoulder, he retied the frayed ribbon that secured the neckline. "Then I'll stop," he said. "Come—I'll take you to the house."

He stayed close to her as they continued through the forest, occasionally moving to push a branch out of the way, or taking her hand to guide her over a rough place on the path. As familiar as she was with the woods of Stony Cross Park, Lottie had no need of his assistance. But she accepted the help with demur. And she did not protest when he paused again, his lips finding hers easily in the darkness. His mouth was hot and sweet as he kissed her compulsively . . . swift kisses, languid ones, kisses that ranged from intense need to wicked flirtation. Drugged with pleasure, Lottie let her hands wander to the thick dishevelment of his hair, the iron-hard nape of his neck. When the blistering heat rose to an untenable degree, Lord Sydney groaned softly.

"Charlotte . . ."

"Lottie," she told him breathlessly.

He pressed his lips to her temple and cuddled her against his powerful body as if she were infinitely fragile. "I never thought I would find someone like you," he whispered. "I've looked for you so long . . . needed you . . ."

Lottie shivered and dropped her head to his shoulder. "This isn't real," she said faintly.

His lips touched her neck, finding a place that made her arch involuntarily. "What's real, then?"

She gestured to the yew hedge that bordered the estate garden. "Everything back there."

His arms tightened, and he spoke in a muffled voice. "Let me come to your room. Just for a little while."

Lottie responded with a trembling laugh, knowing exactly what would happen if she allowed that. "Absolutely not."

Soft, hot kisses drifted over her skin. "You're safe with me. I would never ask for more than you were willing to give."

Lottie closed her eyes, her head spinning. "The problem is," she said ruefully, "I am willing to give you entirely too much."

She felt the curve of his smile against her cheek. "Is that a problem?"

"Oh, yes." Pulling away from him, Lottie held her hands to her hot face and sighed unsteadily. "We must stop this. I don't trust myself with you."

"You shouldn't," he agreed hoarsely.

The sounds of their breathing mingled in the darkness. He was so warm and strong that Lottie could barely keep from flinging herself at him. Instead she forced herself to think rationally. Lord Sydney would be gone soon, and the memory of this night would fade in time. She was not so weak-willed, or foolish, that she could be so easily seduced.

"At least let me walk with you to the house," Lord Sydney urged. "If we are seen together, you can explain it as a chance meeting."

Lottie hesitated, then nodded. "And we'll part company at the back terrace?"

"Yes." Offering her his arm, Lord Sydney accompanied her to the double-sided stone staircase at the back of the manor. They were both silent as they ascended to the terrace that overlooked the main gardens. Abundant light from the great hall shone through the glittering multipaned windows and French doors. The terrace, often the location for guests to smoke and drink port, was unoccupied, as nearly everyone was either in the village or playing cards and billiards inside.

A lone figure relaxed in a chair by the railing. He drew lazily on a cigar, exhaling a thin stream of smoke that drifted in the air like a vanishing wraith. The scent of expensive tobacco tickled Lottie's nostrils as she reached the top step.

Her stomach flipped uneasily as she realized who the man was.

"Lord Westcliff," she murmured, curtsying automatically. Uneasily she wondered what he would make of the fact that she was accompanied by Lord Sydney.

The earl remained seated as he surveyed the two of them. The refracted light from the windows gleamed on his coal black hair and cast angular shadows across his blunt, strong features. "Miss Miller," he said in his gravelly voice, and nodded coolly to her companion. "Sydney. What convenient timing. There is a matter that I wish to take up with you."

Certain that her employer was displeased with her, Lottie lowered her gaze to the stone flagging of the terrace. "My lord, forgive me. I went to watch the festival in the village, and—"

"You did more than watch, it appears," Lord

Westcliff observed mildly, his keen gaze sweeping over her rustic attire.

"Yes, I took part in the Maypole dance. And Lord Sydney offered to escort me home—"

"Of course he did," the earl said sardonically, taking another pull on his cigar. Blue-gray smoke whirled and eddied upward. "There is no need to look so distressed, Miss Miller. As far as I am concerned, you are not prohibited from seeking entertainment in the village—although it would doubtless be wise not to mention such activities to the dowager countess." He gestured with his cigar. "You may go now, while I discuss a few things with Lord Sydney."

Lottie nodded in cautious relief. "Yes, sir." As she began to depart, she was astonished to feel Lord Sydney's light, restraining hand on her arm.

"Wait."

Lottie froze in utter confusion, her face flooding with color. She could not believe that he had dared to touch her in front of the earl. "My lord," she murmured in protest.

Sydney did not return her glance; his gaze was fixed intently on the earl's harsh features. "Before Miss Miller takes her leave, you had better tell me what this is about."

"This is about your so-called family," Lord Westcliff said softly. "And your so-called past." The quiet words rang with condemnation. Lottie realized from the earl's expression that something was very wrong.

If any warmth had lingered from the enchanted moments in the forest, it vanished abruptly.

Bewildered, she stared at Lord Sydney. His face had changed somehow, no longer quite so handsome, but suddenly hard and cold. To behold him now, one would believe that this man was capable of anything. Suddenly, she could not believe that a few minutes ago she had kissed that stern mouth, that his hands had caressed her intimately. When he spoke, even his voice sounded different, his accent a bit coarser. The aristocratic veneer had been stripped away, revealing the stony layers beneath. "I would prefer to discuss this in a more private setting," he said to the earl.

Westcliff inclined his head with icy courtesy. "There is a study in the family wing. Will that serve?"

"Yes." Sydney paused deliberately before adding, "Miss Miller will accompany us."

Lottie stared at him blankly. His request made no sense. Suddenly she felt cold all over, and a shiver chased down her spine. "Why?" she asked through dry lips.

"She has nothing to do with this," Lord Westcliff said curtly, rising from his chair.

Lord Sydney's face was dark and still. "She has everything to do with it."

Lottie felt herself turn white. The entire surface of her body seemed to prickle and burn, as if she had fallen into a frozen pond. She found it difficult to speak or move as a paralyzing suspicion crept over her.

The earl dropped his cigar to the terrace and crushed it with his foot. A touch of uncharacteristic impatience edged his tone. "Miss Miller, will you be so kind as to join us? It seems that we have a small mystery to solve."

Nodding in a puppetlike fashion, Lottie followed the earl into the house, while her instincts screamed for her to flee. She had little choice but to play the scene out, however. Forcing herself to behave calmly, she went with the two men to the private study, its rosewood paneling glowing ruddily in the lamplight. The room was hard and uncompromising, with minimal upholstery and sharp angles, and no ornamentation save for a pristine row of stained glass windows.

As Lord Westcliff closed the door, Lottie took care to keep as great a distance between herself and Sydney as possible. A sense of foreboding nearly made her ill. She could not bring herself to look directly at Lord Sydney, but she was intensely aware of him.

Lord Westcliff spoke. "Will you have a seat, Miss Miller?"

Lottie shook her head dumbly, afraid that if she moved at all, she might collapse.

"Very well." The earl's attention moved to Lord Sydney. "Let us begin with the information I received today. Immediately upon your arrival at Stony Cross Park, I undertook to make certain inquiries about you. I suspected that you were not being entirely truthful in some regard, although I could not quite put my finger on what it was."

Lord Sydney appeared relaxed but watchful, his blue eyes hard as he returned the earl's stare. "And the results of your inquiries, my lord?"

"There is no Viscount Sydney," Westcliff said bluntly, ignoring Lottie's gasp as he continued. "The family line ended approximately twenty years ago, when the real Lord Sydney died *sine prole mascula superstite*—without surviving male children to establish a legitimate claim to the title. Which begs the question . . . who the hell are you? And what is your purpose here?"

"I'm Nick Gentry."

Although Lottie had never heard the name, Lord Westcliff seemed to recognize it. "I see," he said softly. "That explains Sir Ross's involvement. You're about some business for Bow Street, then."

Lottie gasped in astonishment as she realized that the stranger was a Bow Street runner. She had heard of the small, elite force of officers who did everything from solving murder cases to serving as bodyguards for royalty. They were known for their ruthless efficiency and courage, and had even achieved a celebrated status in higher social circles. No wonder this man had seemed so different from the other guests here. *"I hunt,"* he had told her, conveniently omitting the fact that his prey was the two-legged variety.

"Not always," Gentry said in response to Westcliff's question. "Sometimes I accept private commissions." His gaze moved to Lottie's tense face. "Two months ago I was hired by Lord Radnor to find his runaway fiancée, Charlotte Howard, who has been missing for two years."

Lottie was utterly still, while cruel pain burst inside her chest and leaked all through her. Her mouth shook with violent denial, but no words would come out. Instead she heard a high-pitched, incoherent cry, only later realizing it had been her own. She was not aware of moving, but suddenly she was across the room, clawing at Gentry's dark face, while rage and terror swooped around her like attacking buzzards.

A savage curse rang in her ears, and her wrists were snatched in crushing vises, but she did not, could not, stop struggling. Sweat and tears poured down her face, and she breathed in sobbing screams, fighting for her life, for the freedom that was being ripped away from her. Somewhere in her mind she knew that she was acting like a madwoman, that this would do her no good, but she could not seem to stop herself.

"Stop it, Lottie," Gentry snarled, giving her a hard shake. "Calm yourself . . . for God's sake—"

"I won't go back!" she shrieked, panting furiously. "I'll kill you first, oh God, I hate you, *hate you*—"

"Lottie." The cold voice of sanity cut neatly through her writhing torment. It was Lord Westcliff's voice. One of his powerful arms slid around her from behind, and he hauled her away from Gentry. She reared back against him like a terrified animal. "That's enough," Westcliff said against her ear, his arm tightening into a steely band. "He won't take you, Lottie. I swear it. You know that I always keep my word. Now take a deep breath. Another."

Somehow the earl's stern, quiet voice reached her as nothing else could have, and she found herself obeying. He guided her to a chair and forced her to sit. Lowering to his haunches, he pinned her with a steady, black gaze. "Stay still. And keep breathing."

Lottie nodded jerkily, her face still streaming. "Don't let him come near me," she whispered.

Standing, Westcliff shot the Bow Street runner a glance of obsidian ice. "Keep your distance, Gentry. I don't give a damn about who has paid you to do what. You're on my estate, and you'll do nothing without my consent."

"You have no legal claim on her," Gentry said softly. "You can't keep her here."

Westcliff responded with an arrogant snort. Going to the sideboard, he poured a small quantity of amber liquid into a glass. Bringing the liquor to Lottie, he forced her trembling fingers around the vessel. "Drink this," he said curtly.

"I don't—" she began, but he interrupted in a tone of absolute authority.

"Now. Every drop."

Grimacing, she downed the liquid in a few gulps and coughed as her lungs and throat were filled with velvet fire. Her head swam, and she regarded the earl with watering eyes. He extracted a handkerchief from the inside of his coat and gave it to her. The linen was warm from the heat of his body. Blotting her face with it, she sighed shakily. "Thank you," she said hoarsely. She kept her gaze fastened on him, unable to look at Gentry. She had never dreamed that such devastation was possible . . . that her ruin had come in the form of a handsome man with cruel eyes and raffish charm . . . the first man she had ever kissed. The pain of betrayal, the crushing humiliation of it, was too great to bear.

"Now," Westcliff said evenly, taking a chair beside Lottie's, "your reaction to Mr. Gentry's revelation would seem to confirm that you are indeed Charlotte Howard." He waited for her brief nod before continuing. "It is also true that you are betrothed to Lord Radnor?"

Lottie was reassured by the earl's powerful presence, knowing that he was the only thing that kept her safe from the predator who lurked nearby. Staring into Westcliff's blunt features, she struggled for the right words to make him understand her situation. As the earl saw her agitation, he surprised her by reaching out and taking her hand in his square one. His grip, so strong and secure, seemed to drive away the incapacitating fear. Lottie was amazed by his kindness. He had never shown her this kind of consideration . . . had never seemed to take much notice of her, actually.

"It was never my choice," she told him. "It was arranged when I was a child. My parents promised Lord Radnor my hand in return for his financial patronage. I have tried very hard to accept the situation, but Radnor is not rational—not sane—in my opinion. He has made no secret of his plans—he regards me as some kind of animal to be trained to his satisfaction. Suffice it to say that I would be better off dead. You must believe me, I would never have resorted to this otherwise—"

"I believe you." Still retaining possession of her hand, Westcliff glanced at Nick Gentry. "Having been acquainted with Miss Miller for quite some time, I can only assume that her objections to marrying Radnor are valid."

"They are," came the runner's flat response. He lounged near the fireplace with deceptive laziness, resting an arm on the marble mantel. Flames cast tongues of red light over his dark face. "Radnor is a swine. But that is beside the point. Her parents have agreed to the match. Money—a great deal of it—has changed hands. And if I don't retrieve her, Radnor will send a dozen more like me to do the job."

"They won't find me," Lottie said, finally managing to meet his gaze. "I'll go abroad. I'll disappear—"

"You little fool," Gentry interrupted in a low voice. "Do you plan to spend the rest of your life running? He'll send another man after you, and another. You'll never have a moment's peace. You can't go fast enough, or far enough—"

"That's enough," Westcliff said curtly, feeling the shiver that ran through Lottie's body. "No, Lottie will not go abroad, nor will she continue to run from Lord Radnor. We will find a way to resolve the matter so that she may lead a normal life."

"Oh?" One of Gentry's dark brows lifted in a

mocking arch. "This should be interesting. What do you propose to do, Westcliff?"

The earl was silent as he considered the matter.

As Lottie continued to stare at Nick Gentry, she tried to think past the welter of emotions. She would find some way out. She would be damned if she would be taken to Radnor like a lamb to the slaughter. Her thoughts must have been obvious, for Gentry's gaze was suddenly touched with flinty admiration as he stared at her. "As I see it, you have only two options," he said softly.

Her voice shook only a little as she replied. "What are they?"

"With the right inducement, I may be persuaded to let you go, in which case you will continue to hide from Radnor until you're caught again. Or . . . you can remove yourself from his reach permanently."

"What do you mean?"

Lord Westcliff intervened in the taut silence. "He means marriage. Once you are married and legally under another man's protection, Radnor will cease his pursuit."

Lottie's gaze dropped to the strong hand covering hers. "But that is impossible. I don't know any men who would be willing . . ." She stopped, feeling ill and bitter.

"It *is* possible," the earl countered calmly.

As Lottie stared at Westcliff with wondering eyes, Nick Gentry's quiet jeer cut through the air. "Planning to make her your countess, my lord?"

The earl's face was expressionless. "If necessary."

Stunned, Lottie clung to his hand tightly before withdrawing from him. It was inconceivable that Westcliff would be willing to make such a sacrifice. Perhaps she could reconcile herself to the prospect of marrying without love. After all, anything was preferable to becoming Lady Radnor. However, the earl was a good, honorable man, and she would not take advantage of him that way.

"You are remarkably kind, my lord," she told him. "But I would never marry you, as you deserve far better than a marriage of convenience. That is too great a sacrifice for you to make."

"It would hardly be a sacrifice," he replied dryly. "And it is a logical solution to your dilemma."

Lottie shook her head, her fine brows knitting as a new thought occurred to her. "There is a third option."

"What is it?"

A great icy calmness settled over Lottie, and suddenly she felt removed from the scene, as if she were an impartial onlooker rather than a participant. "I would rather not say just yet. If you would not mind, my lord, I would like to have a few minutes alone with Mr. Gentry."

Chapter Five

Nick had known that Lottie would not react passively to the news that he had hunted her down on behalf of Lord Radnor. But the passionate fury of her response when cornered had startled him. Now that she had regained her self-possession, she stared at him with a desperate calculation that he understood all too well. He thought her magnificent.

Although Lord Westcliff clearly did not agree with Lottie's request, he complied with a frown. "I will wait in the next room," he said, as if he expected Nick to fall on her like a ravening animal as soon as the door was closed. "Call out if you require assistance."

"Thank you, my lord," Lottie murmured, giving the earl a grateful smile that caused Nick to boil with jealousy. He would have required little provocation to drive his fist into Westcliff's aristocratic face, especially at the moment when he had taken Lottie's hand to comfort her. Nick had never been possessive of anyone in his life, but he could barely tolerate the sight of Lottie accepting another man's touch. Something was happening to him—he had lost control of the situation, and he was not certain how to regain it. All he knew for certain was that Lottie was necessary to him . . . that if he could not have her, this endless feeling of being hungry, unsatisfied, cold, would never leave him.

Nick remained by the fire, relaxed except for his clenched fist on the mantel. Silently he damned Westcliff for this turn of events. Nick had planned to impart the news to Lottie in a gentle way, and soothe her fears before she had a chance to fly into a panic. Now Westcliff had fouled things up considerably, and Lottie was understandably hostile.

She turned to him, her face pale, her eyes reddened from her tears. Her expression was composed, however, and she looked at him with unsettling intensity, as if she were trying to see inside his mind. Her searching gaze made him feel oddly threatened.

"Was it all an act?" she asked quietly.

Nick blinked. He, who had endured countless hours of scrutiny and interrogation and even torture, was completely thrown off by the question.

"I know that some of it was," Lottie said. "It was part of your job to gain my trust. But you went quite a bit farther than necessary." She approached him with hypnotic slowness. "Why did you say those things to me tonight?"

God help him, he couldn't answer. Worse, he couldn't look away from her, and she seemed to be staring through his eyes into his soul.

"The truth, Mr. Gentry," she insisted. "If I can bring myself to ask, surely you can bring yourself to answer. Did you mean any of it?"

Nick felt a light sweat break out on his face. He tried to close her away, to deny her, but it was impossible. "Yes," he said hoarsely and clamped his mouth shut. The devil take her if she wanted him to say anything more than that.

For some reason, the admission seemed to make Lottie relax. Nick couldn't begin to imagine why. Finally managing to rip his gaze away from hers, he stared blindly into the dancing firelight. "Now," he muttered, "perhaps you can explain what the third option is."

"I need protection from Lord Radnor," she said bluntly. "Few men would be able to hold their own against him. I believe that you could."

The statement was matter-of-fact . . . there was nothing complimentary in her tone. Nevertheless, Nick felt a flicker of masculine pride that she recognized his abilities.

"Yes, I could," he said evenly.

"Then in return for your protection and financial support, I would be willing to be your mistress. I would sign a legally binding contract to that effect. I think that would be enough to keep Lord Radnor at bay—and then I would no longer have to stay in hiding."

His mistress. Nick had never anticipated that she would be willing to lower herself that way. However, it seemed that Lottie was ultimately a pragmatist, recognizing when she could not afford to keep her principles.

"You'll let me bed you in return for my money and protection," he said, as if the word *mistress* required definition. He threw a cautious glance at her. "You will live with me, and accompany me in public, regardless of the shame it causes you. Is that what you're saying?"

Her cheeks turned bright red, but she did not look away from him. "Yes."

Desire flooded every part of his body with primal heat. The realization that he was going to have her, that she would give herself to him willingly, made him light-headed. His mistress . . . but that wasn't enough. He needed more of her. All of her.

Deliberately he went to the settee, a somewhat utilitarian piece upholstered in stiff burgundy leather, and he sat with his legs spread. He let his gaze travel over her with pure sexual appraisal. "Before I agree to anything, I want a sample of what you're offering."

She stiffened. "I think you've sampled quite enough already."

"You're referring to our interlude in the woods

this evening?" He made his voice very soft, while his heart pounded violently in his chest. "That was nothing, Lottie. I want more than a few innocent kisses from you. Keeping a mistress can be an expensive proposition—you'll have to prove that you're worth it."

She came to him slowly, her slim form silhouetted in the firelight. Clearly she knew that he was playing some kind of game with her, but she hadn't yet realized what the stakes were. "What do you want from me?" she asked softly.

What he'd had from Gemma. No, *more* than Gemma had ever given him. He wanted someone to belong to him. To care about him. To need him in some way. He didn't know if that was possible . . . but he was willing to gamble everything on Lottie. She was his only chance.

"I'll show you." Nick reached out and caught her wrist, pulling until she half-sat, half-toppled beside him. Sliding a hand behind the nape of her neck, he bent over her, finding her pulse with the tip of his tongue. At the same time, he brought her hand to his crotch, cupping her slender fingers around the straining shape of his erection. She stiffened and gasped, suddenly leaning against his chest as if her strength had deserted her. Gently he drew her hand up the length of his shaft, to the round head that pushed impatiently against the taut broadcloth.

A ragged sound escaped him, and he tugged at her blouse, filled with gratitude to whoever had designed a garment that made a woman's body so mercifully accessible. Her exposed breasts gleamed in the firelight, their tips soft and pale pink. Lottie turned her face to the side, her eyes tightly closed. Pulling her farther over his lap, Nick cradled her in one arm, while her bottom rested on the rigid mound of his erection. His calloused fingers slipped beneath one bare breast, lifting the silken weight to position her for the slow descent of his mouth. A quiver went through her as he opened his lips over the tender nipple, stroking until it strained against his tongue. Lottie's hands half-raised as if to push him away, but suddenly her fingers clutched around the lapels of his coat, and she let out a whimper of pleasure. The sound electrified him. He used his tongue to trace circles around the stiffening nipple, making her writhe like a cat in his arms.

While he continued to suckle and tease her breasts, he slid his hand beneath her skirts, finding the plain hem of her drawers and the thick cotton garter that fastened her stockings. Becoming aware of the hand that intruded beneath her skirts, Lottie clenched her legs together, a crimson blush spreading over her face and breasts. He caressed her over the crumpled linen, sliding his palm over her hip and stomach, then moving to the soft curls lower down.

"Don't," she said, her eyes still closed.

Nick kissed the pink curve of her throat and the fine edge of her jaw. Her skin was so thin and satiny that it was almost translucent. He wanted to kiss her from head to toe. "That's not how a mistress talks," he whispered. "Are you reneging on your offer, Lottie?"

She shook her head, unable to speak as his palm pressed on her mound.

"Then spread your legs."

She complied jerkily, her thighs parting, her head falling back against his supportive arm. He caressed her over the fragile fabric, gently rubbing the hot furrow until the linen became damp beneath his fingers. He was aroused by her efforts to stay quiet and still, her face turning scarlet, her legs stiffening as he teased her intimately. Finally she moaned and clutched at his wrist imploringly.

"That's enough," she gasped.

His cock pulsed violently beneath her. "Is it?" he whispered, sliding his fingers into the open slit of her drawers. "I think you want more."

Her body jerked in his lap as he found softly matted hair . . . plump silken flesh . . . the wet entrance to her body. Kissing the arch of her throat, Nick played with the velvety thicket. "Sweet little curls," he breathed near Lottie's ear. "What color are they, I wonder? Blond, like the hair on your head? Or darker?"

Shocked by the question, Lottie stared at him with an unfocused gaze.

"It's all right," he said, opening the soft cleft. "I'll find out for myself . . . later."

She arched as he found the tender peak that had been hidden by the protective folds. "Oh . . . oh, God—"

"Shhhh." He nipped the lobe of her ear. "You don't want Westcliff to hear, do you?"

"Stop that," she said shakily.

But nothing would stop him now. He caressed her skillfully, circling the point of delicate fire. Her buttocks lifted away from the hard length of his erection as her hips strained toward his hand. He brushed the swollen bud with the calloused tip of his thumb and slid his middle finger inside her, until it was completely submerged in the luscious channel.

Lottie's breath shortened, and her thighs clamped around his hand as he thrust and withdrew his finger in an easy rhythm. He felt her inner muscles tauten as she labored and twisted, fighting instinctively for release from the excruciating tension. Nick lowered his head to her breasts once more. The tips were taut and rosy now, and he blew against one of them softly before drawing it into his mouth. With his finger sunk inside her, and her nipple throbbing against his tongue, he experienced a triumph he had never known before.

Lottie struggled helplessly as climax remained elusive, a moan of frustration escaping her. Withdrawing his finger from the sweet depths of her body, Nick settled his damp hand on her taut stomach, rubbing in soothing circles. "I'll take care of you later," he murmured. "I promise."

Lottie moaned again, arching desperately against his hand. He knew what she wanted, and he longed to give it to her. His nostrils flared as he detected the heady perfume of female desire. Heat pumped through him, and he nearly lost all self-control as he thought of burying his face between her thighs, plunging his tongue inside her . . .

He shuddered as he forced himself to pull her skirts down, covering the sweet flesh he craved. Westcliff was waiting nearby, and now was not the time or place to indulge himself further. Later there would be time to make love to Lottie at his leisure. *Patience*, he counseled himself, taking a few steadying breaths.

Lottie crawled from his arms and huddled at the opposite end of the settee. She was gorgeously tousled, her cheeks dewy and deeply flushed in the flickering light. Fumbling with her bodice, she covered her breasts.

Their gazes met, hers bright with shame, his frankly calculating. And then Nick went in for the kill. "I do want you," he said. "In fact, I would probably stoop at nothing to get you. But I don't want you as a mistress. I want full, irrevocable ownership. Everything that you would have given to Radnor, or Westcliff."

Realizing what he meant, Lottie stared at him as if he were a lunatic. It took a full half-minute for her to recover enough to speak. "Do you mean marriage? What difference would there be between marrying you or Lord Radnor?"

"The difference is that I'm letting you choose."

"Why would you be willing to shackle yourself to me for a lifetime?"

The truth was something that Nick could never

admit to her. "Because I want the convenience of a wife," he lied. "And you'll do as well as any other woman."

She sucked in a breath of outrage.

"Make your choice," Nick advised. "You can keep running, or you can become someone's wife. Mine or Radnor's."

She gave him another one of those long, searching stares that made the hair on the back of his neck rise. Damn, he hated it when she did that. Once again he could not blink or look away, and she appeared to read his thoughts in spite of his will to conceal them.

"Yours," she said stiffly. "I'll be yours."

And he let out a slow, nearly imperceptible sigh of relief.

Lottie struggled from his lap and straightened her clothes. She went to pour herself some brandy from the crystal decanter at the mahogany sideboard. She was dizzy, and her knees felt like jelly, which were good indications that more spirits were the last thing she needed. Moreover, she was still technically Lord Westcliff's servant, and no one in such a position would ever think of helping herself to some of the master's liquor. On the other hand, such distinctions had become blurred after the stunning revelations of the evening. She was bemused by the realization that she had received two marriage proposals in one night from vastly different men.

And the things that Nick Gentry had just done to her—no, she would not think about that now, while her body still throbbed with the echoes of shameful pleasure. Filling the glass liberally, Lottie grimaced and gulped the fine vintage.

Gentry came to her, taking the glass after she had downed half its contents. "In a minute you're going to be as drunk as a wheelbarrow."

"Does it matter?" she asked hoarsely, watching as he finished the brandy for her.

"I suppose not." As she swayed before him, he set aside the empty snifter and caught her waist in his hands. A self-mocking smile touched his lips. "God knows any woman would need to fortify herself after agreeing to become my wife."

A demanding thump rattled the door, and Lord Westcliff entered the room. His sharp gaze settled on the two of them standing so close together, and one thick brow arched quizzically.

Gentry's hands tightened on Lottie's waist as she tried to step away from him. "You may be the first to congratulate us," he told the earl, in a nasty parody of a gentlemanly announcement. "Miss Howard has done me the honor of bestowing her hand on me."

Lord Westcliff's eyes narrowed as he glanced at Lottie. "*That* is the third option?"

"As it turns out," she said unsteadily, "yes."

Lottie knew that the earl did not understand why she would be willing to make a bargain with the devil. Returning his gaze, she begged him silently not to request an explanation, as she would be unable to account for her reasons. She was tired of hiding, worrying, and being afraid. Nick Gentry had offered her sanctuary. He was unprincipled, callous, and worldly—exactly the kind of man who could protect her from Radnor. But all of that would not have been sufficient to compel her to marry him. One other factor had made the difference— her awareness that Gentry felt something for her. He was not able to hide it despite his efforts to the contrary. And against all better judgment, she wanted him. Or at least, she wanted the man he had pretended to be . . . the one who had stared at her with such desperate intensity as they'd stood by the wishing well . . . the one who had kissed her in the forest and whispered that he needed her.

Frowning, the earl came forward and reached for her. "I want a word with you, Lottie."

She nodded obediently, out of long-standing habit. "Yes, sir." When Gentry did not release her, she shot him a challenging gaze. "I haven't married you yet," she said beneath her breath. "Let me go."

His hands slid from her waist. Lottie went to the earl, who took her elbow in a light grasp and drew her with him to the corner. His respectful touch was strikingly different from Gentry's rampant possessiveness.

Lord Westcliff looked down at her, a lock of dark hair tumbling over his broad forehead. "Lottie," he said quietly, "you can't make such a decision without understanding more about the man you're giving yourself to. Do not be deceived by the fact that Gentry is a Bow Street runner. No doubt you think his profession imparts a certain sense of honor, even heroism. In Nick Gentry's case, the opposite is true. He is, and always has been, a figure of public controversy."

"In what way?" Lottie asked, glancing at the dark figure on the other side of the room. Gentry was drinking another brandy, pretending to inspect a row of books. The sullen curve of his mouth made it clear that he knew perfectly well what Westcliff was telling her.

"Gentry has only been a runner for the past two or three years. Before that, he was a crime lord masquerading as a private thief-taker. He ran an infamous corporation of thieves and was arrested numerous times for fraud, thievery, receivership, and manufacturing evidence. I can guarantee that he is acquainted with every criminal of note in England. Despite his apparent reformation, there are many who believe that he still has illicit dealings with many of his former cohorts in the underworld. He is not to be trusted, Lottie."

She tried to show no reaction to the information, but she was inwardly stunned. Glancing around Westcliff's broad shoulder, she viewed the Bow Street runner's menacing form as he lounged in the darkest corner of the study. He seemed more comfortable in the shadows, his eyes gleaming like a cat's. How could a man only in his late twenties have had such a varied career? Crime lord, thief-taker . . . what in God's name *was* he?

"Miss Howard . . . Lottie . . ." The earl recaptured her attention with a quiet murmur. "You must consider my proposal once more. I believe the arrangement would benefit us both. I give you my word that I would be a kind husband, and that you would want for nothing—"

"My lord," she interrupted earnestly, "I hope you will not regard my refusal as an indication of anything other than my great respect for you. You are the most honorable man I have ever known—and that is why I would never consign you to a loveless marriage. You cannot deny, my lord, that I would not be your first choice, were you seeking a wife. And if I did you the injustice of accepting your offer, we would both regret it someday. Mr. Gentry and I are far more suited to each other, as neither of us will regard it as a true marriage, but rather as a business transaction in which . . ." Her cheeks burned as she forced herself to finish. "In which one service is exchanged for another."

Westcliff's face was grim. "You're not cynical or hardened enough to tolerate such an arrangement."

"Unfortunately, my lord, I am indeed that hardened. Because of Lord Radnor, I've never had the hopes and dreams that many other women do. I've never expected to be happy in marriage."

"You still deserve better than this," he insisted.

She smiled without humor. "Do you think so? I'm not so certain." Breaking away from him, Lottie strode to the center of the study and stared at Gentry expectantly. She made her manner brisk. "When shall we leave?"

Gentry emerged from the corner. She saw from the flicker in his eyes that he had half-expected her to change her mind after speaking with Westcliff. Now that her choice had been reaffirmed, there was no turning back.

"Now," he said softly.

Her lips parted in the beginnings of an objection. Gentry intended to sweep her away without allowing any opportunity to say good-bye to anyone in the household, not even Lady Westcliff. On the other hand, it would be easier for her to simply disappear without having to explain anything to anyone. "Isn't it rather dangerous to travel at night?" she asked, then quickly answered her own question. "Never mind. If we met with a highwayman, I would probably be safer with him than you."

Gentry grinned suddenly. "You may be right."

His momentary amusement was wiped away by Lord Westcliff's crisp announcement. "If I cannot change Miss Howard's mind, I will at least require proof that the ceremony is legal. I will also demand evidence that she will be satisfactorily provided for."

Lottie realized that in all her considerations, she had actually not given a thought as to what kind of life she would have with Gentry. Good Lord. What kind of a living did a Bow Street runner earn? No doubt his salary was minimal, but surely with private commissions, he would make enough to live in a decent style. She did not require much—a room or two in a safe area of London would be sufficient.

"I'll be damned if I have to account for my ability to provide for my own wife," Gentry said. "All you need to know is that she won't starve, and she'll have a roof over her head."

The journey to London would last approximately twelve hours, which meant they would travel through the night and arrive in early afternoon. Lottie rested against the rich brown velvet upholstery of Gentry's well-appointed vehicle. Once they were on their way, Gentry moved to extinguish the small carriage lamp that illuminated the interior. "Do you want to sleep?" he asked. "It's a long time until morning."

Lottie shook her head. Despite her weariness, she was too agitated to relax.

Shrugging, Gentry left the lamp burning. He rested one of his legs on the upholstery, grimacing slightly. Clearly it was uncomfortable for a man of his size to be confined in a relatively small area.

"Is this yours?" Lottie asked. "Or did you hire it as part of your deception?"

Realizing that she referred to the carriage, he gave her a mocking smile. "It's mine."

"I wouldn't have thought a professional man could afford such a vehicle."

The runner played idly with the fringed edge of

the little window curtain nearby. "My work requires frequent travel. I prefer to do it in comfort."

"Do you often use an assumed name when you go about your investigations?"

He shook his head. "Most of the time there is no need."

"I wonder that you didn't choose a better disguise," she said. "One that could not be disproved so easily. It did not take long for Lord Westcliff to discover that there is no Viscount Sydney."

A strange expression crossed his face, amusement interlaced with discomfort, and he seemed to engage in a silent debate about whether or not to tell her something. Finally his mouth twisted, and he let out a brief sigh. "Westcliff was wrong. There *is* a Viscount Sydney. At least, there is a legitimate successor to the title."

Lottie regarded him skeptically. "Who is he? And if what you say is true, why has he not come forward to claim his title and property?"

"Not everyone wants to be a peer."

"Of course they do! Besides, a peer isn't given the choice. One either is, or isn't. He can't deny his birthright any more than he can change his eye color."

"Damned if he can't," came his scowling reply.

"There is no need to be cross," Lottie said. "And you haven't yet told me who and where this mysterious viscount is, which leads me to believe that you're making it up."

Gentry changed position, shifting uncomfortably, his gaze carefully averted from hers. "It's me."

"*What?* Are you trying to fool me into thinking that you are some long-lost peer? *You*, a crime lord and thief-taker, are a secret viscount?" Lottie shook her head decisively. "I don't think so."

"I don't give a damn if you believe it or not," Gentry said evenly. "Especially when it has no bearing on the future, as I will never claim the title."

Lottie stared at his hard profile in astonishment. He certainly seemed to believe what he was saying. But how could it be possible? If there was any truth to his claim, how had a son of the aristocracy come to this turn? One did not begin life as a member of the nobility and end up as a ... whatever he was. She couldn't keep from pelting him with questions. "You are John, Lord Sydney? The son of the Viscount Sydney who died twenty years ago, supposedly without an heir? Do you have any proof of this? Is there anyone who would corroborate it?"

"My sister, Sophia. And her husband, Sir Ross Cannon."

"The magistrate? The former head of Bow Street is your *brother-in-law*?"

Gentry responded with a single nod. Lottie was utterly confounded. She supposed she had no choice but to believe him, since the story could easily be discredited if it were untrue. But it was so fantastical, so absurd, that she couldn't begin to make sense of it.

"I was seven years old, perhaps eight, when my parents died," Gentry explained gruffly. "Other than me, there were no male relatives who could lay legitimate claim to the title or lands. Not that there was much to inherit, as my father was in debt, and the estate was in disrepair. My older sister Sophia and I knocked about the village for a while, until she was finally taken in by a distant cousin. But I had become a hellion, and the cousin was understandably reluctant to take me under her roof. So I ran off to London, and became a footpad, until I was imprisoned for my crimes. When another boy died in prison, I took his name so that I could gain early release."

"He must have been the real Nick Gentry, then," Lottie said.

"Yes."

"And you took his identity and let everyone believe that you had died?"

A defiant gleam entered his eyes. "He had no more use for the name."

"But certainly later you must have thought about reclaiming your true name . . . your rightful position in society . . ."

"I have exactly the position in society that I want. And Nick Gentry has become my name more than it ever was his. I intend to let Sydney rest in peace." He smiled sardonically. "Sorry for the loss of prestige, but you're going to be known as Mrs. Nick Gentry, and no one save my sister and her husband will be aware of the truth. Do you understand?"

Lottie nodded with a puzzled frown. "I don't care about a loss of prestige. If I did, I would have married Lord Radnor."

"You don't mind being the wife of a commoner, then," Gentry said, watching her intently. "One with limited means."

"I am used to living in humble circumstances. My family is of good blood, but as I mentioned once before, we are poor."

Gentry studied the polished tips of his boots. "Lord Radnor was a damned stingy benefactor, if the condition of Howard House is anything to judge by."

Lottie inhaled swiftly. "You've been to my family's home?"

He glanced into her wide eyes. "Yes, I visited your parents to question them. They knew that I was searching for you."

"Oh," Lottie said in dismay. Of course her parents would have cooperated with the investigation. They had been aware that Lord Radnor wanted to find her, and as always, they had acceded to his wishes. The news should not have come as a surprise. And yet she could not help feeling betrayed. Had they taken even one moment to consider her interests, rather than Radnor's? Her throat tightened, and she could not seem to swallow properly.

"They answered every question in detail," Gentry continued. "I've seen the dolls you once played with, the storybook you drew in . . . I even know the size of your shoes."

Filled with terrible vulnerability, Lottie wrapped her arms around herself. "It seems odd that you have seen my family, when I have been away from them for two years. H-how are my sisters and my brothers? How is Ellie?"

"The sixteen-year-old? Quiet. Pretty. In good health, it seems."

"Sixteen," Lottie murmured, unsettled by the realization that her siblings had grown older, just as she had. They had all changed during the time they had been apart. Her head ached suddenly, and she rubbed her forehead. "When my parents spoke of me, did they seem to . . ."

"What?"

"Do they hate me?" she asked distractedly. "I've so often wondered . . ."

"No, they don't hate you." His voice became oddly gentle. "They're concerned for their own hides, of course, and they seem to entertain a sincere belief that you would benefit from a marriage to Radnor."

"They've never understood what he is really like."

"They don't want to. They've profited far more by deceiving themselves."

Lottie was tempted to rebuke him even though she had thought the same thing a thousand times before. "They needed Lord Radnor's money," she said dully. "They have expensive tastes."

"Is that how your father lost the family fortune? By living outside his means?"

"I don't believe there was much of a fortune to begin with. But my parents certainly spent whatever was available. I remember that when I was a child, we had the best of everything. And then when the money was gone, we nearly starved. Until Lord Radnor intervened." She continued to rub her forehead, letting her fingers drift to her aching temples. "The argument could easily be made that I've benefitted from his interest. Because of Radnor, I was sent to the most exclusive girls' school in London, and he paid for my food, my clothes, and even hired a maid to attend me. I thought he wanted to make a lady of me. At first I was even grateful that he took such care to prepare me for being his wife."

"But it became more complicated than that," Gentry murmured.

She nodded. "I was treated like a pet on a leash. Radnor decided what I could read, what I was allowed to eat . . . he instructed the teachers that my baths were to be ice cold, as he believed it was more conducive to good health than hot water. My diet was limited to broth and fruit whenever *he* decided that I needed slimming. I had to write a letter to him every day, to describe my progress on the subjects he wished me to study. There were rules for everything . . . I was never to speak unless my thoughts were well formed and gracefully expressed. I was never to offer an opinion about anything. If I fidgeted, my hands were tied to the seat of my chair. If I became sun-browned, I was kept indoors." She let out a strained sigh. "Lord Radnor wanted to make me into another person entirely. I could not fathom what it would be like to live with him as his wife, or what would happen when he finally realized that I could never attain the standards of perfection he set." Lost in the dark memories, Lottie twisted her fingers together and spoke without being fully aware of what she revealed. "How I dreaded coming home on holidays. He was always there, waiting for me. He barely allowed me time to see my brothers and sisters before I had to go with him and . . ."

She stopped suddenly, realizing that she had been about to confide the secret that had caused her parents to erupt in fury when she had tried to tell them. It had seethed at the bottom of her soul for years. They had somehow made it clear without words that the family's survival, and hers, depended entirely on her silence. Choking back the forbidden words, Lottie closed her eyes.

"You had to go with him and . . ." Gentry prompted.

She shook her head. "It doesn't matter now."

"Tell me." His voice was soft. "I assure you, nothing you say could shock me."

Lottie regarded him cautiously, realizing it was true. With all that Gentry had seen and heard and done, nothing would disgust him.

"Go on," he murmured.

And Lottie found herself telling him what no one had ever wanted to hear.

"Every time I came home, I had to go into a private room with Radnor, and account to him for my behavior at school, and answer his questions about my studies and my friends, and . . ." She stared into Gentry's inscrutable face, finding that his lack of re-action made it easy for her to continue. "He made me sit on his lap while we talked. He touched me, on my chest and beneath my skirts. It was repul-sive, allowing him to . . . but I couldn't stop him, and my parents . . ." She shrugged helplessly. "They wouldn't listen when I tried to tell them. It went on for years. My mother slapped me once, and told me that I belonged to Lord Radnor, and that he was going to marry me anyway. She said I must let him do as he liked. The family's safety de-pended on his pleasure and goodwill." Shame infused her voice as she added, "And then I ran from him any-way, and by doing so I threw them all to the wolves."

Gentry spoke carefully, as if she were still an inno-cent child rather than a woman of twenty. "Did it go farther than touching, Lottie?"

She stared at him without comprehension.

His dark head tilted slightly, his voice remaining soft as he persisted. "Did he bring you or himself to climax, while you sat on his lap?"

Her face turned hot as she understood what he was referring to . . . the mysterious ecstatic culmina-tion that some of the girls had described with naughty laughs. A physical pleasure that she cer-tainly could never have felt with Radnor. "I don't think so."

"Believe me, you would know if either of you had," he said sardonically.

Lottie thought of the way that Gentry had touched her in the firelight, the coiling sensation she had felt in her breasts and loins and stomach, the sweet aching frustration that had tormented her so. Had that been climax, or was there more she had yet to experience? She was sorely tempted to ask her companion, but she kept silent out of fear that he might mock her for her ignorance.

The sway of the well-sprung carriage lulled her, and she yawned tightly behind her hand.

"You should rest," Gentry said quietly.

Lottie shook her head, reluctant to abandon herself in slumber while he watched. How silly to fear that small intimacy after all that had happened between them. She sought for a new topic of conversation.

"Why did you become a Bow Street runner? I can't believe you chose such a profession willingly."

A laugh rustled in his throat. "Oh, I was willing enough, considering the alternative. I made a deal with my brother-in-law, Sir Ross, three years ago. At the time he was chief magistrate of Bow Street, and he had evidence in his possession that would have had me dancing in the wind, had it ever been presented at a trial."

"Dancing in the wind," Lottie repeated, puzzled by the unfamiliar expression.

"Hanging. Dangling at the end of a rope. Believe me, I should have been drawn and quartered for some of the things I did in my underworld career." Pausing to observe the effect of his words, Gentry smiled slightly at her obvious unease. "In an effort to avoid the uncomfortable position of having to execute his wife's brother," he continued, "Sir Ross offered to conceal the damning evidence against me, if I would double-cross my underworld associates and become a runner."

"For how long?"

"Indefinitely. Naturally I agreed, as I had no loyalty to my former companions, and I didn't fancy having my neck stretched."

Lottie frowned. "Why did Sir Ross want you to become a runner?"

"I believe he had the mistaken impression that a few years of public service would reform me." Gentry grinned suddenly. "It hasn't yet."

"Isn't it rather hazardous for you to hunt criminals in such places, after you have betrayed them?"

"More than a few people would like my head on a silver platter," he admitted with reckless confidence. "In fact, you may not have to endure me for long. Everyone who knows me will vouch for the fact that I'm going to die young."

"I probably won't be that fortunate," she said sardonically. "But one can hope."

Immediately after Lottie said the words, she was inundated with shame. It wasn't like her to stoop to such nastiness. "I'm sorry," she said at once. "I shouldn't have said that."

"That's all right," he said easily. "I've inspired people to say much worse, with less cause."

"That I can believe," she replied, and he laughed.

"I'm going to snuff the light," he said. "I have to take my rest when and where I can find it. And tomorrow promises to be busy."

The silence that followed was surprisingly comfortable. Lottie settled into the corner, exhausted and dazed by the unforeseen direction her life had taken. She had expected that sleep would be elusive, with all the thoughts buzzing through her mind. However, a deep slumber soon overtook her, and she sagged against the seat cushions. Shifting, twisting restlessly, she sought a more comfortable position. She felt herself being gathered up and held like a child, and the dream was so soothing that she couldn't help but surrender to the insidious pleasure. Something soft brushed her forehead, and the last few pins that anchored her coiffure were gently drawn from her hair. She inhaled a wonderful scent, the crispness of wool and shaving soap overlaying the essence of clean male skin.

Realizing that she was lying in Gentry's arms, snuggled in his lap, she stirred groggily. "What . . . what . . ."

"Sleep," he whispered. "I won't harm you." His long fingers moved through the loose locks of her hair.

The part of Lottie's mind that protested such a circumstance grappled with the rest of her brain, which pointed out that she was exhausted, and at this point it hardly mattered what liberties she allowed him. However, she stubbornly tugged free of him and pushed away from the inviting warmth of his body. He released her easily, his eyes a dark glitter in the shadows.

"I'm not your enemy, Lottie."

"Are you my friend?" she parried. "You haven't behaved like one so far."

"I haven't forced you to do anything you didn't want to do."

"If you hadn't found me, I would still be residing happily at Stony Cross Park—"

"You weren't happy there. I'll wager you haven't been happy a day in your life since you met Lord Radnor."

Oh, how she longed to contradict him! But it was pointless to lie, when the truth was obvious.

"You'll find life a hell of a lot more enjoyable as my wife," Gentry continued. "You won't be anyone's servant. You can do as you please, within reasonable limits. And you won't have to fear Lord Radnor any longer."

"All for the price of sleeping with you," she muttered.

He smiled, all velvety arrogance as he replied. "You may come to enjoy that part of it most of all."

Chapter Six

~~~~

When Lottie emerged from her slumber, daylight was leaking through the gaps in the window curtains. Bleary-eyed, disheveled, she glanced at her husband-to-be, whose clothes were rumpled but who was remarkably alert.

"I don't require much sleep," he said, as if reading her thoughts. Reaching for her hand, he deposited her hairpins in her palm. Her fingers curled around the bits of wire, which had retained the heat of his skin. Mechanically she proceeded to braid and coil her hair with an efficiency born of long-standing habit.

Drawing aside the curtain, Gentry glanced at the swarming city outside the carriage window. A stray shaft of sunlight caught his eyes, turning them to a shade of blue that seemed almost unnatural. Even sitting in an enclosed carriage, Lottie could sense his familiarity with the city, the fearlessness that made no corner or rookery too dangerous for him to venture into.

No aristocrat she had ever encountered—and there had always been plenty of them at Stony Cross Park—had ever possessed such a street-seasoned look, the hardened demeanor that suggested he would be willing to do anything, no matter how abhorrent, to accomplish his goals. Well-bred men were able to draw the line at certain matters . . . they had principles and standards . . . things that Gentry had so far not displayed.

If he was indeed a peer, Lottie thought it was wise of him to reject his heritage and "let Sydney rest in peace," as he had put it. She was certain that had he chosen otherwise, he would have found it difficult, even impossible, to make a place for himself in London's rarefied upper crust.

"Lord Westcliff told me that you were the head of a corporation of thieves," she commented. "He also said that you—"

"I regret to say that I wasn't nearly as powerful a figure as everyone makes me out to be," Gentry interrupted. "The stories are exaggerated more each time they're told. A few chapbook writers have done their best to make me as menacing as Attila the Hun. Not that I'm claiming innocence, of course. I ran a hell of a good smuggling operation. And although I admit my methods were questionable, I was a better thief-taker than any of Cannon's runners."

"I don't understand how you could direct thieves

and smugglers and be a thief-taker at the same time."

"I planted spies and informers all over London, and beyond. I had evidence on everyone from Gin Alley to Dead Man's Lane. Whenever someone got in the way of what I wanted, I turned him in and collected the bounty. As a runner, I find the business of thief-taking a bit more difficult, as the chief magistrate insists that I do things his way. But I'm still the best man he's got."

"And not shy about saying so," Lottie said dryly.

"I'm not one for false modesty. And it happens to be the truth."

"I don't doubt it. You managed to find me when Lord Radnor's men failed after two years of trying."

He surveyed her with unnerving intensity. "The more I learned about you, the more curious I became. I wanted to see what kind of girl had the courage to create a new life for herself, with no help from anyone."

"Courage," she repeated dubiously. "Strange, that you should call it that, when I've always considered it cowardice."

He was about to reply when the carriage made a sharp turn and traveled along a well-paved street. It was sided by a landscaped green with trees and garden walks. Tidy three-story homes of mellow brick lined the secluded lane, which featured a surprisingly pastoral atmosphere in the midst of the bustling city. "Betterton," Gentry said, identifying the street. "The

Bow Street office is located to our south, and Covent Garden just beyond that."

"Is the market within walking distance?" Lottie asked, anticipating the prospect of exploring her new surroundings. Although Maidstone's was established in west London, the students had never been allowed to go anywhere.

"Yes, but you won't be walking anywhere without me."

"I am in the habit of going out every morning," she said, wondering if that small but necessary pleasure was going to be withheld from her.

"I'll walk with you, then. Or a footman will accompany you. But I won't have my wife wandering outside unprotected."

My wife. The casual phrase seemed to knock the breath from Lottie's lungs. Suddenly the idea of marrying him . . . accepting his authority, submitting to his wishes . . . seemed entirely real, whereas it had only been an abstract notion before. It seemed that Gentry had surprised himself as well, for he clamped his mouth shut and stared out the window with a frown. Lottie wondered if the prospect of marriage had also just become real to him . . . or, God help her, if he was having second thoughts.

The carriage stopped before a house designed in the symmetrical early Georgian style, with white Doric columns and folding glazed doors that opened to a domed entrance hall. The small but elegant residence went so far beyond Lottie's expectations that she stared at it in wordless amazement.

Exiting the carriage first, Gentry helped her descend, while a footman hastened up the front steps to alert the servants to the master's arrival.

Grimacing at her cramped leg muscles, Lottie relied on the support of Gentry's arm as they approached the door. A middle-aged housekeeper greeted them. She was a plump woman with warm eyes and smooth silver hair.

"Mrs. Trench," Gentry said with sudden mischief dancing in his eyes, "as you can see, I've brought a guest with me. Her name is Miss Howard. I will counsel you to treat her well, as she has just convinced me to marry her."

Catching the implication that *she* was the one who had pressed for marriage, Lottie gave him a speaking glance, and he grinned.

Mrs. Trench could not hide her astonishment. Clearly it was difficult to twist one's brain around the concept of a man like Nick Gentry getting married. "Yes, sir." She curtsied to Lottie. "Welcome, Miss Howard. Congratulations, and much joy to you."

"Thank you," Lottie returned with a smile, then looked cautiously at Gentry. No mention had been made of how he expected them to behave in front of the servants. For heaven's sake, she hadn't even known that he *had* servants. She supposed that the household would know quite soon that theirs was a marriage of convenience, so there was little sense in pretending any kind of affection for him.

"Have a room readied, and tell the cook to prepare something for Miss Howard," he said to Mrs. Trench.

"Will you require a plate as well, sir?"

Gentry shook his head. "I intend to leave soon, to make some arrangements."

"Yes, sir." The housekeeper hurried to follow his wishes.

Glancing down at Lottie, Gentry tucked a loose tendril of hair behind her ear. "I will be gone for only a short time. You're safe here, and the servants will do exactly as you tell them."

Did he think she might be distressed by his absence? Surprised by his concern, Lottie nodded. "Of course."

"Tell Mrs. Trench to show you the house in my absence." He hesitated briefly. "Naturally I will have no objection if you wish to change anything that is not to your liking."

"I'm certain that I shall find it acceptable." Their surroundings were tasteful and elegant—the entranceway, with its marble floor patterned in geometric designs, the little staircase hall beyond, and a set of paneled mahogany doors opening to reveal a low-ceilinged drawing room. The walls were tinted a pale shade of green and hung with a few simple groupings of paintings, while the furniture had clearly been chosen for ease and comfort in lieu of formality. It was a handsome, elegant house, far superior to the one she had grown up in. "Who decorated the house? Not you, surely."

He smiled at that. "My sister Sophia. I told her it wasn't necessary, but she seemed to be of the opinion that my judgment is lacking in such matters."

"Didn't it cause gossip, for her to visit your home?"

"She always brought Sir Ross with her." The twist of his mouth conveyed how little he had enjoyed those visits. "The two of them also undertook to choose a household staff for me, as they weren't especially fond of my hirelings from the flash house. They particularly didn't like Blueskin or Wapping Bess."

"Wapping? What does that mean?"

He looked both amused and perturbed by her ignorance of the word. "It means swiving. Frigging." At her continuing puzzlement, he shook his head ruefully. "Having sexual relations."

Her confusion rapidly transformed into disapproval. "What in heaven's name would you have employed her for in this house? No, don't tell me, I'm sure I should be sorry to know." She frowned at his amusement. "How many servants do you have?"

"Eight, including Mrs. Trench."

"You led me to believe that you were a man of limited means."

"I am, compared to Lord Westcliff. But I can keep you in a comfortable style."

"Do the other runners live in this manner?"

That made him laugh. "Some do. In addition to the assignments from Bow Street, most of us take private commissions. It would be impossible to live exclusively on the salary the government allots."

"Commissions such as the one from Lord Radnor?" The thought of him made Lottie's stomach twist with anxiety. Now that she was in London, easily within Radnor's reach, she felt like a rabbit that had been flushed from its burrow. "Has he already paid you for finding me? What will you do with the money?"

"I'll return it to him."

"What about my family?" she whispered apologetically. "Might something be done for them? Lord Radnor will withdraw his patronage . . ."

Gentry nodded. "I had already considered that. Of course I will take care of them."

Lottie hardly dared to believe her ears. It was asking a great deal of any man to support his wife's entire family, and yet Gentry seemed to accept the burden without apparent resentment. "Thank you," she said, nearly breathless with sudden relief. "That is kind of you."

"I can be very kind," he replied softly, "given the right incentive."

Lottie stood still as he fingered her earlobe and stroked the hollow just behind it. A rush of heat spread over her face . . . such a small, almost innocuous caress, and yet he had found a place so susceptible that she gasped at the brush of his fingertip. He bent his head to kiss her, but she turned her face away. He could have anything he wanted of her, except that. To her, a kiss held a meaning beyond the physical, and she did not want to give that part of herself to him.

His lips touched her cheek instead, and she felt

the warm curve of his smile. Once again, he showed an uncanny ability to read her thoughts. "What can I do to earn a kiss from you?"

"Nothing."

His mouth slid lightly over the edge of her cheek-bone. "We'll see about that."

To most people, the dingy, well-worn Bow Street public office, smelling of sweat, brass polish, and charge-books, was not an inviting place. But during the past three years, Nick had become so familiar with every inch of the office that it felt like home. An outside visitor would be hard-pressed to believe that the small, unassuming buildings—Bow Street Nos. 3 and 4—were the center of criminal investigation in England. Here was where Sir Grant Morgan held court and directed the force of eight runners under his command.

Wearing a relaxed smile, Nick returned the greetings of clerks and constables as he made his way through No. 3 Bow Street. It had not taken long for the force at Bow Street to appreciate his finer points, most particularly his willingness to go to the rookeries and flash houses that no one else dared to venture into. He didn't mind taking the most dangerous assignments, as he had no family of his own to consider, and he wasn't particular in any case. In fact, through some quirk of his character that even Nick didn't understand, he required a frequent amount of risk, as if danger were an addictive drug that he had no hope of renouncing. The past two months of tame investigative work had filled him with a raw energy that he could barely contain.

Reaching Morgan's office, Nick looked askance at the main court clerk, Vickery, who gave him an encouraging nod. "Sir Grant has not yet gone to morning sessions, Mr. Gentry. I am certain that he will wish to see you."

Nick knocked on the door and heard Morgan's rumbling voice. "Come in."

As massive as the battered mahogany desk was, it appeared like a piece of children's furniture compared to the size of the man who sat behind it. Sir Grant Morgan was a spectacularly large man, at least five inches taller than Nick's own height of six feet. Although Morgan was fast approaching the age of forty, no hint of silver had yet appeared in his short black hair, and his distinctive vitality had not faded since the days that he himself had served as a Bow Street runner. As well as having been the most accomplished runner of his day, Morgan was easily the most popular, as he had once been the subject of a string of best-selling ha'penny novels. Before Morgan, the government and the public had regarded the entire Bow Street force with the innate British suspicion toward any form of organized law enforcement.

Nick had been relieved by Sir Ross's decision to appoint Morgan as his successor. An intelligent and self-educated man, Morgan had worked his way through the ranks, beginning in the foot patrol and working his way to the exalted position of chief magistrate. Nick respected that. He also liked Morgan's characteristic blunt honesty and the fact that he seldom bothered with splitting ethical hairs when a job needed to be done.

Morgan guided the runners with an iron hand, and they respected him for his toughness. His only apparent vulnerability was his wife, a small but lovely woman whose mere presence could make her husband start purring like a cat. One could always tell when Lady Morgan had visited the offices at Bow Street, leaving a bewitching trace of perfume in the air and a happily bemused expression on her husband's face. Nick was amused by Sir Grant's obvious weakness where his wife was concerned, and he was determined to avoid such a trap. No female was ever going to lead him around by the nose. Let Morgan and Sir Ross make fools of themselves over their wives—he was much smarter than they.

"Welcome back," the magistrate said, leaning back in his chair to regard him with sharp green eyes. "Have a seat. I assume your return means that you have concluded your business with Lord Radnor?"

Nick took the chair across the desk. "Yes. I found Miss Howard in Hampshire, working as a lady's companion to the dowager countess of Westcliff."

"I am acquainted with Lord Westcliff," Morgan remarked. "A man of honor and good sense—and perhaps the only peer in England who doesn't equate modernity with coarseness."

For Morgan, the comments were akin to wildly effusive praise. Nick made a noncommittal grunt, having little desire to discuss the many virtues of Westcliff. "After tomorrow, I will be ready for new assignments," he said. "I just have one last matter to clear away."

Although Nick had expected that Morgan would be pleased by the information—after all, he had been absent for two months—the magistrate received his words in a surprisingly distant manner. "I'll see if I can find something for you to do. In the meantime—"

"What?" Nick stared at him with open suspicion. The magistrate had never displayed such diffidence before. There was *always* something to be done . . . unless the entire London underworld had elected to go on leave at the same time Nick had.

Looking as though he wanted to discuss some volatile matter but had not been given permission to do so, Morgan frowned. "You need to visit Sir Ross," he said abruptly. "There is something that he wants to communicate with you."

Nick didn't like the sound of that at all. His suspicious gaze met with Morgan's. "What the hell does he want?" As one of the few people who knew about Nick's secret past, Morgan was well aware of the agreement Nick had made three years earlier and the difficulties between him and his esteemed brother-in-law.

"You'll have to learn that from Sir Ross," Morgan replied. "And until you do, you will receive no assignments from me."

"What have I done now?" Nick asked, suspecting

that some kind of punishment was being inflicted on him. Swiftly he mulled over his actions of the past few months. There had been the usual minor infractions, but nothing out of the ordinary. He found it infuriating that Sir Ross, despite his so-called retirement, still had the ability to manipulate him. And Morgan, damn his eyes, would never go against Sir Ross's wishes.

Amusement flickered in Morgan's eyes. "To my knowledge, you've done nothing wrong, Gentry. I suspect that Sir Ross wishes to discuss your actions at the Barthas house fire."

Nick scowled. Two months earlier, just before taking the commission from Lord Radnor, he had received an on-duty summons to run to the fashionable quarter near Covent Garden. A fire had started in a private house belonging to Nathaniel Barthas, a rich wine merchant. Being the first constable to arrive on the scene, Nick had been informed by onlookers that no one in the family had been seen to exit the burning building.

Without stopping to think, Nick had dashed inside the inferno. He had found Barthas and his wife on the second floor, overcome by smoke, and their three children crying in another room. After managing to rouse the couple, Nick had ushered them from the home while carrying the three screaming imps beneath his arms and on his back. In what seemed a matter of seconds afterward, the house had exploded into flames, and the roof had caved in.

To Nick's chagrin, the *Times* had published an extravagant account of the incident, making him out to be some grand, heroic figure. There had been no end of friendly needling from the other runners, who had adopted expressions of mock worship and exclaimed adoringly whenever he'd entered the public office. To escape the situation, Nick had requested a temporary leave from Bow Street, and Morgan had given it to him without hesitation. Thankfully, the public was possessed of a short memory. During the past eight weeks of Nick's absence, the story had disappeared, and things had finally returned to normal.

"The damned fire is irrelevant now," he said brusquely.

"Sir Ross is not of that opinion."

Nick shook his head in annoyance. "I should have had the sense to stay out of the place."

"But you didn't," Morgan returned. "You went inside, at great peril to yourself. And because of your efforts, five lives were saved. Tell me, Gentry, would you have reacted the same way three years ago?"

Nick kept his face smooth, although the question startled him. He knew the answer at once . . . no. He would not have seen the value in taking such a risk, when there would have been no material benefit in saving the lives of ordinary people who were of no use to him. He would have let them die, and although it might have bothered him temporarily, he would have found a way to put it out of his mind.

He had changed in some inexplicable way. The realization made him ill at ease.

"Who knows," he muttered with an insouciant shrug. "And why should it matter to Sir Ross? If I am being summoned so that he can give me a pat on the head for a job well done—"

"It's more than that."

Nick scowled. "If you're not going to explain or give me some work, I'm not going to waste my time sitting here."

"I will not keep you, then," the magistrate said equably. "Good day, Gentry."

Nick headed for the door, paused as he remembered something, and turned back to Morgan. "Before I go, I need to ask a favor. Will you use your influence with the registrar to get a civil license by tomorrow?"

"A marriage license?" The only sign of Morgan's puzzlement was the subtle narrowing of his eyes. "Doing errands for Lord Radnor, are you? Why does he wish to marry the girl with such haste? And why would he condescend to wed in the registrar's office, rather than have a church ceremony? Furthermore—"

"The license isn't for Radnor," Nick interrupted. The words suddenly stuck in his throat like a handful of thistles. "It's for me."

An interminable silence followed as the magistrate worked things out for himself. Finally recovering from an attack of jaw-dropping astonishment,

Morgan fastened his intent gaze on Nick's reddened face. "Just *whom* are you marrying, Gentry?"

"Miss Howard," Nick muttered.

A snort of disbelieving laughter escaped the chief magistrate. "Lord Radnor's bride?" He regarded Nick with mingled amusement and wonder. "My God. She must be an unusual young woman."

Nick shrugged. "Not really. I've just decided that having a wife will be convenient."

"In some ways, yes," Morgan said dryly. "In other ways, no. You might have done better to give her to Radnor and find some other woman for yourself. You've made a considerable enemy, Gentry."

"I can handle Radnor."

Morgan smiled with an amused resignation that annoyed Nick profoundly. "Well, allow me to offer my sincere felicitations. I will notify the superintendent-registrar, and the license will be waiting at his office tomorrow morning. And I urge you to speak to Sir Ross soon thereafter, as his plans will be all the more relevant in light of your marriage."

"I can hardly wait to hear them," Nick said sarcastically, making the chief magistrate grin.

Grimly wondering what kind of scheme his manipulative brother-in-law was devising, Nick took his leave of the Bow Street office. The sunny April day had rapidly become overcast, the air turning cool and damp. Maneuvering nimbly through the mass of carriages, wagons, carts, and animals that clogged the streets, Nick rode away from the river, toward the west. Abruptly Knightsbridge quickly gave way to open country, and enormous stone mansions on large tracts of land replaced the rows of terrace-houses built on neat squares.

As the aggressive outlines of Lord Radnor's weighty Jacobean mansion loomed before him, Nick spurred his horse to a more urgent gait. The chestnut's iron shoes crunched steadily over the long graveled drive that led to the house. The last and only time Nick had come here was to accept Radnor's commission. All business thereafter had been conducted with the earl's agents, who'd forwarded Nick's occasional reports to him.

As he felt the small weight of the enameled miniature case in his coat pocket, Nick briefly regretted the fact that he would have to return it to Radnor. He had carried it, stared at it, for two months, and it had become a sort of talisman. The lines of Lottie's face, the shade of her hair, the sweet curve of her mouth, had been carved into his brain long before he had met her. And yet the likeness—that of a pretty but rather ordinary face—had captured nothing of what made her so desirable. What was it about her that moved him so? Perhaps it was her mixture of fragility and valiance . . . the intensity that simmered beneath her quiet exterior . . . the electrifying hints that she possessed a sensuality that rivaled his own.

It made Nick uncomfortable to acknowledge that

his desire for Lottie was no less acute than Radnor's. And yet they each wanted her for entirely different reasons.

"No expense is too great in my quest to create the perfect woman," Radnor had told him, as if Lottie were destined to play Galatea to his Pygmalion. Radnor's idea of female perfection was something entirely different than Lottie. Why had he fixed his attentions on her, rather than on someone who was far more tractable? It would have been infinitely easier to dominate a woman who was submissive by nature . . . but perhaps Radnor was irresistibly attracted to the challenge that Lottie presented.

Arriving at the front entranceway, Nick handed the reins of his horse to a servant and slowly made his way up the flight of narrow stone steps. A butler greeted him, asked his business there, and seemed galvanized by Nick's reply.

"Tell Lord Radnor that I have news about Charlotte Howard."

"Yes, sir." The butler left with circumspect haste and returned in one minute. He was slightly out of breath, as if he had run back to the entrance hall. "Lord Radnor will see you at once, Mr. Gentry. If you will follow me, please."

As the butler led him across the entrance and through a narrow hallway, the mansion seemed to swallow Nick in its dark crimson interiors. It was stifling and poorly lit, though luxuriously appointed. Nick recalled that Radnor was sensitive to light. At their first meeting, he had mentioned that strong illumination strained his eyes. Now, as then, the windows were shrouded in heavy velvet that obscured every hint of daylight, and the thick carpets muffled all sound as a servant led him deeper into the maze of small compartmented rooms.

Nick was shown to the library. The earl was seated at a mahogany table, his narrow, harshly planed face illuminated by the flame trapped in a nearby lamp.

"Gentry." Radnor's avid gaze fastened on him. He did not invite Nick to take a chair, only waved him closer, while the butler retreated and closed the door with an ineffable click. "What news have you for me? Have you located her? I warn you, my patience is nearly at an end."

Withdrawing a bank draft from his pocket, Nick flattened it on the table, leaving it beside the lamp. "I am returning your money, my lord. Unfortunately I won't be able to oblige you where Miss Howard is concerned."

The earl's fingers curled, sending clawlike shadows across the gleaming table. "You have not found her, then. You have proven yourself to be an inept fool, just like the rest. How can one insolent girl have eluded every man that I have sent to retrieve her?"

Nick smiled casually. "I didn't say that she had eluded me, my lord. As a matter of fact, I've brought her to London with me."

Radnor bolted from his chair. *"Where is she?"*

"That is no longer your concern." Suddenly Nick

was enjoying himself. "The fact is, Miss Howard has elected to marry another man. It seems that in this case, absence has not made the heart grow fonder."

"Whom?" was all Radnor seemed to be able to bring himself to ask.

"Me."

The air around them seemed saturated with poison. Nick had rarely seen such fury on another man's face. He had no doubt that Radnor would have murdered him had the means been at his disposal. Instead, the earl stared at him with the dawning comprehension that Lottie had been permanently removed from his reach.

"You can't have her," Radnor finally whispered, his face veined with murderous choler.

Nick's reply was just as soft. "You can't stop me."

The muscles in the earl's face twitched in frenzied spasms. "How much do you want? Obviously this is a means to extort money from me . . . well, you may have it and be damned. Tell me your price."

"I didn't come to have my palms greased," Nick assured him. "The fact is, I want her. And she appears to prefer my offer to yours." He took the miniature of Lottie from his pocket and sent it skittering across the table, until it spun to a rest beside the earl's rigid arm. "It seems this is all you'll ever have of Charlotte Howard, my lord."

It was obvious that Radnor found the situation incomprehensible, that it was difficult for him to speak through an attack of throat-seizing rage. "You will both suffer for this."

Nick held his gaze. "No, *you* will suffer, my lord, if you accost Lottie in any way. There will be no communication with her, and no reprisal against her family. She's under my protection now." He paused, and felt it necessary to add, "If you understand anything of my history, you won't take my warning lightly."

"You ignorant whelp. You dare to warn me away from her? I *created* her. Without my influence, Charlotte would be a bovine in the country with a half-dozen children at her skirts . . . or spreading her legs for every man who dropped a coin between her breasts. I've spent a fortune to make her into something far better than she was ever meant to be."

"Why don't you send me a bill?"

"It would beggar you," Radnor assured him with raw contempt.

"Send it anyway," Nick invited gently. "I'll be interested to learn the cost of creating someone."

He left Radnor sitting in the dark room like a reptile in dire need of sunning.

Chapter Seven

As Lottie consumed a plate of salty mutton stew, she enjoyed the serene atmosphere of the small dining room, the shining floorboards redolent with beeswax, the sideboard loaded with good white china.

Mrs. Trench appeared in the doorway, a comfortable presence with a sturdy physique, her pleasant expression tempered by a touch of wariness. Lottie sensed the questions in the woman's mind . . . the housekeeper was wondering if she was truly going to marry Nick Gentry, if a trick was being played on her, if the match had been made out of love, convenience, or necessity . . . if Lottie was a figure to be pitied or a force to be reckoned with.

"Is your dinner satisfactory, Miss Howard?"

"Yes, thank you." Lottie gave her a friendly smile.

"How long have you worked for Mr. Gentry, Mrs. Trench?"

"For three years," came the ready reply. "Ever since he began working at Bow Street. Sir Ross himself interviewed me for the position, as he wished to help the master establish a proper household. Mr. Gentry is a protégé of Sir Ross's, you might say."

"Why would Sir Ross take such an interest in him, I wonder?" Lottie asked, trying to discern if the housekeeper knew about the secret kinship between them.

Mrs. Trench shook her head, seeming genuinely perplexed. "It's a great mystery, especially as they were once bitter enemies. Many people criticized Sir Ross for bringing Mr. Gentry to Bow Street. But Sir Ross's judgment has since been proven right. Mr. Gentry is the one they call for when there is the most danger involved. He fears nothing. A cool head and fast feet—that's what Sir Grant says about him. No one cares to find himself the object of Mr. Gentry's pursuit."

"Indeed," Lottie said dryly, but the sardonic note in her voice escaped the housekeeper.

"A brave, bold man, Mr. Gentry is," Mrs. Trench continued, "and no one would dispute that now, after the Barthas fire."

"What fire?"

"You didn't hear of it? Not long ago, the master saved a wine merchant and his entire family in a house fire. They would have perished for certain, had Mr. Gentry not rushed in to find them. The *Times* reported the story, and the master was the most talked-about man in London. Why, even the queen commended him and requested that he guard the prince consort at the annual Literary Fund dinner."

"Mr. Gentry didn't mention a word about it," Lottie said, finding it difficult to reconcile the information with what she already knew of him.

It appeared that Mrs. Trench desired to say more, but she kept her silence on the subject. "If you will excuse me, Miss Howard, I will make certain that the guest room has been properly aired and that your things have been put away."

"Yes, of course." After finishing her stew, Lottie drank a glass of watered-down wine. Nick Gentry, risking his life for someone else . . . it was difficult to imagine. How much easier it would have been to think of Gentry as purely a villain. Good Lord, one could ruminate about him for weeks and still not come to a definite conclusion—was he a good man acting as a bad one, or a bad man acting as a good one?

The wine made her drowsy. Eyes half-closed, Lottie leaned back in her chair as a footman appeared to clear the table. A humorless smile grazed the corners of her lips as she reflected on the oddity of marrying one man to avoid marrying another. The prospect of being Mrs. Nick Gentry was far more appealing than continuing to hide from Lord Radnor and his henchmen. Moreover, as Gentry had demonstrated, the arrangement would not be without its pleasures.

As she thought of his hands on her body, heat prickled across her face and deep in her stomach. She couldn't help remembering the touch of his mouth on her breast. The silky brush of his hair against her inner arms. The long, rough-textured fingers slipping gently over—

"Miss Howard."

Stiffening, she turned to the door. "Yes, Mrs. Trench?"

"The guest room is ready. If you are finished with your meal, a maid will help you to change from your traveling clothes."

Lottie nodded in thanks. "I would like a bath, if possible." Although she did not wish to trouble the maids with the task of running up and down stairs with ewers of hot water, she was dusty and sore from traveling, and she longed to be clean.

"Certainly. Shall you wish to take a shower-bath, miss? Mr. Gentry has installed one in the bathing room upstairs, with piped hot and cold water."

"Has he?" Lottie was intrigued, as she had heard of many well-to-do households that featured shower-baths, but she had never actually seen one. Even Stony Cross Park, with all its amenities, had not yet been fitted with hot-water piping. "Yes, I would very much like to try it!"

The housekeeper smiled at her enthusiasm. "Harriet will attend you."

Harriet was a bespectacled young housemaid with a white mobcap covering her dark hair. She was polite but friendly as she showed Lottie to the upstairs rooms. The dressing and bathing rooms branched off from the largest bedchamber, which clearly belonged to the master of the household. It contained a bed with polished, exposed wooden framework and columns supporting the amber silk canopy above. Although the bed was large, the base was lower than usual, requiring no steps to climb up to the mattress. Stealing a glance at the lavish arrangement of pillows and bolsters, Lottie felt a cramp of nervousness in her stomach. Her attention moved to the walls, which were covered with hand-painted paper featuring Chinese birds and flowers. A porcelain washstand on a tripod foot was positioned beside a tall mahogany wardrobe, topped with a small, square looking glass. It was a handsome and very masculine room.

A subtle fragrance drifted through the air, luring her to investigate. She discovered that the source of the smell was his shaving soap, contained in a marble box on the washstand. As she replaced the top on the box, a bit of soap residue transferred to her fingers, leaving them aromatic and spicy. She had inhaled this scent before, from the warm, slightly prickly skin of Nick Gentry's jaw.

Good God, in less than a week, she had been wrenched from her hideaway and brought to London . . . she was standing in a stranger's bedroom, already familiar with the scent of his body. Suddenly she could no longer be certain of who she was, or where she belonged. Her inner compass had been damaged somehow, and she was unable to negotiate between what was wrong and what was right.

The maid's voice broke through her uneasy pondering. "Miss Howard, I've started the water. Shall I 'elp you into the shower-bath? The 'eat doesn't last long."

Obeying the prompting, Lottie ventured into the blue-and-white tiled bathing room, noting the porcelain tub with its exposed pipes, a dressing-stand and a chair, and the shower-bath neatly fitted into the space of a tall but narrow cupboard. The tight confines of the room explained why the wash-stand remained in the bedchamber.

With Harriet's help, Lottie undressed quickly and let down her hair. Covered in only a blush, she stepped over the raised threshold of the shower-bath. Viewing the steaming water that poured lavishly from the perforated projection directly overhead, she hesitated. A cold draft curled around her, raising gooseflesh on her skin.

"Go on, miss," the maid encouraged, seeing her irresolution.

Taking a breath, Lottie walked straight into the fall of water, while the door closed gently behind her. A startling suffusion of heat, a moment of watery blindness, until she maneuvered far enough that her face was no longer directly in the spray. Wiping her streaming eyes with her hands, Lottie laughed in sudden pleasure. "It's like standing in the rain," she exclaimed.

The loud spattering of water on tile made the housemaid's reply inaudible. Standing still, Lottie absorbed the exhilarating sensation, the needling warmth on her back, the steam that saturated her lungs. The door opened a crack, and a bar of soap and a sponge were extended to her. She soaped her hair and body and turned in slow circles, her face uplifted, eyes and mouth tightly closed. Hot water slid everywhere, over her breasts and stomach, down her thighs, between her toes. It was a surprisingly sensual experience, making her feel at once enervated and relaxed. She wanted to stand there for hours. However, all too soon the water began to cool. With a regretful sigh, Lottie stepped away from the shower-stream before she became completely chilled.

"It's cold now," she called to Harriet, who twisted the valve outside the door before handing her a towel that had been warmed on the hot-water pipe.

Shivering in the cool air, Lottie blotted her face and hair, and wrapped the towel around herself. "If only it could have lasted a bit longer," she said wistfully, making Harriet smile.

"In three hours, there will be enough hot water for another, miss."

Lottie followed the maid to the adjoining dressing room, where her dark blue dress and fresh linens had been set out for her on a narrow daybed. "It would almost be worth marrying Mr. Gentry just for his shower-bath," she said.

The remark earned a cautiously inquiring glance from Harriet. "It's true, then, miss? You are going to marry the master?"

"It would seem so."

It was obvious that the housemaid was eaten up with curiosity but somehow managed to remain respectfully silent. Lottie dropped her wet towel and pulled on her drawers and chemise with modest haste. When she was decently covered, she sat on the velvet-covered daybed and began to tug her thick cotton stockings over her calves. She couldn't help wondering how many women had bathed and dressed and slept here. Gentry's bed must be as busy as a brothel. "I suppose you've attended quite a few female guests at Mr. Gentry's home," she commented, reaching for a garter.

Harriet stunned her by saying, "No, Miss 'Oward."

Lottie nearly dropped the garter in surprise. "What?" She raised her brows as she stared at the housemaid. "Surely I am not the first woman that he has brought here."

"Ye are as far as I know, miss."

"But that can't be true." She paused and added with deliberate bluntness, "I am certain that Mr. Gentry has entertained no less than a harem's worth in his bedroom."

The housemaid shook her head. "I've never seen any ladies visit the 'ouse . . . not in that way. O' course, after the Barthas fire, many lady admirers sent letters an' made calls." A sly grin touched Harriet's lips. "The 'ole street was filled with carriages, an' poor Mr. Gentry couldn't go through 'is own front door, as a crowd waited for 'im ewery morning."

"Hmmph." Lottie fastened her garter neatly over her stocking and reached for the other one. "But he's never brought a mistress here?"

"Oh, no, miss."

Evidently Gentry was more scrupulous than she had expected—or at least, he wished to keep his home completely private. It must be that he satisfied his sexual needs at a brothel, or—distasteful thought—perhaps his appetites were base enough that he sought the services of alleyway prostitutes. But he seemed more discerning than that. The way he touched her bespoke the appreciation of a connoisseur rather than a simple brute. Her face flamed, and she tried, as she dressed, to cover her discomfiture by asking further questions of the housemaid.

Lottie quickly discovered that Harriet was far more voluble on the subject of Gentry than Mrs. Trench had been. According to the housemaid, Gentry was something of a mystery even to his own servants, as one never knew what to expect from him. He comported himself like a gentleman in private but did not shrink from the violence of his profession. He could be scathing or kind, brutal or gentle, his moods infinitely mercurial. Like the other Bow Street runners, Gentry kept odd hours and could be summoned at any moment to assist at some disaster, or investigate a murder, or apprehend a particularly dangerous fugitive. There was little structure or routine to his days, and he did not like to make plans. And curiously, he did not sleep well, and was occasionally tormented by nightmares.

"Nightmares about what?" Lottie asked, fascinated.

"He won't say, not even to 'is valet, Dudley. But he makes the most fearsome noises in 'is sleep sometimes, and then 'e wakes 'imself, and won't go back to bed for the rest o' the night. Dudley says it must be from things that Mr. Gentry remembers from . . ." Pausing, Harriet glanced at Lottie warily.

"From his days in the underworld?" Lottie asked calmly. "Yes, I am aware of Mr. Gentry's criminal past."

" 'E weren't a criminal, miss. Not 'xactly. 'E was a thief-taker. But 'e owned a flash house near Fleet Ditch, and 'e was put in the stone jug a time or two."

"Imprisoned, you mean?"

Harriet nodded, adding with a boastful note in her voice, "Escaped twice, Mr. Gentry did. They say there's not a prison that can 'old 'im. The second time, 'e was weighted wiv three 'undred pounds o' chains, right in the Devil's Closet, in the center o' Newgate. An' 'e slipped out an' shuttered off easy as ye please."

Lottie was not surprised by the information, knowing what she did of Gentry's unusual agility, physical strength, and wily nature. Perhaps the image of her soon-to-be husband as a hardened criminal should have alarmed her, but instead it was oddly reassuring. She was more convinced than ever that he would not be intimidated or easily outwitted by Lord Radnor. He was quite possibly the best protection she could have enlisted.

Yawning, she went with Harriet to the guest room, a room with soft blue walls, an exquisite tent bed enclosed with gray-and-blue curtains, and a large Hepplewhite wardrobe with a row of cunning little drawers for gloves, stockings, and other small necessities. She found her comb in one of the drawers, and she approached the hearth as the housemaid lit a fire in the grate. "Thank you, that is lovely," she said. "That will be all for now, Harriet."

"Yes, miss. The bellpull is there, if ye needs anyfing."

Sitting beside the hearth, Lottie combed her fine, straight hair until the long blond strands were warm from the heat of the fire. From somewhere in the house, a clock chimed four times. As she glanced at the gray sky outside the window and the raindrops that scattered against the glass panes, she shivered. For just a little while, she would push away her concerns about the future. Setting aside the comb, she crawled onto the bed, drew the hangings closed, and rested against the pillows.

She fell asleep rapidly, swimming through a haze of pleasant images . . . walking through the forest in Hampshire . . . dangling her feet in a cool pond on a hot day . . . pausing in the kissing gate, while the smell of sun-warmed meadowsweet rose thickly to her nostrils. She closed her eyes and tilted her chin upward, relishing the sultry rays, while a butterfly's wings brushed lightly against her cheek. Entranced by the delicate tickle, she held very still. The silken strokes moved over the tip of her nose, the sensitive periphery of her upper lip, the tender corners of her mouth.

Searching blindly, she lifted her face to the brushes of warmth and was rewarded by a gentle pressure that opened her lips and drew a moan from the upper part of her lungs. Lord Sydney was standing with her in the kissing gate, his arms trapping her against the painted ribs of latticework. His mouth searched hers so gently, his body firm against hers, and she writhed in a mute plea for him to hold her more tightly. Seeming to know exactly what she wanted, he pushed his knee into her skirts, right against the place that felt swollen and yearning. Gasping, she curled her fingers in his glossy hair, and he whispered for her to relax, that he would take care of her, satisfy her—

"Oh." Blinking hard, she stirred from the sensuous dream as she realized that she was not alone. The bed curtains had been drawn aside, and Nick Gentry's long body was entangled with hers. One large hand was cupped beneath her hips, while his leg wedged more intimately between hers. His breath surged against her ear, filling the shell with moist heat, and then his lips wandered back to hers in a searing path. He absorbed her protest as he kissed her, his tongue searching her mouth, his body levering over hers. She felt the hard length of his erection, nudging against the cleft between her thighs until she could feel it distinctly through the layers of their clothing . . . a restrained thrust . . . another . . . another . . . each rhythmic insinuation was so maddeningly good that she could not bring herself to stop him. She was filled with a physical agitation that penetrated to her soul, and every part of her demanded that she pull him harder, closer, tighter.

Instead Lottie pushed at him, ripping her mouth free with a sob. "No."

He released her, and she rolled to her stomach, resting on her clenched fists. As her lungs moved in violent inhalations, she was aware of him right behind her, the powerful length of his body pressing against her from neck to heels.

"You took advantage of me while I was sleeping," she said breathlessly. "That's not fair."

Gentry's hand moved over her hip in a slow circle. "I seldom play fair. It's usually easier to cheat."

A sudden laugh bubbled in Lottie's throat. "You are the most shameless man I've ever encountered."

"Probably," he conceded, pushing her hair aside and lowering his smiling mouth to the back of her neck. She inhaled sharply as she felt him nuzzle the fragile wisps of hair at her nape. "How soft you are," he breathed. "Like silk. Like kitten fur."

The touch of his lips sent a ripple through the overheated core of her body. "Nick, I—"

"Mrs. Trench told me that you tried the shower-bath." His hand coasted from her hip to the indentation of her waist. "Did you like it?"

"It was very refreshing," Lottie managed to say.

"I'm going to watch you the next time."

"Oh, no you won't!"

He laughed quietly and offered, "I'll let you watch me, then."

Before she could stop herself, Lottie imagined him standing in the shower-bath, the water coursing and gliding over his skin, darkening his hair, steam veiling his sapphire eyes. The image was a vague one, as she had never seen a naked man, only the engraved images in an anatomy book she had found in Lord Westcliff's library. She had pored over the drawings with fascination, wishing that certain details had been more fully articulated.

Soon she would not have to wonder.

He seemed to read her thoughts. "It's not wrong to like it," he said, stroking her midriff with his palm. "Whom will it benefit if you deny yourself pleasure? You're paying the price for my protection—you may as well get some enjoyment out of it."

"But you're a stranger," she said ruefully.

"What husband isn't a stranger to his wife? Courtship consists of a dance at a ball, a chaperoned drive through the park, and a conversation or two in the garden. Then the parents agree on the match, the ceremony is performed, and the girl finds herself in bed with a man she hardly knows. There isn't much difference between that scenario and ours, is there?"

Lottie frowned and rolled to face him, knowing

there was a flaw in his reasoning, but she was unable to identify it. Gentry was reclining on his side, propped up on one elbow, the broad outline of his shoulders obscuring most of the light shed by the bedside lamp. His body was so large and sheltering, his self-confidence so substantial, that it seemed as if she could wrap it around herself like a blanket and stay safe forever.

Shrewdly, he understood her Achilles' heel—that terrible need for sanctuary—and he did not hesitate to make use of it. He slid his arm over her waist, his hand resting on the middle of her back, his thumb brushing along the stiff arc of her spine. "I'll take care of you, Lottie. I'll keep you safe and provide all the comforts you require. All I want in return is for you to enjoy yourself with me. That isn't so terrible, is it?"

He had Lucifer's own skill of making what he wanted sound perfectly reasonable. Discerning her weakness, he leaned over until the solid weight of his body was poised above her and his thigh pressed into the mattress between her legs. "Kiss me," he whispered. The sweet, drugging spice of his breath and skin sent her thoughts scattering like dry leaves in the wind.

She shook her head, even though the most tender parts of her body had begun to throb in acute longing.

"Why not?" he asked, his fingertips teasing the edge of her hairline.

"Because a kiss is something that a woman gives to a sweetheart . . . something you are not."

He trailed the backs of his fingers lightly over her throat, between her breasts, down over her stomach. "You kissed me at Stony Cross Park."

A fierce blush enveloped her. "I didn't know who you were then."

His hand settled perilously low on her stomach. Were she not clothed, his fingers would have been resting at the top of the triangle between her thighs. "I'm the same man, Lottie." His hand began to stray even lower, until she caught at his wrist and shoved it away.

Gentry chuckled, and then sobered as he moved back to look at her. "I saw Lord Radnor today."

Although Lottie had expected it, she still felt a chill of alarm. "What happened? What did you tell him?"

"I returned his money, informed him of your decision to marry me, and warned him not to bother you or your family in the future."

"How angry was he?"

He held his thumb and forefinger a mere millimeter apart. "He was this close to apoplexy."

The thought of Radnor's anger filled her with satisfaction, but at the same time, she could not quell a sudden shiver. "He won't give up. He'll cause trouble for both of us, in every way possible."

"I've dealt with worse characters than Radnor," he said evenly.

"You don't know him as well as you think you do."

His lips parted as he prepared to argue. But as he

saw the trembling of her chin, the aggressive gleam faded from his eyes. "Don't be afraid." He startled her by settling his palm on her chest, on the smooth reach between her throat and her breasts. She inhaled deeply, her chest rising beneath the soothing weight of his hand. "I meant it when I told you that I would take care of you and your family," he said. "You're giving Radnor more importance than he merits."

"You couldn't possibly understand the way he has overshadowed my entire life. He—"

"I do understand." His fingers drifted to her throat, stroking the tender place where he could feel her swallowing. Such a powerful hand—he could crush her so easily, and yet he touched her with incredible gentleness. "And I know that you've never had anyone to defend you from him. But from now on I will. So stop turning pale every time his name is mentioned. No one is ever going to dominate you again, least of all Radnor."

"No one except *you*, you mean."

He smiled at the pert accusation, toying with a lock of her hair. "I have no desire to dominate you." Leaning over her, he kissed the tiny pulse in her throat and touched it with his tongue. Lottie held very still, her toes curling inside her stockings. She wanted to put her arms around him, touch his hair, press her breasts upward into his chest. The effort to hold back made her entire body stiffen.

"After we wed tomorrow, I'll take you to meet my sister Sophia," he said against her neck. "Will that be agreeable?"

"Yes, I would like that. Will Sir Ross be there as well?"

Gentry lifted his head. "Probably." He sounded distinctly less than thrilled by the prospect. "I received a warning today that my brother-in-law is hatching some plan, as usual, and wants to see me."

"Is there no liking at all between you?"

"God, no. Sir Ross is a manipulative bastard who has plagued me for years. Why Sophia saw fit to marry him is still beyond any hope of understanding."

"Does she love him?"

"I suppose," he said reluctantly.

"Do they have children?"

"One daughter, so far. A tolerable brat, if one likes children."

"And is Sir Ross faithful to your sister?"

"Oh, he's a saint," Gentry assured her dourly. "When they met, he was a widower who had been celibate ever since the death of his wife. Too honorable to lie with a woman outside of wedlock."

"He sounds quite chivalrous."

"Yes. Not to mention honest and ethical. He insists that everyone around him follow the rules . . . *his* rules. And as his brother-in-law, I receive an ungodly amount of his attention."

Having a fair idea of how well Gentry received Sir Ross's attempts to reform him, Lottie bit the inside of her lower lip to suppress a sudden smile.

Seeing the twitch of her lips, Gentry gave her a glance of mock warning. "That amuses you, does it?"

"Yes," she admitted, and yelped in surprise as he nudged a sensitive spot beneath her ribs. "Oh, don't! I'm ticklish there. Please."

He moved over her with easy grace, his thighs straddling her hips, his hands catching at her wrists to pull them over her head. Lottie's amusement disappeared at once. She felt a pang of fear, as well as a confusing rush of excitement, as she stared at the large male above her. She was stretched beneath him in a primal position of submission, helpless to prevent him from doing whatever he wanted. Despite her anxiety, however, she did not ask him to release her, only waited tensely with her gaze locked on his dark face.

His grip on her wrists loosened, and his thumbs dipped gently into the humid cups of her palms. "Shall I come to you tonight?" he whispered.

Lottie had to lick her dry lips before she could answer. "Are you posing a question to me or yourself?"

A smile flickered in his eyes. "You, of course. I already know what I want."

"I'd rather you stayed away, then."

"Why prolong the inevitable? One more night isn't going to make a difference."

"I would prefer to wait until after we are married."

"Principle?" he mocked, his thumbs tracing slowly along her inner arms.

"Practicality," Lottie countered, unable to prevent a gasp as he touched the delicate creases inside her elbows. How was it that he could elicit sensation from such ordinary parts of her body?

"If you think I might change my mind about marrying you after one night of lovemaking . . . you're wrong. My appetite isn't satisfied nearly that easily. In fact, having you once is only going to make me want you more. It's a pity that you're a virgin. That will limit the number of things I can do with you . . . for a while, at least."

Lottie scowled. "I'm so sorry for the inconvenience."

Gentry grinned at her annoyance. "That's all right. We'll do the best we can, in light of the circumstances. Perhaps it will be less of a hindrance than I expect. Never having had a virgin before, I won't know until I try one."

"Well, you will have to wait until tomorrow night," she said firmly, wriggling beneath him in an effort to free herself.

For some reason he froze and caught his breath at the movement of her hips beneath his.

Lottie frowned. "What is it? Did I hurt you?"

Shaking his head, Gentry rolled away from her. He dragged a hand through his gleaming brown hair as he sat up. "No," he muttered, sounding a bit strained. "Although I may be permanently debilitated if I don't get some relief soon."

"Relief from what?" she asked, while he left the bed and fumbled with the front of his trousers.

"You'll find out." He glanced over his shoulder, his blue eyes containing both a threat and a delicious promise. "Put yourself to rights, and let's have supper downstairs. If I can't satisfy one appetite, I may as well attend to the other."

Chapter Eight

As a wedding to Lord Radnor had figured prominently in Lottie's nightmares for years, she had inevitably come to regard such a ceremony with suspicion and dread. She was gratified, therefore, that the rite in the superintendent-registrar's office turned out to be fast and efficient, consisting of signing her name, exchanging obligatory vows, and paying a fee. There were no kisses, no long glances, no hint of emotion to color the businesslike atmosphere, and for that she was grateful. However, she felt no more married upon leaving the registrar's office than she had when entering it.

She had just become the wife of a man who did not love her and was probably incapable of such an emotion. And by marrying him, she had just removed all possibility of ever finding love for herself.

However, there would be consolations in this union, the greatest one being her escape from Lord Radnor. And truth be told, Nick Gentry was fascinating company. He did not bother to conceal his faults as everyone else did but instead boasted about them, as if there were some merit in being amoral and mercenary. He was a foreigner to her, coming from a world she had only heard about in whispers . . . a world populated with scavengers, thieves, dispossessed people who resorted to violence and prostitution. Gentlemen and ladies were supposed to pretend that the underworld did not exist. But Nick Gentry answered Lottie's questions with stunning frankness, explaining exactly what occurred in the rookeries of London, and the difficulties the Bow Street runners encountered in trying to bring criminals to justice.

"Some of the alleyways are so narrow," he told her as their carriage traveled to Sir Ross's home, "that a man has to turn sideways to squeeze between the buildings. Many times I've lost a fugitive simply because he was thinner than I. And then there are masses of buildings that are connected—roof, yard, and cellar—so a thief can slip through them like a rabbit in a warren. I usually accompany the new constables who don't have much experience, as they can get lost in less than a minute. And once a runner is lost, he can stumble right into a trap."

"What kind of trap?"

"Oh, a group of thieves or costers will be waiting

to bash a pursuing officer's skull, or stab him. Or they'll cover a cesspool with a few rotten boards, so when he sets a foot on it, he'll drown in a vat of sewage. That kind of thing."

Her eyes widened. "How dreadful!"

"It's not dangerous when you learn what to expect," he assured her. "I've been in every corner of every rookery in London, and I know every dodge and trap there is."

"You almost seem to enjoy your work . . . but you couldn't possibly."

"I don't enjoy it." He hesitated before adding, "I need it, though."

Lottie shook her head in confusion. "Are you referring to the physical exertion?"

"That's part of it. Jumping over walls, climbing onto rooftops, the feeling of catching a fugitive and bringing him to the ground . . ."

"And the fighting?" Lottie asked. "Do you enjoy that part of it?" Although she expected him to deny it, he nodded briefly.

"It's addictive," he said. "The challenge and excitement . . . even the danger."

Lottie twined her fingers together in her lap, reflecting that someone needed to tame him enough so that he could live in a peaceful manner someday— or his prediction of being short-lived would fulfill itself rather quickly.

The carriage traveled along a drive lined with plane trees, their intricately lobed leaves providing dense cover for the underplantings of white snowdrops and spiky green-stemmed cornuses. They stopped before a large house, handsome in its stately simplicity, the entrance guarded by wrought-iron railings and arched lamp standards. The pair of attentive footmen, Daniel and George, helped Lottie alight from the carriage and went to alert the household of their arrival. Noticing that the letter C had been worked into the designs of wrought iron, Lottie paused to trace it with her fingers.

Gentry smiled sardonically. "The Cannons aren't members of the peerage, but one wouldn't know it to look at them."

"Is Sir Ross a very traditional sort of gentleman?"

"In some regards, yes. But politically speaking, he's a progressive. Fights for the rights of women and children, and supports every reformist cause you can name." With a short sigh, Gentry guided her toward the front steps. "You'll like him. All women do."

As they ascended the stone staircase, Gentry surprised Lottie by fitting his arm behind her back. "Take my hand. That step is uneven." He navigated her carefully over the irregular surface, releasing her only when he was certain that her balance was perfect.

They walked into a large entrance hall painted in eggshell shades, with gleaming gold ormolu swags that bordered the lofty ceiling. A half-dozen doorways connected the hall to six principal rooms, while a horseshoe-shaped staircase led to the private apartments above. Lottie scarcely had time to appreciate the graceful design of the house's interior before they were approached by a lovely woman.

The woman's blond hair was much darker than her own, the color of aged honey. It had to be Lady Cannon, whose face was a delicate copy of Gentry's severely handsome features. Her nose was less bold, her chin defined but not quite as decisive as her brother's, her complexion fair instead of tanned. The eyes, however, were the same distinctive blue; rich, dark, and fathomless. Lady Cannon was so youthful in appearance that one would never have guessed that she was older than her brother by four years.

"Nick," she exclaimed with an exuberant laugh, coming forward and lifting up on her toes to receive his kiss. He enclosed her in a brief hug, rested his chin on the crown of her head, then drew back to look at her appraisingly. In that one instant, Lottie saw the remarkable depth of feeling between the two, which had somehow survived years of distance, loss, and deception.

"You're expecting another one," Gentry said after a moment, and his older sister laughed.

"How did you know? Sir Grant must have told you."

"No. But your waist is thicker—or else your corset strings have come loose."

Pulling away, Lady Cannon laughed and swatted at his chest. "You tactless wretch. Yes, my waist is thicker, and will continue to increase until January, at which time you'll have a new niece or nephew to dandle on your knee."

"God help me," he said with feeling.

Lady Cannon turned toward Lottie, her face softening. "Welcome, Charlotte. Nick sent word to me about you yesterday—I have been terribly impatient to meet you." She smelled like tea and roses, a fragrance that was as soothing as it was alluring. Sliding a slender arm around Lottie's shoulders, she turned to address Gentry. "What a lovely sister you've brought me," she remarked. "Mind you treat her well, Nick, or I shall invite her to live here with me. She appears far too well-bred to keep company with the likes of you."

"So far, I have no complaints about Mr. Gentry's treatment of me," Lottie replied with a smile. "Of course, we've only been married for an hour."

Lady Cannon frowned at her brother. "Marrying this poor girl in the registrar's office, of all places! I wish to heaven you had waited and allowed me to arrange something here. Why, you haven't even given her a ring! Honestly, Nick—"

"I didn't want to wait," he interrupted brusquely.

Before Lady Cannon could reply, a small child toddled into the entrance hall, followed by an aproned nanny. The dark-haired little girl, with her blue eyes and dimpled cheeks, could not have been much older than two. "Unca Nick!" she shrieked, rushing at him headlong, her curls flying in a wild, tangled mass.

Gentry caught her and swung her up in the air, grinning at her screams of delight. As he hugged her close, his strong affection for the child was more than obvious, belying his earlier description of her as a "tolerable brat."

Wrapping her plump arms around his neck, the little girl growled playfully, kissing him and pulling at his hair.

"God, what a savage," Gentry said, laughing. He turned her upside down, making the child squeal in excitement.

"Nick," his sister reproved, although she was laughing as well. "Don't, you'll drop her on her head."

"I will not," he said lazily, righting the child and holding her against his chest.

"Candy," the little girl demanded, plunging inside his coat as busily as a ferret. Finding what she had been searching for, she extracted a small paper parcel and crowed with excitement as her uncle opened it for her.

"What are you giving her this time?" Lady Cannon asked with resignation.

"Cinder toffee," he said cheerfully, while his niece popped a large sugary wad into her cheek. His eyes continued to sparkle as he glanced at Lottie. "Would you like some?"

She shook her head, while her heart gave a peculiar extra thump. Just now, when he had looked at her that way, his face gentle, his smile quick and easy, he had been so devastatingly handsome that Lottie had felt a shot of pleasure from the back of her neck down to her toes.

"Amelia," Gentry murmured, bringing her to Lottie. "Say hello to your aunt Charlotte. I married her this very morning."

Suddenly shy, the little girl laid her head on Gentry's shoulder and smiled at Lottie. Lottie smiled back at her, uncertain of what to say. She had little experience with children, as she had lived away from home for so many years.

Lady Cannon came to retrieve her sticky-faced daughter, smoothing back her knotted curls. "My darling," she murmured. "Won't you let Nanny brush your hair?"

The round little chin protruded obstinately. "No," she said around the mouthful of cinder toffee, punctuating her refusal with a drooling grin.

"If you won't let her brush out the tangles, they'll become so impossible that we'll have to cut them out."

Gentry added in a coaxing tone, "Let Nanny brush your hair, sweets. And the next time I come to visit, I'll bring you a pretty blue ribbon."

"And a doll?" Amelia asked hopefully.

"A doll as big as you," he promised.

Squirming down from her mother's arms, the little girl tottered off to the waiting nanny.

"She is a beautiful child," Lottie remarked.

Lady Cannon shook her head with a rueful smile,

her eyes filled with maternal pride. "And spoiled beyond reason." Returning to Lottie, she took her hand. "You must call me Sophia," she said warmly. "Let's not bother with formal terms of address."

"Yes, my . . . yes, Sophia."

"My husband will be joining us quite soon in the parlor—"

"Oh, splendid," came Gentry's surly voice from behind them.

Sophia continued as if she hadn't heard him. "—and I will send for some refreshments. I have just acquired an exquisite chocolate service—do you like chocolate, Charlotte?"

Lottie accompanied her newfound sister-in-law to a sumptuous parlor, one side of which was lined with glass panels that provided a view of a lushly planted indoor conservatory. "I've never had it before," she replied. The beverage had never been served at Maidstone's—and even if it had been, Lord Radnor would never have allowed her to have it. And certainly the servants at Stony Cross Park had rarely, if ever, enjoyed such luxuries. Butter and eggs were seldom allotted to servants, much less something as dear as chocolate.

"Never? Well, then, you shall try some today." Sophia's smile contained an impish quality as she added, "I happen to be a great authority on the subject."

The parlor was decorated in warm shades of burgundy, gold, and green, the heavy mahogany furniture upholstered in brocade and velvet. Small tables with leather tops were scattered throughout the room, bearing tempting loads of folio books, novels, and newspapers. At Sophia's direction, Lottie sat on an overstuffed couch, against a row of pillows embroidered in patterns of animals and flowers. Nick sat beside her after Sophia took a nearby chair.

A housemaid approached Sophia, received a few whispered directions, and left the room discreetly.

"My husband will be here momentarily," Sophia informed them serenely. "Now, Charlotte, do tell me how you and Nick met. His note was quite brief, and I am eager for details." Lottie opened and closed her mouth like a landed fish, unable to form a reply. She did not want to lie to Sophia, but the truth—that their marriage was a cold, practical arrangement—was too embarrassing to admit. Gentry answered for her, his large hand covering hers.

"We met in Hampshire during an investigation," he told his sister, playing with Lottie's fingers as he spoke. "Lottie was affianced to Lord Radnor, and she went into hiding to avoid him. He hired me to find her, and when I did . . ." He shrugged and let Sophia draw her own conclusions.

"But Lord Radnor is at least three decades older than Charlotte," Sophia said, wrinkling her nose. She glanced at Lottie with frank sympathy. "And having met him on one or two occasions, I find him to be quite odd. No wonder you didn't suit." She glanced at Gentry. "And were you immediately taken with Charlotte, when you found her?"

"Who wouldn't be?" Gentry parried with a bland smile. He drew a slow circle on Lottie's palm, stroked the insides of her fingers, brushed his thumb over the delicate veins of her wrist. The subtle exploration made her feel hot and breathless, her entire being focused on the fingertip that feathered along the tender flesh of her upper palm. Most disconcerting of all was the realization that Gentry didn't even know what he was doing. He fiddled lazily with her hand and talked with Sophia, while the chocolate service was brought to the parlor and set out on the table.

"Isn't it charming?" Sophia asked, indicating the flowered porcelain service with a flourish. She picked up the tall, narrow pot and poured a dark, fragrant liquid into one of the small cups, filling the bottom third. "Most people use cocoa powder, but the best results are obtained by mixing the cream with chocolate liquor." Expertly she stirred a generous spoonful of sugar into the steaming liquid. "Not liquor as in wine or spirits, mind you. Chocolate liquor is pressed from the meat of the beans, after they have been roasted and hulled."

"It smells quite lovely," Lottie commented, her breath catching as Gentry's fingertip investigated the plump softness at the base of her thumb.

Sophia turned her attention to preparing the other cups. "Yes, and the flavor is divine. I much prefer chocolate to coffee in the morning."

"Is it a st-stimulant, then?" Lottie asked, finally managing to jerk her hand away from Gentry. Deprived of his plaything, he gave her a questioning glance.

"Yes, of a sort," Sophia replied, pouring a generous amount of cream into the sweetened chocolate liquor. She stirred the cups with a tiny silver spoon. "Although it is not quite as animating as coffee, chocolate is uplifting in its own way." She winked at Lottie. "Some even claim that chocolate rouses the amorous instincts."

"How interesting," Lottie said, doing her best to ignore Gentry as she accepted her cup. Inhaling the rich fumes appreciatively, she took a tiny sip of the shiny, dark liquid. The robust sweetness slid along her tongue and tickled the back of her throat.

Sophia laughed in delight at Lottie's expression. "You like it, I see. Good—now I have found an inducement to make you visit often."

Lottie nodded as she continued to drink. By the time she reached the bottom of the cup, her head was swimming, and her nerves were tingling from the mixture of heat and sugar.

Gentry set his cup aside after a swallow or two. "Too rich for my taste, Sophia, although I compliment your skill in preparing it. Besides, my amorous instincts need no encouragement." He smiled as the statement caused Lottie to choke on the last few drops of chocolate.

"Would you like some more, Charlotte?" Sophia offered.

"Oh, yes, please."

Before Sophia poured more of the magical liquid, however, a tall, black-haired man entered the room. He spoke in an extraordinary voice, deep and gently abraded, his accent exquisitely cultured. "Pardon me for taking so long to join you. It was necessary to conclude some business with my estate agent."

Somehow Lottie had expected that Sir Ross would be settled and solid and pompously middle-aged. He was, after all, in his early forties. However, Sir Ross appeared to be more fit and virile than most men half his age. He was handsome in an aloof way, his natural authority so potent a force that Lottie instinctively shrank backward into the cushions. He was tall and lean, possessing a combination of self-assurance and vitality that made callow youth seem entirely graceless. His innate elegance would have been apparent even if he had been dressed in rustic peasant garb. As it was, he was clad in a crisply tailored black coat and matching trousers, with a charcoal silk necktie knotted deftly around his collar. His gaze swept over the scene, touching briefly on Lottie, lingering a bit longer on Gentry, then settling on his wife. What strange eyes he had . . . a gray so piercing and brilliant that it made her think of lightning trapped in a bottle.

Amazingly, Sophia spoke to the remarkable creature as if he were an ordinary man, her tone decidedly flirtatious. "Now that you're here, I suppose we'll have to discuss something dull, like politics or judicial reform."

Sir Ross laughed as he bent to kiss her cheek. It would have been an ordinary husbandly gesture except for the way he finished the kiss with a soft, nearly imperceptible nuzzle. Sophia's eyes closed briefly, as if the feel of his mouth on her skin recalled tantalizing memories.

"I'll try to be entertaining," he murmured with a caressing smile. As he straightened, the light played on the ebony blackness of his hair and picked out the silver streaks at his temples.

Gentry was stone-faced as he stood to shake his brother-in-law's hand. "Sir Grant told me that you wished to see me," he said without preamble. "What are you planning, Cannon?"

"We'll discuss that later. First I wish to become acquainted with your intrepid young bride."

Lottie laughed at Sir Ross's implication—that any woman would have to be intrepid, to marry such a notorious man as Nick Gentry. She curtsied as the former magistrate came around the table to her. Taking her hands in his large, warm ones, Sir Ross spoke with engaging gentleness. "Welcome to the family, Mrs. Gentry. Be assured that if you ever require assistance of any kind, you have only to ask. I am at your disposal."

As their gazes met, Lottie knew instinctively that he meant what he said. "Thank you, Sir Ross. I regret the necessity of keeping our kinship a secret, as I would be quite proud to claim you and Lady Cannon as relatives."

"Perhaps we can do something about that," he replied enigmatically.

Suddenly Lottie felt Gentry's hands close around her waist, and he tugged her away from Sir Ross. "I doubt it," Gentry said to his brother-in-law. "Since there is no way in hell that I would ever allow such information to be made public."

Sophia interceded quickly. "Since it is rather too late to have the traditional wedding breakfast, I propose that we enjoy a wedding luncheon. Cook is preparing lamb cutlets, early-season asparagus, and several varieties of salad. And pineapple cream for dessert."

"How wonderful," Lottie said, joining her in the effort to keep the atmosphere tranquil. She sat once more on the couch and carefully arranged her skirts. "I've never had asparagus, and I've always wanted to try it."

"Never had asparagus?" Sophia asked in disbelief.

As Lottie searched for a way to explain her unfamiliarity with such delicacies, Gentry sat beside her and took her hand again. "I'm afraid my wife was served a rather spartan diet at school," he told his sister. "She attended Maidstone's for several years."

Sir Ross occupied a chair beside Sophia's and gazed at Lottie intently. "A well-known institution, with the reputation of turning out very accomplished young ladies." His tone became gently encouraging. "Tell me, did you enjoy your years there, Mrs. Gentry?"

"Please call me Lottie," she invited with a shy

smile. As she proceeded to describe her experiences at the school, Sir Ross listened attentively, although Lottie had no idea why the subject would be of such interest.

Soon luncheon was served in the conservatory, at a table laden with glittering crystal and flowery china, while two footmen attended them. Lottie was delighted by the indoor trees and the lavish spills of delicate tea roses that scented the air. Even Gentry's mood seemed to lighten in the convivial atmosphere. Relaxing back in his chair, he regaled them with stories about the Bow Street office, including an account of how the runners had been assigned to inspect the dirty undergarments and shirts of prisoners being held in the strong room. Apparently the prisoners often penciled secret messages in their clothes, which were then given to relatives, who brought new garments for them to wear when they saw the magistrate. The condition of the prisoners' clothing was often so foul that the runners had resorted to drawing straws to decide who should be given the disgusting task. By the time Gentry had finished describing the fury of a particular runner who always seemed to draw the short straw, even Sir Ross was laughing richly.

Eventually Sir Ross and Gentry launched into a conversation about the problems concerning the "New Police," which had been created approximately ten years earlier. Since then, Bow Street had remained separate from the New Police, as Sir

Grant's force of constables and runners were far better trained and more effective than the "raw lobsters."

"Why are the New Police called raw lobsters?" Lottie could not resist asking.

Sir Ross replied with a faint smile. "Because raw lobsters are blue—the color of the new uniforms—and lobsters also pinch."

The comment made Gentry laugh.

As the police discussion continued, Sophia drew closer to Lottie. "Do you think that my brother will wish to continue at Bow Street, now that you've married?"

"He gave me the impression that he has no choice," Lottie replied carefully. "The bargain with Sir Ross . . ."

"Yes, but that arrangement was never intended to last forever. And now that Nick has married, perhaps Sir Ross will release him from the agreement."

"Why would our marriage have any effect on Mr. Gentry's position at Bow Street?"

Sophia glanced cautiously at the men across the table. "The answer to that is too private—and complicated—to discuss now. May I call on you soon, Lottie? We could have a nice long chat—and perhaps we'll go on a shopping excursion."

Lottie smiled. She had never expected that Gentry's sister would turn out to be so personable. And it seemed that Sophia was quite willing to shed some light on Gentry's mysterious past, which would help Lottie understand him much better. "Yes, I would like that very much."

"Lovely. I expect we shall have great fun."

Overhearing his sister's last remark, Gentry arched a dark brow. "What are you arranging, Sophia?"

"Oh, a simple stroll along Oxford Street," she replied cheerfully.

Gentry snorted. "There are at least a hundred and fifty shops on Oxford. I suspect you'll do more than simply stroll."

Sophia laughed. "You must open accounts for Charlotte at the drapers, and Wedgwood, and naturally the jewelers, as well as the bookshop and—"

"Oh, my lady . . . er, Sophia," Lottie interrupted uncomfortably, wondering why she didn't seem to realize that their finances were quite meager, compared to the Cannons' affluence. "I'm certain it will not be necessary to open accounts on my behalf."

Gentry spoke to Sophia with a slight smile. "Lottie may have credit wherever she likes. But first take her to your dressmaker. To my knowledge, she has no wedding trousseau."

"I don't need any new gowns," Lottie protested. "Perhaps one nice gown, but that is all." The last thing she desired was for Gentry to spend a great deal on clothes for her. Her memories of her parents' extravagant spending habits, and their resulting descent into poverty, were still very clear in her mind. She had an instinctive fear of spending large amounts of money, and she knew better than anyone how even a comfortable fortune could be squandered in a short time. "Please, I must insist that you don't—"

"It's all right," Gentry interrupted, touching her shoulder. His gaze conveyed the message that now was not the time to debate the issue.

Flushing, Lottie fell silent. His hand lingered at her shoulder, then slid to her elbow, squeezing lightly.

Thankfully, the silence at the table was relieved by the appearance of a footman, who cleared the dishes while another set out plates of dessert and tiny glasses of sweet wine. The dessert plates were arranged with delicate biscuits and pineapple cream served in cunning little glazed pots.

Sir Ross introduced a new topic of conversation concerning some recently proposed amendments to the Poor Law, which both he and Gentry supported. Surprisingly, Sophia offered her own opinions on the subject, and the men listened attentively. Lottie tried to conceal her astonishment, for she had been taught for years that a proper woman should never express her opinions in mixed company. Certainly she should say nothing about politics, an inflammatory subject that only men were qualified to debate. And yet here was a man as distinguished as Sir Ross seeming to find nothing wrong in his wife's speaking her mind. Nor did Gentry seem displeased by his sister's outspokenness.

Perhaps Gentry would allow her the same freedom. With that pleasant thought in her mind, Lottie consumed her pineapple cream, a rich, silky custard with a tangy flavor. Upon reaching the bottom of the pot, she thought longingly of how nice it would be to have another. However, good manners and the fear of appearing gluttonous made it unthinkable to request seconds.

Noticing the wistful glance Lottie gave her empty dish, Gentry laughed softly and slid his own untouched dessert to her plate. "You have even more of a taste for sweets than little Amelia," he murmured in her ear. His warm breath caused the hair on the back of her neck to rise.

"We didn't have desserts at school," she said with a sheepish smile.

He took his napkin and dabbed gently at the corner of her mouth. "I can see that I'll have a devil of a time trying to compensate for all the things you were deprived of. I suppose you'll want sweets with every meal now."

Pausing in the act of lifting her spoon, Lottie stared into the warm blue eyes so close to hers, and suddenly she felt wreathed in heat. Ridiculous, that all he had to do was speak with that caressing note in his voice, and she could be so thoroughly undone.

Sir Ross studied the pair of them with an all-engulfing glance. "Gentry, there is a matter I would take up with you. Undoubtedly there are better ways to reveal my thoughts concerning your future, but I confess that I can't think of them. Your circumstances are unusual." He paused and smiled ruefully. "That is an understatement, of course. The twists and turns of your life have been nothing if not bizarre."

Gentry sat back with languid grace, appearing relaxed, but Lottie sensed the apprehension that coiled inside him. "I haven't asked you to consider my future."

"I have, nonetheless. During the past three years that I have followed your career—"

"Followed?" Gentry interrupted dryly. "More like manipulated, meddled, and interfered."

Inured to semantics after so many years on the bench, Sir Ross shrugged. "I've done as I thought best. Bear in mind that in my dealings with you, I've also had Sophia's interests to consider. She is the only reason I kept you from the gallows. She believed there was potential for goodness in you. And though I didn't see it back then, I am willing to admit now that she was right. You are not the complete villain I thought you to be."

Gentry smiled coolly, aware that he was being damned with faint praise. "In return, let me say that you are not completely the hypocritical cold fish I thought you to be."

"Nick," Sophia scolded, and laid her slender hand over Sir Ross's large one. "My husband has never had a hypocritical thought in his life. And as for his being a cold fish, I can assure you most definitely that he is not. Furthermore—"

"Sophia," Sir Ross interrupted softly, "you don't have to defend me, my love."

"Well, you're *not*," she insisted.

His hand turned palm up to grip hers, and for just a moment the pair stared at their interlaced fingers with a shared pleasure that seemed unspeakably intimate. Lottie felt a peculiar ache in her chest. What must it be like to love that way? The two of them seemed to take such enormous delight in each other.

"All right," Gentry said impatiently. "Let's get to the point, Cannon. I have no desire to spend my entire wedding day with you."

That elicited a grin from the former magistrate. "Very well, I will try to be succinct. Ever since you joined the Bow Street force, Sir Grant has kept me informed of your accomplishments; the detective operations, the work with the foot patrols, the pursuits that you've undertaken at the hazard of your life. But it wasn't until the Barthas house fire that I realized how much you have changed."

"I haven't changed," Gentry said warily.

"You've learned to value others' lives as much as your own," Sir Ross continued. "You've met the challenge I presented to you three years ago, and you've contributed greatly to the public welfare. And now you've even taken a wife. Interestingly enough, she is the kind of young woman you might have married had circumstances not deprived you of your title and position so long ago."

Gentry's eyes narrowed. "I never gave a damn about the title. And God knows I have no use for it now."

The older man toyed with his spoon, wearing an

expression befitting a chess player in the middle of a long game. "There is something you've never quite understood about your title. It's yours, whether you want it or not. A title doesn't disappear merely because one chooses to ignore it."

"It does if one chooses to become someone else."

"But you're not someone else," Sir Ross rejoined. "The real Nick Gentry died fourteen years ago. You are Lord Sydney."

"No one knows that."

"That," Sir Ross said calmly, "is about to change."

Gentry went very still as he absorbed the statement. "What the hell does that mean?"

"After a great deal of deliberation, I decided to begin the process of dignification on your behalf. Recently I explained the particulars of your situation to the offices of the Crown and the Lord Chancellor. Not only did I assure them that you are indeed the long-lost Lord Sydney, I also confirmed that you are financially equipped to manage the title. In approximately a fortnight, the Clerk of the Crown will issue a Writ of Summons, calling you to the House of Lords. At which time I will introduce you publicly as Lord Sydney, at a ball that will be given in your honor."

Gentry shot up from the table, his chair falling back and clattering to the floor. "Go to hell, Cannon!"

Lottie started at the burst of hostility. Gentry reacted as if his very life were being threatened. However, the danger he faced was not the physical peril he was accustomed to . . . it was intangible, insidious . . . the one prison he could not escape. Lottie sensed the thoughts that writhed behind his set expression, the way his clever mind analyzed the sudden predicament and considered various ways to evade it.

"I'll deny everything," Gentry said.

Sir Ross made a temple of his hands, regarding him steadily. "If you do, I will respond with depositions from myself, Sir Grant, your sister, and even your wife, testifying to the fact that you have privately confessed yourself to be Lord Sydney. Those, combined with circumstantial oddities such as missing burial records and inconsistent reports of your death, form what is known in English law as a *fecundatio ab extra*—a rare but not impossible occurrence."

Gentry looked as if he wanted to murder the former Bow Street magistrate. "I'll petition the House of Lords to be allowed to renounce the title. God knows they'll be overjoyed to get rid of me."

"Don't be a fool. Do you really believe they would ever allow you to disclaim your title? To their minds, such a renunciation would challenge the very institution of the peerage. They would fear that the distinctions between the classes—no, the monarchy itself—would be threatened."

"You don't believe in privilege based on birth," Gentry shot back. "Why force a damned title on me? *I don't want it.*"

"This has nothing to do with my political beliefs. This is a matter of simple fact. You are Sydney, no matter what you call yourself. You are not going to be able to overturn seven hundred years of hereditary principle, nor will you be able to avoid your obligations as Lord Sydney any longer."

"Obligations to what?" Gentry sneered. "To an estate that has been held in abeyance for fourteen years?"

"You have a responsibility to the tenants who are trying to eke out a living on ramshackle government-managed lands. To the House of Lords, where your seat has gone vacant for two decades. To your sister, who is obligated to keep her relationship with her own brother a secret. To your wife, who will enjoy far more respect and social advantage as Lady Sydney than she ever would as Mrs. Gentry. To the memory of your parents. And to yourself. For half of your life you've been hiding behind a false name. It is time for you to acknowledge who you are."

Gentry's hands clenched. "That's not for you to decide."

"If I don't force the issue, you'll spend the rest of your life avoiding it."

"That is my right!"

"Perhaps. But regardless, you will find it impossible to remain a runner. Sir Grant concurs with my opinion, and therefore he will no longer require your services at Bow Street."

A wash of color spread over Gentry's face. His throat worked violently as he realized that his days as a runner had just come to an end. "Then I'll spend my time taking private commissions."

"That would be a novelty, wouldn't it?" Sir Ross asked sardonically. "The crime-solving viscount."

"Nick," Sophia broke in softly, "you know what Papa and Mama would have wanted."

He appeared bitter and miserable, and above all, outraged. "I've been Nick Gentry too long to change."

Sophia replied with great care, seeming to understand why he would consider it impossible. "It will be difficult. No one would deny that. But you have Lottie to assist you."

Nick did not spare Lottie a glance but made a scornful sound.

"Lottie, dear," Sophia said with a gentle inflexibility that betrayed the strong will beneath her delicate facade. "How many years did you attend Maidstone's?"

"Six," Lottie said, casting a wary glance at her husband's hard profile.

"If Maidstone's reputation holds true, those six years were filled with an education that included rigorous training in deportment, grace, the art of polite entertaining, the skills of household budgeting and management, the elements of style and good taste, the rituals of morning calls and after-dinner assemblies . . . the thousands of little points of etiquette that separate the first tier from the other layers of society. I suspect you could easily regulate a household of any size, no matter how large. No doubt you were also taught how to dance, ride, play a musical instrument, speak French and perhaps a smattering of German . . . am I mistaken?"

"You are correct," Lottie said shortly, hating the sudden feeling that she was part of the trap that was closing around Gentry. He was being forced to become something he had no desire to be, and she understood his feelings all too well.

Nodding in satisfaction, Sophia turned to her glowering brother. "Lottie is a great asset to you. She will prove invaluable in helping you adjust to your new life—"

"I'm not going to adjust to a damned thing," he growled and threw a commanding glance to Lottie. "Come, we're leaving. Now."

She rose automatically, and Sir Ross stood as well. Troubled, Lottie glanced at her brother-in-law. There was no glint of victory in his eyes. She did not believe that his motives had anything to do with vengeance or ill will. She was certain that Sir Ross— and Sophia—thought it quite necessary that Gentry reclaim his former identity. She longed to discuss the matter with them, but it was clear that Gentry was barely maintaining his self-control. Any other man would have been gratified to recover his title, his lands, and family possessions. However, it was obvious that to Gentry this was a nightmare.

Lottie held her silence during the carriage ride home. Her husband was utterly still, trying to contain his explosive outrage, and most likely struggling to comprehend the suddenness with which his life had changed. Not unlike her own mood upon leaving Stony Cross Park, she thought wryly.

The moment they arrived at the house on Betterton Street, Gentry practically leapt from the carriage, leaving Lottie to accept the footman's help in descending from the vehicle. By the time she reached the front door, he was nowhere to be seen.

The housekeeper was in the entrance hall, her perplexed expression betraying that she had just seen Gentry storm inside the house.

"Mrs. Trench," Lottie said calmly, "did you happen to see where Mr. Gentry went?"

"I believe he is in the library, miss. That is . . . Mrs. Gentry."

Good Lord, how strange it was to be called that. And it was stranger still to contemplate the very strong possibility that before long she would be called Lady Sydney. Frowning, Lottie glanced from the staircase to the hall leading toward the library. Part of her wanted to retreat to the safety and seclusion of her room. However, the other part was irresistibly drawn to find Gentry.

After Mrs. Trench took her bonnet and gloves, Lottie found herself walking to the library. She knocked at the closed door before entering. The library was paneled in dark cherrywood, and fitted with carpets woven with gold medallions on a brown background. Multipaned windows stretched up to the top of the ceiling, which was at least eighteen feet high.

Gentry's broad-shouldered form was at one of the windows, his back tensing visibly as he heard her approach. A brandy snifter was clenched in his hand, the delicate bowl of the glass looking as if it might shatter in his long fingers.

Lottie hesitated beside one of the towering cherrywood bookshelves, noticing that the library was strangely bereft of volumes.

"Your library is nearly empty," she commented.

Gentry stood at the window, his stare brooding and vacant. He tossed back the remainder of his brandy with a stiff-wristed motion. "Buy some books, then. Fill it from floor to ceiling if you like."

"Thank you." Encouraged by the fact that he had not yet told her to leave, Lottie ventured closer. "Mr Gentry . . ."

"Don't call me that," he said in a burst of irritation.

"I'm sorry. Nick." She drew closer to him. "I wish to correct something that Sir Ross said—you have no responsibility to make me Lady Sydney. As I told you before, I do not care if you are a peer or a commoner."

He was quiet for a long time, then he let out a tense sigh. Striding to the sideboard, he poured another brandy.

"Is there any way of stopping Sir Ross from carrying out his plans?" Lottie asked. "Perhaps we might seek some legal counsel—"

"It's too late. I know Sir Ross—he has thought of every possible countermove. And his influence extends everywhere; the judiciary, law enforcement, Parliament, the Crown office . . . that writ of summons is going to arrive, no matter what the hell I do to avoid it." He uttered an unfamiliar word that sounded quite foul. "I'd like to break every bone in Cannon's body, the insufferable ass."

"What can I do?" she asked quietly.

"You heard my sister, didn't you? You're going to play lady of the manor and help me pretend to be a viscount."

"You managed quite well at Stony Cross Park," she pointed out. "You gave a convincing appearance of nobility."

"That was only for a few days," he said bitterly. "But now it appears I'll have to play the role for the rest of my life." He shook his head in furious disbelief. "God! I don't want this. I'm going to kill someone before long."

Lottie tilted her head as she regarded him speculatively. No doubt she should fear him when he was in this mood. He did indeed look as though he was ready to commit murder, his eyes gleaming with bloodlust. But curiously she was filled with sympathy, and even more than that, a sense of partnership. They were both floundering, both facing a life they had neither planned nor asked for.

"How did you feel at Stony Cross Park, when you introduced yourself as Lord Sydney?" she asked.

"At first I found it amusing. The irony of masquerading as myself. But after the first day, it became a weight on my shoulders. The mere mention of the name annoys the hell out of me."

Lottie wondered why he was so antagonized by

the name he had been born with. There had to be some reason other than the ones he had given so far.

"Nick, what did Sir Ross mean when he said that you were financially equipped to manage the title?"

His mouth twisted. "He meant that I could afford the cost of maintaining a large estate and the kind of lifestyle required of a peer."

"How could he know such a thing?"

"He doesn't know for certain."

"He is wrong, of course."

"No," Nick muttered, "he's not wrong. Before I came to Bow Street, I made a few investments, and I have some holdings here and there. All in all, I have about two hundred put away."

Silently Lottie reflected that two hundred pounds in savings was not bad, but it did not offer the kind of security one could have wished for. She only hoped that his investments would not depreciate in value. "Well, that seems quite satisfactory," she said, not wishing to hurt his feelings. "I think we shall do fairly well if we economize. But I do not think the circumstances allow for a wedding trousseau. Not at this time. Perhaps in the future—"

"Lottie," he interrupted, "we don't need to economize."

"Two hundred pounds is a fine sum, but it will be difficult to maintain a household with—"

"Lottie." He glanced at her with an odd expression. "I was referring to thousands. Two hundred thousand pounds."

"But . . . but . . ." Lottie was astonished. It was an immense sum, a fortune by anyone's standards.

"And about five thousand a year from investments and private commissions," he added, stunning her further. His face darkened. "Although it seems my days of private commissions are over."

"Why, you must be as rich as Lord Radnor," she said dazedly.

He made a choppy gesture with his hand, as if consideration of money was completely irrelevant, compared to his far greater problem. "Probably."

"You could afford a dozen houses. You could have anything you—"

"I don't need a dozen houses. I can only sleep under one roof at a time. I can only eat three meals a day. And I don't give a damn about impressing anyone."

Lottie was surprised by the realization that he was not motivated to acquire wealth. His fortune had come as a consequence of his need to outwit everyone from the underworld to Bow Street. And now that the profession of law enforcement had been taken from him, he would be in urgent need of something to do. He was a tremendously active man, not at all suited for the cultivated indolence of aristocratic life. How in heaven's name was he going to adjust to living as a peer?

His thoughts must have mirrored hers, for he gave a groan of hopeless anger and raked his hand roughly through his hair. A stray lock fell on his forehead, and Lottie was startled by her sudden urge to play with the thick chocolate-colored strands, smooth them back, slide her fingers into the warm silk.

"Lottie," he said gruffly, "I'm going out for a while. I probably won't be back until morning. You have a reprieve for tonight."

"What are you going to do?"

"I don't know yet." He stepped back from her with a restlessness that contained an edge of panic, as if a heavy net had dropped over him.

Lottie knew that she should not care if he went out and drank, or struck up a fight with someone, or did any of the numerous foolish things that men in search of amusement did. She should not want to soothe his barely contained fury. But she did.

Without allowing herself time to consider her actions, Lottie approached him, touching the fine broadcloth of his coat with her palm. Her hand smoothed over the fabric and eased inside. His waistcoat was the same inky black as his coat, but the material was silkier, slipping a little over the hard delineation of his chest muscles. She thought of how hot his skin must be, to impart such warmth to the thick garment.

Nick was suddenly motionless, his breath changing to a slower, deeper rhythm. Lottie did not look at his face but concentrated instead on the knot of his gray necktie as her fingers explored the snowy, fragrant folds of his shirt.

"I don't want a reprieve," she said eventually and tugged at the knot until it slid loose.

As the necktie unraveled, it seemed that his self-control became similarly undone. He breathed more heavily, and his hands clenched at his sides. Inexpertly she unfastened the stiff collar of his shirt and spread it wide to reveal the amber sheen of his throat. She glanced up at his face and saw with a quake of sudden nervousness that his fury was transforming rapidly into pure sexual need. Color crept across his cheekbones and the bridge of his nose, a burnished glow that made his eyes look like blue fire.

His head lowered very slowly, as if he were giving her every opportunity to flee. She stayed where she was, her eyes closing as she felt the barely perceptible touch of his mouth on the side of her neck. His lips brushed the sensitive skin, parted, and the silken tip of his tongue stroked her in a delicate, hot circle. With a shaky sigh, Lottie leaned forward into his body as her legs wobbled beneath her. He did not touch her with his hands, only continued to explore her neck with exquisite leisure. She held onto him, her arms locking around his lean waist.

His hands came to her shoulders, gripping softly. He seemed undecided as to whether he wanted to pull her closer or push her away. His voice was hoarse as he asked, "What are you doing, Lottie?"

Her heart was hammering so wildly that she could barely summon the breath to speak. "I suppose I am encouraging you to finish what you started in Lord Westcliff's library."

"Be certain," he said roughly. "I haven't had a

woman in six months. If you suddenly decide to stop, I'm not going to take it well."

"I won't tell you to stop."

He stared at her, his gaze fever-bright, his face hard. "Why now, when you didn't want to last night?"

That was beyond her ability to explain. After the events of this afternoon, he suddenly seemed vulnerable to her. She was beginning to see the ways in which he needed her, needs that went beyond sexual desire. And the challenge of taming him, matching his powerful will with her own, was too tempting to resist.

"We're married now," she said, seizing on the first excuse she could think of. "And I would prefer to . . . to have done with this, so that I won't have to dread it."

She saw the predatory flicker in his eyes. He wanted her. He did not waste time asking questions, only extended his hand. "Come upstairs, then."

Carefully Lottie placed her hand in his. "Nick, there is just one thing . . ."

"What?"

"It's not dark yet."

"And?"

"Is it appropriate to do this in the afternoon?"

The question pulled an unsteady laugh from him. "I don't know. And I damn well don't care." Keeping her hand in his, he guided her from the library to the entrance hall, and up the grand staircase.

Chapter Nine

Lottie went upstairs with him, her hand caught fast in his, her legs feeling like rubber when they finally reached his bedroom. The curtains were parted, admitting soft gray light through the windows. She would have much preferred darkness. The thought of being naked in the unforgiving daylight caused her to shake all over.

"Easy," Nick murmured, standing behind her. His hands closed gently around her upper arms. His voice was lower, thicker than usual. "I'll be careful. I can make it pleasant for you, if . . ."

"If?"

"If you'll trust me."

They were both still and silent. Lottie moistened her lips, reflecting that she hadn't trusted anyone in years. And to put her faith in Nick Gentry . . . the most unscrupulous man she had ever met . . . it was not folly, it was insanity. "Yes," she said, surprising herself. "Yes, I will trust you."

He made a soft sound, as if the words had caught him off guard.

Gradually his hand slid across the upper part of her chest, exerting a gentle pressure that caused her to lean back against him. She felt his mouth on the back of her neck, his lips playing through the tender wisps at her nape. He tasted the downy skin, then pressed the edge of his teeth in a sensitive spot that made her squirm against him in pleasure. Working his way to the side of her neck, he nibbled his way to the tip of her earlobe, while his hands moved over the front of her gown. The bodice parted, the sides listing to reveal the framework of the light corset beneath. His fingertips drifted to her throat, caressed the vulnerable curve, then traveled to the wing of her collarbone.

"You're beautiful, Lottie," he whispered. "The way you feel and taste . . . your skin, your hair . . ." He took the pins from her hair, sent them skittering to the carpet, and sank his fingers into the pale silken locks that fell over her shoulder. Bringing her hair to his face, he rubbed it against his cheek and chin. Heat played in her body, rising, intensifying, and she leaned back against the solid form behind her.

He eased her gown to her waist, helping her to extract her arms from the sleeves, his fingertips running lightly from her elbows to her underarms. Turning her to face him, Nick deftly unhooked the corset, releasing her from the wrapping of stays and laces. Her breasts, which had been propped artificially high in the boned supports, were left unconfined, the tips hardening against the thin crushed muslin of her chemise. His hand lifted, and he touched her through the sheer fabric. Sliding his fingers beneath the fullness of her breast, he drew his thumb over the shape of her nipple. His touch was very light, lingering at the tip until it burned.

Gasping, Lottie grasped his shoulders for balance. He slid a solid arm behind her back as he continued to toy gently with her body, taking the peak in his fingers, stroking softly. An ache of pleasure formed deep in her stomach as he cupped her breast in his hand, containing the roundness in his palm. Suddenly she wanted him to touch her other breast. She wanted his mouth on her, everywhere, and to slide her own lips across the heat of his skin, and to feel his unclothed body against hers. Frustrated and eager, she tugged at his coat, until his choppy laugh ruffled through her hair.

"Slowly," he whispered. "There's no need to hurry." He removed his coat . . . waistcoat . . . stockings and shoes . . . trousers . . . shirt . . . and finally the linens that had obscured the startling sight of his erection.

Suddenly Lottie didn't know where to look. He should have appeared vulnerable in his nakedness, but he seemed more powerful now than when he'd had his clothes on. His body was hewn with brutal grace, large and muscular and superbly fit. His bronze tan ended at his waistline, fading into the paler skin of his hips. A wealth of thick dark hair covered his chest, and there was another heavy patch of it at his groin, around the dark, upthrust length of his erection.

Nick's fingertip traced the side of her scarlet cheek. "Do you know what is going to happen?"

Lottie nodded jerkily. "Yes, I think so."

He stroked the underside of her chin, his fingertip leaving a trail of fire. "Who told you about it? Your mother?"

"Oh, no. She was going to explain everything to me the night before my wedding to Lord Radnor. But of course that never transpired." Lottie closed her eyes as he caressed the side of her neck, his hand warm and a bit raspy from callouses. "I heard gossip at school, though. A few of the girls had . . . done things . . . and they told the rest of us about it."

"Done what things?"

"Met in private with gentlemen friends, or cousins, and allowed them liberties." Lottie opened her eyes and met his smiling gaze, refusing to look below the level of his collarbone.

"How far did the liberties go? As far as we went the other night?"

"Yes," she forced herself to admit.

"Did you enjoy the way I touched you?" he asked softly.

Color blazed in her face, and she managed a jerking nod.

"You'll enjoy the rest of it, too," he promised, reaching for the hem of her chemise.

Obeying his wordless urging, she lifted her arms and let him strip away the garment. She kicked off her slippers and stood before him in her long drawers and stockings, with her arms crossed over her bare breasts.

He stood over her, his hand trailing over her back, raising gooseflesh on every inch of her skin. "Put your arms around me, Lottie."

She obeyed awkwardly, bringing her body fully against his. Her nipples sank into the coarse mat of curls on his chest. His body was incredibly hot, his erection burning through the muslin drawers. It prodded against her stomach, until he slid his hand beneath her buttocks and hitched her upward. His hand slid between her buttocks to hold her compactly against him, and she felt him press against her sex. A shock of sensation went through her, followed by a surge of lust so acute that she could hardly bear it. Gripping his neck, she pushed her face against the dense muscle of his shoulder. His fingers slid farther between her thighs. The linen beneath his fingers became damp as he stroked the soft furrow in a lazy rhythm. For a long, blissful minute he held her like that, warming her with his own body until she began to strain against the ridge of his erection.

Reaching between their bodies, he pulled at the tapes of her drawers. He let the garment drop to the floor and picked her up, carrying her to the bed with astonishing ease. As Lottie reclined on the embroidered counterpane, Nick's gaze slid over her. A smile tugged at his lips. "I've never seen anyone blush from head to toe before."

"Well, I've never been naked in front of a man," Lottie said, abashed. It was inconceivable that she should be conversing with someone while she wasn't wearing a stitch of clothing, except for her stockings.

His hand closed gently around her ankle. "You're adorable," he whispered, and climbed over her.

He tugged at one of her garters with his teeth, loosening the ribbon that fastened it. She gasped as he kissed the red marks left by the tie, and soothed them with his tongue. Unrolling the stockings from her legs, he pushed her thighs wide apart. Increasingly uncomfortable, Lottie used her hand to conceal herself from his view. His head moved over her, his hot breath fanning her skin. His thumbs swept over the pulse in the fragile crease between her thigh and groin.

"Don't cover yourself," he coaxed.

"I can't help it," she said, wriggling to evade the tiny flicks of his tongue, which ventured in places she had never imagined a man would want to put his mouth. Somehow she managed to dislodge the bedclothes enough to dive beneath them in search of sanctuary. She shivered at the cool slickness of the linens against her naked body.

Following with a low laugh, Nick slid beneath the

bedclothes, until they tented over the broad outline of his shoulders. His head disappeared, and she felt his hands on her knees, pushing them apart once more.

Lottie stared blindly at the dark canopy overhead. "Nick," she asked raggedly, "is this the usual way that people h-have relations?"

His voice was muffled. "What is the usual way?"

She inhaled sharply as he nipped at the inner curve of her thigh. "I'm not entirely certain. But I don't think this is it."

His voice thickened with amusement. "I know what I'm doing, Lottie."

"I was not implying that you didn't . . . oh, *please* don't kiss me there!"

Then she felt him shake with suppressed laughter. "For someone who has never done this before, you're rather opinionated. Let me make love to you the way I want, hmmn? The first time, at least." He grasped both her wrists and pinned them at her sides. "Lie still."

"Nick . . ." She started as his mouth descended to the nest of blond curls. "Nick . . ."

But he did not listen, completely absorbed in her salt-scented female flesh. His breath filled the moist cleft with steamy heat. A moan rose in her throat, and her wrists twisted in his grasp. His tongue searched through the springy curls until he reached the rosy lips hidden beneath. He licked one side of her sex, then the other, the tip of his tongue teasing delicately.

His mouth ravished her so gently, his tongue slipping over her melting flesh to find the secret entrance to her body, filling her with silky heat . . . withdrawing . . . filling. Lottie went weak all over, her sex pulsing urgently. As he nuzzled and played with her, she tried to angle her body so that he would touch the peak that throbbed so desperately. He seemed not to understand what she wanted, licking all around the sensitive spot but never quite reaching it.

"Nick," she whispered, unable to find words for what she wanted. "Please. Please."

But he continued to deny her, until she realized that he was doing it deliberately. Frustrated beyond bearing, she reached down to his head, and she felt the puff of his brief laugh against her. Immediately his mouth slid away and traveled downward, tasting the damp creases of her knees, moving to the hollows of her ankles. By the time he made his way back to her loins, her entire body was sweltering. His head hovered over the place between her legs again. Lottie held her breath, aware of a hot trickle of moisture from her body.

His tongue brushed the peak of her sex in a tentative lap. Lottie could not hold back a wild cry as she arched into his mouth.

"No," he murmured against her damp flesh. "Not yet, Lottie. Wait just a little longer."

"I can't, can't, oh, don't stop . . ." She pulled at his dark head frantically, groaning as he feathered his tongue over her once more.

Catching her wrists, Nick pulled them over her

head and settled his body between her thighs, taking care not to crush her. His shaft was cradled in the hot valley between her legs. His dark blue eyes stared directly into hers as he released her hands. "Leave them there," he said, and she obeyed with a sob.

He kissed her breasts, moving from one to the other. With each incendiary swirl of his tongue, she nearly rose off the sheet. His sex slid against her in disciplined thrusts that teased and rubbed and tormented, while his mouth drew hungrily on her nipples. She arched upward with supplicating moans. Stunning pleasure built inside her, gaining intensity . . . she hovered on the brink, waiting, waiting . . . *oh, please* . . . until the culmination was finally upon her. She cried out in bashful amazement as rich spasms spread from the center of her body.

"Yes," he whispered against her taut throat, his hips working gently over hers. The sensation eased into long shivers as he smoothed her hair back from her damp forehead.

"Nick," she told him between deep gulps of air, "s-something happened . . ."

"Yes, I know. You climaxed." His voice was tender and vaguely amused. "Shall I do it again?"

"No," she said instantly, making him laugh.

"Then it's my turn." He slid an arm beneath her neck so that her head rested in the crook of his elbow. He mounted her again, the muscular weight of his thighs pushing between hers, and she felt the broad head of his shaft press against the vulnerable cove between her legs. He skimmed it through the moisture in deliberate circles, then nudged against her until Lottie felt a slight burn. Instinctively she shrank from the pressure. Holding still, Nick gazed down at her, his face suddenly taut and intent. He bent his head and touched his mouth to the delicate space between her brows. "I'm sorry," he said quietly.

"Why—" she began, and gasped as he invaded her in a single determined thrust. She recoiled from the pain, her legs closing instinctively, but she could do nothing to prevent him from sliding deeper. She was trapped beneath his body, impaled with hardness and heat.

Carefully he pushed farther. "I'm sorry," he said again. "I thought it might be easier for you if I did it quickly."

It hurt more than Lottie had expected. It was a curious sensation, having part of someone else's body inside her own. It was so remarkable that she almost forgot the pain. She sensed the effort it took for him to hold still. He was trying to wait until she became accustomed to him, she realized. But the discomfort persisted, and she knew that no matter how much time he gave her, it was not going to improve. "Nick," she said unsteadily, "would it be possible for you to finish this part of it right away?"

"God," he muttered ruefully. "Yes, I can do that." Cautiously he tightened his hips, and Lottie realized in consternation that he was advancing even deeper. As the crown of his shaft pressed against her womb, she flinched in distress. Immediately he drew back a little, his hand stroking from her breast to her hip. "The next time will be better," he said, keeping his thrusts shallow. "You're so warm, Lottie, so sweet . . ." He became breathless, his eyes closing tightly, his hands clenching against the mattress. Despite the pain his movements caused, Lottie experienced a curious feeling of protectiveness . . . of tenderness, even. Her hands slid over his back, following the deep arch of his spine. She tightened her knees on his hips as she contained his large body, hugging him to herself, listening to the way his breath hitched. Suddenly he buried his entire length inside her and held still. She felt him jerk violently as he released his passion with a harsh groan. Stroking his back, she let her inquisitive fingers wander lower, lower, until she found the tightly muscled curves of his buttocks, harder than she had thought human flesh could be.

Finally Nick sighed and opened his eyes, a blaze of unearthly blue in his passion-flushed face. The way he murmured her name sent shivers down her back. After tucking the linen neatly beneath her arms, Nick rose on one elbow to look down at her. A small frown pleated the space between his thick brows. "Are you all right?"

"Yes." A drowsy smile curved her lips. "It wasn't bad at all. Until the end, I thought it was even better than a shower-bath."

He made a sound of amusement. "Yes, but was it as good as chocolate?"

Lottie reached up to stroke the high plane of his

cheekbone. She couldn't resist teasing him. "Not quite."

Another chuckle escaped him. "My God, you're hard to please." He turned his mouth into her hand, kissing the damp hollow of her palm. "As for me, I'm more content than a sailor at fiddler's green."

Lottie continued to explore the bold contours of his face with her fingertips. With a flush lingering high in his cheeks, and the brackets around his mouth softened, he looked younger than usual. "What is fiddler's green?" she asked.

"A place in heaven for sailors. Nothing but wine, women, and song all day and night."

"What is your idea of heaven?"

"I don't believe in heaven."

Lottie's eyes widened. "I'm married to a pagan?" she asked, and he grinned.

"You may yet be sorry you didn't marry Radnor."

"Don't joke about that," she said, turning away from him. "It's not a subject for humor."

"I'm sorry," he interrupted, his arm sliding around her waist. He pulled her into the shelter of his body, her back fitting against his hairy chest. "I didn't mean to nettle you. Here, rest against me." He nuzzled into the pale streamers of her hair. "What a fiery little wench you are."

"I'm not fiery," Lottie protested, for that quality was hardly something that befitted a ladylike graduate of Maidstone's.

"Yes, you are." His hand curved possessively

over her hip. "I've known it from the moment we met. It's one of the reasons I wanted you."

"You said you wanted me merely for convenience."

"Well, there is that," he said with a grin, and reacted swiftly as she tried to elbow him. "But in truth, convenience had nothing to do with it. I wanted you more than any woman I've ever met."

"Why did you insist on marriage, when I offered to be your mistress?"

"Because being a mistress wasn't good enough for you." He paused before adding quietly, "You deserve everything I can give you, including my name."

A sobering thought dimmed Lottie's pleasure in the compliment. "After everyone learns that you are Lord Sydney, you will be quite sought after," she said. A man with his looks, a fortune, and a title to boot was an irresistible combination. He would undoubtedly receive a great deal of attention from women who would want to tempt him into having an affair.

"I won't stray from you," Nick said, surprising her with his perceptiveness.

"You can't be certain. A man with your personal history . . ."

"What do you know of my personal history?" He pressed her flat on her back and loomed over her, one long leg sliding between hers.

"It is obvious that you are very experienced in the bedroom."

"I am," he admitted. "But that doesn't mean that I've been indiscriminate. In fact . . ."

"In fact?" Lottie prompted.

He looked away. "Nothing."

"You were going to tell me that you haven't had all that many women, I suppose." Her tone was loaded with skepticism. "Although the concept is obviously subjective. What is 'many' for you, I wonder? A hundred? Fifty? Ten?"

"It doesn't matter," he said with a scowl.

"I wouldn't believe you if you claimed anything less than twenty."

"You would be wrong, then."

"How far off the mark would I be, then?"

"I've been with only two women," he said curtly. "Including you."

"You have not," she exclaimed with a disbelieving laugh.

"Believe what you like," he muttered, rolling away from her.

He was clearly annoyed, as if he regretted what he had just told her. As he left the bed and strode to the wardrobe, Lottie watched him in slack-jawed astonishment. She couldn't quite bring herself to accept his claim, and yet there was no reason for him to lie to her. "Who was the other one?" she couldn't resist asking.

His broad, well-muscled back flexed as he shrugged into a burgundy velvet robe. "A madam."

"French, you mean?"

"No, the kind of madam that owns a whore-house," he replied bluntly.

Lottie nearly toppled from the edge of the bed. She managed to keep her face relatively composed as he turned toward her. "Was it a long . . . friendship?"

"Three years."

Lottie absorbed the information silently. She realized with dismay that the heaviness in her chest was caused by jealousy. "Were you in love with her?" she brought herself to ask.

"No," he said without hesitation. "But I liked her. I still do."

A frown worked across her forehead. "Why do you no longer see her?"

Nick shook his head. "After a while, Gemma believed there was nothing more to be gained on either side by continuing the arrangement. I've since come to realize that she was right. And I haven't slept with anyone else, until you. So you see, I don't have a problem keeping my trousers buttoned."

A tide of relief swept over her. Just why she was so pleased at the notion that she might be able to keep him all to herself was not something she wished to ponder too closely. Leaving the bed, she hurried to pick up her discarded dress from the floor, and held it over her front. "I will admit that I am surprised," she said, trying to appear casual with her nudity. "You are certainly not predictable in any regard."

He approached her and closed his hands over her bare shoulders. "Neither are you," he replied. "I never expected to receive such pleasure from a rank novice." Taking the dress from her hands, Nick dropped it to the floor and pressed her body against the velvet front of his robe. Her skin tingled at the plush softness that caressed her from breasts to knees. "Maybe it's because you're mine," he mused, his hand covering her pale, round breast. "No one's ever belonged to me before."

Lottie smiled wryly. "You make me sound like a horse you've just bought."

"A horse would have been cheaper," he replied, and grinned as she attacked him in mock outrage.

She pounded at his chest, and he twisted her wrists neatly behind her back, causing her breasts to thrust forward. "Save your strength," he advised, smiling against her hair. Releasing her wrists, he rubbed the small of her back with one hand. "You must be sore. I'll draw a hot bath for you. When you finish, we'll have something to eat."

A hot bath would be wonderful. However, the thought of lacing herself into a corset and dressing for dinner was distinctly unappealing.

"Shall I have a supper tray sent up here?" Nick asked.

"Yes," Lottie said immediately and gave him a quizzical glance. "How do you do that? You always seem to know what I'm thinking."

"Your face shows everything." Removing his robe, he placed it around her, the heavy velvet warming her with the lingering heat of his body.

"I've only eaten in my bedroom once, when I was ill," she told him as he tied the robe around her. "And that was years ago."

Nick bent to whisper in her ear. "My passionate bride . . . later I'll show you that the bedroom is the best possible place to dine."

He bathed her himself, kneeling by the tub with the sleeves of his robe rolled up to reveal the wet, dark hair of his forearms. Eyes half-closed, Lottie let her gaze drift from the tanned column of his throat to the dark hair that filled the open vee of his robe. He was such a robustly masculine creature, and yet he touched her with incongruous gentleness. Veils of steam rose from the water, making the air hot and iridescent. She felt drugged with heat and sensuality as his strong, soapy hands glided into the intimate places of her body.

"Does it hurt here?" he asked, his fingers slipping over the swollen entrance of her sex.

"A little." She leaned back against his arm, her head lolling on the polished wooden rim of the huge porcelain bathtub.

Nick kneaded lightly with his fingertips, as if he could heal her with his touch. "I tried to be gentle."

"You were," she managed to say, her thighs floating apart.

Nick's thick lashes lowered as he stared at the shimmering blur of her body beneath the water. His handsome features were carved with such severity that his face could have been molded from bronze. The edge of his rolled-up sleeve dragged in the water, the velvet turning hot and sodden.

"I won't ever hurt you again," he said. "That's a promise."

Lottie caught her breath as he parted the tender folds between her thighs and investigated the fragile plumpness they had concealed. Her hips lifted, while her hands fought for purchase on the slippery surface of the tub. He slid a supportive arm behind her back, holding her securely.

"Lean back," he murmured. "Let me pleasure you."

No, she thought skeptically, not in a bathtub, with a thick wall of porcelain between them. But she relaxed in his hold and opened for him as his free arm moved across her body. She grasped his wrist lightly, feeling the movement of tendons and muscles as he ran his thumb over each side of her vulva. He rubbed the silken flanges of her inner lips together, his touch tender and light. Softly he spread her, stroking his middle fingertip along the tender seam, brushing the rosy nub of her sex each time. He smiled slightly as he saw bright patches of color appear on her face and chest. "The Chinese call this the jewel terrace," he whispered. Gently his finger slipped inside her, advancing only an inch, circling softly. "And here, the lute strings . . . and here . . ." He reached to the most secret recesses of her body. "The flower heart. Does it hurt when I touch you this way?"

"No," she gasped.

His lips brushed her ear. "The next time we lie together, I'll show you a position called Stepping
Tigers. I'll enter you from behind and go deep inside . . . and rub against the flower heart over and
over . . ." He suckled her earlobe, catching it lightly
between his teeth. A hum of pleasure climbed from
Lottie's chest to her throat. She was floating, weight-
less, yet clasped securely by the arm at her back and
the hand between her thighs.

"How do you know such things?" she asked unsteadily.

"Gemma collects books on erotic techniques. One
of her favorites is a translation of a text written during the Tang dynasty. The book counsels men to increase their stamina by forestalling their own
pleasure as long as possible." His finger withdrew,
and he stroked her inner thighs with the lightness of
butterfly wings. "And it gives prescriptions for
health benefits . . . to strengthen the bones . . . enrich
the blood . . . ensure long life."

"Tell me some of them," Lottie said, swallowing
hard as his hand cupped over her, the base of his
palm nudging rhythmically into the place where she
was most sensitive.

He nuzzled her cheek. "There's the Soaring
Phoenix, which is said to make a hundred illnesses
disappear. And Cranes Entwining Necks—reputedly
very good for promoting healing."

"How many have you tried?"

"Only about forty. The ancient masters would
consider me a novice."

Lottie drew back to stare at him in astonishment, her movement causing a wave to slosh close to the rim of the tub. "How many are there, for heaven's sake?"

"Fifteen coital movements applied to thirty-six basic positions . . . which provides about four hundred variations."

"That s-seems rather excessive," she managed to say.

Amusement curled through his voice. "It would keep us busy, wouldn't it?"

Lottie winced as she realized that he was trying to slide two fingers inside her. "Nick, I can't—"

"Take a deep breath and exhale slowly," he whispered. "I'll be gentle." And as she obeyed, he eased his middle fingers past the tight entrance. His thumb teased her sex and swirled in a steady rhythm.

Moaning, Lottie buried her face against his velvet-covered arm while her inner muscles grasped helplessly at the gentle invasion. After the initial sting faded, she began to squirm and gasp at each penetrating glide. "You hold me so sweetly in here," Nick said huskily. "I want to go deeper and deeper . . . lose myself in you . . ."

His words were drowned out by the thundering of her own heartbeat, and she was racked with shudders of bliss, her senses lit with white-hot fire.

A long time later, after the bath had cooled, Lottie dressed in a fresh white nightgown and approached the bedroom table, where Nick was standing. She felt herself color as he stared at her with a half-smile. "I like the way you look in this," he said, brushing his fingers over the high-necked bodice of the gown. "Very innocent."

"Not any longer," Lottie said with an abashed smile.

He lifted her against his body, his face rubbing into the cool dampness of her hair. His beguiling mouth found her neck. "Oh, yes, you are," he said. "It's going to require a great deal of time and effort to debauch you completely."

"I have every faith you'll succeed," she said, and sat before a plate loaded with ham, vegetable pudding, potatoes, and open-faced tarts.

"To our marriage," Nick said, pouring a glass of wine for her. "May it continue in a better vein than it started."

They raised their glasses and clinked the crystal gently. Lottie sipped cautiously, discovering a rich, spicy flavor that balanced the saltiness of the ham.

Setting his glass aside, Nick took her hand in his and regarded her bare fingers thoughtfully. "You have no ring. I'm going to remedy that tomorrow."

Lottie experienced a shameful spark of interest in the idea. She had never owned a piece of jewelry. However, it had been drilled into her at Maidstone's that a lady should avoid the appearance of acquisitiveness. She managed to adopt an impassive expression that would have pleased her former teachers excessively. "It isn't necessary," she said. "Many married women do not wear rings."

"I want anyone who looks at you to know that you're taken."

Lottie gave him a brilliant smile. "If you insist, I suppose I can't stop you."

He grinned at her obvious eagerness. His thumb brushed over the fine points of her knuckles. "What kind of stone would you like?"

"A sapphire?" she suggested hopefully.

"A sapphire it is." He kept her hand as they talked, absently toying with the tips of her fingers and the close-trimmed crescents of her nails. "I suspect you'll want to see your family soon."

Lottie's attention was immediately diverted from the subject of the ring. "Yes, please. I fear that Lord Radnor may have already told my parents about what I've done. And I don't want them to worry that they'll be left destitute now that I have married someone else."

"There is no need to look so guilty," Nick said, tracing the thin veins inside of her wrist. "You had no part in making the bargain—it wasn't your fault that you didn't wish to uphold it."

"But I benefitted from it," Lottie pointed out reluctantly. "All those years at Maidstone's . . . my education cost a great deal. And now Lord Radnor has nothing in return."

He arched a dark brow. "If your point is that Radnor has been ill used—"

"No, it's not that, precisely. It's just . . . well, I didn't do the honorable thing."

"Yes, no doubt you should have fallen on the sword for the rest of the family," he said sardonically. "But your parents will be just as well served this way. I couldn't possibly be a worse son-in-law than Radnor."

"You are certainly preferable as a husband," she said.

He smiled at that, lifting her fingers to his mouth. "You would prefer *anyone* to Radnor as a husband— you've made that quite clear."

Lottie smiled, thinking privately that in marrying Nick, she had ended up with a far different husband than she had expected. "What will you do tomorrow?" she asked, remembering their earlier confrontation with Sir Ross. She was certain that Nick would not relinquish his position at Bow Street without objection.

Releasing her hand, Nick frowned. "I'm going to visit Morgan."

"Do you think that he will take your side against Sir Ross's?"

"Not a chance in hell. But I'll at least have the satisfaction of telling Morgan what a damned rotten traitor he is."

Lottie leaned forward to touch the lapel of his robe. "Have you considered the possibility that they both are doing what they think is best for you? That it might be in your own interests to reclaim the title?"

"How could it be? My God, I'll be living in a gilded cage."

"I'll be there with you."

He stared at her, seemingly arrested by the words. He looked at her so intensely, for so long, that Lottie was finally moved to ask, "What? What are you thinking?"

Nick smiled without humor. "I was just reflecting on how much better prepared you are for my life than I am."

Although Lottie had tentatively invited him to stay the night with her, Nick left after supper, retreating to the guest room a few doors away.

I'll be there with you. Her words had affected Nick curiously, just as her casual remarks at the wishing well had. She possessed a terrible knack of unraveling him with a simple phrase . . . words so commonplace, and yet invested with significance.

He didn't know what to make of Lottie. Despite the way he had deceived her initially, she seemed fully prepared to act as his partner. She responded to him with passion and generosity, and in her arms he had been able to forget the secrets that had haunted him for fourteen years. He craved more of that sweet oblivion. The past few hours had been extraordinarily different from what he had experienced with Gemma. When he made love to Lottie, his lust was enmeshed with a deep tenderness that made his physical responses unbearably acute.

She kept reaching through his defenses without even seeming to know what she was doing, and he could not allow anyone that kind of intimacy. At this rate, it was only a matter of time before Lottie discovered the demons that lurked inside him. And if that happened, she would withdraw from him in horror. He had to keep a certain distance between them, otherwise she would eventually come to regard him with disgust. Or pity. The thought made his skin crawl.

He had to maintain his detachment, while even now he longed to go back to her. In all his twenty-eight years, he had never felt this painful need for someone. Just to be in the same room with her.

My God, he thought with dull horror, going to the window and staring blindly into the night. *What is happening to me?*

Sir Grant Morgan looked up from his desk as Nick burst into his office before morning sessions. There was no trace of apology in his hard green eyes. "I see you've spoken to Sir Ross," he said.

Nick proceeded to give vent to his outrage in the coarsest words ever conceived in the history of the English language, leveling accusations that would have caused any other man either to cower in terror or to reach for the nearest pistol. Morgan, however, listened as calmly as if Nick were offering a description of the weather.

After an extensive rant speculating on the likelihood that Morgan was nothing but a puppet while Sir Ross pulled the strings, the chief magistrate sighed and interrupted.

"Enough," he said shortly. "You're beginning to

repeat yourself. Unless you have anything new to add, you may as well spare yourself the breath. As to your last charge—that this situation is all of Sir Ross's making—I can assure you that the decision to remove you from the force was fully as much mine as his."

Until that moment, Nick had never realized that Morgan's opinion was so important to him. But he experienced a genuine stab of pain, a killing sense of betrayal and failure. "Why?" he heard himself ask hoarsely. "Was my performance so unsatisfactory? What more could I have done? I solved every case and caught almost every man you sent me after— and I did it by the rules, the way you wanted. I did everything you asked. More, even."

"There has never been a problem with your performance," Morgan said quietly. "You've discharged your duties as ably as anyone could have. I've never seen any man match you for bravery or wits."

"Then back me against Sir Ross," Nick said roughly. "Tell him to shove that writ of summons up his arse—that you need me at Bow Street."

Their gazes clashed and held, and then something in Morgan's face changed. Damned if he didn't look almost fatherly, Nick thought with sullen fury, despite the fact that Morgan was only about ten years older than he.

"Have a seat," Morgan said.

"No, I don't—"

"Please." The invitation was uttered with steely politeness.

Please? Nick occupied the nearest chair, practically reeling in shock. Morgan had never used that word before—Nick wouldn't have thought it was part of his vocabulary. Gripping the arms of the scarred leather chair, Nick gazed at him warily.

The magistrate began to speak. In their three-year acquaintance, Morgan had never talked to him like this, with a friendly, rather paternal, concern. "I don't want you at Bow Street any longer, Gentry. God knows it has nothing to do with your effectiveness. You're the best runner I've ever seen. Since you came here, I've tried to offer what modicum of guidance I thought you'd accept, and I've watched you change from a self-serving bastard into a man I consider to be both dependable and responsible. But there is one thing that I regret to say has not altered. From the beginning, you've taken suicidal risks in the course of your work because you don't give a damn about yourself or anyone else. And in my opinion, you'll continue to do so if you remain here—at the cost of your own life."

"Why do you give a damn?"

"I was a runner for ten years, and I've seen many men die in the course of their duties. I myself came close to it more than once. There comes a time when a man has tweaked the devil's nose once too often, and if he's too stubborn or slow-witted to realize it, he'll pay with his own blood. I knew when to stop. And so must you."

"Because of your famous instincts?" Nick mocked angrily. "Damn it, Morgan, you stayed a runner until you were thirty-five! By that count, I still have seven years to go."

"You've tempted fate many more times in the last three years than I did in ten," the magistrate countered. "And unlike you, I didn't use the job as a means to exorcize demons."

Nick remained expressionless, while the frantic question *What does he know?* buzzed and stung in his head. Sophia was the only one who knew about the full ugliness of his past. She had probably told Cannon, who in turn might have said something to Morgan—

"No, I don't know what those demons are," Morgan said softly, his eyes warming with a flicker of either pity or kindness. "Although I can make a competent guess. Unfortunately I have no advice to offer about how to reconcile yourself with the past. All I know is that this way hasn't worked, and I'll be damned if I let you kill yourself on my watch."

"I don't know what the bloody hell you're talking about."

Morgan continued as if he hadn't heard him. "I'm rather inclined to agree with Sir Ross's opinion that you'll never find peace until you stop living behind the shield of an assumed name. As difficult as it may be to face the world as Lord Sydney, I think it for the best—"

"What am I supposed to do as a viscount?" Nick asked with an ugly laugh. "Collect snuffboxes and neckties? Read papers at the club? Advise the tenants? Christ, I know as much about farming as you do!"

"There are thousands of ways a man can be of use to the world," Morgan said flatly. "Believe me, no one expects or desires for you to lead an indolent life." He paused and took an ink blotter in his huge hand, regarding it thoughtfully. "The runners will be disbanded soon, in any event. You would eventually have had to find something else to do. I'm merely precipitating the matter by a few months."

Nick felt the color drain from his face. "What?"

Morgan grinned suddenly at his expression. "Come, that should be no surprise to you, even in light of your disinterest in politics. When Cannon left the magistracy, it was only a matter of time until the runners were dismissed. He was the heart and spirit of this place—he devoted every waking moment to it for years, until . . ." He paused tactfully, leaving Nick to fill the silence.

"Until he met my sister," Nick said sourly. "And married her."

"Yes." Morgan did not seem at all regretful about Cannon's departure from the public office. In fact, his blade-hard features softened, and his smile lingered as he continued. "The best thing that ever happened to him. However, it was hardly a boon for Bow Street. Now that Cannon has retired, there is a movement in Parliament to strengthen the Metropolitan Police Act. And many politicians believe that the New Police would become more popular with the public if the runners weren't here to compete with them."

"They intend to leave all of London to that bunch of half-wits?" Nick asked incredulously. "Good God— half of the New Police have no experience to speak of, and the other half are black sheep or idiots—"

"Be that as it may, the public will never fully support the New Police while the runners remain. The old instruments cannot be installed in the new machine."

Stunned by the finality in the chief magistrate's voice, Nick fixed him with an accusing stare. "You're not going to fight for this place? You have an obligation—"

"No," the chief magistrate said simply. "My only obligation is to my wife. She and my children are more important to me than anything else. I made it clear to Cannon that I would never surrender my soul to Bow Street the way he did for so long. And he understood that."

"But what will become of the runners?" Nick asked, thinking of his comrades . . . Sayer, Flagstad, Gee, Ruthven . . . talented men who had served the public with courage and dedication, all for a mere pittance.

"I imagine one or two will join the New Police, where they are much needed. Others will turn to other professions entirely. I may open a private investigative office and employ two or three for a while." Morgan shrugged. Having made a relative fortune in his years at Bow Street, he had no need to work, other than at his own whim.

"My God, I left to attend to *one* private case, and I've come back to find the entire damned public office falling apart!"

The magistrate laughed softly. "Go home to your wife, Sydney. Start making plans. Your life is changing, no matter how you try to prevent it."

"I will not be Lord Sydney," Nick growled.

The green eyes gleamed with friendly irreverence. "There are worse fates, my lord. A title, land, a wife . . . if you can't make something of that, there is indeed no hope for you."

Chapter Ten

"Something in pale yellow, I think," Sophia said decisively, sitting in the midst of so many fabrics that it appeared as if a rainbow had exploded in the room.

"Yellow," Lottie repeated, chewing the side of her lower lip. "I don't think that would flatter my complexion."

As this was at least the tenth suggestion that Lottie had rejected, Sophia sighed and shook her head with a smile. She had commandeered the back room in her dressmaker's shop at Oxford Street specifically for the purpose of ordering a trousseau for Lottie.

"I am sorry," Lottie said sincerely. "I don't mean to be difficult. Clearly I have little experience with this sort of thing." She had never been allowed to choose the styles or colors of her gowns. According to Lord Radnor's dictates, she had always worn chaste designs in dark colors. Unfortunately it was now difficult to envision herself in rich blue, or yellow, or, heaven help her, pink. And the idea of exposing most of her upper chest in public was so discomfiting that she had cringed at the daring pattern-book illustrations that Sophia had showed her.

Nick's older sister, to her credit, was remarkably patient. She focused on Lottie with a steady blue gaze and a persuasive smile that bore an uncommon resemblance to her brother's.

"Lottie, dear, you are not being difficult in the least, but—"

"Fibber," Lottie responded immediately, and they both laughed.

"All right," Sophia said with a grin, "you are being confoundedly difficult, although I am certain that it is unintentional. Therefore I am going to make two requests of you. First, please bear in mind that this is not a life-or-death matter. Choosing a gown is not so very difficult, especially when one is being advised by an astute and very fashionable friend— which would be me."

Lottie smiled. "And the second request?"

"The second is . . . please trust me." As Sophia held her gaze, it was clear that the magnetism of the Sydney family was not limited to the males. She radiated a mixture of warmth and self-confidence that was impossible to resist. "I will not let you look frowzy or vulgar," she promised. "I have excellent taste, and I have been out in London society for some time, whereas you have been . . ."

"Buried in Hampshire?" Lottie supplied helpfully.

"Yes, quite. And if you insist on dressing in drab styles that are appropriate for a woman twice your age, you will feel out-of-place among your own crowd. Moreover, it would undoubtedly reflect badly on my brother, as the gossips will whisper that he must be stingy with you, if you go about so plainly garbed—"

"No," Lottie said automatically. "That would be unfair to him, as he has given me leave to buy anything I wish."

"Then let me choose some things for you," Sophia coaxed.

Lottie nodded, reflecting that she was probably far too guarded. She would have to learn how to rely on other people. "I'm in your hands," she said resignedly. "I'll wear whatever you suggest."

Sophia fairly wriggled in satisfaction. "Excellent!" She hefted a pattern book to her lap and began to insert slips of paper between the pages she particularly liked. The light played over her dark golden hair, bringing out shades of wheat and honey in the shining filaments. She was an uncommonly pretty woman, her delicate, decisive features a feminine echo of Nick's strong face. Every now and then she paused to give Lottie an assessing gaze, followed either by a nod or a quick shake of her head.

Lottie sat placidly and drank some tea that the dressmaker's assistant had brought. It was raining heavily outside and the afternoon was gray and cool, but the room was cozy and peaceful. Intricate feminine things were draped or heaped everywhere . . . spills of lace, lengths of silk and velvet ribbon, cunning artificial flowers, their petals adorned with crystal beads to simulate dewdrops.

Occasionally the dressmaker appeared, conferred with Sophia and made notes, then tactfully disappeared. Some clients, Sophia had told Lottie, required the dressmaker to attend them every minute. Others were far more decided in their preferences and liked to make decisions without interference.

Lost in a peaceful reverie, Lottie almost started when Sophia spoke. "You cannot imagine how thrilled I was when Nick wrote that he was taking a bride." Sophia held two fabrics together and examined them critically, turning them to see how the light affected the weave. "Tell me, what was it about my brother that first attracted you?"

"He is a fine-looking man," Lottie said cautiously. "I could not help but notice his eyes, and dark hair, and . . . he was also very charming, and . . ." She paused, her mind returning to those still, sun-warmed moments by the kissing gate near the forest . . . how world-weary he had looked, how much in need of comfort. "Desolate," she said, almost under her breath. "I wondered how such an extraordinary man could be the loneliest person I had ever met."

"Oh, Lottie," Sophia said softly. "I wonder why you could see that in him, when everyone else considers him to be invulnerable." Leaning forward, she held a length of pale amber silk beneath Lottie's chin, testing it against her complexion, then lowered it. "For most of his life, Nick has had to fight for survival. He was so young when our parents died . . . and he became so rebellious afterward . . ." She gave a quick little shake of her head, as if to elude a sudden swarm of painful memories. "And then he ran off to London, and I heard nothing of him, until one day I learned that he had been convicted of some petty crime and sentenced to a prison hulk. A few months after that, I was told that he had died of disease aboard ship. I grieved for years."

"Why did he not come to you? He could have at least sent a letter of some kind, to spare you such unnecessary distress."

"I believe that he was too ashamed, after what had happened to him. He tried to forget that John, Lord Sydney, had ever existed. It was easier to close everything away and create a new life for himself as Nick Gentry."

"After *what* had happened?" Lottie asked, perplexed. "Are you referring to his imprisonment?"

Sophia's dark blue eyes searched hers. Seeming to realize that Lottie had not been told about something significant, she turned secretive. "Yes, his imprisonment," she said vaguely, and Lottie knew that Sophia was protecting her brother in some mysterious way.

"How did you learn that he was still alive?"

"I came to London," Sophia replied, "to take revenge on the magistrate who had sentenced him to the prison hulk. I blamed him for my brother's death. But to my dismay, I soon found myself falling in love with him."

"Sir Ross?" Lottie stared at her in amazement. "No wonder Nick dis—" Realizing what she had been about to say, she stopped abruptly.

"Dislikes him so?" Sophia finished for her with a rueful smile. "Yes, the two of them have no fondness for each other. However, that has not prevented my husband from doing everything he can to help Nick. You see, even after Nick joined the runners, he was . . . quite reckless."

"Yes," Lottie acknowledged cautiously, "he has quite a vigorous constitution."

Sophia smiled without humor. "I'm afraid it was more than that, my dear. For three years Nick has taken insane chances, not seeming to care if he lives or dies."

"But why?"

"Certain events in Nick's past have made him rather embittered and detached. My husband and Sir Grant have both endeavored to help him change for the better. I haven't always agreed with their methods. I can assure you, Sir Ross and I have engaged in some spirited debates on the matter. However, as time has passed, it seems that my brother has improved in many ways. And Lottie, I am very much encouraged by the fact that he has married you." She took Lottie's hand and squeezed it warmly.

"Sophia . . ." Lottie averted her gaze as she spoke reluctantly. "I do not think the marriage could truly be characterized as a love match."

"No," the other woman agreed softly. "I am afraid that the experience of loving and being loved is quite foreign to Nick. It will no doubt take some time for him to recognize the feeling for what it is."

Lottie was certain that Sophia meant to be reassuring. However, the idea of Nick Gentry falling in love with her was not only improbable but alarming as well. He would never let his guard down to that extent, never allow someone such power over him, and if he did, he might very well become as obsessive and domineering as Lord Radnor. She did not want anyone to love her. Although it was clear that some people found great joy in love, such as Sophia and Sir Ross, Lottie could not help but regard it as a trap. The arrangement that she and Nick had devised was much safer.

Nick found himself strangely adrift after he left the public office. It had begun to rain, and the burgeoning clouds promised a heavier deluge yet to come. Hatless, striding along the slick pavement, he felt the cold, fat splashes of water sinking through his hair and pelting the broadcloth weave of his coat. He should seek shelter somewhere . . . The Brown Bear, a tavern located across from Bow Street No. 3 . . . or perhaps Tom's coffeehouse, where the runners' preferred physician, Dr. Linley, was wont to appear. Or his own home . . . but he shied from that thought instantly.

The rain fell harder, in cold, soaking sheets that drove street sellers and pedestrians to huddle beneath shop awnings. Scrawny boys darted into the street to fetch cabs for gentlemen who had been caught unawares by the rain. Umbrellas snapped open, their frames strained by strong gusts of wind, while the sky was partitioned by jagged shafts of lightning. The air lost its characteristic stable-yard odor and took on the freshness of spring rain. Brown currents ran through the drains, washing them clear of the foul matter that the night-soil men had failed to remove during evening rounds.

Nick walked without direction, while the rain slid down his face and dripped from his chin. Usually in his off-time he went somewhere with Sayer or Ruthven to exchange stories over ale and beefsteaks, or they would attend a prizefight or a bawdy comedy at Drury Lane. Sometimes they would patrol the streets in a small pack, leisurely inspecting the thoroughfares and alleys for any sign of disruption.

Thinking of the other runners, Nick knew that soon he would lose their companionship. It was folly to hope otherwise. He could not move in their world any longer—Sir Ross had made that impossible. But why? Why couldn't the interfering bastard have left well enough alone? Nick's mind chased in circles, failing to apprehend the answer. Perhaps it had something to do with Sir Ross's unfailing pur-

suit of rightness, of order. Nick had been born a viscount and therefore must be restored to his position,
no matter how unsuited he was for it.

Nick considered what he knew of the peerage, of
their habits and rituals, the countless rules of con-
duct, the inescapable removal of landed aristocrats
from the reality of common life. He tried to imagine
spending the majority of his time lounging in parlors
and drawing rooms, or rustling his freshly ironed
newspaper at the club. Making speeches at the Lords
to demonstrate one's social conscience. Attending
soirees, and prattling about art and literature, and exchanging gossip about other silk-stockinged gentlemen.

A sense of panic filled him. He hadn't felt this
trapped, this overwhelmed, since he had been lowered into the dark, stinking hold of the prison hulk
and chained alongside the most degraded beings
imaginable. Except that then he had known that
freedom lay just outside the hulls of the anchored
ship. And now there was no place to escape.

Like an animal in a cage, his mind cast about in
angry sweeps, hunting for some kind of refuge.

"Gentry!" The friendly exclamation interrupted
his thoughts.

Eddie Sayer approached Nick with his customary
hail-fellow-well-met grin. Big, dashing, and congen-
ial in nature, Sayer was liked by all the runners, and
he was the one that Nick most trusted in a tight situation. "You're finally back," Sayer exclaimed, ex-

changing a hearty handshake. His brown eyes twin-
kled beneath the brim of his dripping hat. "I see
you've just come from the public office. No doubt Sir
Grant's given you a devil of an assignment to make
up for your long absence."

Nick found that his usual arsenal of ready quips
was depleted. He shook his head, finding it difficult
to explain how his life had turned upside down
within the space of a week. "No assignment," he
said hoarsely. "I've been dismissed."

"What?" Sayer stared at him blankly. "You mean
for good? You're the best man Morgan's got. Why
the hell would he do that?"

"Because I'm going to be a viscount."

Suddenly Sayer's puzzlement disappeared, and
he laughed. "And I'm going to be the duke of Dev-
onshire."

Nick did not crack a smile, only stared at Sayer
with a grim resignation that caused the other man's
amusement to fade slightly.

"Gentry," Sayer asked, "isn't it a bit early for you
to be this fox-faced?"

"I haven't been drinking."

Ignoring the statement, Sayer gestured to Tom's
coffeehouse. "Come, we'll try to sober you with
some coffee. Perhaps Linley is there—he can help
figure out what has made you so addlepated."

After numerous cups of coffee that had been liberally sweetened with lumps of brown sugar, Nick felt

like a pocket watch that had been wound too tightly. He found little comfort in the company of Sayer and Linley, who clearly did not know what to make of his implausible claim. They pressed him for details that he was unable to give, as he could not bring himself to discuss a past that he had spent a decade and a half trying to forget. Finally he left them at the coffeehouse and walked back out into the rain. Bitterly he thought that the only period of his life in which he had been able to make decisions for himself had been his years as a crime lord. It would be damned easy to overlook the violent squalor of those years and think only of the savage enjoyment he'd taken in outwitting Sir Ross Cannon at every turn. Had someone told him back then that he would someday be working for Bow Street, and *married*, and compelled to take up the cursed family title . . . holy hell. He would have taken any and all measures to avoid such a fate.

But he could not think of what he could have done differently. The bargain with Sir Ross had been unavoidable. And from the moment he had seen Lottie standing on that wall on the river-bluff in Hampshire, he had wanted her. He knew also that he would never stop wanting her, and he should probably abandon all attempts to puzzle out why. Sometimes there were no reasons—a thing was just so.

Thinking of his wife's sweetly erotic scent and her eloquent brown eyes, he suddenly found himself before a jeweler's shop. The place was devoid of customers, save one who was preparing to dash out into the downpour beneath the questionable cover of a battered umbrella.

Nick went inside just as the other man plunged out. Pushing the dripping hair out of his eyes, he glanced around the shop, noting the felt-covered tables and the door that led to the safe room in back.

"Sir?" A jeweler approached him, his neck hung with a large magnifying loupe. He gave Nick a glance of pleasant inquiry. "May I assist you?"

"I want a sapphire," Nick told him. "For a lady's ring."

The man smiled. "You have done well to come here, then, as I have recently imported a magnificent selection of Ceylon sapphires. Is there a particular weight you have in mind?"

"At least five carats, without flaws. Something larger, if you have it."

The jeweler's eyes gleamed with patent eagerness. "A fortunate lady, to receive such a generous gift."

"It's for a viscount's wife," Nick said sardonically, unfastening his rain-soaked coat.

It was afternoon by the time Nick returned to Betterton Street. Dismounting at the entrance of his house, he gave the reins to the footman, who had dashed out into the storm with an umbrella.

Refusing the umbrella, which would do him little good at this point, Nick sloshed up the front steps. Mrs. Trench closed the door against the bluster of the storm, her eyes widening at the sight of him.

Then Lottie appeared, neat and dry in her dark gray gown, her hair silvery in the lamplight.

"Good Lord, you're half-drowned," Lottie exclaimed, hurrying forward. She enlisted a maid to help tug the sodden coat from his shoulders and bid him remove his muddy boots right there in the hall. Nick barely heard what she said to the servants, all his awareness focused on Lottie's small form as he followed her upstairs.

"You must be cold," she said in concern, glancing over her shoulder. "I'll start the shower-bath to warm you, and then you can sit before the fire. I was out earlier with your sister—she came to call, and we went to Oxford Street and spent a delightful morning at the dressmaker's. I vow, you will regret giving me carte blanche with your credit, as I allowed Sophia to persuade me into ordering a shocking number of gowns. A few were positively scandalous—I fear I shall never have the courage to wear them outside the house. And then we made an excursion to the bookshop, and it was there that I *truly* lost my head. No doubt I've made paupers of us now . . ."

An extensive description of her various purchases ensued, while she nudged him into the changing-room and bid him to remove his wet clothes. Nick moved with unusual care, his intense awareness of her making him almost clumsy. Lottie ascribed his slowness to a chill taken from outside, saying something about the health risks of walking about in a storm, and that he must drink a cup of tea with brandy after the shower-bath. He was not cold at all. He was burning inside, remembering details from the night before . . . her breasts, her open thighs, the places where silken smoothness flowed into light, intimate curls.

He could not simply fall on her the moment he entered the house, as if he had no modicum of self-control. But oh, how he wanted to, he thought with a wry smile, fumbling with the fastenings of his clothes. The wet garments came off with difficulty. Despite his inner heat, he realized that he was indeed chilled. He heard the rattle of pipes as Lottie started the shower-bath, and then her hesitant tap at the door.

"I've brought your dressing robe," came her muffled voice. Her hand appeared around the doorframe with the burgundy velvet clutched between her fingers.

Nick looked at her small hand, the tender inside of her wrist with the little tracing of veins. Last night it had been easy to find every throb of her pulse, every vulnerable place of her body. He found himself reaching out, ignoring the robe in favor of wrapping his fingers around her delicate wrist. He pushed the door fully open and pulled her in front of him, looking down into her flushed face. It was not difficult for her to see what he wanted.

"I don't need a robe," he said gruffly, pulling the garment from her hand and dropping it to the floor.

"The shower-bath . . ." Lottie murmured, falling silent as he reached for the front placket of buttons on her gown. His fingers became swift and self-assured, peeling the bodice apart to reveal the construction of linen and stays that molded her flesh. He pushed down her sleeves, taking the straps of the chemise with them, and set his mouth to the bare curve of her shoulder. Miraculously she relaxed in his hold with a willingness he had not expected. Inflamed, he tasted the fine skin of her shoulder, kissed and licked his way to her throat, while he coaxed her hands free of the gown and pushed it over her hips.

The shower-bath began to heat, saturating the air with steam. Nick unhooked the front of the corset, briefly compressing the hard edges of the garment, then releasing them completely. Lottie held onto his shoulders as she moved to help him strip away the rest of her undergarments. Her eyes were closed, her translucent lids trembling slightly as she began to breathe in long sighs.

Hungrily, Nick pulled her with him into the hot rain of the shower-bath. Turning her face out of the stream of water, Lottie rested her head on his shoulder, standing passively as his hands slid over her body. Her breasts were small but plump in his hands, the nipples turning hard in the clasp of his fingers. He shaped his hands over her unrestricted waist, the swell of her hips, her round backside . . . caressing her everywhere, moving her against the engorged length of his sex. Moaning, she parted her thighs in compliance with his exploring hand, pushing her delicate flesh against his stroking thumb. As he entered her with his fingers, she gasped and instinctively relaxed at the gentle penetration. He caressed her, stroking in deep, secret places that brought her to the brink of climax. When she was ready to come, he lifted her against the tiled wall, one arm beneath her hips, the other behind her back. She made a sound of surprise and clung to him, her eyes widening as he pushed his cock inside her. Her flesh closed tightly around him, swallowing every inch of his shaft as he let her settle against him.

"I've got you," he murmured, her slippery body locked securely in his arms. "Don't be afraid."

Breathing fast, she rested her head back against his arm. With the hot water falling against his back, and the lush female body impaled on his, every lucid thought promptly evaporated. He filled her in heavy upward surges, again and again, until she cried out and clamped around him in luxurious contractions. Nick held still, feeling her quiver around him, the depths of her body becoming almost unbearably snug. Her spasms seemed to pull him deeper, drawing waves of pleasure from his groin, and he shuddered as he spent inside her.

Releasing her slowly, he let her drift down his body until her feet touched the tiled floor. He cupped a hand around her wet head and rubbed his mouth over her sodden hair, her saturated lashes, the round tip of her nose. Just as he reached her lips, she turned her face away, and he growled in frustration, dying for the taste of her. He had never wanted anything so badly. For a split second he was tempted to hold her head in his hands and crush his mouth on hers. But that wouldn't satisfy him . . . he could not get what he wanted from her with force.

Carrying Lottie from the shower-bath, he dried them both before the hearth in the bedroom and combed Lottie's long hair. The fine strands were dark amber when wet, turning to a pale shade of champagne when they were dry. Admiring the contrast of the shining locks against his velvet robe, he smoothed them with his fingers.

"What was said between you and Sir Grant?" Lottie asked, leaning back against his chest as they sat on the thick Aubusson rug. She was wearing another of his robes, which was at least three times her size.

"He supported Sir Ross's decision, naturally," Nick said, inwardly surprised to realize that his bitter desperation of the morning had faded considerably. It seemed that his mind was reconciling itself to the prospect of what lay ahead, however unwillingly. He told her what Morgan had said about the runners being disbanded soon, and Lottie twisted to look at him with a thoughtful frown.

"London without the Bow Street runners?"

"Things change," he said flatly. "So I'm learning."

Lottie sat to face him, unthinkingly curving her arm around his propped-up knee for support. "Nick," she said cautiously, "as Sophia and I were talking today, she mentioned something that I believe you will wish to know, even though it is supposed to be a surprise."

"I don't like surprises," he muttered. "I've had enough of them lately."

"Yes, that's what I thought."

Her eyes were clear, dark brown, like cups of shimmering caravan tea. Nick stared into her sweetly curved face, the chin too pointed, the nose too short. The little imperfections made her beauty unique and endlessly interesting, whereas more classically shaped features would have bored him quickly. His body reacted with pleasure to the pressure of the slim arm hooked around his leg and the side of her breast brushing his knee.

"What did my sister tell you?" he asked.

Lottie smoothed the loose folds of the silk robe. "It concerns your family estate in Worcestershire. Sophia and Sir Ross are having it restored, as a gift to you. They are repairing the manor and landscaping the grounds. Sophia has taken great pains to select fabrics and paints and furnishings that closely resemble the ones she remembered. She says it is rather like taking a journey back in time . . . that when she walks through the front entrance, she half-expects to hear your mother's voice calling her, and to find your father smoking in the library—"

"My God," Nick said through his teeth, rising to his feet.

Lottie remained before the fire, extending her hands toward its warmth. "They want to take us there after the writ of summons arrives. I thought it best to give you advance warning, to allow you time to prepare yourself."

"Thank you," Nick managed to say tautly. "Although no amount of time would be sufficient for that." The family manor . . . Worcestershire . . . he had not been back there since he and Sophia had been orphaned. Was there no damned escape from this? He felt as if he were being hauled inexorably toward a bottomless pit. The Sydney name, the title, the estate, the memories . . . he wanted none of it, and it was being shoved upon him regardless.

A sudden suspicion spread through him. "What else did my sister tell you?"

"Nothing of significance."

Nick would have been able to see if his sister had confided in her. But it seemed that Sophia had not betrayed him in that way. And if she had not told Lottie by now, she would probably continue to hold her silence. Relaxing marginally, he scrubbed his fingers through his disheveled hair. "Damn everyone and everything," he said in a low voice. But as he saw the indignant expression on Lottie's face, he added, "Except for you."

"I should hope so," she retorted. "I am on your side, you know."

"Are you?" he asked, drawn to the idea in spite of himself.

"Your life isn't the only one that's been turned topsy-turvy," she informed him. "And to think that I was worried about the problems that *my* family would cause!"

Nick was tempted to smile in the midst of his aggravation. He went to where she sat and lowered a hand to her. "If the rain stops," he said, pulling her up, "we'll visit your parents tomorrow."

Lottie's expressive face betrayed both consternation and eagerness. "If it isn't convenient . . . that is, if you have other plans . . . I am willing to wait."

"I have no plans," Nick said, thinking briefly of his dismissal. "Tomorrow will be as convenient as any other day."

"Thank you. I do want to see them. I only hope—" Lottie fell silent, her brows knitting together. The hem of the robe dragged in a long train as Lottie went to the fire. Nick followed immediately, wanting very much to cuddle and reassure her, to kiss her lips until they softened beneath his.

"Try not to think about it," he advised. "Distressing yourself won't change anything."

"It won't be a pleasant visit. I can't think of a situation in which two parties could feel more mutually betrayed. Although I am certain that most people would hold me at fault."

Nick stroked the sides of her arms over the silk sleeves. "If you had it to do over again, would you have stayed to marry Radnor?"

"Certainly not."

Turning Lottie to face him, he smoothed her hair back from her forehead. "Then I forbid you to feel guilty about it."

"*Forbid?*" she repeated, arching her brows.

Nick grinned. "You promised to obey me, didn't you? Well, do as I say, or face the consequences."

"Which are?"

He unfastened her robe, dropped it to the floor, and proceeded to demonstrate exactly what he meant.

The Howard family lived in a hamlet two miles west of fashionable London, a residential outgrowth surrounded by farming land. Nick remembered the well-structured but shabby house from his much earlier visit, at the beginning of his search for Lottie. The irony of returning to them as their new, very much unwanted son-in-law would have made him smile, as the situation contained strong elements of farce. However, his private amusement was tamped down by Lottie's impenetrable silence. He wished he could spare her the difficulty of seeing her family. On the other hand, it was necessary for Lottie to face them and at least try to make peace.

The small Tudor-style home was one in a row of architecturally similar houses. It was fronted with small, overgrown garden plots, its red brick exterior sadly dilapidated. The front door was raised four steps from the ground, the narrow entrance leading to two downstairs rooms that served as parlors. Beside the entrance, another set of stone steps led to the cellar below, which contained a kitchen and a water-storage tank filled from the main in the road.

Three children played in the garden plots, brandishing sticks and running in circles. Like Lottie, they were flaxen blond, fair skinned, and slim of build. Having seen the children before, Nick had been told their names, but he could not recall them. The carriage stopped on the paved coachway, and the small faces appeared at the front gate, staring through the peeling slats as Nick helped Lottie descend from the carriage.

Lottie's face was outwardly calm, but Nick saw how tightly clenched her gloved fingers were, and he experienced something he had never known before—concern for someone else's feelings. He didn't like it.

Lottie stopped at the gate, her face pale. "Hullo," she murmured. "Is that you, Charles? Oh, you've grown so, I can scarcely recognize you. And Eliza, and—good gracious, is that baby Albert?"

"I'm not a baby!" piped the toddler indignantly.

Lottie flushed, poised on the verge between tears and laughter. "Why, no indeed. You must be three years old by now."

"You're our sister Charlotte," Eliza said. Her serious little face was sided by two long braids. "The one who ran away."

"Yes." Lottie's mouth was touched with sudden melancholy. "I don't wish to stay away any longer, Eliza. I have missed all of you so very much."

"You were supposed to marry Lord Radnor," Charles said, regarding her with round blue eyes. "He was very angry that you wouldn't, and now he's going to—"

"Charles!" A woman's agitated voice came from the doorway. "Hush and come away from the gate at once."

"But it's *Charlotte*," the boy protested.

"Yes, I'm aware of that. Come now, children, all of you. Tell the cookmaid to make you some toast with jam."

The speaker was Lottie's mother, a breakably slender woman in her early forties, with an unusually narrow face and light blond hair. Nick recalled that her husband was of stocky build with full cheeks. Neither of the pair was particularly handsome, but by some trick of nature Lottie had inherited the best features of each.

"Mama," Lottie said softly, gripping the top of the gate. The children promptly fled, eager for the promised treat.

Mrs. Howard regarded her daughter with a dull gaze, harsh lines scored between her nose and mouth, and across her forehead. "Lord Radnor came not two days ago," she said. The simple sentence contained both an accusation and indictment.

Bereft of words, Lottie looked back over her shoulder at Nick. He went into action immediately, joining her at the gate and unlatching it himself. "May we come in, Mrs. Howard?" he asked. He ushered Lottie toward the house without waiting for permission. Some devil prompted him to add, "Or shall I call you Mama?" He put a mocking emphasis on the last syllable of the word, as Lottie had.

For his effrontery, Lottie surreptitiously knocked an elbow into his ribs as they entered the house, and he grinned.

The interior of the house smelled musty. The

drapes at the windows had been turned many times, until both sides were unevenly sun-bleached, while the aged carpets had been worn so thin that no regular pattern was discernable. Everything from the chipped porcelain figures on the mantel to the grimy paper on the walls contributed to the picture of decayed gentility. Mrs. Howard herself gave the same impression, moving with the weary grace and self-consciousness of someone who had once been accustomed to a far better life.

"Where is Father?" Lottie asked, standing in the center of the parlor, which was hardly bigger than a closet.

"Visiting your uncle, in town."

The three of them stood in the center of the room, while awkward silence thickened the air. "Why have you come, Charlotte?" her mother finally asked.

"I've missed you, I—" Lottie paused at the resolute blankness she saw on her mother's face. Nick sensed his wife's struggle between stubborn pride and remorse as she continued carefully. "I wanted to tell you that I'm sorry for what I did."

"I wish I could believe that," Mrs. Howard replied crisply. "However, I do not. You do not regret abandoning your responsibilities, nor are you sorry for placing your own needs above everyone else's."

Nick made the discovery that it was not easy for him to listen to someone criticizing his wife—even if that person happened to be her own mother. For Lottie's sake, however, he concentrated on keeping his mouth shut. Clasping his hands behind his back, he focused on the indistinct design of the ancient carpet.

"I regret causing you so much pain and worry, Mama," Lottie said. "I am also sorry for the two years of silence that have passed between us."

Finally Mrs. Howard displayed some sign of emotion, her voice edged with anger. "That was your fault—not ours."

"Of course," her daughter acknowledged humbly. "I would not presume to ask you to forgive me, but—"

"What's done is done," Nick interrupted, unable to tolerate Lottie's chastened tone. He would be damned if he stood by while she was brought to her knees in contrition. He placed a hand at Lottie's neatly corseted waist in a possessive gesture. His cool, steady gaze caught Mrs. Howard's. "There is nothing to be gained by talking about the past. We've come to discuss the future."

"You have no involvement in our future, Mr. Gentry." The woman's blue eyes were icy with contempt. "I blame you for our situation fully as much as my daughter. I never would have talked with you, answered your questions, if I had known that your ultimate design was to take her for yourself."

"It was not my plan." Nick let his fingers nestle in the curve of Lottie's waist, remembering the delicious softness beneath the confining stays. "I had no idea that I would want to marry Lottie until I met her. But it was obvious then—as it is now—that Lottie will be better served by a marriage to me than to Radnor."

"You are very much mistaken," Mrs. Howard snapped. "Arrogant scoundrel! How dare you compare yourself to a peer of the realm?"

Feeling Lottie stiffen at his side, Nick squeezed her subtly in a silent message not to correct her mother on that point. He was damned if he would use his own title to compare himself in any way with Radnor.

"Lord Radnor is a man of great wealth and refinement," Mrs. Howard continued. "He is highly educated and honorable in every regard. And if it weren't for my daughter's selfishness and your interference, Charlotte would now be his wife."

"You've omitted a few points," Nick said. "Including the fact that Radnor is thirty years older than Lottie and happens to be as mad as cobbler's punch."

The color on Mrs. Howard's face condensed into two bright patches high on her cheeks. "He is not mad!"

For Lottie's sake, Nick struggled to control his sudden fury. He imagined her as a small, defenseless child, being closed alone in a room with a predator like Radnor. And this woman had allowed it. He vowed silently that Lottie would never again go unprotected. He gave Mrs. Howard a hard stare. "You saw nothing wrong in Radnor's obsessive attentions to an eight-year-old girl?" he asked softly.

"The nobility are allowed their foibles, Mr. Gentry. Their superior blood accommodates a few eccentricities. But of course, you would know nothing about that."

"You might be surprised," Nick said sardonically. "Regardless, Lord Radnor is hardly a model for rational behavior. The social attachments he once enjoyed have withered because of his so-called foibles. He has withdrawn from society and spends most of his time in his mansion, hiding from the sunlight. His life is centered around the effort to mold a vulnerable girl into his version of the ideal woman—one who isn't allowed even to draw breath without his permission. Before you blame Lottie for running from that, answer this question in perfect honesty—would *you* want to marry such a man?"

Mrs. Howard was spared from having to reply by the sudden arrival of Lottie's younger sister Ellie, a pretty sixteen-year-old girl with a full-cheeked face and heavily lashed blue eyes. Her hair was much darker than Lottie's, light brown instead of blond, and her figure was far more generously endowed. Coming to a breathless halt in the doorway, Ellie beheld her prodigal sister with a crow of excitement. "Lottie!" She rushed forward and seized her older sister in a tight embrace. "Oh, Lottie, you're back! I missed you every day, and thought of you, and feared for you—"

"Ellie, I've missed you even more," Lottie said with a choked laugh. "I didn't dare write to you, but oh, how I wanted to. One could paper the walls with the letters I wished to send—"

"Ellie," their mother interrupted. "Return to your room."

She was either unheard or ignored, as Ellie drew back to look at Lottie. "How beautiful you are," she exclaimed. "I knew you would be. I knew . . ." Her voice trailed away as she caught sight of Nick standing nearby. "Did you *really* marry him?" she whispered with a scandalized delight that made Nick grin.

Lottie glanced at him with a curious expression. Nick wondered if she disliked having to acknowledge him as her husband. She didn't seem disgruntled, but neither did she sound wildly enthusiastic. "Mr. Gentry," Lottie said, "I believe you have met my sister?"

"Miss Ellie," he murmured with a slight bow. "A pleasure to see you again."

The girl flushed and curtsied, and looked back at Lottie. "Will you be living in London?" she asked. "Will you have me there for a visit? I so long to—"

"Ellie," Mrs. Howard said meaningfully. "Go to your room now. That is quite enough nonsense."

"Yes, Mama." The girl threw her arms around Lottie for one last hug. She whispered something in her older sister's ear, a question that Lottie answered with a comforting murmur and a nod. Guessing that it had been another request to be invited for a visit, Nick suppressed a smile. It seemed that Lottie was not the only willful daughter in the Howard family.

With a shy glance at Nick, Ellie left the room and heaved a sigh as she walked away from the parlor.

Heartened by her sister's obvious delight in seeing her again, Lottie sent Mrs. Howard a glance of entreaty. "Mama, there are so many things I must tell you—"

"I am afraid there is no point in further discussion," her mother said with brittle dignity. "You have made your choice, and so have your father and I. Our connection with Lord Radnor is too entrenched to break. We will fulfill our obligations to him, Charlotte—even if you are unwilling."

Lottie stared at her in confusion. "How would you accomplish that, Mama?"

"That is no longer your concern."

"But I don't see—" Lottie began, and Nick interrupted, his gaze fastened on Mrs. Howard. For years he had successfully negotiated with hardened criminals, overworked magistrates, the guilty, the innocent, and everyone in-between. He would be damned if he couldn't come to some sort of compromise with his own mother-in-law.

"Mrs. Howard, I understand that I am not your first choice as a husband for Lottie." He gave her the wry, charming smile that worked well with most women. "The devil knows that I wouldn't be anyone's preference. But as things stand, I will prove a far more generous benefactor than Radnor."

He glanced deliberately at their dilapidated surroundings and returned his gaze to hers. "There is
no reason you shouldn't make improvements to the
house and refurbish it to your satisfaction. I will
also pay for the children's education and see to it
that Ellie has a proper coming-out. If you like, you
can travel abroad and spend the summer months at
the coast. Tell me whatever you want and you shall
have it."

The woman's expression was frankly disbelieving. "And why would you do all that?"

"For my wife's pleasure," he replied without hesitation.

Lottie turned to him with a round-eyed gaze of
wonder. Casually he fingered the collar of her
bodice, thinking that it was a small price to pay for
what she gave him.

Unfortunately the intimate gesture seemed to
harden Mrs. Howard against him. "We want nothing from you, Mr. Gentry."

"I understand that you're in debt to Radnor,"
Nick persisted, feeling there was no way to address
the issue other than with bluntness. "I will take care
of that. I've already offered to repay him for Lottie's
years at school, and I will assume your other financial obligations as well."

"You can't afford to keep such promises," Mrs.
Howard said. "And even if you could, the answer
would still be no. I bid you take your leave, Mr. Gentry, as I will not discuss the matter any more."

Nick gave her a searching stare, detecting desperation . . . uneasiness . . . guilt. His every instinct warned him that she was hiding something. "I will call on you again," he said gently, "when Mr. Howard is at home."

"His answer will be no different than mine."

Nick did not indicate that he had heard the refusal. "Good day, Mrs. Howard. We take our leave with every wish for your health and happiness."

Lottie's fingers clenched tightly through Nick's coat sleeve as she fought to master her emotions. "Good-bye, Mama," she said huskily and walked out with him.

Nick handed her carefully into the carriage and glanced back at the empty garden plot. All the windows of the house were vacant, except for one on the upper floor, where Ellie's round face appeared. She waved forlornly and rested her chin on her hands as the carriage door closed.

The vehicle pulled away with a jolt before the horses settled into their rhythm. Lottie leaned her head back against the velvet upholstery, her eyes closed, her mouth trembling. The glitter of unshed tears appeared beneath her rich gold lashes. "Foolishly I had hoped for a warmer reception," she said, trying for an ironic tone and failing completely as a half sob escaped her throat.

Nick sat there unnerved and damnably helpless, his body tensing all over. The sight of his wife crying filled him with alarm. To his relief, she managed to gain control over her emotions, and she pressed the heels of her gloved hands to her eyes.

"They couldn't afford to turn down my offer," Nick said, "unless they were still receiving money from Radnor."

Lottie shook her head in confusion. "But it makes no sense that he would continue to support my family now that I've married you."

"Do they have any other source of income?"

"I can't think of one. Perhaps my uncle may be able to give them a little. Not enough to keep them indefinitely, however."

"Hmmm." Considering various possibilities, Nick leaned back into the corner of his seat, his gaze fixed on the scenery that jostled past the window.

"Nick . . . did you really tell Lord Radnor that you would repay my school tuition for all those years?"

"Yes."

Strangely, Lottie did not ask why, only occupied herself with arranging her skirts and tugging her sleeves down to cover her wrists. Removing her gloves, she folded them and set them beside her on the carriage seat. Nick watched her through half-closed eyes. When she could find nothing left to adjust or straighten, she brought herself to look at him. "What now?" she asked, as if preparing for a new round of difficulties.

Nick considered the question, feeling a tug in the center of his chest as he saw the resolution in her expression. She had endured the past few days with an equanimity that was extraordinary for a girl her age. No doubt any other young woman would have been reduced to a sobbing heap by now. He wanted to remove the strained look from her eyes and for once see her carefree and relaxed.

"Well, Mrs. Gentry," he said, moving to the space beside her, "for the next day or two, I propose that we have some fun."

"Fun," she repeated, as if the word were unfamiliar. "Forgive me, but my capacity for enjoyment is rather diminished at present."

Nick smiled and settled his hand on the outline of her thigh. "You're in the most exciting city in the world," he murmured, "in the company of a virile young husband and his ill-gotten gains." He kissed her ear, making her shiver. "Believe me, Lottie, there is a great deal of fun to be had."

Lottie would not have thought that anything could shake her from her despondency after the cold reception from her mother. However, Nick engaged her so thoroughly during the next few days that she found it difficult to think about anything but him.

That night Nick took her to a theatrical tavern where music and comical acts were staged to draw in customers. Located in Covent Garden, the Vestris—named after a once-popular Italian opera dancer—was a meeting ground for theatrical folk, slumming nobles, and all manner of colorful characters. The place was dirty and reeking of wine and smoke, the floor so sticky that Lottie was in danger of walking right out of her shoes. She crossed the threshold with reluctance, as young women of quality were never seen in such places unless in the company of their husbands—and even then it was highly questionable. Nick was immediately hailed by the occupants of the tavern, many of them appearing to be complete ruffians. After a brief interval of backslapping and an exchange of friendly insults, Nick took Lottie to a table. They were served a dinner of beefsteak and potatoes, a bottle of port, and two mugs of something called "heavy wet."

Although Lottie had never eaten in public before and felt absurdly self-conscious, she gamely attacked a beefsteak that could easily have served a family of four. "What is this?" she asked, gingerly taking her mug and peering into the foaming brown depths.

"Ale," Nick replied, resting his arm along the back of her chair. "Try some."

Obediently she took a sip of the thick grain-flavored beverage, and her entire face wrinkled in distaste. Laughing at her expression, Nick told a nearby barmaid to fetch her some gin punch. More patrons crowded into the building, mugs were clanked heavily on the battered wooden tables, and barmaids moved busily among the crowd with large pitchers.

At the front of the tavern, a comic musical ditty was being performed by a slender woman wearing men's clothing and a portly gentleman with a luxuriant moustache who was dressed as a country maid, with a huge false bosom that swayed from side to side as he moved. As the "lad" chased the "maid" around the tavern, singing a soulful love song that praised her beauty, the place erupted in bellows of laughter. The sheer silliness of the performance was impossible to resist. Tucked against her husband's side, with a cup of astringent gin punch in her hands, Lottie tried without success to stifle a fit of giggles.

More performances followed . . . bawdy songs and dances, comic verse, even a display of acrobatic tumbling and juggling. The hour grew late, the corners of the tavern became shadowy, and in the relaxed atmosphere, more than a few couples began to indulge in some indiscreet fondling and kissing. Lottie knew that she should have been shocked, but the gin punch had made her sleepy and thick-headed. She discovered that she was sitting on Nick's lap, her legs tucked between his, and that the only reason she was able to sit upright was the fact that his arms were around her.

"Oh, dear," she said, staring into her nearly empty cup. "Did I drink all of that?"

Nick took the cup from her and set it on the table. "I'm afraid so."

"Only you could undo my years of training at Maidstone's in one evening," she said, making him grin.

His gaze lowered to her mouth, and he traced the edge of her jaw with his fingertip. "Are you completely corrupted now? No? Then let's go home, and I'll finish the job."

Feeling unsteady and very warm, Lottie giggled as he guided her through the tavern. "The floor is uneven," she told him, leaning hard against his side.

"It's not the floor, sweetheart, it's your feet."

Pondering that, Lottie glanced from his amused face to her own feet. "They do feel as if they've been put on the wrong legs."

Nick shook his head, his blue eyes gleaming with laughter. "You have no tolerance for gin, do you? Here, let me carry you."

"No, I don't wish to be a spectacle," she protested as he lifted her against his chest and carried her out to the street. Catching sight of them, a waiting footman hurried to the end of the street, where their carriage waited in a long row.

"You'll be more of a spectacle if you fall on your face," Nick replied.

"I'm not *that* far gone," Lottie protested. However, his arms were so solid and his shoulder so inviting that she snuggled against him with a sigh. The slightly musky scent of his skin mingled with the crisp smell of starch from his necktie, a blend so alluring that she inched closer to inhale deeply.

Nick stopped by the side of the street. His head turned, his shaven cheek brushing hers and making her skin tingle. "What are you doing?"

"Your smell . . ." she said dreamily. "It's wonderful. I noticed it the first time we met, when you nearly knocked me off the wall."

A laugh stirred in his throat. "I saved you from falling, you mean."

Intrigued by the scratchy texture of his skin, Lottie pressed her lips beneath his jaw. She felt him swallow hard, the movement rippling against her mouth. It was the first time she had ever made an advance to him, and the small gesture was surprisingly effective. He stood there holding her tightly, his chest rising and falling in increasingly labored breaths. Intrigued by the notion that she could arouse him so easily, Lottie tugged at the knot of his necktie and kissed the side of his throat.

"Don't, Lottie."

She drew the tip of her fingernail over the hair-roughened skin, scraping delicately.

"Lottie . . ." he tried again. Whatever he had intended to say was forgotten as she kissed his ear and took the lobe between her teeth in a soft bite.

The carriage stopped before them, and the footman busied himself with setting out the removable step. Schooling his features into a blank mask, Nick thrust Lottie inside the carriage and climbed in after her.

As soon as the door closed, he hauled her into his lap and tugged roughly at the front of her gown. She reached up to play with his hair, tangling her fingers in the thick sable locks. Unlacing the top of her corset, he eased one breast out and fastened his mouth over the soft nipple. The teasing suction caused her to arch against him with a whimper of pleasure. His hands delved frantically beneath her skirts, slipping past masses of broadcloth and linen to find the damp slit of her drawers. His hand was too large to slip inside the undergarment, and he ripped it with an ease that made her gasp. Her thighs spread in helpless welcome, and her vision blurred as one long finger eased inside her. Cradled in his lap, with his hand working gently between her legs, she felt her inner muscles begin to tighten rhythmically.

A groan escaped him, and he pulled her hips over his, fumbling roughly with the front of his trousers. "You're so wet . . . I can't wait, Lottie, let me . . . sit in my lap, and put your legs . . . oh, God, yes, right there . . ."

She straddled him willingly, sucking in her breath as he penetrated her, his hands urging her hips down until he had buried himself to the hilt. He was deliciously hard and thick inside her, holding still while the motion of the carriage jostled their bodies together. Surreptitiously Lottie rubbed the aching peak of her sex against him, feeling waves of heat rising from the place they were joined. One of his hands passed gently over her upper back.

Lottie gasped as a vigorous jolt of the carriage wheels impelled him farther inside her. "We don't have long," she managed to say against his throat. "The tavern is very close to home."

Nick responded with a tortured groan. "The next time I'll make the driver take us around the whole of London . . . twice." He slid his thumb to the top of her wet sex and flicked it with soft, rapid strokes, building her pleasure rapidly until she curled against him with a sob, overwhelmed by explosive sensation. Hitching his hips upward in desperate thrusts, he growled and buried his face in the curve of her neck, his passion reaching a blinding culmination.

They both breathed in long gasps, while their naked flesh was locked together beneath the layers of disheveled clothing. "It's never enough," Nick said gruffly, his hand cupping over her soft buttocks, holding her firmly against him. "It feels too good to stop."

Lottie understood what he was attempting to express. The unquenchable need between them was more than mere physical craving. She found a satisfaction in being together that went far beyond the joining of their bodies. Until this moment, however, she hadn't known that he felt it too . . . and she wondered if he was as afraid to acknowledge the feeling as she was.

Chapter Eleven

London was so vastly different from the seren-
ity of Hampshire that Lottie could scarcely believe it was in the same country. It was a world of
high fashion and endless amusements, with a sharp
juxtaposition of poverty and wealth, and crime-
ridden alleys tucked behind the streets of prosperous markets and shops. There was the area past
Temple Bar called the City, and the west side, referred to as "town," and an abundance of gardens,
walks, concert halls, and shops featuring luxuries
that she could never have imagined.

As the second week of their marriage began, Nick
seemed to find it amusing to indulge Lottie as if she
were a child he was bent on spoiling. He took her to
a confectioner's shop at Berkeley Square and bought
her an ice made of pureed chestnuts mixed liberally
with candied cherries. Afterward they proceeded to

Bond Street, where he purchased her a selection of French powders and scented waters, and a dozen pairs of embroidered silk stockings. Lottie tried to stop him from buying a fortune's worth of white gloves and handkerchiefs from the linen-draper's, and she objected strongly to a pair of pink silk shoes with gold tassels that would have cost a full month's tuition at Maidstone's. However, Nick ignored her protests as he continued to purchase whatever caught his fancy. Their final stop was at a tea shop, where he ordered a half-dozen exotic teas in beautiful jars, bearing intriguing names such as "gunpowder," "congou," or "souchong."

Envisioning the mountain of packages that would be delivered later that day to the house on Betterton, Lottie begged him to desist. "I need nothing else," she said firmly, "and I refuse to set foot in one more shop. There is no reason for such immoderation."

"Yes, there is," Nick replied, escorting her to their waiting carriage, piled high with parcels and boxes.

"Oh? What is it?"

He responded with a maddening smile. Surely he didn't think that he was purchasing her sexual favors, as she had been more than acquiescent in that regard. Perhaps he simply wanted her to feel obligated to him? But why?

Life with Nick Gentry was turning out to be quite puzzling, consisting of moments of searing closeness interspersed with small reminders that they were still complete strangers in most regards. She did not understand why Nick left her bed every night after making love to her, never allowing himself to drift to sleep beside her. After everything else they had shared, that seemed harmless enough. But he refused her awkward invitations to stay, stating that he preferred to sleep alone, and they would both be more comfortable that way.

Lottie quickly discovered that certain subjects set off Nick's temper like a flame held to gunpowder. She learned never to question him about any part of his boyhood, and that any reference to the days before he took the name of Nick Gentry would earn his certain wrath. When he became angry, he did not shout or throw things, but instead was coldly quiet and left the house, and did not return until long after she had gone to bed. She learned also that Nick never allowed himself to be vulnerable in any way. He preferred to stay in complete control of himself and his environment. He considered it unmanly for someone not to be able to hold his liquor—she had yet to see him drink to excess. Even sleep seemed to be a luxury he did not like to indulge in too often, as if he could not afford to relax into unguarded slumber. In fact, according to Sophia, Nick had never even allowed physical injuries to hamper him—he stubbornly refused to yield to pain or weakness.

"Why?" Lottie had asked Sophia in genuine bewilderment, as they went for dress fittings and waited for the gowns to be brought out. "What does he fear, that he cannot allow himself to be unprotected for one moment?"

For a moment, Nick's older sister had stared at her with an obvious longing to reply. Her deep blue eyes were filled with sadness. "I hope that someday he will confide in you," she said softly. "It is a great burden to bear alone. I am certain that he fears your reaction, once you are told."

"Told what?" Lottie persisted, but to her frustration, Sophia would not answer.

Some great fearful secret. Lottie could not fathom what it might be. She could only suppose that he had killed someone, perhaps in a fury—that was the worst thing she could think of. She knew that he had committed crimes in his past, that he had done things that would probably horrify her. He was so guarded and self-possessed that it seemed she would never come to know him fully.

In other ways, however, Nick was an unexpectedly tender and generous husband. He coaxed her to tell him all the rules that had been drilled into her at school, and then he proceeded to make her break every single one of them. There were nights when he launched a gentle assault on her modesty, undressing her in the lamplight and making her watch as he kissed her from head to toe . . . and others when he made love to her in exotic ways that shamed and excited her beyond bearing. He could arouse her with a single glance, a brief caress, a soft word whispered in her ear. It seemed to Lottie that entire days passed in a haze of sexual desire, her awareness of him simmering beneath everything they did.

After the crates of books she had ordered arrived,

she read to Nick in the evenings, as she sat in bed
and he lounged beside her. Sometimes while he listened, Nick would pull her legs into his lap and
massage her feet, running his thumbs along her in-
step and playing gently with her toes. Whenever
Lottie paused in her reading, she always found his
gaze fastened securely on her. He never seemed to
tire of staring at her . . . as if he were trying to un-
cover some mystery that was hidden in her eyes.

One evening he taught her to play cards, claiming
sexual liberties as forfeits each time she lost. They
ended up on the carpeted floor in a tangle of limbs
and clothing, while Lottie breathlessly accused him
of cheating. He only grinned in reply, thrusting his
head beneath her skirts until the issue was entirely
forgotten.

Nick was an exciting companion—a fascinating
storyteller, a superb dancer, a skilled lover. He was
playful but not at all boyish, never quite losing the
seasoned look that proclaimed he had seen and
done enough to last several lifetimes. He escorted
Lottie around London with an energy that far
eclipsed her own, seeming to know and be known
by practically everyone. More than once, at a sub-
scription dance, or a private party, or even walking
through the park, Lottie could not help but be aware
of the attention he attracted. Nick was regarded as
either a hero or a devil, depending on one's view,
and everyone wanted to be seen with him regardless. Innumerable men came to shake his hand, and
to seek his opinions on various matters. Women, on

the other hand, trembled and giggled and flirted shamelessly with him, even in Lottie's presence. Lottie witnessed such overtures with surprised disgruntlement, realizing that she felt very much like a jealous wife.

At the invitation of some friends, Nick and Lottie attended a play at Drury Lane that staged naval battles using complicated machinery and light displays to thrilling effect. Actors dressed like sailors hurled themselves from the sides of the "ship" in perfect conjunction with the bursts of cannon-fire, their shirts blotched with red paint to resemble blood. The results were so realistic that Lottie clapped her hands over her ears and hid her face against Nick's chest, disregarding his laughing efforts to make her watch the action.

Perhaps it was the violence of the display, or the aftereffects of the wine she had drunk with supper, but Lottie felt apprehensive as they left their box seats at the first intermission. Theatergoers mingled in the hall downstairs, partaking of refreshments and chattering excitedly about the graphic onstage battles they had just witnessed. As the atmosphere in the crowded room became stifling, Nick left Lottie in the company of friends as he went to fetch her a glass of lemonade. Lottie forced a smile to her lips as she half-listened to the conversation around her, hoping that he would return soon. How quickly she had become accustomed to Nick's reassuring presence beside her, she thought.

It was ironic. After so many years of being told

that she belonged to Lord Radnor, she had never been able to accept it. And yet it felt entirely natural to belong to a virtual stranger. She remembered Lord Westcliff's warning about Nick Gentry. *He is not to be trusted*, Westcliff had said. But the earl had been wrong. Regardless of Nick's shadowy past, he had been gentle and considerate with her, and more than worthy of her trust.

As Lottie cast a glance around the assemblage, hoping to catch sight of him, her attention was caught by a figure standing several yards away from her.

Radnor, she thought, while a shower of icy needles seemed to rain down on her. Every muscle locked . . . she was frozen with the same fear she had felt during two years of being hunted. His face was partially averted from her horrified gaze, but she saw his iron-gray hair, the haughty tilt of his head, the black slashes of his brows. And then he turned in her direction, as if he sensed her presence in the crowded hall.

Immediately her silent terror turned to bewilderment . . . no, it was not Radnor, only a man who resembled him. The gentleman nodded and smiled to her, as strangers sometimes did when their gazes happened to meet. He turned back to his companions, while Lottie looked down at her clenched hands in their pale pink gloves and tried to calm the thrashing of her heart. The aftereffects of the shock hit her . . . a touch of nausea, a dousing of cold sweat, a trembling that refused to abate. *How ridicu-*

lous you are, she told herself, disgusted by the fact that the mere glance of a man who looked like Radnor could have elicited such an overreaction.

"Mrs. Gentry," came a nearby voice. It was Mrs. Howsham, a pleasant and soft-spoken woman whom Lottie had only recently met. "Are you feeling ill, dear? You look rather queer."

She looked into Mrs. Howsham's face. "It's rather stifling in here," she whispered. "And I think I've laced a bit too tightly this evening."

"Ah, yes," the woman said in wry understanding, familiar with the complaints that corset strings often induced. "The perils of fashion we must suffer . . ."

To Lottie's relief, Nick appeared at her side, a glass of lemonade in hand. Instantly perceiving that something was wrong, he slid a supportive arm behind her. "What is it?" he asked, staring alertly at her pale face.

Mrs. Howsham took it upon herself to answer. "Tight-lacing, Mr. Gentry . . . I suggest that you take her somewhere a bit more secluded than this. A breath of fresh air often helps."

Keeping his arm around Lottie, Nick guided her through the hall. The night air caused Lottie to shiver as her sweat-soaked garments turned clammy. Carefully Nick drew her to the lee of a massive column that blocked the light and noise coming from inside the building.

"It was nothing," Lottie told him sheepishly. "Nothing at all. I feel like an idiot, making a fuss for no reason." Accepting the lemonade from him, she drank thirstily, not stopping until the glass was drained.

Nick bent to set the empty glass on the ground and rose to face Lottie once more. His face was taut as he took a handkerchief from his coat and wiped the trickling perspiration from her cheeks and forehead. "Tell me what happened," he said quietly.

Lottie flushed in embarrassment. "I thought I saw Lord Radnor in there. But it was only a man who looked like him." She sighed tensely. "Now I've revealed myself to be an utter coward. I'm sorry."

"Radnor rarely goes out in public," Nick murmured. "It's not likely that you would encounter him at an event like this."

"I know," she said ruefully. "Unfortunately I didn't stop to think about that."

"You're not a coward." There was concern in his dark blue eyes . . . concern overlaying some richer, more mysterious emotion underneath.

"I reacted like a child who's afraid of the dark."

His fingers slid beneath her chin, forcing her to meet his gaze. "It's conceivable that you will encounter Radnor someday," he said softly. "But I'll be with you when or if that happens, Lottie. You don't have to fear him anymore. I'll keep you safe."

She felt a rush of wonder at the tender gravity of his expression. "Thank you," she replied, taking a full breath for the first time since they had left the hall.

Continuing to stare into her pale, damp face, Nick shook his head with a slight frown, as if the sight of her distress was painful to him. Seeming unable to help himself, he reached out and pulled her against him, his arms wrapping around her as he tried to comfort her with his body. There was nothing sexual about the embrace, but somehow it was more intimate than anything they had ever done together. His arms were strong and possessive, holding her steady while his breath fell in moist, hot surges against her neck.

"Shall I take you home?" he whispered.

Lottie nodded slowly, while a lifetime of loneliness transformed into a sense of inconceivable comfort. A home . . . a husband . . . things she had never let herself hope for. Surely this illusion couldn't last—somehow, someday, it would be taken away from her. But until that happened, she would cherish every moment.

"Yes," she said, her voice muffled against his coat. "Let's go home."

Gradually emerging from a deep sleep, Lottie became aware of odd noises in the house. Thinking that perhaps the sounds were a remnant of a dream, she blinked and sat up slowly in bed. It was the middle of the night, and the bedroom was pitch black. There it was again . . . a growl, a garbled phrase . . . as if someone were in the midst of an argument. Recalling that Nick was occasionally troubled by nightmares, Lottie sprang from the bed. Carefully she lit a lamp, replaced the glass, and carried it with her down the hall.

Shadows fled before her as she approached the guest room where Nick slept. Pausing at the closed door, she tapped on it cautiously. There was no reply. After a moment, she heard a violent rustling from within. Lottie turned the knob and entered the bedroom.

"Nick?"

He was stretched out on the bed, lying on his stomach with the sheet twisted at his hips. Breathing rapidly, he clenched his fists and muttered incoherently, his dark face gleaming with sweat. Staring at him in puzzled concern, Lottie wondered what unseen monsters could cause his long body to twitch with what was either suppressed rage, or fear, or both. She set the lamp on the bedside table and approached him.

"Nick, wake up. It's only a dream." Reaching out to him, she laid a gentle hand on the brutal curve of his shoulder. "Nick—"

Suddenly she was caught in an explosion of violence. A startled cry escaped her as she was seized and flung halfway across the bed. Nick was on her in an instant, straddling her with his powerful thighs. Hearing a murderous growl, Lottie looked up into the harsh, shadowed mask of his face and saw one huge hand draw back in a fist.

"No!" she gasped, shielding her face with her arms.

The strike never came. All went still. Trembling, Lottie lowered her arms and looked up to see Nick's face change, the nightmarish mask dropping, sanity and awareness creeping back into his expression. He lowered his fist and stared at it blankly. Then his gaze fell to Lottie's slim form, and the fury and terror in his eyes made her cringe.

"I could have killed you," he snarled, his white teeth gleaming like an animal's. "What are you doing here? Don't *ever* touch me while I'm sleeping, damn you!"

"I didn't know, I . . . what in heaven's name were you dreaming about?"

He rolled away from her in a lithe movement and left the bed, panting. "Nothing. Nothing at all."

"I thought you needed something—"

"All I need is for you to stay the hell away from me," he snapped. Finding his discarded clothes on a chair, he jerked his trousers on.

Lottie felt as if she had been struck. She hated it that his words had the power to hurt her. Even more than that, she was anguished for him, wishing he did not have to bear such torment alone.

"Get out of here," he said, pulling his shirt and coat on, not bothering with a waistcoat or necktie.

"Are you leaving?" Lottie asked. "There is no need. I will go back to bed, and—"

"Yes, I'm leaving."

"Where are you going?"

"I don't know." He didn't spare her a glance as he

picked up his stockings and shoes. "And don't ask when I'll return. I don't know that, either."

"But why?" Lottie took a halting step toward him. "Nick, please stay and tell me—"

He shot her a warning glance, his eyes bright with the ferocity of a wounded animal. "I told you to get out."

Feeling the blood drain from her face, Lottie nodded and went to the door. Pausing at the threshold, she spoke without a backward glance. "I'm sorry."

He made no reply.

Lottie bit the insides of her lips, damning herself as she felt the sting of tears at the corners of her eyes. She left swiftly, retreating to her room with the shreds of her dignity.

Nick did not return all the next day. Anxious and bewildered, Lottie tried to find ways to occupy herself. However, no distraction proved sufficient to stop her from worrying. She took a long walk with a footman in tow, attended to needlework, read, and helped Mrs. Trench make tallow candles.

The housekeeper and servants were quietly deferential to Lottie. Predictably, not one word was mentioned about the previous night, although they were all certainly aware that some disturbance had taken place. Servants knew everything, but none of them would ever admit to knowledge of the intimate details of their master's life.

Wondering where her husband had gone, Lottie feared that perhaps he had done something reckless. She consoled herself that he was quite good at taking care of himself, but that did not ease her distress. He had been so very upset, and she suspected that his anger had stemmed from the fear that he might have hurt her.

However, she was his wife, and she deserved better than to be abandoned with no explanation. The day was relentlessly long, and Lottie was relieved when evening finally approached. After dining alone, she took a long bath, donned a fresh white nightrail, and read from a stack of periodicals until she finally felt able to sleep. Exhausted by the endless circling of her thoughts and the tedium of the past hours, she sank into deep slumber.

Long before morning, she was roused from the thick mist of sleep by the realization that the weight of the blankets had been drawn from her. Stirring, she became aware of a solid presence behind her, the mattress dipping slightly. Nick, she thought in drowsy relief, yawning as she turned toward him. The room was so dark that she could not quite distinguish him. The familiar warmth of his hands pressed her back to the bed, one large palm resting gently on the center of her chest . . . and then he drew her wrists over her head.

Lottie murmured in surprise, awakening fully as she felt him loop something around each wrist. Before she realized what was happening, the bonds were secured to the headboard, stretching her tautly beneath him. Her breath stopped in amazement. Nick moved over her, crouching like a cat, his breath coming in rough surges. He touched her body over the cotton veil of her gown, his fingers slipping beneath the curve of her breast, the indentation of her waist, the swell of her hip and thigh. His weight shifted, and his mouth sought her breast, wetting the gown, licking the rising peak of her nipple. He was naked, the scent and heat of warm male skin surrounding her.

Dazedly Lottie realized that he wanted to take her like this, with her hands fastened over her head. The idea made her fearful. She did not like being restrained in any way. But at the same time she understood what he wanted . . . her helplessness, her absolute trust . . . the knowledge that he could do anything he wanted to her without restrictions. He rolled her distended nipple against his tongue, excited the tight peak with long, dragging licks, and sucked hard through the wet cotton until she gasped. She squirmed in a mute plea for him to remove her gown, but he only slid farther down her body, his muscular arms braced on either side of her.

Curling her thumb and forefinger over one of the bonds that fastened her wrists, Lottie discovered that Nick had used her silk stockings. The light tension on her arms seemed to intensify her response to him, sensation racing through her in electric charges.

His mouth was at her stomach, his breath burning through the delicate gown. He nibbled at her body, his caresses languid, while the pace of his breathing betrayed his excitement. He made a space between her thighs, pushing them apart with his hands. His mouth rooted gently between her legs, against the cotton fabric. Lottie strained toward him, her fingers opening and closing helplessly, her heels digging hard into the mattress. He played with her leisurely, then rose again to find her breasts, kissing and fondling her through the clinging nightrail until she thought she would go mad if he didn't remove it. Every inch of her skin was hot and oversensitive, the fine fabric seeming to chafe her unbearably.

"Nick," she said frantically, "my gown, take if off, please take it . . ."

He hushed her with his fingers, resting two of them lightly against her lips. When she quieted, his thumb brushed over the curve of her cheek in a whisper-soft caress. Reaching for the hem of the gown, he pulled it upward, and she sobbed with gratitude. Her legs twitched as they were exposed to the cool air, and her wrists tugged at the silken bonds as she writhed to help him. The cotton was raised over her chest, catching slightly at the stiff tips of her nipples.

Nick's hand slid carefully over her stomach, traveling to the tender flesh of her inner thighs. His fingertip stroked through the curly hair, found the welling moisture, and brushed softly against the smoldering, delicate flesh. Her legs spread, her body throbbing with anticipation. She gave a pleading sob as his hand left her. The tip of his

middle finger traced the sensitive edge of her upper lip. His finger was damp with the salty elixir of
her own body, leaving the fragrance wherever he
touched. Suddenly her nostrils were filled with the
scent of her own arousal, filling her lungs with
every breath.

Slowly Nick turned her to her side, his hand running over her arms to check their tension. His body
settled behind hers, his mouth caressing the back of
her neck. Lottie strained backward, her bottom
pressing into his turgid shaft. She wanted to touch
him, to twist around and stroke the coarse, thick hair
on his chest, and then to grasp the hard weight of his
sex and let the silken barrel of it push through the
circle of her fingers. But her position made movement impossible, and her only choice was to wait
helplessly for his pleasure.

He hooked one arm beneath her top leg, lifting it
slightly, and she felt the swollen tip of his sex nudge
inside her. He entered her only an inch, teasing her,
withholding the full possession she craved. Lottie
trembled violently, pleading with wordless gasps as
he kissed the back of her neck. With the head of his
shaft lodged just inside her entrance, his hand wandered over her . . . an exquisite tug at her nipple, a
circling stroke of her navel. Gradually his caresses
became more purposeful, his gentle, clever fingers
delving into the thicket of curls.

Sweating, moaning, Lottie undulated against his
sweetly provoking fingertips. She felt his shaft slide
all the way inside her, filling her completely, and she

cried out sharply, her body shaken with tremors of delight.

Nick waited until she quieted. He began to pump inside her, his movements steady and deliberate, flooding her with pleasure. She breathed in open-mouthed sighs, her wrists pulling hard at the silk loops as she climaxed again with a long, shuddering moan. He thrust harder then, his loins meeting hers in delicious impacts, his breath rushing through his clenched teeth. The bed shook from his movements. Lottie felt at once vulnerable and strong, possessing him as surely as he did her, with her heart beating against his hand, and her flesh surrounding his. He tensed inside her, his organ jerking and pulsing, his lips parting as he gasped against her neck.

For a long time she lay against his large, hard body, giving a soft moan when he released her wrists. He rubbed them gently, and then his hand came down to cup her wet sex. His breathing slowed, and at the thought that he was drifting to sleep beside her, Lottie quivered in longing. Suddenly nothing was more desirable in the world than to have him stay in her bed for an entire night. But he rose eventually, leaning to kiss her breast, his tongue swirling around the tender peak.

As Nick left the bed, Lottie bit her lip to keep from asking him to stay, knowing that he would only deny her as always. The door closed, leaving her in solitude. And although her body was sated and weary and her flesh tingled pleasantly, she felt tears welling behind her eyelids. She felt sorrow . . . not for herself, but for him. And longing . . . the dangerous need to comfort him, even though he would bitterly resent her for doing so. And last of all, a deep tenderness for a man she barely knew—a man who needed to be rescued far worse than she ever had.

The following morning a parcel arrived from Sir Ross, containing a sheaf of documents bearing elaborate seals and an invitation to a ball to be held in one week's time. As Lottie entered the dining room, she saw Nick sitting alone at the table, a half-finished breakfast plate before him. His gaze lifted from the thick sheet of parchment in his hand, his eyes darkening as he saw her. He rose to his feet, staring at her without blinking.

Lottie felt a brilliant tide of red sweep over her face. On the mornings after an unusually passionate evening, Nick usually teased her, or smiled as he made some commonplace remark to ease her discomfort. Today, however, his face was taut and his eyes were bleak. Something had changed between them—the ease of their former interactions was gone.

Awkwardly she gestured to the paper in his hand. "It has arrived?"

There was no need to clarify what "it" was.

Nick nodded briefly, his gaze returning to the summons.

Striving to maintain an appearance of normalcy, Lottie went to the sideboard and served herself from the covered dishes. Nick helped her into the chair beside him and resumed his seat. He regarded the remains of his breakfast with unusual concentration, while a maid came to set a cup of steaming tea before Lottie.

They were both silent until the maid left the room.

"The ball will be given next Saturday," Nick said brusquely, not looking at her. "Will you have an appropriate gown by then?"

"Yes. I've already been fitted for a ballgown, and there were only a few minor alterations to be made."

"Good."

"Are you angry?" Lottie asked.

He picked up his knife and regarded it moodily, scraping the tip of the blade against the calloused pad of his thumb. "I'm beginning to feel oddly resigned to the situation. Now the news is leaking from the offices of the Crown and the Lord Chancellor. It's all been set in motion, and there is nothing anyone could do to stop it now. Sir Ross will introduce us at the ball as Lord and Lady Sydney . . . and from then on, Nick Gentry will be dead."

Lottie stared at him intently, struck by his odd phrasing. "You mean the name will no longer be used," she said. "You, as Lord Sydney, will be very much alive. Shall I begin to call you John in private?"

A scowl pulled at his features, and he set the knife down. "No. I'll be Sydney to the rest of the world, but in my own home I'll answer to the name that *I* choose."

"Very well . . . Nick." Lottie stirred a generous lump of sugar into her tea and sipped the hot, sweet liquid. "The name has served you well for many years, hasn't it? I daresay you've given it far more renown than the original Gentry ever would have." Her idle remark earned a peculiar glance from him, somehow rebuking and beseeching at the same time. A sudden realization flashed through her mind—the real Nick Gentry, the boy who had died of cholera aboard the prison hulk, was at the heart of the secret that tormented her husband. Lottie stared absently into her tea, striving to keep her tone casual as she asked, "What was he like? You haven't yet told me."

"He was an orphan, whose mother was hanged for thievery. He lived in the streets for most of his life, starting as a pudding shammer and eventually acquiring his own gang of ten."

"Pudding shammer," Lottie repeated, puzzled.

"Stealing food to survive. That's the lowest of the low, except for beggars. But Gentry learned fast, and he became a proficient thief. Finally he was caught robbing a house, and he was sentenced to the prison hulk."

"And then you became friends," Lottie prompted.

Nick's expression became distant as long-buried memories recalled him to the past. "He was strong, shrewd . . . with sharp instincts from living so long in the streets. He told me things I needed to know to stay alive in the hulk . . . protected me some-times . . ."

"Protected you from what?" Lottie whispered. "The guards?"

Nick jerked out of his trance, blinking the remoteness from his eyes. He glanced down at his hand, which was gripping the knife handle too tightly. Carefully he set the gleaming object on the table and pushed his chair back.

"I'm going out for a while," he said, his voice stripped of all nuance. "I expect I will see you at dinner this evening."

Lottie responded in the same carefully neutral tone. "Very well. Have a pleasant day."

During the week that ensued, the days and nights were dizzying in their contrast. Lottie's daytime hours were occupied with errands and small practical matters. She was never quite certain when she would see Nick, for he came and went at will. At supper they would discuss meetings that he'd had with investment partners and bankers, or his occasional visits to Bow Street, as Sir Grant occasionally consulted with him on matters pertaining to past cases. In the daytime, Lottie's interactions with Nick were cordial, the conversation pleasant and yet slightly impersonal.

The nights, however, were a far different story. Nick made love to her with an almost desperate intensity. He did things that shocked her, leaving no part of her body untouched in his passion. At times their lovemaking was urgent and primitive, while other times it was languid and slow, with both of them reluctant to let it end. There were also unexpected moments of humor, as Nick played with her,

teased her, and coaxed her to try positions so undignified that she dissolved into mortified giggles.

No matter what enjoyment the nights held, however, each day brought them closer to the time when
Sir Ross would make the announcement that would
change the course of their lives. Lottie knew that her
husband dreaded the ball, and that the months afterward would be quite difficult as he tried to adjust to
his new circumstances. She was certain, however,
that she could be of some help to him. When she had
entered into the marriage, she had never suspected
that he might need her in any way, nor had she
thought that she would take any satisfaction in helping him. And yet, she felt very much like a help-
mate . . . a partner . . . and sometimes, for just a
moment or two, a wife.

As the night of the ball finally arrived, Lottie was
thankful that she'd accepted Sophia's advice at the
dressmaker's. Sophia had helped her choose styles
that were youthful but ladylike, in soft colors that
flattered her immensely. The gown Lottie had decided to wear tonight was a pale blue satin overlaid
with white tulle, with a daring scooped neckline that
bared the tops of her shoulders. Lottie stood in the
center of the bedroom while Mrs. Trench and Harriet
pulled the billowing gown over her head and helped
guide her arms through the puffed sleeves of stiffened satin. It was a gown as beautiful—no, more
beautiful—than any she had seen during the parties
in Hampshire. Thinking of the ball she was about to

attend, and Nick's reaction when he saw her, Lottie was nearly giddy with excitement.

Her light-headedness was no doubt encouraged by the fact that her corset was laced with unusual tightness, to enable Mrs. Trench to fasten the close-fitting gown. Wincing in the confinement of stays and laces, Lottie stared into the looking glass as the two women adjusted the ballgown. The transparent white tulle overslip was embroidered with sprays of white silk roses. White satin shoes, long kid gloves, and an embroidered gauze scarf were the final touches, making Lottie feel like a princess. The only flaw was her stick-straight hair, which refused to hold a curl no matter how hot the tongs were. After several fruitless attempts to create a pinned-up mass of ringlets, Lottie opted for a simple braided coil atop her head, encircled with fluffy white roses.

When Harriet and Mrs. Trench stood back to view the final results of their labors, Lottie laughed and did a quick turn, making the blue skirts whirl beneath the floating white tulle.

"You look beautiful, my lady," Mrs. Trench commented with obvious pleasure.

Pausing in mid-whirl, Lottie stared at her with a wondering smile. As Nick had not brought himself to make any kind of announcement to the servants about reclaiming his family name and title, it had been left to Lottie to tell them about their master's noble origins. After their initial amazement had faded, the servants had seemed more than a little pleased by the turn of events. If they were to become servants of a peer's household, their own status in the world would be greatly enhanced.

"Thank you, Mrs. Trench," Lottie replied. "As always, you have been invaluable this evening. We couldn't manage without you, especially in the days to come."

"Yes, my lady." The housekeeper wore an expression of frank anticipation. As they had previously discussed, a brand-new household would have to be established in Worcestershire, with at least thirty servants to start with. Mrs. Trench would be largely responsible for selecting and hiring the new staff.

Lottie left the room, her gown swishing and rustling as she moved. As she descended the grand staircase, she saw Nick waiting in the entrance hall, his body as tense as that of a panther about to strike. His broad-shouldered form was dressed to perfection in the formal scheme of a dark coat, silver waistcoat, and a charcoal silk necktie. With his dark brown hair neatly brushed and his face gleaming from a close shave, he was both virile and elegant. His head turned toward her, and suddenly his narrow-eyed impatience was replaced by an arrested expression.

Lottie felt a rush of elation at the look in his eyes. She deliberately took her time about reaching him. "Do I look like a viscountess?" she asked.

His lips quirked wryly. "No viscountess I've ever seen looks like you, Lottie."

She smiled. "Is that a compliment?"

"Oh, yes. In fact . . ." Nick took her gloved hand

and assisted her down the last step. He held her gaze compulsively, his fingers tightening around hers, and he answered her light question with a gravity that stunned her. "You are the most beautiful woman in the world," he said huskily.

"The *world*?" she repeated with a laugh.

"When I say you're beautiful," he murmured, "I refuse to qualify the statement in any way. Except to add that the only way you could be more so is if you were naked."

She laughed at his audacity. "I am afraid that you will have to reconcile yourself to the fact that I'm going to remain fully clothed tonight."

"Until after the ball," he countered. He tugged at the fingertips of her left glove, loosening them one by one.

"What are you doing?" Lottie asked, suddenly breathless.

His blue eyes taunted her. "Removing your glove."

"For what purpose?"

"To admire your hand." Drawing the glove completely away, he draped it over the nearby banister of the stairs and lifted her tapered fingers to his mouth. Lottie watched as he kissed them each in turn, his lips warm on her skin. By the time he finished with a soft kiss in the center of her palm, her entire arm was tingling. Lowering her hand, Nick regarded it thoughtfully. "It lacks something." Reaching into his pocket, he murmured, "Close your eyes."

Lottie obeyed with a slight smile. She felt something cool and heavy slide over her fourth finger, fitting snugly at the base. Realizing what it was, she opened her eyes and caught her breath.

The ring was a huge, dome-shaped sapphire, a blue that nearly approached the dark, sparkling depth of her husband's eyes. The gem was set in gold, with a ring of smaller diamonds surrounding it. What made the sapphire so remarkable, however, was the star that danced on the silky surface of the gem, appearing to slide across it with the light. Awestruck, Lottie looked up into Nick's dark face.

"Does it please you?" he asked.

Words eluded her. She tightened her fingers on his, her mouth opening and closing before she could manage to speak. "I've never seen anything so lovely. I didn't expect anything like this. Oh, how generous of you!" Impulsively she threw her arms around his neck and kissed his cheek.

Nick's arms closed around her. She felt his hot breath on the side of her neck, while his hand drew gently over her lace-covered back. "Don't you know that I would give you anything you wanted?" he said softly. "Anything at all."

Afraid to let him see her expression, Lottie remained close against him, her face averted. He had spoken without thinking. Either that, or the words could not possibly reveal what she thought they did. Nick stiffened, as if realizing what he had just said, and he stepped back from her quickly. Risking a glance at him, Lottie saw the careful blankness of his face, and she remained silent, giving him control of the moment.

Nick shook his head as he painstakingly reassembled his self-possession. When his gaze returned to hers, his eyes were bright with self-mockery. "Shall we depart, Lady Sydney?"

"Yes, Nick," she whispered, and reached for his proffered arm.

Sir Ross had prevailed on a friend in the first tier of society, the duke of Newcastle himself, to host the ball at which the long-lost Lord Sydney would be introduced. The duke and duchess were a distinguished pair, a well-respected couple who had been married for forty years. Their unimpeachable reputations would be quite useful in this situation, for a man as infamous as Nick would certainly need sponsors who were above reproach.

The duke's London estate featured what was tactfully referred to as an "important" house, one so mammoth in scale that visitors frequently lost their way from one circuit of rooms to another. There were innumerable parlors, rooms for breakfasting, supping, or taking coffee, a library, dining hall, and a hunting hall, rooms for studying, smoking, and music. The drawing room was floored with what seemed to be acres of highly polished parquet-work, reflecting light from a half-dozen celestial chandeliers hung two stories above. Lined with balconied galleries above and below, the room provided many pockets of privacy for gossip and intrigue.

The ball was attended by at least five hundred guests, many of them chosen for their glittering social status. As Sophia had remarked dryly to Nick, the invitations to this particular event had become such a mark of distinction that no one dared *not* to attend, in case it was perceived that they had not been asked.

Nick assumed a properly grateful expression as he was introduced to the duke and duchess, both of whom had known his parents. "You bear a striking resemblance to your late father," the duchess remarked as Nick bent over her gloved hand. She was a small but elegant woman, her silver head adorned with a diamond tiara, her neck weighted with ropes of pearls so massive that they threatened to topple her off-balance. "Had I not been told of your parentage," the duchess continued, "I would have known it at once, just by looking at you. Those eyes . . . yes, you are indeed a Sydney. Such a tragedy for you to lose both parents at once. A boating accident, was it not?"

"Yes, Your Grace." As Nick had been told, his mother had drowned when a boat had overturned at a water party. His father had died trying to save her.

"A great pity," the duchess said. "And such a devoted couple, as I recall. But perhaps in that light, it may have been a blessing for them to be taken together."

"Indeed," Nick said blandly, concealing a flare of annoyance. In the days just after his parents' death, the same sentiment had been voiced countless times—how kind fate had been in that regard, to let them die together. Unfortunately neither of the Sydneys' children had shared that romantic sentiment, wishing instead that at least one of their parents had survived. Nick's gaze shot to his sister, who stood nearby with Sir Ross. Overhearing the duchess's comment, Sophia's eyes narrowed slightly, and she exchanged a subtle, grim smile with Nick.

"Your Grace," Lottie murmured, smoothing over the moment, "how very kind it is of you to extend your hospitality to us. Lord Sydney and I will always attach the memory of your generosity to this special occasion."

Obviously flattered, the duchess paused to speak with Lottie for a few moments, while the duke favored Nick with a congratulatory smile. "An exceptional choice for a wife, Sydney," the elderly man remarked. "Poised, unaffected, and quite lovely. You are quite fortunate."

No one would have disagreed with that, least of all Nick. Lottie was a revelation this evening, her gown stylish but not too sophisticated, her smile easy, her posture as regal as that of a young queen. Neither the grandeur of their surroundings nor the hundreds of curious gazes seemed to disturb her composure. She was so polished and immaculately pretty that no one suspected the layer of steel beneath her exterior. No one would ever guess that she was the kind of young woman who would have defied her parents and lived by her own wits for two years . . . the kind of woman who could hold her own against a hardened Bow Street runner.

As the duke continued to receive guests, the duchess continued to speak with Lottie, the gray head inclined toward the pale golden one.

Sophia drifted closer to Nick, employing her fan to mask the movement of her lips as she murmured to him, "I told you so."

Nick smiled wryly, recalling his sister's claim that Lottie would prove to be a great asset to him. "Those are without doubt the four most irritating words in the English language, Sophia."

"She is a dear creature, and far too good for you," his sister informed him with amusement dancing in her eyes.

"I've never claimed otherwise."

"And she seems rather fond of you," Sophia continued, "so if I were you, I would not take my good fortune for granted."

"Fond," Nick repeated warily, aware of a sudden increase of his pulse. "Why do you say that?"

"Well, the other day she—" Sophia broke off as she caught sight of a newly arrived couple. "Oh, there is Lord Farrington! Excuse me, dear, as Lady Farrington has been ailing for the past month, and I want to ask after her health."

"Wait," Nick demanded. "Finish what you were going to say!" But Sophia had already glided away with Sir Ross in tow, leaving Nick to seethe in frustration.

When Lottie was released from the duchess's attentions, she took Nick's arm and accompanied him as they mingled with various groups. She was adept at light social conversation, talking amiably without becoming drawn into a lengthy discussion, moving gracefully among the guests and remembering people they had met on previous occasions. It was clear that had Nick wished to leave her while he joined his friends in the smoking and billiards rooms, Lottie would have been perfectly comfortable. However, as Nick saw the number of covetous gazes following his wife's every movement, he remained close beside her, occasionally resting his hand at the small of her back in a territorial gesture that was well understood by every man who saw it.

An ebullient melody filled the air, provided by an orchestra that was carefully concealed by a forest of potted plants in one of the upper balconies. As they made their way through the crowded ballroom, Lottie flirted with Nick discreetly, laying her hand on his chest in provocative little touches, rising to whisper in his ear until her lips brushed his skin. Semi-aroused and thoroughly fascinated, Nick breathed in the scent of white roses from her hair and stood close enough to see the faint dusting of perfumed powder that had collected in the gentle valley between her breasts.

Suddenly Lottie's attention was caught by a small group of women, two of whom were staring at her with obvious excitement. "Nick, I see some friends that I haven't set eyes on since I was at

Maidstone's. I must speak with them—why don't you join your gentlemen friends? You certainly don't want to listen to us gossip about our school days."

Nick was disgruntled by his wife's clear desire to be rid of him. "Fine," he said curtly. "I'll go to the billiards room."

Lottie shot him a provocative glance from beneath her lashes. "Promise you will come find me for the first waltz?"

Realizing that he was being adeptly managed, Nick grumbled an assent and watched Lottie glide toward the group of waiting women. To his astonishment, he stood there feeling completely bereft. He was so mesmerized by one small woman that he could scarcely think straight. He, who was so eternally self-assured, was in danger of being led around by the nose by his own wife.

Brooding over the alarming discovery, Nick heard his brother-in-law's deep voice beside him.

"It happens to the best of us, Sydney."

Nick turned to face Sir Ross. Uncannily, Sir Ross seemed to understand exactly what he was feeling. His gray eyes gleamed with amusement as he continued in a tone that was not unsympathetic. "No matter how strong our resolve, we eventually find ourselves enslaved by the compulsive preference for one particular woman. You've been caught, my friend. You may as well reconcile yourself to it."

Nick did not bother trying to deny it. "I was going to be so much smarter than you," he muttered.

Sir Ross grinned. "I prefer to think that intelligence has nothing to do with it. For if a man's intellect is measured by his ability to remain untouched by love, I would be the greatest idiot alive."

The word *love* made Nick flinch. "What would it take to make you shut your gob, Cannon?"

"A glass of 1805 Cossart-Gordon would probably do it," came the amiable reply. "And if I'm not mistaken, they've just brought out a case in the billiards room."

"Let's go, then," Nick said, and they strode from the ballroom together.

"Lottie Howard!" Two young women rushed over to her, and they clasped hands tightly, sharing grins of barely suppressed glee. Were it not for their strict training at Maidstone's, the three of them would have squealed in a most unladylike manner.

"Samantha," Lottie said warmly, gazing at the tall, attractive brunette who had always been like a kind older sister to her. "And Arabella!" Arabella Markenfield looked exactly the same as she had at school ... pretty and a bit plump, with strawberry blond ringlets that were perfectly arranged on her porcelain forehead.

"I'm Lady Lexington now," Samantha informed her with considerable pride. "I caught an earl, no less, with a good, sound fortune." Slipping an arm around Lottie's waist, she turned her slightly. "He's standing right there, close to the conservatory doors. The tall, balding one. Do you see him?"

Lottie nodded as she caught sight of a somber-looking gentleman who appeared to be in his early forties, with large eyes that seemed slightly out of proportion to his long, narrow face. "He looks to be a very pleasant gentleman," Lottie remarked, and Samantha laughed.

"Very tactful, dear. I'll be the first to admit that the earl is not much to look at, and he has no sense of humor. However, men with a sense of humor often tend to grate on one's nerves. And he is an impeccable gentleman."

"I'm so glad," Lottie said sincerely, knowing from past conversations with Samantha that such a marriage was very much what she had desired. "And you, Arabella?"

"I married into the Seaforths last year," Arabella confided with a giggle. "You've heard of them, I'm sure . . . do you remember, one of the daughters was in the class ahead of us . . ."

"Yes," Lottie said, recalling that the Seaforths were a great untitled family with a considerable quantity of rich farming land. "Don't say you married her brother Harry?"

"Just so!" The girl's ringlets danced merrily on her forehead as she continued with great animation. "Harry is quite fine-looking, though he's grown as round as a bait-pot since our wedding. And he is ever so charming. Of course I'll never have a title, but there are compensations . . . my own carriage . . . a real French lady's maid, not one of those Cockney maids who throw out a see-voo-play or a bon-joor every once in a while!" She giggled at her own wit, and sobered enough to regard Lottie with round, curious eyes. "Dear Lottie, is it true that you are Lady Sydney now?"

"Yes." Lottie glanced in the direction of her husband, who was walking from the ballroom in the company of Sir Ross, their long legs matched at an equal pace. She felt an unexpected rush of pride at the sight of him, so virile and graceful, his bold good looks displayed to their best advantage in the elegant evening clothes.

"Handsome as the devil," Samantha commented, following her gaze. "Is he as wicked as they say, Lottie?"

"Not in the least," Lottie lied. "Lord Sydney is as mild-tempered and obliging a gentleman as could be found anywhere."

It was a case of unfortunate timing that at that moment, Nick happened to glance in her direction. His gaze encompassed her in a smoldering sweep that threatened to singe her clothing to ashes. Knowing what that look meant, and what would happen in the evening hours after the ball, Lottie felt a thrill deep inside, and she struggled to maintain her composure.

Samantha and Arabella, meanwhile, had snapped open their fans and were employing them vigorously. "Good heavens," Samantha exclaimed in a low voice, "the way he looks at you is positively indecent, Lottie."

"I don't know what you mean," Lottie said demurely, though she felt her own cheeks heating.

Arabella giggled behind her own painted silk fan. "The only time I've ever seen that expression on my Harry's face is when a plate of Yorkshire pudding is set before him."

Samantha's dark eyes were keen with interest. "I was under the impression that Lord Radnor owned you part and parcel, Lottie. How did you escape him? And where have you been these past two years? And most of all, how in heaven's name did you manage to catch a man like Nick Gentry—and is this long-lost-lord business some bit of trickery?"

"No," Lottie said instantly, "he truly is Lord Sydney."

"Did you know that he was a viscount when you married?"

"Well, no." Lottie strove to offer the simplest explanation possible. "To start with, you know that I left school to avoid marrying Lord Radnor—"

"The definitive scandal of Maidstone's," Arabella interrupted. "They still talk of it, I'm told. None of the teachers or staff could conceive that sweet, obedient Charlotte Howard would simply disappear like that."

Lottie paused in momentary embarrassment. She was far from proud of her actions—it was simply that she'd had no other choice. "To avoid being found, I changed my name and went to work as a companion to Lady Westcliff in Hampshire—"

"You *worked*?" Arabella repeated in awe. "My word, how you must have suffered."

"Not unduly," Lottie replied with a wry smile. "The Westcliffs were kind, and I liked the dowager countess quite well. It was while I was in her employ that I made the acquaintance of Mr. Gentry—er, Lord Sydney. He proposed quite soon after we met, and . . ." She paused, an image flashing in her mind of that evening in Lord Westcliff's library, the fire-light playing over Nick's face as he bent to her breast . . .

"And I accepted," she said hastily, feeling her face turn fiery red.

"Hmmm." Samantha smiled at Lottie's discomfiture, seeming to guess the reason behind it. "Apparently it was a memorable proposal."

"Were your parents terribly put out with you?" Arabella asked.

Lottie nodded, reflecting with sad irony that "put out" was singularly inadequate to describe her family's reaction.

Samantha's face was grave with understanding. "They won't be angry forever, dear," she said with a pragmatism that was far more comforting than sympathy would have been. "If your husband is half as wealthy as the rumors indicate, the Howards will eventually prove more than happy to claim him as a son-in-law."

The three of them conversed for a while, eagerly becoming reacquainted and making plans to call on each other soon. Lottie was unaware of time passing until she heard the orchestra begin to play a newly popular waltz called "Blossoms in the Spring," a melody that immediately inspired a host of eager couples to begin whirling through the room. Wondering if Nick would remember to dance the first waltz with her, Lottie decided to look for him at the side of the room. Excusing herself from the company of her friends, she walked along one of the first-floor galleries, which was separated from the dance floor by carved wooden railings and bowers of greenery and pink roses. A few couples were absorbed in private conversations, half-concealed by the massive flower arrangements, and Lottie averted her gaze with a slight smile as she passed them.

She was startled by a sudden touch on her arm, and she stopped with a jolt of anticipation, expecting that Nick had found her. But as she glanced down at the growing pressure on her gloved wrist, she did not see Nick's large, square hand. A set of long, almost skeletal fingers had wrapped around her wrist, and with a shock of cold horror, she heard the voice that had haunted her nightmares for years.

"Did you think you could avoid me forever, Charlotte?"

Chapter Twelve

Bracing herself, Lottie looked up into the face of Arthur, Lord Radnor. Time had wrought an astonishing difference in him, as if ten years had passed rather than two. He was unnaturally pale, his skin the color of sun-bleached bone, his dark brows and eyes standing out in jarring contrast. Harsh grooves of bitterness divided his face into angular sections.

Lottie had known the inevitability of seeing Lord Radnor someday. In the back of her mind, she had assumed that he would regard her with hatred. But what she saw in his eyes was far more alarming. Hunger. A voracity that had nothing to do with sexual desire but something far more consuming. Instinctively she understood that his longing to own her had only intensified during her absence, and

that her betrayal of him had given him the deadly resolve of an executioner.

"My lord," she acknowledged, her voice steady
even though her lips were trembling. "You are im-
portunate. Release my arm, please."

Ignoring her request, Radnor pulled her into the
concealment of a greenery-laded column, his fingers
tightening into a bruising vise. Lottie went with him
easily, determined that this ugliness from her past
would not result in a scene that would mar an evening so important for her husband. Ridiculous, that
she should be so afraid in a room filled with people.
Radnor certainly could not, would not, harm her
here. If they were alone, however, she believed that
he would feel absolutely justified in wrapping those
long fingers around her throat and choking the last
breath from her.

His gaze sliced over her. "My God, what has he
turned you into? I can smell the lust on you. Only
the thinnest veneer separated you from the ill-bred
provincials you came from, and now it has vanished
completely."

"In that case," Lottie replied, her imprisoned
hand balling into a numb fist, "you will disassociate
yourself from me at once, as I'm certain you will not
wish to be contaminated by my presence."

"Stupid girl," Radnor whispered, his black eyes
lit with cold fire, "you cannot begin to understand
what you've lost. Do you know what you would be
without me? *Nothing.* I *made* you. I lifted you from

the bowels of society. I was going to turn you into a creature of grace and perfection. And instead you betrayed me and turned your back on your family."

"I did not ask for your patronage."

"All the more reason you should have knelt to me in gratitude. You owe me everything, Charlotte. Your very life."

Lottie saw that it would be pointless to debate his insane certainty. "Be that as it may," she said softly, "I belong to Lord Sydney now. You have no claim on me."

His mouth twisted in a malevolent sneer. "My claim on you goes far beyond some piddling marriage vows."

"Have you deluded yourself into thinking that you could purchase me like some bit of goods in a shop window?" she asked scornfully.

"I own your very soul," Radnor whispered, clenching her wrist until she felt the delicate bones flex, and tears of pain came to her eyes. "I purchased it at the expense of my own. I've invested more than ten years of my life in you, and I will be repaid."

"How? I am another man's wife. And I feel nothing for you now—not fear, not hatred—only indifference. What can you possibly think you will recoup from me?"

Just as Lottie thought her arm would break, she heard a quiet snarl from behind her. It was Nick, moving swiftly between them. His arm descended in a blur, and whatever he did, it caused Lord Rad-

nor to let go of her with a grunt of pain. The abrupt
release sent Lottie stumbling backward, and Nick
caught her hard against his chest. Automatically she
turned into the crook of his arm, and she heard the
deep rumble of his voice as he spoke to Lord Radnor.

"Don't come near her again, or I'll kill you." It
was a quiet statement of fact.

"Insolent swine," Radnor said hoarsely.

Risking a glance at Radnor from the safety of her
husband's arms, Lottie saw a grayish-purple tide
sweep over his pallid face. It was clear that the sight
of Nick's hands on her was more than he could
bear. Nick touched the back of her neck and slid his
fingers along the top of her spine, taunting the earl
deliberately.

"Very well," Radnor whispered. "I leave you to
your debasement, Charlotte."

"Leave," Nick said. *"Now."*

Radnor walked away, his frame stiff with the
righteous fury of a deposed monarch.

Cradling her throbbing wrist with her free hand,
Lottie saw that they had drawn more than a few curious stares from people passing through the gallery.
In fact, some guests in the ballroom were becoming
keenly aware of the scene. "Nick—" she whispered,
but he went into action before she needed to say another word.

Keeping a supportive arm around her, Nick mo-
tioned to a servant who was passing with a tray of
empty glasses. "You," he said tersely. "Come here."

The dark-haired footman obeyed with haste. "Yes, my lord?"

"Tell me where I can find a private room."

The footman thought rapidly. "If you proceed along that hallway, my lord, you will come to a music room that I believe is unoccupied at present."

"Fine. Bring some brandy there. Quickly."

"Yes, my lord!"

Dazedly Lottie went with Nick as he guided her through the hallway. Chaotic thoughts filled her mind, while the elegant din of the ballroom receded behind them. Her body was charged with peculiar battle-readiness. The long-dreaded confrontation with Lord Radnor had left her ill, elated, furious, and relieved. How was it possible to feel so many things at once?

The music room was quietly lit, the outlines of a piano, harp, and several assorted music stands casting deep shadows on the wall. Nick closed the door and turned to Lottie, his broad shoulders looming over her. She had never seen his face so hard.

"I'm all right," Lottie said, and the unusually high pitch of her own voice actually drew a giggle from her throat. "Really, there's no need to look so—" She paused with another uncontainable laugh, seeing that Nick clearly thought she had taken leave of her senses. She would never be able to explain the wild sense of freedom that flooded her, after having faced her greatest fear.

"I'm sorry," she said giddily, even as tears of relief dampened her eyes. "It's just. . . . I've been so afraid of Lord Radnor for my entire life . . . but as I saw him just now, I realized that his power over me is gone. He can do nothing to me. I don't feel any obligation to him wh-whatsoever . . . and I don't even feel guilty about it. The burden of it is gone, as well as the fear, and it feels so strange . . ."

As she trembled and laughed and blotted her eyes with her gloved fingers, Nick took her into his arms and tried to soothe her. "Easy . . . Easy . . . ," he whispered, while his hands moved gently over her shoulders and back. "Take a deep breath. Hush, everything's all right." The warm brand of his mouth pressed against her forehead, her wet lashes, her cheeks. "You're safe, Lottie. You're mine, my wife, and I'll take care of you. You're safe."

As Lottie tried to explain that she wasn't afraid, he murmured for her to be quiet, to rest against him. She began to breathe deeply, as if she had just run for miles without stopping, and lay her head on the center of his chest. Nick tore off his gloves and placed his warm hands on her chilled skin, his strong fingers kneading the rigid muscles of her neck and upper shoulders.

Someone knocked at the door.

"The brandy," Nick said quietly and guided Lottie to an armchair.

Lottie sank into the chair, listening to the footman's appreciative exclamation as Nick gave him a coin in return for his trouble. Returning with a tray bearing a bottle and a snifter, Nick set it on a nearby table.

"I don't need that," Lottie said with a wan smile.

Ignoring her, Nick poured a finger of brandy into the snifter and held the bowl of the glass between his palms. After warming the spirits with his hands, he gave it to her. "Drink."

Obediently Lottie took the snifter. To her surprise, her hands trembled so badly that she could barely hold it. Nick's face darkened as he saw her difficulty. He sank to his knees before her, his muscular thighs spread on either side of her legs. Covering her fingers with his own, Nick steadied her hands and helped guide the rim of the snifter to her lips. She took a sip, grimacing as the brandy scalded her throat.

"More," Nick murmured, forcing her to take another swallow, and another, until her eyes watered from the velvet fire.

"I think it's a bit off," she said scratchily.

Nick's eyes flickered with sudden amusement. "It's not off. It's a Fin Bois '98."

"It must have been a bad year."

He grinned at that, his thumbs caressing the backs of her hands. "Someone should tell the wine merchants, then, as it usually goes for fifty pounds a bottle."

"Fifty pounds?" Lottie echoed, aghast. Closing her eyes, she finished the brandy in a few determined gulps and coughed as she gave him the empty glass.

"Good girl," Nick murmured, sliding a hand around the back of her neck and squeezing gently. She could not help reflecting that although Nick's hand was much larger and infinitely more powerful than Radnor's, he had never caused her a single moment of pain. Nick's touch had given her only pleasure.

She winced as she rested her sore wrist on the arm of the chair. Subtle as the movement was, Nick detected it immediately. He swore beneath his breath as he took her arm and began to peel away the long glove.

"It's nothing," Lottie said. "Really, I would prefer to leave the glove on . . . Lord Radnor did take hold of my arm, but it wasn't all that—" She broke off with a gasp of discomfort as Nick eased the glove from her hand.

Nick froze as he saw the black finger marks that had been left by Lord Radnor's vicious grip. The murderous fury that suffused his face caused Lottie to start in alarm. "I bruise quite easily," she said. "You mustn't look like that. The marks will be gone in a day or two, and then—"

"I'm going to kill him." Nick bared his teeth in feral rage. "When I get through with him, all that will be left is a stain on the ground, damn him to everlasting hell—"

"Please." Lottie laid a soft hand on his stiff cheek. "Lord Radnor intended to ruin this evening for both of us, and I refuse to let him succeed. I want you to bind my wrist with a handkerchief, and help me to put my glove back on. We must hurry back before we're missed. Sir Ross will be making his speech, and we—"

"I don't give a damn about that."

"I do." Regaining her composure, Lottie stroked his cheek with soft fingertips. "I want to go out there and waltz with you. And then stand by your side while Sir Ross tells everyone who you really are." Her lashes lowered as she glanced at his mouth. "And then I want you to take me home and carry me to bed."

As Lottie had intended, Nick was momentarily distracted. His savage gaze began to soften. "And then what?"

Before she could answer, the door vibrated with a demanding thump. "Sydney," came a muffled voice from the other side.

"Yes," Nick said, rising to his feet.

Sir Ross's tall form filled the doorway. His face was expressionless as he looked at the two of them. "I was just told of Lord Radnor's presence." He went directly to Lottie, crouching before her much as Nick had. Seeing her bruised arm, Sir Ross gestured toward it carefully. "May I?" His voice was more gentle than she had ever heard it.

"Yes," Lottie murmured, allowing him to take her hand in his. Sir Ross examined the darkened wrist with a gathering frown. His face was very close, and his gray eyes were so kind and concerned that Lottie wondered how she could have ever thought him aloof. She recalled his reputed compassion for women and children—a focal point of his magisterial career, Sophia had told her.

Sir Ross's mouth flexed in a faint, reassuring

smile as he released her hand. "This won't happen again—I can promise you that."

"Wonderful party," Nick said sarcastically. "Perhaps you can tell us who the hell included Lord Radnor on the guest list?"

"Nick," Lottie interceded, "it's all right, I am certain that Sir Ross did not—"

"It is not all right," Sir Ross countered quietly. "I hold myself responsible for this, and I humbly beg your forgiveness, Charlotte. Lord Radnor was most certainly *not* included on the guest list that I approved, but I will find out how he managed to obtain an invitation." His brow creased as he continued. "Lord Radnor's behavior tonight was irrational as well as reprehensible . . . it bespeaks an obsession with Charlotte that will likely not end with this incident."

"Oh, it's going to end," Nick said darkly. "I have several methods in mind that will cure Radnor's obsession. To start with, if he hasn't left the premises by the time I go back out there—"

"He's gone," Sir Ross interrupted. "Two of the runners are here—I bid them to remove him in as discreet a manner as possible. Calm yourself, Sydney—it will do no good for you to rampage like a maddened bull."

Nick's eyes narrowed. "Tell me how calm *you* would be if someone had left those bruises on Sophia."

Sir Ross nodded with a short sigh. "Point taken." His dark brows drew together as he continued. "Obviously it is your right to deal with Radnor as you will, Sydney, and I would not presume to stop you, or to interfere. But you should be aware that I intend to approach him myself and make it clear that Charlotte is under my protection as well as yours. The fact that Radnor would dare accost a member of my family is an untenable outrage."

Lottie was touched by his concern. She had never imagined that she would have two such powerful men to defend her from Lord Radnor—not only her husband but her brother-in-law as well. "Thank you, Sir Ross."

"No one would blame you if you wished to go home now," he told her. "As for the speech I had planned to give this evening, other arrangements can be made—"

"I'm not going anywhere," Lottie said steadily. "And if you do not give your speech tonight, Sir Ross, I vow I will do it in your stead."

He smiled suddenly. "All right, then. I would hate to gainsay your wishes." He sent Nick a questioning look. "Will you return to the ballroom soon?"

Nick's mouth twisted. "If Lottie wishes it."

"Yes," she said decisively. Despite the pain in her wrist, she felt ready to confront the devil himself, if need be. She saw the glances the two men exchanged as they silently agreed to discuss the problem of Radnor at a more appropriate time.

Sir Ross left them in private once more, and Lottie

stood resolutely. Nick was at her side immediately, his hands framing her waist as if he feared she would topple over. Lottie smiled at his overprotectiveness. "I am fine now," she told him. "Truly."

She waited for the familiar glimmer of wry humor to appear in Nick's eyes, for him to return to his usual insouciant self, but he remained tense, his gaze searching her face with strange gravity. He looked as though he wanted to wrap her in cotton wool and carry her far away from here.

"You're staying by my side for the rest of the evening," he told her.

Lottie tilted her head back to smile at him. "That might be wise, as the brandy seems to have gone to my head."

Warmth kindled in his eyes, and one of his hands slipped upward to cradle the shape of her breast. "Do you feel dizzy?"

She relaxed into the cupping pressure of his fingers, his touch releasing a glow of sensuality from her susceptible flesh. The pain in her wrist was nearly forgotten, her nerves tingling wildly as his thumb teased her nipple into a thrusting point. "Only when you touch me like that."

Finishing the tantalizing caress with a gentle rotation of his palm, Nick returned his hand to safer territory. "I want this damned evening to be done with," he said. "Come . . . the sooner we go out there, the sooner Cannon can make his bloody speech."

Extending her bare hand, Lottie steeled herself

not to flinch as he eased the tight-fitting glove over her swollen wrist. By the time he was finished, Lottie was white-faced, and Nick was sweating profusely, as if the pain had been his rather than hers. "Damn Radnor," he said raspily, going to pour her another brandy. "I'm going to tear his throat out."

"I know something that would hurt him far more than that." Carefully Lottie raised a folded handkerchief to blot his damp brow.

"Oh?" His brows arched in sardonic inquiry.

Her fingers closed around the handkerchief, compressing it into a ball. She paused for a long moment before replying, while a wave of hope rose in her throat and nearly threatened to choke her. Taking the brandy from him, she took a bracing swallow. "We could try to be happy together," she said. "That is something he could never understand . . . something he'll never have."

She could not bring herself to look at him, afraid that she might see mockery or rejection in his eyes. But her heart slammed heavily in her chest as she felt his mouth drift along the top of her head, his lips playing with white rose petals as they fluttered against the pinned-up silk of her braid.

"We could try," he agreed softly.

After the two glasses of brandy, Lottie's head was swimming pleasantly, and she was grateful for Nick's steady guidance as they returned to the ballroom. The hardness and strength of his arm fasci-

nated her. No matter how heavily she leaned on
him, he took her weight easily. He was a strong
man . . . but until tonight, she had not suspected
that he was capable of offering her such tender comfort. Somehow she did not think that he had suspected it of himself, either. Their reactions had been
unthinking—hers, to turn to him, and his, to engulf
her in reassurance.

They walked into the ballroom and approached
Sir Ross. Ascending a moveable step to become easily visible to the huge crowd in the ballroom, Sir
Ross signaled the musicians to stop playing, and
asked for the guests' collective attention. He possessed the kind of elegant, innately authoritative
voice that any politician would have envied. An ex-
pectant hush fell over the ballroom, while more
guests poured in from the outside circuits, and a virtual army of servants moved rapidly through the assemblage with trays of champagne.

Sir Ross began the speech with a reference to his
magisterial career and the satisfaction it had always
given him to see that certain wrongs were put right.
He followed with a string of approving remarks
about the inviolable traditions and obligations of
hereditary peerage. The remarks obviously gratified
the gathering, which was liberally salted with vis-
counts, earls, marquesses, and dukes.

"I was under the impression that Sir Ross was not
a great supporter of hereditary principle," Lottie
whispered to Nick.

He smiled grimly. "My brother-in-law can be quite a showman when he wishes. And he knows that reminding them of their strict adherence to tradition will help them to swallow the idea of accepting me as a peer."

Sir Ross went on to describe an unnamed gentleman who had been deprived for far too long of a title that was rightfully his. A man who was in the direct line of descent of a distinguished family, and who in the past few years had devoted himself entirely to public service.

"Therefore," Sir Ross concluded, "I am grateful for the rare privilege of announcing Lord Sydney's long overdue reclamation of his title, and the seat in the Lords that accompanies it. And I have every expectation that he will continue to serve the country and queen in the role that is his by birth." Raising a glass in the air, he said, "Let us toast Mr. Nick Gentry—the man who shall be known to us from now on as John, Viscount Sydney."

A ripple of amazement went through the crowd. Although most of them had already known what Sir Ross would announce, it was startling to hear the words spoken aloud.

"To Lord Sydney," came hundreds of obedient echoes, followed by as many cheers.

"And to Lady Sydney," Sir Ross prompted, drawing another enthusiastic response to which Lottie curtsied in gracious recognition.

Rising, Lottie touched Nick's arm. "Perhaps you should offer a toast to Sir Ross," she suggested.

He gave her a speaking glance but complied, lifting his glass toward his brother-in-law. "To Sir Ross," he said in a resonant voice, "without whose efforts I would not be here tonight."

The crowd responded with a round of hurrahs, while Sir Ross grinned suddenly, aware that Nick's carefully worded toast did not include the barest hint of gratitude.

Toasts to the queen, the country, and the peerage itself ensued, and then the orchestra filled the room with buoyant melody. Sir Ross came to claim Lottie for a waltz, while Nick went to dance with Sophia, who wore an irrepressible smile as she sailed into his arms.

Beholding the pair, one so fair, one so dark, and yet both so similar in their striking attractiveness, Lottie smiled. She turned to Sir Ross and carefully rested her sore hand on his shoulder as they began to waltz. As might have been expected, he was an excellent dancer, self-assured and easy to follow.

Feeling a mixture of liking and gratitude, Lottie studied his severely handsome face. "You've done this to save him, haven't you?" she asked.

"I don't know that it will," Sir Ross said quietly.

The words sent a fearful pang through her. Did he mean that he still believed Nick was in some kind of peril? But Nick was no longer a Bow Street runner— he had been removed from the hazards that his profession had entailed. He was safe now . . . unless Sir Ross was implying that the greatest danger to Nick came from somewhere inside himself.

* * *

In the days following the public revelation of Nick's identity, the house on Betterton was under siege from callers. Mrs. Trench spoke to everyone from Nick's old underworld cohorts to representatives of the queen. Cards and invitations were brought to the front door until the silver tray on the entrance hall table was laden with a mountain of paper. Periodicals dubbed him "the reluctant viscount," recounting his heroism as a former Bow Street runner. As reporters followed the lead that Sir Ross had established, Nick was generally depicted as a selfless champion of the public who would have modestly preferred to serve his common man rather than accept his long-dormant title. To Lottie's amusement, Nick was outraged by his new public image, for no one seemed to regard him as dangerous any longer. Strangers approached him eagerly, no longer intimidated by his air of subtle menace. For a man who was so intensely private, it was nearly intolerable.

"Before long, their interest in you will fade," Lottie said in consolation after Nick had to push through an admiring throng to reach his own front door.

Harried and scowling, Nick shed his coat and flopped onto the parlor settee, his long legs spread carelessly. "It won't be soon enough." He glared at the ceiling. "This place is too damned accessible. We need a house with a private drive and a tall fence."

"We have received more than a few invitations to visit friends in the country." Lottie came beside him and sank to the carpeted floor, the skirts of her printed muslin skirts billowing around her. Their faces were nearly level as Nick reclined on the arm of the low-backed settee. "Even one from Westcliff, asking if we would stay a fortnight or so at Stony Cross Park."

Nick's face darkened. "No doubt the earl wants to assure himself that you're not being maltreated by your husband from hell."

Lottie couldn't help laughing. "You must admit that you were not at your most charming then."

Nick caught at her fingers as she reached over to loosen his necktie. "I wanted you too badly to bother with charm." The pad of his thumb stroked over the smooth tips of her fingernails.

"You implied that I was interchangeable with any other woman," she chided.

"In the past I learned that the best way to get something I wanted was to pretend that I didn't want it."

Lottie shook her head, perplexed. "That makes no sense at all."

Smiling, Nick released her hand and toyed with the lace edge of her scooped neckline. "It worked," he pointed out.

With their faces close together and his vivid blue eyes staring into hers, Lottie felt a blush climbing her face. "You were very wicked that night."

His fingertip eased into the shallow valley between her breasts. "Not nearly as wicked as I wanted to be . . ."

The sound of the front door being soundly

rapped echoed through the entrance hall and drifted into the parlor. Withdrawing his hand, Nick listened as Mrs. Trench went to answer the door, telling the visitor that neither Lord Sydney nor his wife was receiving callers.

The reminder of their beleaguered privacy caused Nick to scowl. "That does it. I want to get out of London."

"Whom shall we visit? Lord Westcliff would be perfectly—"

"No."

"All right, then," Lottie continued, unruffled. "The Cannons are in residence at Silverhill—"

"God, no. I'm not spending a fortnight under the same roof as my brother-in-law."

"We could go to Worcestershire," Lottie suggested. "Sophia says that the restoration of the Sydney estate is nearly complete. She has made no secret of the fact that she wants you to view the results of her efforts."

He shook his head instantly. "I have no desire to see that accursed place."

"Your sister has gone to great effort—you wouldn't want to hurt her feelings, would you?"

"No one asked her to do all that. Sophia took it upon herself, and I'll be damned if I have to shower her with gratitude for it."

"I've heard that Worcestershire is quite beautiful." Lottie let a wistful note enter her voice. "The air would be so much nicer there—London in summer is dreadful. And someday I would like to see the place where you were born. If you do not wish to go now, I understand, but—"

"There are no servants," he pointed out triumphantly.

"We could travel with a skeleton staff. Wouldn't it be pleasant to stay in the country at our own home, rather than visit someone else? Just for a fortnight?"

Nick was silent, his eyes narrowing. Lottie sensed the conflict in him, the desire to please her warring with his fierce reluctance to return to the place he had left all those years ago. To confront those memories and recall the pain of being orphaned so suddenly would not be pleasant for him.

Lottie lowered her gaze before he could see the compassion that he would surely misread. "I will tell Sophia that we will accept her invitation some other time. She will understand—"

"I'll go," he said brusquely.

Lottie looked at him in surprise. He was visibly tense, clad in invisible armor. "It isn't necessary," she said. "We'll go somewhere else, if you prefer."

He shook his head, his mouth twisting sardonically. "First you want to stay in Worcestershire, then you don't. Damn, but women are perverse."

"I'm not being perverse," she protested. "It's just that I don't want you to go and then be vexed with me for the entire stay."

"I'm not vexed. Men don't get 'vexed.' "

"Annoyed? Exasperated? Irked?" She offered him a tender smile, wishing that she could protect him from nightmares and memories and the demons inside himself.

Nick began to reply, but as he stared at her, he seemed to forget what word he would have chosen. Reaching for her, he suddenly checked the movement. As Lottie watched him, he stood from the settee and left the parlor with startling swiftness.

The journey to Worcestershire would normally last a full day, long enough that most travelers of reasonable means would elect to travel for part of one day, stay overnight at a tavern, and arrive later in the morning. However, Nick insisted that they make the trip virtually without stopping, except to change horses and obtain a few refreshments.

Although Lottie tried to take the arrangement in stride, she found it difficult to maintain a cheerful facade. The carriage ride was arduous, the roads were of uneven quality, and the constant rattling and swaying of the vehicle made her slightly nauseous. As Nick saw her discomfort, his expression became grim and resolute, and the atmosphere disintegrated into silence.

A skeleton staff had been sent the day before their arrival, to stock the kitchen and ready the rooms. As had been previously agreed, the Cannons would visit the estate the following morning. Conveniently, Sir Ross's country seat at Silverhill was only an hour away.

The last faint glow of the setting sun was retreating from the sky by the time the carriage reached

Worcestershire. From what Lottie could see, the
county was fertile and prosperous. Rich green
meadows and tidily groomed farms covered the
level earth, occasionally giving way to verdant hills
covered with fat white sheep. The webbing of canals
that spread from the rivers graced the area with easy
routes for trade and commerce. Any average visitor
to Worcestershire would surely react to the scenery
with pleasure. However, Nick became increasingly
morose, emanating sullen reluctance from every
pore with each turn of the wheels that brought them
closer to the Sydney lands.

At last they turned onto a long, narrow drive that
extended for a mile before a stately house came into
view. Light from the outside lamps cast a warm
glow over the entranceway and caused the front
windows to glitter like black diamonds. Eagerly Lottie pushed aside the curtains at the carriage windows to obtain a better view.

"It's lovely," she said, her heart beating fast with
excitement. "Just as Sophia described." The large
Palladian-style house was handsome, if unexcep-
tional, the combination of red brick, white columns,
and precise pediments designed with tidy symme-
try. Lottie loved it at first sight.

The carriage stopped before the entranceway.
Nick was expressionless as he descended from the
vehicle and helped Lottie down. They climbed the
steps to the double doors, and Mrs. Trench wel-
comed them into a large, oval-shaped hall floored
with gleaming rose-colored marble.

"Mrs. Trench," Lottie said warmly, "how are you?"

"Very well, my lady. And you?"

"Tired, but relieved to be here at last. Have you encountered any difficulties with the house so far?"

"No, my lady, but there is much to be done. A single day was scarcely sufficient to prepare things . . ."

"That is all right," Lottie said with a smile. "After the long journey, Lord Sydney and I will require nothing more than a clean place to sleep."

"The bedrooms are in order, my lady. Shall I show you upstairs at once, or will you want some supper . . ." The housekeeper's voice trailed away as she glanced at Nick.

Following her gaze, Lottie saw that her husband was staring at the main hall of the house as if transfixed. He seemed to be watching a play that no one else could see, his gaze following invisible actors as they crossed the stage to speak their lines. His face was flushed, as if from fever. Wordlessly he wandered through the hall as if he were alone, exploring with the hesitancy of a lost young boy.

Lottie did not know how to help him. One of the hardest things she'd ever have to do was to summon a casual tone as she replied to the housekeeper, but somehow she managed it.

"No, thank you, Mrs. Trench. I don't believe that we will require supper. Perhaps you will have some water and a bottle of wine sent to our room. And have the maids take out just a few things for tonight.

They can unpack the rest of it tomorrow. In the meanwhile, Lord Sydney and I will have a look around."

"Yes, my lady. I will see that your personal articles are set out immediately." The housekeeper strode away, calling out instructions to a pair of maids, who rushed quickly through the hall.

As the overhead chandelier had been left unlit, the shadowy atmosphere was relieved by only two lamps. Following her husband, Lottie approached the archway at one end of the hall, which opened to a portrait gallery. The air was laced with the crisp scents of new wool carpeting and fresh paint.

Lottie studied Nick's profile as he gazed at the conspicuously bare walls of the gallery. She guessed that he was remembering the paintings that had once occupied the empty spaces. "It seems we'll have to acquire some artwork," she remarked.

"They were all sold to pay off my father's debts."

Moving closer, Lottie pressed her cheek against the broadcloth of his coat, where the edge of his shoulder flowed into the hard swell of his muscular arm. "Will you show me the house?"

Nick was silent for a long moment. When he glanced into her upturned face, his eyes were bleak with the knowledge that there was nothing left of the boy who had once lived here. "Not tonight. I need to see it alone."

"I understand," Lottie said, slipping her hand into his. "I am quite fatigued. Certainly I would prefer to tour the house tomorrow morning, in the daylight."

His fingers returned the pressure with a barely discernable squeeze, and then he let go. "I'll take you upstairs."

She pressed her lips into the shape of a smile. "No need. I'll have Mrs. Trench or one of the servants accompany me."

A clock from somewhere in the house chimed half past midnight by the time Nick finally entered the bedroom. Unable to sleep despite her exhaustion, Lottie had retrieved a novel from one of her valises and had stayed up reading until the book was half finished. The bedroom was a cozy haven, the bed richly appareled with an embroidered silk counterpane and matching hangings, the walls painted in a soft shade of green. Becoming absorbed in the story, Lottie read until she heard the creak of a floorboard.

Seeing Nick in the doorway, Lottie set the novel on the bedside table. Patiently she waited for him to speak, wondering how many memories had been stirred by his walk through the house, how many silent ghosts had traversed his path.

"You should sleep," he said eventually.

"So should you." Lottie turned back the covers. After an extended pause, she asked, "Will you come to bed with me?"

His gaze slid over her, lingering on the ruffled front of her nightrail, the kind of prim, high-necked gown that never failed to arouse him. He looked so alone, so disenchanted . . . very much the way he had appeared when they had first met.

"Not tonight," he said for the second time that evening.

Their gazes caught and held. Lottie knew that she would be wise to maintain a facade of relaxed unconcern. To be patient with him. Her demands, her frustrations, would only drive him away.

But to her horror, she heard herself say baldly, "Stay."

They both knew that she was not asking for a few minutes, or a few hours. She wanted the entire night.

"You know I can't do that," came his soft reply.

"You won't harm me. I'm not afraid of your nightmares." Lottie sat up, staring at his still face. Suddenly she could not stem a flood of reckless words, her voice becoming raw with emotion. "I want you to stay with me. I want to be close to you. Tell me what I should do or say to make that happen. Tell me, please, because I can't seem to stop myself from wanting more than you're willing to give."

"You don't know what you're asking for."

"I promise you that I would never—"

"I'm not asking for reassurances or promises," he said harshly. "I'm stating a fact. There is a part of me that you don't want to know."

"In the past you've asked me to trust you. In return I ask you to trust me now. Tell me what happened to give you such nightmares. Tell me what haunts you so."

"No, Lottie." But instead of leaving, Nick remained in the room, as if his feet would not obey the dictates of his brain.

Suddenly Lottie understood the extent of his tortured longing to confide in her, and his equally potent belief that she would reject him once he did. He had begun to sweat heavily, his skin gleaming like wet bronze. A few strands of sable hair adhered to the moist surface of his forehead. Her longing to touch him was untenable, but somehow she remained where she was.

"I won't turn away from you," she said steadily. "No matter what it is. It happened on the prison hulk, didn't it? It has to do with the real Nick Gentry. Did you kill him, so that you could take his place? Is that what torments you?"

She saw from the way Nick flinched that she had struck close to the truth. The crack in his defenses widened, and he shook his head, trying to navigate past the breach. Failing, he gave her a glance filled with equal parts of rebuke and desperation. "It didn't happen that way."

Lottie refused to look away from him. "Then how?"

The lines of his body changed, relaxing into a sort of wretched resignation. He leaned one shoulder against the wall, facing partially away from her, his gaze arrowing to some distant point on the floor.

"I was sent to the hulk because I was responsible for a man's death. I was fourteen at the time. I had joined a group of highwaymen, and an old man died when we robbed his carriage. Soon afterward we were all tried and convicted. I was too ashamed to tell anyone who I was—I simply gave my name as John Sydney. The other four in the gang were hanged in short order, but because of my age, the magistrate handed me a lesser sentence. Ten months on the *Scarborough*."

"Sir Ross was the magistrate who sentenced you," Lottie murmured, remembering what Sophia had told her.

A bitter smile twisted Nick's mouth. "Little did either of us know that we would someday be brothers-in-law." He slouched harder against the wall. "As soon as I set foot on the hulk, I knew that I wasn't going to last a month there. A quick hanging would have been far more merciful. Duncombe's Academy, they called the ship, Duncombe being the officer in command. Half of his prisoners had just been cleared out by a round of gaol fever. They were the lucky ones.

"The hulk was smaller than the others anchored just offshore. It was fitted for one hundred prisoners, but they crammed half again that amount into one large area belowdeck. The ceiling was so low that I couldn't stand fully upright. Prisoners slept on the bare floor or on a platform built on either side of the deck. Each man was allowed to have sleeping space that was six feet long, twenty inches wide. We were double-ironed much of the time, and the constant rattling of chains was almost more than I could stand.

"The smell was the worst of it, though. We were

seldom allowed to wash—there was always a short-age of soap, and we had to rinse with seawater. And no through ventilation, just a row of portholes left open on the seaward side. As a result, the reek was so powerful that it would overcome the guards who first opened the hatches in the mornings—once I even saw one of them faint from it. During the time that we were locked down from early evening until the hatches were opened at daybreak, prisoners were left entirely to themselves, with no guards or officers to observe them."

"What did the prisoners do then?" Lottie asked.

His lips parted in a feral grin that made her shiver. "Gambled, fought, made escape plans, and bug-gered each other."

"What does that word mean?"

Nick shot her a swift glance, seeming startled by the question. "It means rape."

Lottie shook her head in bewilderment. "But a man can't be raped."

"I assure you," Nick said sardonically, "he can. And it was something I had a rather strong desire to avoid. Unfortunately boys of my age—fourteen, fifteen—were the most likely victims. The reason I stayed safe for a time was because I had made friends with another boy who was a bit older and a damned sight more hard-bitten than I."

"Nick Gentry?"

"Yes. He watched over me when I slept, taught me ways to defend myself . . . he made me eat to stay alive, even when the food was so foul that I could barely swallow it. Talking with him kept my mind occupied during the days when I thought I would go insane from having nothing to do. I wouldn't have lived without him, and I knew it. I was terrified of the day he would leave the hulk. Six months after I'd boarded the *Scarborough*, Gentry told me that he was due to be released in a week." The look on his face caused Lottie's insides to tighten into cold knots. "Only one week left, after surviving two years in that hellhole. I should have been glad for him. I wasn't. All I could think about was my own safety, which wasn't going to last five minutes after he left."

He stopped, sliding deeper into the memories.

"What happened?" Lottie asked quietly. "Tell me."

His face went blank. His soul had clenched hard around the secrets, refusing to release them. A strange, cold smile flickered on his lips as he spoke with utter self-contempt. "I can't."

Lottie stiffened her legs to keep from leaping out of bed and rushing to him. The heat of unshed tears filled her eyes as she stared at his dark, shadowed form. "How did Gentry die?" she asked.

His throat worked, and he shook his head.

Faced with his silent struggle, Lottie sought for some way to tip the balance. "Don't be afraid," she whispered. "I'll stay with you no matter what."

Averting his face, he squinted fiercely, as if he had just been exposed to brilliant light after spending too long in the dark. "One night I was attacked by one of the prisoners. His name was Styles. He dragged me off the platform while I was sleeping and pinned me to the floor. I fought like hell, but he was twice my size, and no one was going to interfere. They were all afraid of him. I called out to Gentry, to pull the bastard off of me before he could—" Breaking off, he made a strange sound, a shaky laugh that contained no trace of humor.

"And did he help you?" Lottie asked.

"Yes . . . the stupid bastard." His breath caught in a low sob. "He knew there was no point in doing a damn thing for me. If I wasn't buggered right then, I would be after he was released. I shouldn't have asked for his help, and he shouldn't have given it. But he drove Styles off, and . . ."

Another long silence passed. "Did Nick die during the fight?" Lottie made herself ask.

"Later that night. He'd made an enemy of Styles by helping me, and retribution wasn't long in coming. Just before morning, Styles strangled Nick in his sleep. By the time I realized what had happened, it was too late. I went to Nick . . . tried to make him wake up, to breathe. He wouldn't move. He turned cold in my arms." His jaw shook, and he cleared his throat roughly.

Lottie couldn't let it end there, without knowing the full story. "How did you switch places with Gentry?"

"Every morning the assistant medical officer and one of the guards came down to collect the bodies of the men who had died during the night, of disease, or starvation, or something they called 'depression of the spirits.' Those who hadn't finished dying were taken up to the forecastle. I pretended to be ill, which wasn't difficult at that point. They took us both up to the deck, and asked who I was, and if I knew the dead man's name. The guards knew hardly any of the prisoners—to them we were all the same. And I had changed clothes with his . . . his corpse, so they had little reason to doubt me when I told them I was Nick Gentry, and the dead boy was John Sydney. For the next few days I stayed in the forecastle, feigning illness so I wouldn't be sent back down to the prison deck. The other men who'd been brought there were too sick or weak to give a damn what I called myself."

"And soon you were released," Lottie said quietly, "in Gentry's place."

"He was buried in a mass grave near the docks, while I went free. And now his name is more real to me than my own."

Lottie was overwhelmed. No wonder he had wanted to keep Nick Gentry's name. In some way he must have felt that he could keep a part of him alive by retaining it. The name had been a talisman, a new beginning. She couldn't begin to understand the amount of shame he had attached to his true identity, believing that he was responsible for his friend's death. It wasn't his fault, of course. But even if she could make him admit the flaws in his reasoning, she could never expunge his guilt.

Lottie slipped out of bed, the thick-piled wool carpeting prickling beneath her bare soles. As she approached him, she was swamped in a sense of utter inadequacy. If she treated him with kindness, he would receive it as pity. If she said nothing, he would take it as a sign of scorn or disgust.

"Nick," she said softly, but he would not face her. She went to stand before him, listening to the broken pattern of his breathing. "You did nothing wrong in calling out for help. And he wanted to help you, as any true friend would. Neither of you did anything wrong."

He dragged his sleeve over his eyes and drew a shuddering breath. "I stole his life."

"No," she said urgently. "He wouldn't have wanted you to stay there—whom would it have served?" A hot trickle touched the corner of her lips, flavoring them with salt. How well she understood guilt, the self-hatred it caused, especially in the absence of forgiveness. And the person that Nick needed forgiveness from was dead. "He can't be here to absolve you," she said. "But I'm going to speak for him. If he could, he would tell you, 'You're forgiven. It's all right now. I'm at peace, and you should be as well. And it is long past time for you to forgive yourself.'"

"How do you know he would say that?"

"Because anyone who cared for you would. And he did care for you, or he wouldn't have risked his life to protect you." Stepping forward, Lottie put her arms around his rigid neck. "I care for you, too." She had to use her full weight to make him bend to her.

"I love you," she whispered. "Please don't turn me away." And she brought her mouth to his.

It took a long time for him to respond to the soft pressure of her lips. He made a faint sound in his throat, and slowly his shaking hands came to her face, holding her still while his mouth molded over hers. His cheeks were wet with sweat and tears, and his kiss was bruising in its fervor.

"Does it help to hear those words?" Lottie whispered when his mouth lifted.

"Yes," he said hoarsely.

"Then I'll say them whenever you need to hear them, until you begin to believe." She slid her hand behind his neck and tugged his head down for another kiss.

Nick startled her with his sudden wildness. Picking her up with frightening ease, he carried her to the bed and dropped her to the mattress. He tore his own clothes off, ripping plackets of buttons rather than take the time to unfasten them. Climbing over her swiftly, he straddled her and split the front of her gown with his hands. Dimly she realized that Nick's need to be inside her was so violent that he had lost all self-control. Kneeing her legs wide apart, he pushed the head of his sex against her, demanding entry. Her body was unprepared, her flesh dry and tight despite her willingness to receive him.

Sliding down her body, Nick took her with his mouth, his large hands gripping her hips and pressing them firmly to the bed as she arched upward in surprise. His tongue plunged into her, wetting and softening the tender flesh. Finding the delicate peak just above the vulnerable opening, he drew the flat of his tongue against it, over and over, until he caught the intimate scent of her desire. Levering his body upward, he mounted her again, and drove his hard organ inside her.

As soon as Nick entered her warm body, his blind ferocity seemed to drain away. He hung over her, his muscular arms braced on either side of her head, his chest moving in deep, irregular breaths. Lottie was pinned beneath him, her flesh throbbing around the thick shaft that impaled her.

His mouth came to hers again, this time gentle as he possessed her with long, teasing kisses, the tip of his tongue stroking the insides of her mouth. She had secretly cherished the memory of his other kisses, the sweetly fervent brushes of a stranger's lips . . . but this was so different, dark and heady and powerful. She ached for his touch, gasping with relief at the soft tugs of his fingers on her nipples. He used all his skill to arouse her, teasing her with shallow strokes that enticed rather than satisfied. Wanting more, Lottie tried to pull him closer. He resisted, maintaining the languid rhythm, hushing her with kisses when she protested. Suddenly he plunged inside her with one long drive. Bewildered, Lottie stared at his intent face. "What are you doing?" she asked faintly.

His mouth brushed over hers with kisses of soft fire. And as he possessed her, she gradually came to understand the pattern he was working within her . . . eight shallow thrusts, two deep . . . seven shallow, three deep . . . progressing until he finally gave her ten heavy, penetrating plunges. Lottie cried out with wrenching pleasure, her hips lifting against his sleek weight as she was filled with volatile sensation. When the burning delight had begun to fade, Nick altered their positions subtly, moving farther over her, nudging her knees wider, adjusting the angle of his sex. He thrust deeply, sealing their bodies together, and circled his hips in a slow, steady rhythm.

"I can't," Lottie said breathlessly, realizing what he wanted, knowing that it was impossible.

"Let me," Nick whispered, tireless and wickedly adept as he continued the gentle circling, using his body to pleasure her.

She was astonished by how quickly the heat rose again, her senses welcoming the patient stimulation, her sex turning slick and swollen as he moved inside her, over her, against her. "Oh . . . oh . . ." The sounds were torn from her throat as she reached another crest, her limbs jerking, her cheek pressed hard against his shoulder.

And then he began the entire cycle again. Nine shallow, one deep . . .

Lottie lost count of how many times he brought her to ecstasy, or how much time passed while he made love to her. He whispered in her ear . . . endearments . . . intimate praise . . . telling her how hard she made him . . . how sweet she felt around him . . . how much he wanted to satisfy her. He gave her more pleasure than it seemed possible to bear, until finally she begged him to stop, her body trembling with exhaustion.

Nick complied with reluctance, pushing deep inside one last time, releasing his pent-up desire with a shuddering groan. Compulsively he kissed her again, as he withdrew from her sated body. Lottie barely had the strength to lift her hand, but she caught at his arm and murmured thickly, "Will you stay?"

"Yes," she heard him say. "Yes."

Relieved and tired, she sank quickly into a fathomless sleep.

Chapter Thirteen

Sunlight streamed in through the windows, which Lottie had left open the night before to admit the cool air. She yawned and stretched, wincing uncomfortably at the strained muscles in her thighs and the unusual ache she felt in her—

Suddenly remembering the previous night, Lottie rolled over. A shiver of pleasure went through her as she saw Nick sleeping on his stomach beside her, his long muscular back gleaming in the rising light. His head was half-buried in a pillow, his lips slightly parted as he slumbered. The growth of a thick night-beard shadowed his jaw, lending a disreputable cast to his handsome face. Lottie had never experienced this kind of passionate interest in anyone or anything . . . this keen desire to know every detail of his mind, body, and soul . . . the pure delight of being in his presence.

Propping herself up on one elbow, Lottie realized that she'd never had the opportunity to view him at her leisure. The lines of his body were sleek and strong, his broad back tapering to a lean waist and hips, his flesh densely muscled yet smooth. She admired the solid curve of his buttocks, covered by the sheet that lay low on his hips.

And she wanted to see more of him. Glancing cautiously at his peaceful face, she reached down to the edge of the white linen and began to ease it away from his backside. Lower and lower . . .

With a swiftness that made her gasp, Nick reached out and seized her wrist. His eyes opened to study her drowsily, and a smile lit the depths of warm blue. When he spoke, his voice was sleep-roughened. "It's not fair to ogle a man while he's asleep."

"I wasn't ogling," Lottie said impishly. "Women don't ogle." She gave him a boldly appraising glance. "But I do like the way you look in the morning."

Releasing her, Nick shook his head with a snort of disbelief, scrubbing his fingers through his disheveled hair. He rolled to his side, revealing a chest covered with thick dark curls.

Tempted beyond her ability to resist, Lottie wriggled closer to him, until her breasts were pressed into the wealth of warm fur. "Did you ever spend the night with your friend?" she asked, entwining her legs with his.

"You mean with Gemma? God, no."

"Then I'm the first woman you've ever slept with," she said, pleased.

He touched her softly, his fingertips tracing the silken curve of her shoulder. "Yes."

Lottie made no protest as he rolled her to her back, his head lowering to her breasts. They were tender and sensitive from his attentions, and she gasped as she felt his hot, gentle tongue swirling over the rosy nipple. Relaxing beneath him, she luxuriated in the tangle of sunshine and white linen, her arms curving around his dark head . . .

"Nick, we can't," she said suddenly. Her gaze shot to the clock on the mantel. "Good Lord, we're late!"

"Late for what?" he asked in a muffled voice, resisting as she attempted to push his heavy body away.

"Sophia and Sir Ross promised to be here at ten o'clock. There's barely enough time to bathe and dress—oh, do get off me, I must hurry!"

With a surly frown, Nick allowed her to squirm out from beneath him. "I want to stay in bed."

"We can't. We're going to tour the house with Sophia and Sir Ross, and you're going to make yourself agreeable and praise your sister for the splendid job she's done, and thank them both for their generosity. And then we'll entertain them for an early supper, after which they will return to Silverhill."

Nick lounged on his side as he watched her descend from the bed. "That's going to be at least twelve hours from now. I'm not going to be able to keep my hands off of you for that long."

"Then you'll have to devise some means of—" Lottie broke off and inhaled sharply as she stood upright.

"What is it?" he asked alertly.

Lottie blushed from her head to her toes. "I'm sore. In . . . in places that I'm not usually sore."

Nick understood immediately. An abashed grin touched his lips, and he hung his head in an unconvincing effort at penitence. "I'm sorry. An aftereffect of Tantric lovemaking."

"Is that what it was?" Lottie hobbled to a chair near the hearth, where she had left her robe. Hastily she wrapped it around herself.

"An ancient Indian art form," he explained. "Ritualized methods designed to prolong intercourse."

Lottie's high color persisted as she recalled the things he had done to her in the night. "Well, it certainly was prolonged."

"Not really. Tantric experts often have sexual relations for nine or ten hours at a time."

She gave him an appalled glance. "Could you do that, if you wished?"

Standing from the bed, Nick walked over to her, completely unself-conscious in his nakedness. He took her into his arms and nuzzled her soft blond hair, playing with the loose braid that hung down her back. "With you, I wouldn't mind trying," he said, smiling against her temple.

"No, thank you. I can barely walk as it is." She searched through the tantalizing hair on his chest, finding the point of his nipple. "I'm afraid I'm not going to encourage any of your Tantric practices."

"That's all right," he replied amiably. "There are other things we can do." His voice lowered seductively. "I haven't begun to show you the things I know."

"I was afraid of that," she said, and he laughed.

His big hand cupped around the back of her head, tilting it until her face was lifted to his. Lottie was amazed by the expression in his eyes, the heat that smoldered in the fathomless blue wells. His mouth lowered to hers slowly, as if he thought she might twist away. She realized that he feared her willingness to kiss him might have evaporated with the morning light. Holding still for him, she let her eyes close as she felt the velvety warmth of his mouth cover hers.

Nick hardly recognized himself in the days that followed. His confession to Lottie, and her astonishing reaction to it, had changed everything. She should have been repulsed by the things he had told her, and instead she had embraced him, accepted him, without hesitation. He didn't understand why. He watched her carefully for signs of regret, thinking that she would come to her senses. But the expected rejection did not come. Lottie opened herself to him in every way, sexually and emotionally. Her trust terrified him. His own need for her terrified him. God, to realize the extent to which his independence had been compromised . . .

However, he could not seem to stop it from happening.

Faced with this inevitability, Nick had no choice but to give in to it. And day after day, he let it drift farther inside him—this precarious, giddy warmth that he could only identify as happiness. He was no longer bedeviled and driven, no longer hungry for things he couldn't have. For the first time in his life, he was at peace. Even his nightmares seemed to have retreated. He slept more deeply than he ever had in his life, and if his dreams began to trouble him, he awakened to find Lottie's small body snuggled against his, her silken hair trailing over his arm. He had never been this idle . . . lazing in bed, making love to his wife, taking long rides or walks with her, even going on a damned picnic and enjoying himself despite the feeling that he should be in London with Morgan and the runners, doing something useful.

It began to bother him, though . . . the old familiar urge to prowl the rookeries, the addictive excitement of pursuit and capture. He did not know how to be a viscount, and he felt vaguely out of place here, at his own childhood home. No magical change had occurred with the arrival of the writ of summons. Blue blood or no, he was a product of the streets.

"I've been thinking about what you need," Lottie told him one morning as they strode away from the house along a paved rose walk that overlooked a long, formal pool adorned with water lilies. Beyond the pool, a broad curving lawn led to a chain of artificial lakes bordered by a forest of cedar and elm. Nick had taken her on a shortcut he had used often as a boy, circumventing the lawn by jumping over a short stone wall and heading straight into the forest.

Smiling at Lottie's statement, Nick lifted his arms to help her descend from the wall. Although she could easily have jumped by herself, she accepted his help, resting her hands on his shoulders as he took hold of her waist.

"What is it that I need?" he asked, letting her slide down his front until her feet touched the ground.

"A cause."

"A what?"

"Something worthwhile for you to pursue. Something not related to estate management."

Nick let his gaze wander blatantly over Lottie's small, trim form, clad in a peach-colored walking-dress trimmed with chocolate brown. "I already have that," he said and settled his mouth over hers. He felt her smile before she accommodated the warm pressure of his mouth, opening for the gentle exploration of his tongue.

"I mean something that would keep you busy in your spare time," she said breathlessly when he ended the kiss.

He slid his hand along the side of her uncorseted waist. "So do I."

Lottie pulled away from him with a laugh, her flat ankle boots tromping on the carpet of leaves as she strode into the forest. Thin shafts of sunlight filtered through the ancient canopy of foliage-laden branches overhead, catching the pale gleam of her pinned-up hair and making it flash like silver. "Sir Ross has his interest in judicial reform," she pointed out, "as well as his concerns for the rights of women and children. If you were to take up some pursuit that would benefit the public in some manner, you could put your seat in the Lords to some good use—"

"Wait," he said warily, following her through the maze of trees. "If you're going to start comparing me to my saintly brother-in-law—"

"I merely used him as an example, not as a basis for comparison." Stopping beside a huge elm, she ran her hand along the deep furrows of mottled gray bark. "The point is, you have spent the past few years of your life serving the public and helping people, and for you to stop so suddenly—"

"I haven't been helping people," Nick interrupted, affronted. "I've been rubbing elbows with felons and whores, and chasing fugitives from Tyburn to East Wapping."

Lottie gave him a wry stare, her dark brown eyes filled with an inexplicable tenderness. "And in doing so, you've made London safer, and brought justice to those who deserved it. For heaven's sake, why are you offended at the implication that you may have actually done something good now and then?"

"I don't want to be portrayed as something I'm not," Nick said curtly.

"I see you exactly for what you are," she informed him, "and I would be the last to call you a saint."

"Good."

"On the other hand . . . your work as a runner *did* serve to benefit other people, whether you choose to admit it or not. Therefore, you will now need to find some meaningful activity to occupy your time." Casually Lottie walked on, stepping over a fallen branch.

"You want me to turn into a reformist?" he asked in disgust, following her.

Deliberately ignoring his sudden bad humor, Lottie continued through the trees until the forest opened to reveal a small, glittering lake. "There must be *some* issue that concerns you. Something you want to fight for. What about improving the horrid condition of the Thames. . . . or the workhouses in which the elderly, children, and the insane are all mixed together with no one to tend them . . ."

"Next you'll want me to make speeches in Parliament and give charity balls." He scowled at the thought.

Lottie continued listing problems that needed to be addressed. "Insufficient public education, the cruelty of blood sports, the plight of orphans, or discharged prisoners—"

"You've made your point," Nick interrupted, coming to stand beside her.

"What about prison reform? There's a subject that you can address with some conviction."

Nick froze, unable to believe that Lottie had dared

to say it to him. He kept that part of his past closed in some distant part of his mind. For her to mention it in such a relaxed manner was like an attack. A betrayal. But as he stared into her upturned face and struggled to reply, he saw the absolute gentleness in her expression. *Be comfortable with me*, the soft light in her eyes entreated. *Let me share some of your burden.*

He tore his gaze away, the flare of defensive rage melting into alarm. Holy hell, he wanted to believe in her. To give her the last part of his soul that the world had not yet stained and shredded and ruined. But how could he let himself be that vulnerable?

"I'll think about it," he heard himself say raspily.

Lottie smiled, reaching out to stroke his chest. "I'm afraid that if you don't apply yourself to a worthy cause, you'll go mad from inactivity. You're not a man to spend all of your time pursuing idle amusements. And now that you are no longer working at Bow Street . . ." She paused, seeming troubled by something she saw in his eyes. "You miss it, don't you?"

"No," he said lightly.

"The truth," she insisted with a frown.

Catching her hand in his, Nick drew her along the path beside the lake.

"I do miss it," he admitted. "I've been a thief-taker for too long. I like the challenge of it. I like the feeling of outwitting those bastards on the streets. I know how they think. Each time I hunt down an escaped murderer, or some filthy rapist, and throw him into the Bow Street strongroom, it gives me a satisfaction like nothing else. I . . ." He paused, searching for the right words. "I've won the game."

"Game?" Lottie repeated carefully. "Is that how you think of it?"

"All the runners do. You have to, if you're going to outfox your opponent. You need to stay detached, otherwise you'll get distracted."

"It must have been quite difficult at times, to maintain your detachment."

"Never," he assured her. "It's always been easy for me to shut away my feelings."

"I see."

But while Lottie seemed to understand what he was telling her, there was a barely perceptible edge of skepticism in her tone. As if she doubted that he still had the ability to remain completely emotionless. Troubled and annoyed, Nick fell silent as they continued around the lake. And he told himself that he could hardly wait to leave the idyllic scenery of Worcestershire and return to London.

Chapter Fourteen

"You're going to Bow Street today, aren't you?" Lottie asked, cradling a cup of tea in her hands as she watched Nick devour a large plate of eggs, fruit, and currant bread.

Nick glanced at her with a deliberately bland smile. "Why do you ask?" Since they had returned from Worcestershire three days earlier, he had met with bankers, hired an estate agent, visited his tailor, and spent an afternoon at Tom's coffeehouse with friends. For all Lottie knew, today would proceed in much the same manner—but somehow her intuition had led her to suspect otherwise.

"Because you have a certain look in your eyes whenever you go to meet Sir Grant or anyone else at Bow Street."

Nick could not help grinning at his wife's suspicious expression. She had the instincts and the tenacity of a rat terrier—and he considered that a compliment, though she would probably not. "As it happens, I'm not going to Bow Street," he said mildly. It was the truth, although only in the most technical sense. "I'm just going to visit a friend. Eddie Sayer. I've told you about him before, remember?"

"Yes, he's one of the runners." Lottie's eyes narrowed above the delicate edge of her teacup. "What are the two of you planning? You're not going to do something dangerous, are you?"

Her voice contained an edge of apprehension, and her gaze swept over him with a possessive concern that made his heart knock hard in his chest. Nick struggled to understand what those signs meant. It almost seemed as if she was worried for him, that his safety mattered to her. She had never looked at him that way before, and he was not certain how to react.

Carefully he reached out and pulled her from the chair, settling her on his lap. "Nothing dangerous at all," he said against the softness of her cheek. Intoxicated by the taste of her skin, he worked his way to her ear and touched the delicate lobe with the tip of his tongue. "I would hardly risk coming home to you in less than full working order."

Lottie squirmed in his lap, and the movement drew a surge of heat to his loins. "Where are you and Mr. Sayer going to meet?" she persisted.

Ignoring the question, Nick ran his hand over the bodice of her morning dress, made of a soft white fabric printed with tiny flowers and leaves. The scooped neckline revealed the tender line of her throat, presenting a temptation too potent to resist. Lowering his mouth to her neck, he kissed her sweet, downy skin, while his hand stole beneath the rustling layers of her skirts.

"You're not going to distract me that way," Lottie told him, but he heard the hitch of her breath when he found the smooth reach of her thigh. He made a discovery that sent a wash of sexual interest through his body, his cock rising vigorously against the shape of her bottom.

"You're not wearing drawers," he murmured, his hand wandering avidly over her bare limbs.

"It's too hot today," she said breathlessly, wiggling to evade him, pushing ineffectually at the mound of his hand beneath her dress. "I most certainly did *not* discard them for your benefit, and . . . Nick, stop that. The maid is going to come in at any moment."

"Then I'll have to be fast."

"You're *never* fast. Nick . . . oh . . ."

Her body curled against his as he reached the patch of hair between her thighs, the sweet cleft already rich with moisture as her well-tutored body responded to his touch. "I'm going to do this to you next week at the Markenfields' ball," he said softly, running his thumb along the humid seam of her sex. "I'm going to take you to some private corner . . . and pull up the front of your dress, and stroke and tease you until you come."

"No," she protested faintly, her eyes closing as she felt his long middle finger slide inside her.

"Oh, yes." Nick withdrew his wet finger and ruthlessly tickled the softly straining crest until he felt her body tensing rhythmically in his lap. "I'll keep you quiet with my mouth," he whispered. "And I'll be kissing you when you climax with my fingers inside you . . . like this . . ." He thrust his two middle fingers inside the warm, pulsing channel and covered her lips with his as she moaned and shuddered violently.

When he had siphoned the last few shivers of pleasure from her body, Nick lifted his mouth and smiled smugly into her flushed face. "Was that fast enough for you?"

The brief interlude at the breakfast table left Nick's senses pleasantly awakened and his mind filled with agreeable thoughts about what would happen when he returned home later in the day. In good spirits, he hired a hackney to convey him to his meeting place with Eddie Sayer. It would not have been wise to take a good horse or a private carriage to the Blood Bowl Tavern, a favorite criminal haunt, or "bastard sanctuary."

Nick had long been familiar with the Blood Bowl, as it was part of the area around Fleet Ditch where he had once owned a flash house. Fleet Ditch, London's main sewer, cut through a region of massive criminal activity. It was arguably the heart of the underworld, situated amidst four prisons including Newgate, the Fleet, and Bridewell.

For years Nick had known no other home. At the height of his career as a crime lord, Nick had rented an elegant office in town to meet with upper-class clients and bank representatives who were understandably reluctant to go to Fleet Ditch. However, he had spent the majority of his time in a flash house not far from the ditch, gradually becoming inured to the perpetual stink. There he had schemed, set traps, and skillfully amassed a network of smugglers and informants. He had always expected to die rich and young, having agreed with the words of a criminal he had once seen hanged at Tyburn: "A life has been well-spent if it be short but merry."

But just before Nick had been about to receive his well-deserved comeuppance, Sir Ross Cannon had stepped in with his infamous deal. Much as Nick hated to admit it, the years he had spent as a runner had been the best of his life. Although he had always resented Sir Ross's manipulations, there was no denying that his brother-in-law had changed his life for the better.

Nick glanced curiously at the dark, crowded streets, where swarms of people moved in and out of ramshackle buildings that were seemingly piled one atop the other. Coming here after having just left his clean, pretty wife in the serene little house on Betterton Street was jarring. And strangely, the anticipation of going on the hunt was not half as strong as it used to be. Nick had expected to feel the savage thrill of prowling through the most dangerous area in London, and instead . . .

He was damned if he wasn't half sorry that he had agreed to come help Sayer today.

But why? He was no coward, no pampered aristocrat. It was just . . . he had the perplexing feeling that he did not belong here anymore. He had something to lose, and he did not want to risk it.

Shaking his head in confusion, Nick entered the Blood Bowl and found Sayer waiting at a table in a dark corner. The tavern was as rank and filthy and crowded as ever, smelling like refuse, gin, and bodily odors.

Sayer greeted him with a friendly grin. Young, dashing, and large-framed, Sayer was undoubtedly the best runner that Sir Grant had now that Nick had left the force. Although Nick was glad to see his friend, he had an odd sinking feeling as he saw the gleam of reckless excitement in Sayer's eyes and realized that he did not share it. Nick did not doubt that his abilities and instincts were still there, but he no longer possessed the hunger to hunt. He wanted to be at home with his wife.

Damn, he thought in rising agitation.

"Morgan will gut me like a cod if he finds out that I asked you to do this," Sayer said ruefully.

"He won't find out." Nick joined him at the table, shaking his head in refusal as a barmaid approached them with a jug of ale. The coarse-faced girl pretended to pout, then winked as she sidled away.

"I could do it myself, I think," Sayer said softly,

heedful of the possibility of being overheard. "But I don't know all the ins and outs of Fleet Ditch as well as you do. No one does. And you're the only one who could easily identify the fellow I want to catch, as you've had prior experience with him."

"Who is it?" Nick set his forearms on the table and removed them promptly as he felt his sleeves sticking to the wooden surface.

"Dick Follard."

The name took Nick by surprise. Unlike the average criminal in London, most of whom were opportunists, Follard was of that category considered to be the criminal elite, both skillful and soulless. Nick had arrested Follard two years ago, after the bastard had robbed the house of a prosperous attorney and killed the man and raped his wife when they'd offered resistance. However, Follard had been spared the gallows and been transported instead, in return for offering evidence against his accomplices.

"Follard was sent to Australia," Nick said.

"He's come back," Sayer replied with a grim smile. "Like a dog to its vomit."

"How do you know that?"

"I can't prove it, unfortunately. But there have been rumors of sightings lately, not to mention a string of violent robberies that look exactly like Follard's work. Yesterday I questioned a poor woman who was raped by a thief who had broken into her home and killed her husband. Same method of breaking in, same knife-work on the body, and the woman's description of her attacker matched Follard's—right down to the scar on the right side of the neck."

"Jesus." Frowning, Nick pinched the bridge of his nose as he pondered the information. "I can't believe that Morgan would send you to catch Follard alone."

"He didn't," Sayer said cheerfully. "He wants me to question some of Follard's old cohorts and give him a report. I'd rather just bring Follard in directly."

Nick couldn't help grinning at that, knowing exactly what Morgan's reaction to that would be. "If you succeed, Morgan will flay the hide off you for such damned stupid showmanship."

"Yes . . . and then he'll kiss my bony arse for capturing a returned transportee. And I'll be on the front page of the *Times*, with scores of women begging for my attention."

Nick's smile turned wry. "That's not as enjoyable as you might think," he informed his friend.

"No? Well, I'd like to try it, nevertheless." Sayer cocked his brow expectantly. "Are you game?"

Nick nodded with a sigh. "Where do you want to start looking?"

"Reports are that Follard has been seen in the slums between Hanging Ax Alley and Dead Man's Lane. It's like an anthill with all the holes in the walls, and tunnels between the cellars—"

"Yes, I know the place." Nick kept his face expressionless, although he was aware of cold distaste coiling in his belly. He had gone in those slums before, and even with his high tolerance for the horrors of the underworld, it was a nasty experience. The last time he had visited Hanging Ax Alley, he had seen a mother prostituting her child for gin, while beggars and whores crammed in the narrow lanes like sardines.

"We'll have to search quickly," Nick said. "Once they realize we're in the area, word will spread fast, and Follard will slip away before we ever clap eyes on him."

Sayer grinned with barely repressed enthusiasm. "Let's go, then. You lead the way."

They left the tavern and made their way through streets bisected with open gutters, the stench of dead animals and rotting garbage hanging thick in the air. The decaying buildings leaned against each other as if in exhaustion, groaning with every strong wind that blew against them. There were no signs to identify streets, nor were there numbers on houses or buildings. A stranger to the area could easily become lost and quickly find himself robbed, carved up and left for dead in some dark yard or alley. The poverty of the slum inhabitants was unimaginable, and their only escape was the temporary one to be found in a gin shop. In fact, there was a gin shop on nearly every street.

It bothered Nick to see the wretchedness of the people around him, the skeletal children, the degraded women and desperate men. The only healthy creatures to be found were the rats and mice that scuttled across the street. Until now, Nick had accepted all of this as an inevitable part of life. For the first time, he wondered what could be done for these people. Good God, they needed so much that it nearly overwhelmed him. He remembered what Lottie had said to him only a few days earlier . . . *"There must be some issue that concerns you,"* she had said. *"Something you want to fight for . . ."* Now that he'd had time to consider it, he had to admit that she was right. As Lord Sydney, he could accomplish far more than he ever had as Nick Gentry.

Shoving his hands in his pockets, Nick glanced cautiously at Sayer, who was clearly thinking of nothing more than finding Dick Follard. Just as he should be. No distractions, Nick warned himself, even as another voice filtered through his mind.

"There comes a time when a man has tweaked the devil's nose once too often," Morgan had told him. *"And if he's too stubborn or slow-witted to realize it, he'll pay with his own blood. I knew when to stop. And so must you . . ."*

It was indeed time to stop, although Nick hadn't known it until this moment. After helping Sayer with this one task, Nick would finally let go of his identity as a runner and reinvent himself once more. This time as Lord Sydney . . . a man with a wife, a home, perhaps even children someday.

The idea of seeing Lottie pregnant with his child caused a sweet pang in his chest. Finally he was beginning to understand why Sir Ross had found it so easy to resign from the magistracy when he'd married, and why Morgan valued his family above all else.

"Gentry," Sayer muttered. "Gentry?"

Lost in his thoughts, Nick did not notice until Sayer spoke once more.

"Sydney!"

Nick gave him an inquiring glance. "Yes?"

Sayer was frowning. "Keep your wits about you. You seem a bit distracted."

"I'm fine," Nick said curtly, realizing that he had indeed been preoccupied. In this place, that could be a fatal mistake.

They ventured into the slum district, and Nick assessed the area with a critical glance, trying to remember what he knew of the warren of alleys, tunnels, and crossways between buildings. He passed a hand lightly over his chest, checking the reassuring weight of an iron-filled leather cudgel in his coat pocket.

"Let's start with the buildings on the north side of the street," Nick said. "We'll work our way to the corner."

Sayer nodded, his body tensing visibly as he prepared for action.

They searched the buildings methodically, pausing briefly to ask questions of those who seemed likely to know something. The rooms and burrows were badly lit, not to mention crowded and fetid. Nick and Sayer met with no resistance, although they were the focus of many suspicious and hostile stares.

In a workshop near the end of the street—ostensibly a buckle-maker's shop, but in reality a harbor for coiners and forgerers—Nick saw the betraying flicker in a scrawny old man's eyes when he heard the mention of Follard's name. While Sayer checked through the shop, Nick approached the man with an inquiring gaze.

"Do you know anything about Follard?" Nick asked gently, fingering the edge of his own left sleeve with his opposite hand, in a signal well-known to those in the London rookeries. The subtle gesture was a promise of payment for valid information.

The man's paper-thin lids lowered over his yellowed eyes as he considered the offer. "I might."

Nick crossed his palm with a few coins, and the old man's wrinkled fingers closed over the money. "Can you tell me where I may find him?"

"Ye might try the gin shop on Melancholy Lane."

Nodding in thanks, Nick glanced at Sayer and indicated with a swerve of his gaze that it was time to leave.

Once outside, they headed swiftly to Melancholy Lane, just two streets over from Hanging Ax Alley. As with most gin shops near Fleet Ditch, the place was heavily packed long before noon, with drunken patrons sitting on the ground in a stupor. After conferring briefly, Nick went to the entrance of the shop, while Sayer circled the dilapidated building to find the exit in back.

As soon as Nick entered the shop, a few ugly rumbles went through the crowd inside. It was an unfortunate fact that a runner's height and size made it nearly impossible for him to blend in with a crowd.

It was even more unfortunate that Nick had made countless enemies in the underworld once he had given evidence against his criminal associates and went to serve at Bow Street. That hadn't exactly increased his popularity in Fleet Ditch. Ignoring the threatening murmurs, Nick glanced over the crowd with narrowed eyes.

Suddenly he saw the face he had been looking for. Through his travels from one continent to another, Dick Follard hadn't changed one whit, his ratlike face surmounted with the same shock of oily black hair, his sharp teeth giving his mouth a serrated appearance. Their gazes met in a moment of icy, electric challenge.

Follard was gone in an instant, slipping through the crowd with the ease of a rodent as he headed to the back of the shop. Nick shoved past the mass of bodies in his way, plowing through them with blind determination. By the time he reached the alley, Follard had disappeared into a complex network of fences, walls, and side streets. Sayer was nowhere to be seen.

"Sayer!" Nick shouted. "Where the hell are you?"

"Over here," came the runner's hoarse cry, and Nick spun around to see him climbing a six-foot-high fence in pursuit of Follard.

Following swiftly, Nick clambered over the fence, dropped to the ground, and ran full tilt down a dark alley shadowed by the overhanging eaves of the buildings on either side. The alley came to an abrupt end, and Nick skidded to a halt as he saw Sayer staring upward. Follard was scaling the deteriorated outside wall of an ancient three-story warehouse, resembling an insect as he sought fingerholds in the broken brick surface. After ascending two stories, he finally managed to reach a hole large enough for him to scuttle into. His bony frame disappeared inside the warehouse.

Sayer swore in disgust. "We've lost him," he said flatly. "There's no way in hell that I would try that."

Surveying the wall appraisingly, Nick approached it with a few running strides, launching himself upward. He took the same path Follard had, digging his hands and the toes of his boots into the crumbling holes in the wall, using them to gain purchase. Panting with effort, he climbed after the vanished fugitive.

"Goddamn, Gentry!" he heard Sayer exclaim approvingly. "I'll find some other way to get inside."

Nick continued to scale the wall until he crawled into the gaping second-story opening. Once inside, he went still and listened intently. He heard the sound of footfalls above. His gaze shot to a ladder that led to the top floor of the building, in place of a set of stairs that had crumbled long ago. Nick headed to it with rapid, stealthy strides. The ladder was comparatively new, indicating that the warehouse was being put to use despite its deterioration. Most likely the building served to store smuggled or stolen goods, as well as providing an excellent sanctuary for fugitives. No law enforcement officer with any wits would have dared set foot in the dilapidated place.

The ladder creaked from Nick's weight. Once he reached the third floor, he saw that the floor planks and rafters had mostly rotted away, leaving only a row of support timbers that resembled the ribs of a massive decaying skeleton. Although the edges of the space still bore some flimsy planks, the center of the floor was gone, as was that of the second story, leaving a potentially deadly thirty-foot drop straight through the middle of the building.

As soon as Dick Follard saw Nick, he turned and began to make his way across one of the support timbers. Immediately Nick realized his intentions. The building next door was so close that it would require a three-foot leap at most. All Follard had to do was launch himself from one of the gaping windowholes, and he could escape to the adjoining rooftop.

Gamely Nick followed him, steeling himself to ignore the yawning void beneath the timber. Placing his feet carefully, he pursued Follard's retreating form, gaining confidence as he passed the halfway-mark on the beam. However, just as he was about to reach the end, an ominous crack pierced the silence, and he felt the beam give way beneath him. His weight had been too much for the corroded wood.

With a curse, Nick launched himself toward the next timber, and somehow caught it on his descent. Blindly he clutched at the beam and wrapped his arms around it. A shower of broken timber and brittle planks fell with a thunderous sound, while a stinging rain of dust and powdered wood made Nick's eyes blur. Gasping, he fought to lift himself atop the timber, but a sudden numbing blow to his back nearly caused him to fall. Nick grunted in mingled surprise and pain, and looked into Follard's triumphant face above him.

An evil grin split the bastard's narrow face. "I'll send you to hell, Gentry," he said, venturing farther out onto the beam. He stomped on Nick's hand with his booted foot. The bones in Nick's fingers cracked, drawing a growl of agony from his throat.

Follard laughed in manic glee. "One," he cried. "Two." He stomped again, the crushing force of his foot causing a brilliant burst of pain to shoot up Nick's arm. Follard's boot lifted once more as he prepared for the coup de grace.

"Three," Nick gasped and grabbed at Follard's ankle, jerking him off-balance.

Letting out a shrill scream, Follard toppled from the beam, his body falling two stories to hit the bottom floor with fatal force.

Nick didn't dare look down. Desperately he focused his attention on pulling himself onto the beam. Unfortunately his strength had been depleted, and his left hand was crippled. Writhing like a worm on a hook, he arched helplessly over the fatal drop.

Incredulously, he realized that he was going to die.

* * *

The note trembled in Lottie's hand as she read it again.

Lottie,

Please help me. Mama says that Lord Radnor is coming to take me away. I do not want to go anywhere with him, but she and Papa say I must. They have locked me in my room until he comes. I pray you will not let this happen, Lottie, as you are my only hope.

Your loving sister,
Ellie

A village boy had brought the tear-stained letter not long after Nick had left for the day. The boy claimed that Ellie had bid him to come to her bedroom window and given him the message. "She said if I brought it to ye, I'd get an 'alf crown," he said, shifting his weight uneasily, as if he suspected that the promise would not be honored.

Lottie had gratified the boy by giving him a half sovereign instead, and then sent him to the kitchen with Mrs. Trench for a hot meal. Pacing around the entrance hall, she gnawed frantically on her knuckle as she wondered what to do. She had no way of knowing when Nick would return home. But if she waited too long, Radnor might have already fetched Ellie.

The thought filled her with such distress that Lottie clenched her fists and uttered a cry of outrage.

Her parents, allowing Radnor to come take poor innocent Ellie . . . as if she were an animal to be traded. "She's only sixteen," she said aloud, her face hot with the blood of anger. "How can they? How could they possibly live with themselves?"

And there had been no mention of marriage in the note, which could only lead Lottie to believe that her parents were virtually prostituting Ellie for their own benefit. The realization made her ill.

No, she could not wait for Nick. She would go and collect Ellie herself, before Radnor came. In fact, Lottie was furious with herself for not already having done so. But who could have predicted that Radnor would have wanted Ellie, or that her parents would have given her to him like this?

"Harriet," she called out sharply, striding to the nearest bellpull and tugging it frantically. "Harriet!"

The dark-haired maid appeared at once, having run so fast that her spectacles were a bit askew. "Milady?"

"Fetch my traveling coat and bonnet." Pausing, Lottie considered the footmen in Nick's employ, and decided that Daniel was the largest and most capable man to help her in his absence. "Tell Daniel that he is to accompany me on an errand. I want the carriage to be readied immediately."

"Yes, Lady Sydney!" Harriet rushed to obey, seeming infected by Lottie's urgency.

In less than a minute, Daniel appeared, his tall form clad in black livery. He was a good-natured, robust young man with dark brown hair and sherry-colored eyes. "My lady," he said, making an impeccable bow and waiting for her instructions.

Receiving her bonnet from Harriet, Lottie tied it deftly beneath her chin. "Daniel, we are going to my parents' home to fetch my younger sister. I have no doubt that my family will offer strong objections. There is even a possibility of a physical altercation . . . and while I don't want anyone to be hurt, we must bring my sister back here with us. I trust that I may depend on you?"

He understood what she was asking. "Naturally, my lady."

She smiled slightly, her face pale. "Thank you."

The carriage was prepared in record time, and Lottie clutched the balled-up note in her fist as the vehicle rolled swiftly away from Betterton Street. She tried to make herself think clearly, to understand what was happening.

What did Radnor want with her sister? In the years that Lottie had known him, he had barely seemed to notice Ellie's existence, except to make disparaging comments—that Ellie was plump, simpleminded, unrefined. Why choose her, of all women, to make his mistress? Perhaps because Radnor knew that it was the worst way to hurt Lottie. He knew that she could never be content in her marriage to Nick knowing that her happiness had been purchased at the price of her sister's.

Seething with fear and anger, Lottie twisted her hands in her skirts.

It took only a quarter-hour to reach her parents' home, but to Lottie the wait was unbearable. When they arrived at the street of Tudor houses and Lord Radnor's carriage was nowhere in sight, Lottie allowed herself to feel a glimmer of hope. Perhaps she was not too late.

The vehicle halted, and Daniel helped her down. His calm face helped to steady her frayed nerves as she stepped to the pavement and allowed him to accompany her to the house. The front yard was vacant, her brothers and sisters strangely absent.

At Lottie's nod, Daniel used his fist to knock firmly on the door, alerting the occupants of the house to their arrival. Soon the door was opened by a maid.

"Miss 'Oward," the maid said uneasily, her eyes wide in her freckled face.

"I am Lady Sydney now," Lottie replied and glanced at the footman. "You may wait out here, Daniel. I will call for you if your assistance is needed."

"Yes, milady."

Entering the house, Lottie saw her parents standing in the doorway of one of the receiving rooms . . . her mother, looking pinched and determined, her father hardly able to lift his gaze from the ground. The signs of their guilt fanned her outrage into quiet fury. "Where is Ellie?" she demanded without preamble.

Her mother stared at her without emotion. "That is not your concern, Charlotte. As I made clear during your last visit, you are not welcome here. You cut yourself off from the family with your selfish actions."

A bitter reply rose to Lottie's lips, but before she could utter a word, she heard a determined thumping sound from the back of the house. "Lottie!" came her sister's muffled voice. "Lottie, I'm here! Don't leave me!"

"I'm coming," Lottie called and shot her parents a disbelieving gaze. "Shame on you," she said softly, each word an indictment. "You planned to give her to Radnor, knowing that would ruin any chance for her to have a decent life. How can you live with yourselves?"

Ignoring her mother's vehement outcry, Lottie strode to Ellie's bedroom and turned the key that had been left in the lock.

Ellie burst from the room with a flurry of grateful sobs, throwing herself on Lottie. Her brown hair was matted and tangled. "I knew you'd help me," she gasped, blotting her wet cheeks on Lottie's shoulders. "I knew it. Lottie, take me away at once. He's coming. He'll be here any minute."

Hugging the sobbing girl, Lottie rubbed her back and murmured quietly. "I will always come when you need me, Ellie. Go collect your things, and I'll take you home with me."

The girl shook her head vehemently. "There's no time, we must go *now*."

"All right." Keeping her arm around Ellie, Lottie

To release his grip, and hang suspended, depending entirely on someone else's strength . . .

"No choice," Sayer said through clenched teeth. "Let go, damn it, and let me help you. *Now*."

Nick made himself release his grip on the timber. He swung free for one terrifying moment. He felt Sayer's grip tighten to a crushing vise and a mighty tug upward as the runner hauled him just far enough to balance his weight on top of the crackling wood.

"Move forward," Sayer muttered, retaining his hold on Nick's arm, and together they maneuvered away from the perilous fall. When they had both retreated from the beam and found the safety of some relatively sound planking, they collapsed side by side, gasping violently.

"Damn," Sayer rasped when he had sufficient breath to speak, "you're a heavy bastard, Sydney."

Disoriented, his body racked with pain, Nick tried to make himself comprehend that he was still alive. He drew his sleeve over his sweat-soaked brow and found that his arm was cramping and shaking, the abused muscles going berserk.

Sayer sat up and regarded him with clear anxiety. "It looks like you've strained some muscles. And your hand looks like it's been pushed through a sieve."

But he was alive. It was too miraculous to believe. Nick had gotten a reprieve he didn't deserve, and by all that was holy, he was going to take advantage of it. As he thought of Lottie, he was seized with dark longing.

"Sayer," he managed to say hoarsely, "I've just decided something."

"Oh?"

"From now on, you'll have to find your own fucking way around Fleet Ditch."

Sayer grinned suddenly, seeming to understand the reasons behind his vehemence. "I suppose you think you're too good for this place, now that you're a viscount. I knew it was just a matter of time before you started putting on airs."

Lord Radnor was clearly astonished to see Lottie at her family's home. His hard, black gaze moved from her face to Ellie's, comparing the two of them, cataloging the differences. When he looked back at Lottie, his face was taut with a mixture of hatred and longing.

"You have no right to interfere," he said.

"My sister is an innocent young girl who has done nothing to you," Lottie flared. "She doesn't deserve to suffer because of my actions. Leave her alone!"

"I've invested twelve years of my life in you," Radnor said between clenched teeth, taking a step forward. "And I will be repaid for those years one way or another."

Lottie glanced incredulously at her parents. "You can't truly mean to give her to him! How can you have slipped so far beyond decency? My husband said that he would take care of you and assume your debts—"

"Ellie will have a better life this way," her father mumbled. "Lord Radnor will provide well for her—"

"You don't mind the fact that he intends to make her his mistress?" Lottie glared at them all, while Ellie cowered behind her and sobbed against her back. "Well, I won't have it! I'm leaving now, and taking Ellie with me—and if anyone dares to lay a finger on us, he will answer to Lord Sydney."

The mention of Nick seemed to infuriate Lord Radnor. "How dare you? You have cheated, betrayed, and insulted me beyond all bearing, and now you mean to deprive me of the one recompense I ask for."

"You don't want Ellie," Lottie said, staring at him steadily. "You want to strike back at me. To punish me for marrying someone else."

"Yes," Radnor exploded fiercely, seeming to lose all self-control. "Yes, I want to punish you. I raised you up from the mud, and you have brought yourself low again. You have corrupted yourself, and in doing so, you have deprived me of the only thing I have ever desired." He came to her in a few aggressive strides. "Every night I lie abed imagining you with that swine," he shouted into her face. "How could you choose that loathsome animal over me? The filthiest, most debauched man on—"

Lottie drew back her hand and struck him hard,

her palm smacking the side of his face with numbing force. "You aren't fit to speak his name!"

Their gazes locked, and Lottie saw the last remnants of sanity disappear from Radnor's eyes. He reached out for her, his hands closing around her like a hawk's talons, and he jerked her off her feet until she fell against him. Behind her, Ellie gave a fearful shriek.

Lottie's parents appeared too stunned to move as Lord Radnor dragged her from the house. Caught fast in his grip, Lottie stumbled and tripped down the front steps. Radnor shouted something to his footmen, while she fought and twisted in Radnor's arms, until he cuffed the side of her head, landing a painful blow on her ear. Lottie reared and shook her head to clear a shower of brilliant sparks. Her gaze found Daniel, who had been beset by Radnor's footmen. Despite Daniel's size, he was no match for two of them.

"My lady," Daniel cried, and reeled backward as a heavy fist smashed into his face.

Radnor sank his hand into Lottie's hair and tangled his fingers tightly in the pinned-up locks. Locking his other arm around her neck, he forced her to go with him to his carriage.

"See here, Radnor—" came her father's anxious voice. "We've said you can have Ellie. Release Lottie, and we'll—"

"*This* is what I want," Lord Radnor raged, dragging Lottie with his forearm clamped around her throat, making her choke and gag as she was deprived of air. "No more bargains. No substitutes. I will have Charlotte and be damned to all of you!"

Lottie clawed frantically at the crushing vise of his arm, her lungs feeling as if they would burst. She couldn't breathe . . . she needed air . . . black and red streaks blurred her vision, and she felt herself go limp in Radnor's punishing embrace.

Chapter Fifteen

Lottie did not fully regain her senses until she felt herself being half-dragged, half-carried into Lord Radnor's London home. Her head pounded viciously, and her throat ached as she struggled against his unrelenting grasp. Somewhere beneath her fear and fury, she was aware of a deep relief that Ellie had been spared. Her sister was safe, and now everything had boiled down to the confrontation that Lottie had always known would happen, between her and the man who had dominated most of her life.

Although Lottie was aware of a few exclamations from nearby servants, none of them dared to interfere. They were all fearful of Radnor, and they would not lift a finger to prevent him from doing as he wished. She wondered what his purpose was in bringing her here. His London residence was the first place that would be investigated when it was discovered that she was missing. She would have expected him to take her to a remote place where they could not easily be found.

Radnor hauled her to the library, locked the door shut, and shoved Lottie into a chair. Holding one hand to her bruised throat, she crumpled into the seat. A few moments later, she felt something hard and cold prod against her temple, while one of his hands pulled her head to the back of the chair.

Lottie's heart stopped beating as she understood the reason that Lord Radnor had brought her here. Since he could not have her, he intended to destroy her.

"I loved you," Radnor said quietly, sounding perfectly sane, even as the end of the pistol barrel trembled against her head. "I would have given you everything."

Strangely, Lottie found that she was able to answer in just as rational a tone, as though they were having an ordinary conversation and her life was not about to end with the pull of his finger on the trigger. "You never loved me." It hurt her throat to speak, but she forced herself to continue. "You don't know the meaning of the word."

The pistol shook harder. "How can you say that after all that I have sacrificed for you? Are you really so ignorant?"

"In all the years that we've known each other, you've demonstrated domination, obsession, and desire . . . but those things aren't love."

"Then tell me what love is." His voice was thick with scorn.

"Respect. Acceptance. Selflessness. All the things my husband has shown me in just a few short weeks. My flaws don't matter to him. He loves me without conditions. And I love him the same way."

"You owe your love to *me*," he said harshly.

"Perhaps I could have felt something for you had you ever tried to be kind." Lottie paused, closing her eyes as she felt the pistol nudge harder into her temple. "Strange, but I've never thought it mattered to you, whether I cared for you or not."

"It does," Radnor said furiously. "I deserve that much from you, at least!"

"How ironic." A humorless smile tugged at her dry lips. "You demanded perfection from me— something I could never attain. And yet the one thing I might have given you—affection—you never seemed to want."

"I want it now," Radnor stunned Lottie by saying. Keeping the pistol pressed to her head, he moved in front of her and knelt until their faces were level. His face was ruddy with color that burned not on the surface of his skin but from deep underneath. His eyes were black with rage, or perhaps despair, and his thin mouth was contorted by some powerful emotion. Lottie had never seen him like this. She did not understand what moved him, why he should seem so ravaged by loss, when she knew to the bottom of her soul that he was not capable of love.

His clawlike hand took hers, brought her resisting fingers to his perspiring cheek. She realized with amazement that he was trying to make her caress him . . . here, like this, with a gun held to her head. "Touch me," he muttered feverishly. "Tell me that you love me."

Lottie kept her fingers still and lifeless in his. "I love my husband."

Radnor flushed with baffled anger. "You cannot!"

She almost pitied him as she stared into his uncomprehending eyes. "I'm sorry for you," she said. "You can't conceive of loving anyone who is less than perfect. What a lonely fate that must be."

"I *did* love you," he shouted, his voice striated with rage. "I did, damn your cheating soul!"

"Then you loved someone who never existed. You loved an impossible ideal. Not me." She licked at the beads of sweat on her upper lip. "You don't know anything about me, my lord."

"I know you better than anyone," he said vehemently. "You would be nothing without me. *You belong to me.*"

"No. I am Lord Sydney's wife." She hesitated before giving voice to the thought that had occurred to her more than once in the past few days. "And I am fairly certain that by now I am carrying his child."

Lord Radnor's eyes became two wells of utter

darkness in a face that was skull white. She perceived that she had shocked him deeply, that the thought of her being pregnant with another man's child had never even occurred to him.

Delicately Radnor's fingers withdrew from hers, and he stood. The cold barrel of the gun never left Lottie's temple as he moved behind her once more. She felt the perspiring flat of his palm catch slightly on her hair as he caressed it. "You've ruined everything," he said in a curiously flat tone. The pistol cocked, the heavy click reverberating against her skin. "There's nothing left for me. You'll never be what I wanted."

"No," Lottie agreed softly. "It was always futile." Cold sweat trickled down her face as she waited for him to pull the trigger. In the face of such absolute defeat, Radnor would surely kill her. But she was not going to spend the last moments of her life cowering in fear. She closed her eyes and thought of Nick . . . his kisses, his smiles, the warmth of his arms around her. Tears of regret and gladness prickled behind her lids. If only she could have had a little more time with him . . . if only she could have made him understand what he meant to her. A slow sigh escaped her, and she waited almost peacefully for Radnor to act.

At the sound of her exhalation, the barrel of the pistol lifted from her head. In the weighty silence that followed, Lottie opened her eyes, perplexed by the absolute stillness. Had she not heard the faint rasp of Radnor's breathing, she would have thought that he had left the room. As she began to turn, she was suddenly assaulted with an explosive sound that made her ears ring. She fell backward, her backside hitting the floor, while a curious hot splatter landed on her skirts and arms.

Dazed, she tried to catch her breath, and wiped numbly at the red droplets on her arms until they made long, wine-colored smears. Blood, she thought in amazement, and looked at Radnor's crumpled form. He was lying on the floor a few feet away from her, his body spasming in the throes of death.

Agreeing reluctantly that they would have to report to Morgan, Nick and Sayer went to Bow Street. Nick was in considerable pain, the strained muscles on his side burning, his broken fingers swelling beneath the handkerchief he had bound them with. He was tired and aching, and he could hardly wait to go home to Lottie.

As soon as they entered the comfortably shabby building on Bow Street, they headed straight for Sir Grant's office in the hopes that he had returned from the afternoon court session. The court clerk, Vickery, jumped up from his desk as Nick and Sayer approached. His bespectacled face registered astonishment at their filthy appearance. "Mr. Sayer, and Mr. . . . er, Lord Sydney . . ."

"We had a bit of an altercation near Fleet Ditch," Sayer said. "Is Morgan available to see us, Vickery?"

For some reason, the clerk gave Nick an odd stare.

"He is questioning someone at the moment," he replied.

"How long will that take?" Nick asked with annoyance.

"I have no idea, Lord Sydney. The matter appears to be one of some urgency. Actually the visitor is your footman, my lord."

Nick shook his head as if he hadn't heard correctly. "What?"

"Mr. Daniel Finchley," Vickery clarified.

"What the hell is he doing here?" Instantly concerned, Nick went to Morgan's office and opened the door without knocking.

Morgan's face was grim as he glanced at Nick. "Come in, Sydney. Your arrival is well timed. What happened to your hand?"

"Never mind about that," Nick said impatiently. He saw that the visitor was indeed Daniel, his face bruised and one eye blackened, his livery torn. "Who did that to you?" he asked with a frown of concern. "Why are you here, Daniel?"

"I couldn't find you at home, my lord," the footman replied in agitation. "I didn't know what to do, so I came to tell Sir Grant. Something has happened to Lady Sydney."

A jolt of alarm went through Nick, and he felt his face turn white. "What?"

"Lady Sydney went to visit her family this morning, to fetch her sister. She bade me accompany her, and warned me that there might be some kind of struggle, as the Howards would not want to relinquish the girl." He fumbled in his pocket and produced a crumpled note, handing it to Nick. "Lady Sydney left this in the carriage."

Rapidly Nick scanned the note, his gaze lingering on the first line.

Please help me. Mama says that Lord Radnor is coming to take me away . . .

Cursing, Nick lifted his gaze to the footman's pale face. "Go on," he growled.

"Just a few moments after Lady Sydney and I arrived at the Howards' home, Lord Radnor appeared. He entered the house, and when he came out, he seemed to have taken leave of his senses. He had his arm around Lady Sydney's throat, and he forced her into his carriage. I tried to stop him, but his footmen overpowered me."

A wave of icy horror rolled over Nick. He knew the depth of the earl's dark obsession. His wife was at the mercy of the man she feared most . . . and he was not there to help her. The realization made him insane.

"Where did he take her?" Nick snarled, seizing the footman's coat with his uninjured hand. "Where are they, Daniel?"

"I don't know," the footman replied, trembling.

"I'll kill him," Nick raged, striding to the door. He was going to tear London apart, starting with Radnor's town estate. He was only sorry that a man couldn't be killed more than one time, as he wanted to visit a thousand deaths on the bastard.

"Sydney," Morgan interrupted harshly, moving

so swiftly that he made it to the door at the same time that Nick did. "You're not going to rush out of here like a raving lunatic. If your wife is in danger, she needs you to keep a cool head."

Nick let out an animal-like growl. "Get out of my way!"

"I'm going to organize a search. I can dispatch four runners and at least thirty constables in approximately five minutes. Tell me the most likely places Radnor could have taken your wife, as you have more knowledge of him than I do." Morgan's steady gaze met Nick's, and he seemed to understand his bottomless terror, for his voice softened as he added, "You're not alone in this, Sydney. We'll find her, I swear it."

Just then, a brief tap sounded at the door. "Sir Grant," came Vickery's muffled voice, "you have another visitor."

"Not now," Morgan said curtly. "Tell him to return tomorrow."

There was a brief pause. "Er . . . Sir Grant?"

"What the hell is it, Vickery?" Morgan sent an incredulous glance at the closed door.

"I don't think you want to send this one away."

"I don't give a damn who he is, just tell him . . ." Morgan's voice trailed away as the door swung gently open.

Nick's anguished gaze shot to the visitor, and he nearly fell to his knees at the sight. *"Lottie."*

* * *

Bedraggled and bloodstained, Lottie managed a wan smile as she saw her husband's stark white face. "I've been rather busy today," she said.

The sound of her voice seemed to unleash a flood of savage emotion. Groaning her name, Nick reached her in two strides. He hauled her against him in a brutal embrace that threatened to smother her.

"Blood—" he said incoherently, his large hand moving over her in a frantic search.

"It's not mine. I'm just fine, except for a few—" Lottie broke off, her eyes widening as she saw the bandaged hand he held at his side. "Nick, you've been hurt!"

"It's nothing." Nick tugged her head back, his tormented gaze raking over her face. His trembling fingertips traced the line of her cheek and jaw. "My God. Lottie . . ." As his panicked exploration continued, he discovered the bruises on her throat, and he uttered a cry of fury. "Holy hell! Your neck. He dared to . . . I'm going to *slaughter* that bastard—"

Lottie placed her fingers over his mouth. "I'm all right," she said gently. Feeling the way his large body shook, she drew her hand over his chest in a calming stroke. After the traumatic events of the past hours, it was so wonderful to be with him that her lips curved in a wobbly smile. She gazed into his dusty, sweat-streaked face with concern. "In fact, I believe I may be in better condition than you, my darling."

A primitive groan came from his throat, and he clutched her with his right arm, bending over her hungrily. "I love you," he said in a low, shaken voice. "I love you so much, Lottie." His lips covered hers in a fiercely ardent kiss.

Clearly he was too unsettled to recall that there were others in the room. Lottie turned her face away with a muffled laugh. "I love you, too," she whispered. "Not here, darling. Later, with more privacy, we can—" She was silenced as Nick seized her mouth once more. Suddenly she found herself pushed up against the wall by six feet of aroused, overwrought male. Realizing that there was no hope of subduing him, Lottie stroked his broad back in an effort to soothe him. He possessed her with deep, fervent kisses, while his lungs worked so violently that she could feel his rib cage expanding with each breath. She tried to comfort him, gently rubbing the back of his neck as his mouth worked roughly over hers. His breath came in ragged shivers, and in between kisses he breathed her name as if it were a prayer. "Lottie . . . Lottie . . ." Each time she tried to answer, he dove for her mouth again.

"Sydney," Sir Grant said after some prolonged throat-clearing had failed to capture his attention. "Ahem. Sydney . . ."

After a long time, Nick finally lifted his head.

Lottie pushed at his chest, making him loosen his grip on her. Red-faced and breathless, she saw that Sayer had developed a keenly absorbing interest in the weather outside the window, while Daniel had excused himself to wait outside.

"I am sorry to interrupt your reunion with Lady Sydney, my lord," Sir Grant said ruefully. "However, I must insist on hearing what has occurred with Radnor, and where he is at the moment, especially in light of the condition of Lady Sydney's garments."

Realizing that he was referring to the bloodstains on her dress, Lottie nodded. Nick continued to hold her while she explained. "Lord Radnor died by his own hand," she told the magistrate. "He brought me to his home, and after we talked for a few minutes, he took his own life."

"In what manner?" Sir Grant asked calmly.

"He used a pistol." Lottie felt the tremor that went through Nick's body at the words. "I am at a loss to explain his actions, except to say that he seemed altogether mad. I told his servants to leave his body exactly as it was and not to touch anything, as you might wish to send a runner to investigate the scene."

"Well done, my lady," Sir Grant said. "May I prevail on you to answer just a few more questions?"

"Tomorrow," Nick said roughly. "She's been through enough today. She needs to rest."

"I would be more than happy to tell you every detail," Lottie replied to Sir Grant, "if you will send for a doctor to attend to Lord Sydney's hand, and also have a look at our footman."

The magistrate's green eyes crinkled charmingly at the corners. "We'll send for Dr. Linley at once."

"I'll fetch him," Sayer volunteered and left the office quickly.

"Excellent," Morgan commented, his gaze returning to Nick. "And while we wait for Linley, my lord, perhaps you can explain to me how you came by your injuries—and why you look and smell like you've been tromping through Fleet Ditch."

Much later, when they were at home in bed and had talked for what seemed to be hours, Nick told Lottie about the thoughts he'd had in the perilous moments when he'd thought he would fall to his death in the warehouse. As Lottie listened, she snuggled in the crook of his arm, gently circling her fingertips through the hair on his chest. His voice was deep and drowsy from the effects of the pain medication that Dr. Linley had insisted on giving him before setting and splinting his fingers. Nick had taken it only because the alternative was the undignified prospect of being held to the floor by Sayer and Morgan while the doctor poured the medicine down his throat.

"I never wanted to live so much as I did right then, hanging onto that rotting timber," Nick said. "I couldn't bear the thought of never seeing you again. All I want is time with you. To spend the rest of my life with you. I don't care about anything else."

Murmuring her love to him, Lottie kissed the hard silken skin of his shoulder.

"Remember when I told you once that I needed to be a runner?" he asked.

Lottie nodded. "You said that you were addicted to the challenge and the danger."

"I'm not any longer," he said vehemently.

"Thank God for that," Lottie said with a smile, lifting herself up on one elbow. "Because I have become rather addicted to *you*."

Nick traced the moonlit curve of her back with his fingers. "And I finally know what to wish for."

Puzzled, she gazed down at him while the long locks of her hair trailed over his chest and shoulders. "What?"

"The wishing well," he reminded her.

"Oh, yes . . ." Lottie lowered her face to his chest and nuzzled the soft fur, recalling that morning in the forest. "You wouldn't make a wish."

"Because I didn't know what I wanted. And now I do."

"What do you want?" she asked tenderly.

His hand slipped behind her head, pulling her mouth down to his. "To love you forever," he whispered just before their lips met.

Epilogue

An hour after Master John Robert Cannon was born, Sir Ross carried his infant son to the parlor, where friends and family waited. A chorus of soft, delighted exclamations greeted the sight of the sleeping baby wrapped in a lace-trimmed blanket. Surrendering the bundle to his beaming mother, Catherine, Sir Ross made his way to a chair and lowered himself into it with a long sigh.

Studying his brother-in-law, Nick reflected that he had never seen him look so exhausted and unnerved. Sir Ross had defied convention by staying with his wife while she was in labor, as he was unable to wait outside while she was undergoing the trauma of delivery. With his black hair rumpled and his supreme self-assurance temporarily gone, Sir Ross appeared far younger than usual . . . an ordinary man who was badly in need of a drink.

Nick poured a brandy at the sideboard and brought it to him. "How is Sophia?" he asked.

"A damned sight better than I am," Sir Ross admitted and received the snifter gratefully. "Thank you." Closing his eyes, he took a deep swallow of the brandy, letting it soothe his overwrought nerves. "Good God, I don't know how women do it," he muttered.

Being completely unacquainted with the feminine realm of childbirth, Nick sat in a nearby chair and regarded him with a puzzled frown. "Did Sophia have a difficult time of it?"

"No. But even the easiest of childbirths seems a Herculean effort to me." Seeming to relax slightly, Sir Ross drank more of the brandy. He surprised Nick with his unusual candor. "It makes a husband fearful of ever going back to his wife's bed, knowing what it will all eventually lead to. While she was in labor, I could hardly believe that I was responsible for putting her through that." He smiled wryly. "But then, of course, a man's baser nature eventually wins out."

Nick glanced at Lottie in sudden consternation. Like the other women, she was cooing over the baby, her face soft and radiant. One of her hands rested gently on the curve of her own stomach, where their child was growing. Sensing his stare, Lottie looked up with a smile and wrinkled her nose impishly.

"Damn," Nick muttered, realizing that he was going to be in no better condition than Sir Ross, when his own child was born.

"You'll survive," Sir Ross assured him with a sudden grin, reading his thoughts. "And I'll be there to pour the brandy for you afterward."

They exchanged a friendly stare, and Nick felt an unexpected flicker of liking for the man who had been his adversary for so many years. Shaking his head with a rueful smile, he extended his hand to Sir Ross. "Thank you."

Sir Ross shook his hand in a brief, hard clasp, seeming to understand what Nick was thanking him for. "It was all worth it, then?" he asked quietly.

Settling back in his chair, Nick looked once more at his wife, loving her with an intensity that he never would have believed himself capable of. For the first time in his life he was at peace with himself and the world, no longer haunted by shades of the past. "Yes," he said simply, his soul alight with gladness as Lottie looked back at him once more.

Author's Note

Dear Reader,

I hope you have enjoyed my novels featuring the famed Bow Street runners. They have been a great pleasure for me to write, and I was able to learn some very interesting facts during my research. The Bow Street runners were essentially a private police force, never officially authorized by Parliament. They were not bound by statutory or territorial restrictions—which meant they were virtually a law unto themselves. This dashing group of thief-takers was formed by Henry Fielding in 1753, and when he died one year later, his half brother John Fielding succeeded him as chief magistrate.

After the Bow Street runners faithfully served the public for decades, the first Metropolitan Police Act was passed in 1829, resulting in the creation of the New Police. The Bow Street office continued to operate independently of the New Police for ten years, until the second Metropolitan Police Act expanded the New Police and finally eliminated the Bow Street runners. I humbly ask for your indulgence, as I have taken author's license to extend the runners' existence for another two years, in order to serve the needs of my plot.

I also want to address the fact that I've included a "shower scene" in a historical novel, which I know is unusual. As I researched nineteenth-century plumbing, I learned that the duke of Wellington installed several hundred feet of hot water piping in his home as early as 1833, and by the late 1830s, the duke of Buckingham had equipped his mansion with shower-baths, water closets, and bathrooms. Therefore, Nick Gentry's shower-bath was entirely possible for a well-to-do London gentleman of his time.

Regarding the process of disclaiming one's title . . . it was actually impossible for a peer to do so until the passage of the 1963 peerage act. Only about fifteen or so have actually disclaimed since then.

Wishing you happiness always,

Lisa